Jon Stuart had been angry, really angry.

He'd intended to make good his escape. But something in Cassandra's voice gave h㏌ pause that time, and he swung around.

And there she w.

Falling…

It looked as if she were sailing. In this, as in all other things, she was elegant. She was wearing a white silk dressing gown, and it billowed out around her. Her ebony hair was caught by the golden glory of the sun and shone with blue-black highlights. It struck him that she even fell with dramatic grace and beauty.

And only after a split second of the mindless realization that he could do nothing at all to stop it did h㏌ realize that she was already in the act of dying. S㏌ ㏌㏌㏌ ㏌ing out, shrieking *his* name, plum㏌

She died in the st㏌㏌ ㏌㏌㏌ ㏌㏌㏌ ㏌, like a wayward go㏌㏌ ㏌㏌w-white gown caugh㏌ ㏌㏌ ㏌ she was sleeping, exce㏌

The trident had ㏌㏌ ㏌ the snow-white gown was turning crimson㏌

His heart hammering, he began to shout, running desperately, as if he could reach her, help her, despite the fact that he knew…

He cried out. Cried out her name. Reached her and held her.

As her blood spilled over him.

While her eyes stared into his with an ever silent reproach.

HEATHER GRAHAM
POZZESSERE

NEVER
SLEEP WITH
STRANGERS

MIRA

ISBN 1-55166-445-3

NEVER SLEEP WITH STRANGERS

NEVER SLEEP WITH STRANGERS

Prologue

Cassandra Stuart was beautiful, and she knew it. She could manipulate others, and she knew that, too. If she could just make him turn around and look back at her...

"Jon! *Jon!*"

She knew that he'd heard her, but he didn't stop. He was really furious with her this time. As she watched, he continued down the gravel path that led to the loch. Maybe she had overplayed it this time, but she didn't want to be here in the back of beyond, in this godforsaken, remote patch of Scotland. Despite his famous guests, despite his famous charity game. They were *his* guests; it was *his* game. She hated the country; she wanted to be in London.

But she knew her husband, knew what he was thinking now. He'd known the day would go badly, that she would be rude and impatient and ruin it for them all. But damn him, he still wouldn't give it up! He'd hosted this event every year for the past decade. He'd made his plans; he had a life to live. The week was already underway. Besides, no matter how damned marvelous his wife might be, he'd told her—

sounding awfully damned sarcastic—*he* would be damned if a woman was going to lead him around by the nose. *Any* woman.

"Jon!"

She knew that he didn't want to look back, didn't want to see her.

Because he knew what she was planning. And he had planned ahead himself. He wasn't going to let her play him, wasn't going to let her manipulate him the way she intended to.

She meant to leave. Today. It was the last disruption she had up her sleeve. She hoped her departure would get through to him the way her pouting and petulance had not.

But she wanted him to come back to her first; she wanted to make love, to be passionate and exciting, to remind him that he couldn't exist without her. She would tell him that she needed him, remind him why he had married her. She could make him happy, could make him laugh, and she was damned good in bed, even if she had just taken a lover because she couldn't bear the look in Jon's eyes sometimes, knowing that he might on occasion be thinking of someone else. *Come back!* she thought furiously. *Let me seduce you just one last time so you don't forget, so maybe…*

She would wait until he had slipped away, and then she would pack, leaving behind a letter addressed to "My Dearest Darling," explaining that she would be at the London Hilton, waiting for him when he could escape his dreary associates. And maybe, just maybe, he would come. He could be such a fool! She knew so much more about his guests and household than he did! Who was sleeping with whom. And why. Actually, she thought, and almost smiled, she knew a number of them very well. Intimately, one might say.

And still there was such a wretched hole of jealousy in her heart.

"Jon! Come back!" she called again. She experienced a strange new fear beyond the sense of powerlessness and loss she had been feeling so much lately. "Jon! Please come back! Or I'll make you pay!"

Her voice was both provocative and irritated. But he was still walking. So tall, hair so dark, shoulders broad and muscled. He was a beautiful man, and she was losing him.

Panic seized her. He had guessed she was having an affair with someone here. Did he know that she was trying to goad him, get even with him? Because she was certain he was having an affair, as well.

"Jon! Jon, damn you!"

Her tone was growing more petulant. She stood on the master bedroom's second-floor balcony, overlooking the rear courtyard. The rooms had been handsomely enough appointed, "remodeled" at the end of the seventeenth century and modernized by Jon himself just a few years ago. The balcony was a sweeping, curved affair that boasted views of three corners of the property. Here, in the rear, it looked over an elegant fountain with a priceless marble Poseidon, complete with trident, as its centerpiece. Despite the fact that winter was rapidly approaching, roses still bloomed around the tiled path that encircled the fountain. The path turned to gravel as it passed through the rose arbor and headed toward the loch. In the master chambers themselves, the walls were covered with antique tapestries, and there was a massive fireplace, as well as a state-of-the-art hot-water heating system with generator backup. A four-poster king-size bed sat on a dais, and one level down from the main section of the bedroom, just beyond a medieval archway, was a huge whirlpool bath and sauna. She had a huge dressing room and closet, as did he.

"What's not to like?" Jon had asked her impatiently, offended.

The decor was fine. She just hated the country. No excitement, no sense of life. It wasn't London, Paris, New York or even Edinburgh, for God's sake.

That was exactly why he liked it so much, he'd told her.

He was walking away. Still walking away.

She was amazed to feel tears stinging her eyes. How could he care more about this pile of stones and his imbecilic friends than her? "Jon, Jon! Damn you, *Jon!*"

He'd talked about divorce; he'd said that things just weren't working out. But, he couldn't divorce her. He just *couldn't!* She'd already told him that she would make it impossible. She would drag him through the mud, give away a million filthy secrets about him and his associates.

"Jo—"

She started to say his name, then realized that someone was behind her.

She spun around to see who had slipped in. "You, damn you! Get out! Did he send you? Get the hell out of my room. *Our* room! I'm his wife. I'm the one who sleeps with him. Get out!"

She spun back to stare out from the balcony. "Jon!"

She heard a rush of movement, like a whisper of air, and she turned back.

For a moment she stared into the eyes of her killer, and she knew.

"Oh, God!" she breathed, and, desperate, she began to cry out again.

"Jon! Jon! *Jon!*"

She felt the pressure of the rail at her back. And she screamed.

Because she was falling.

And she could see her own death.

Jon Stuart had been angry, really angry. He'd intended to make good his escape. But something in Cassandra's voice gave him pause that time, and he swung around.

And there she was.

Falling...

It looked as if she were sailing. In this, as in all other things, she was elegant. She was wearing a white silk dressing gown, and it billowed out around her. Her ebony hair was caught by the golden glory of the sun and shone with blue-black lights. It struck him that she even fell with dramatic grace and beauty.

And only after a split second of the mindless realization that he could do nothing at all to stop it did he realize that she was already in the act of dying. Screaming, crying out, shrieking *his* name, plummeting to earth.

She died in Poseidon's arms. Cradled within them, like a wayward goddess. Eyes closed, ebony hair and snow-white gown caught by the breeze. She almost looked as if she were sleeping, except…

The trident had pierced through her.

And the snow-white gown was turning crimson.

His heart hammering, he began to shout, running desperately, as if he could reach her, help her, despite the fact that he knew…

He cried out.

Cried out her name.

Reached her, and held her.

As her blood spilled over him.

While her eyes stared into his with an ever silent reproach.

1

Three years later

The scene was definitely a chilling one. A beautiful woman in medieval dress, her long blond hair waving over the workings of the mechanism, was tied to the implement of torture, with a dark-haired, bearded and mustachioed man standing over her.

The Earl of Exeter's Daughter, also known as the Rack, proclaimed the sign overhead. Named after the Man Most Proficient in the Art of Extracting Confessions from his Victims.

The artist who had created the wax figures had been proficient, as well. The blonde stretched out on the wicked wooden rack was exquisite, with fine, classically molded features and huge blue eyes widened by her fear of her tormentor. Any sane man would long to rescue her. While the fellow standing above her—his features were pure evil. His eyes gleamed in sadistic anticipation of the pain he was about to inflict.

Many of the exhibits in the hall were excellent, retelling ancient tales of man's inhumanity to man. This particular display outdid them all.

So Jon Stuart thought as he stood silently in the shadows, leaning casually against the stone wall, his presence obscured by the darkness of the dungeon. He stared watchfully, contemplatively, at the exhibit—and at the flesh-and-blood blonde now standing in front of it.

She was nearly—in face, coloring and form—a mirror image of the poor beauty stretched out on the rack itself. She was a young woman with a glorious mop of blond hair that cascaded freely over her shoulders and down her back. She was slender and beautifully shaped, doing incredible justice to the jeans and fitted sweater she wore. Her features were very feminine: fine, straight, slender nose; high, chiseled cheekbones; beautiful blue eyes; and full, lushly shaped lips. She was surveying the display with a certain amount of interest—and wariness. She looked as if she wanted to laugh ruefully, reminding herself that she was looking at wax figures, but the scene was scary, and she was alone in the shadows. Or so she thought.

Sabrina Holloway.

He hadn't seen her in more than three and a half years now, and though he was somewhat surprised by her presence; he was glad she had decided to come. She had politely declined his invitation to the last, fateful Mystery Week. The occasion when Cassandra had died.

Whether Sabrina realized it or not, she had most certainly been Joshua's model for the beauty on the rack; she was the victim's spitting image, and Joshua always enjoyed using people he knew in his art. He had mentioned to Jon that he had met Sabrina Holloway in Chicago, and he had sounded entirely infatuated, so Jon had refrained from telling Joshua that he, too, was acquainted with her. It was easy to understand Joshua's head-over-heels reaction; he'd experienced something quite similar when he'd met her himself. Before...

Well, there was a lot to admire—or covet—about Ms. Holloway. Jon hadn't been the only one to fall victim to her charm; she had attracted the attention of Brett McGraff, as well. Jon shook his head. She'd gone off and married McGraff. Whirlwind courtship, whirlwind marriage—scandalous divorce.

Jon watched her now, glad of the distance between them. He stared at her in simple assessment. She possessed a rare grace and beauty. Even though he'd been something of a recluse over the last few years, he'd kept up with her career, reading about her in the papers and tabloids. Reporters had leaped wholeheartedly on Brett McGraff's last, noisy divorce from such a beautiful young creature.

She had been stunning when Jon met her. So innocent, eager, fascinated. He was certain that the rose-colored blinders were gone from her eyes now. She had matured. And now she was...

Spectacular. More elegant than ever. She looked thoughtful, even wise.

And how would you know? Jon taunted himself.

She might well have matured into a hard, ambitious bitch, he reminded himself dryly. Life often did that to people. After all, she'd walked away from him with a will of steel. And she'd been able to stand her ground during the media blitz after her divorce, even in the midst of a shocking situation. Still, she now maintained a strange, compelling air that combined sophistication and innocence, although, God knew, he'd learned the hard way that the most delicate, fragile females could be the worst black widows.

She was a Midwestern farm girl, Jon remembered, and he had to smile. She possessed both warmth and reserve, and yet there had been moments when she'd let down her guard and he'd felt that he had known her forever. He had found her to be both captivating and as down-to-earth as her natural beauty. She'd been twenty-four, fresh from the country, when they met. She'd turned twenty-eight last month. Plenty of time to learn, to harden, to change. If only…

Well, it had been a different time, a different place, a different life. No one had ever been the wiser. He hadn't told tales.

She hadn't wanted any told.

Still…

Jon suddenly felt a deep irritation. His feelings were totally unjustified, he told himself. Brett McGraff was here, as well. She and McGraff had actually been married. Jon had no right himself. And yet…

Hell, it was his place, his party. And he intended to spend time with all his guests. McGraff's presence would only make it a more intriguing enterprise to attempt to get to know Sabrina again.

But was she in over her head? he wondered suddenly. Maybe he should have left her name off the guest list. But then, he hadn't really expected her to come. And they were all in over their heads. Still, he suddenly wished he hadn't taken the chance of making her, like the others, an unwitting pawn in this dark game.

But he'd set this board into motion; he'd had no choice. It was either this or give up his sanity. And there were others to whom he owed both the truth and justice, if not to himself. He wasn't exactly in this alone. He had promised to do things again, exactly this way.

Maybe he should just stay away from Ms. Sabrina Holloway. Of all the people here, she alone was clearly innocent.

He wondered if he could stay away from her. And he reminded himself that she was here by choice. They'd all come willingly enough, ready to play. Some for the fun of it, some for the publicity. Cassie, the inveterate journalist, had once told him, "Never miss a photo op, darling!" He'd noticed that very few writers, actors, musicians or artists ever tended to do so, and, in a manner of speaking, this week was a major photo op. Even the reclusive types who preferred to remain in the shadows wouldn't dare miss this. The world had gotten far too competitive, and name recognition could mean the difference between starvation and healthy income.

Yet, he mused, Sabrina Holloway had inadvertently garnered enough publicity already. Marriage to and divorce from Brett McGraff had put her squarely in the public eye. But she had maintained a steady course, and though her notoriety had given her popular career a jump start, she'd managed to accrue a respectable amount of critical praise for the writing. He hadn't been in the States for a while now, so he wasn't sure who else was doing the talk-show circuit, but apparently she'd hit just the right chord with her Victorian thrillers. She was also young and lovely, and the media loved to hop on a personality with sex appeal and presence.

He was about to approach her when he realized that another woman was walking toward him. Susan Sharp. He groaned inwardly and considered a fast retreat up the secret staircase behind him. His ancestors had been Jacobites and had filled the castle with hidden doors and passages, a multitude of escape routes.

But Jon didn't escape; he didn't want his secrets known as yet, so he stood still while Susan sashayed closer, delighted with her good luck in discovering that he was literally cornered.

"Well, well," she said happily. "Darling! So here you are, in the darkness. How delightful. How wickedly delightful. Do give me a kiss, darling. We've all missed you so much."

Sabrina Holloway stared at the disturbing display, marveling at its realism. The woman on the rack looked as if she were about to open her mouth and cry out. Her eyes were glazed, as if she were trying to deny the terror that was threatening her. Sabrina could almost hear the man demanding that his victim confess her terrible crimes and spare herself the agony of the rack.

A strange tremor snaked up Sabrina's spine.

Whoa. Excellently done. Totally unnerving. There were others ambling around the dungeon displays at Lochlyre Castle, many of them friends, but at the moment she felt thoroughly uneasy in the gloom. Just imagine. If the lights were suddenly to go out...

She would be alone. In the darkness. With him—the dark-haired torturer with the slim mustache and sadistic eyes who looked upon his victim with such pure evil in his heart. The figures were so realistically done that she could easily believe they might come to life in the dark. They would move, walk, stalk, wield their weapons of death and destruction....

Hands landed on her shoulders, and she almost screamed aloud. She jumped, but somehow she choked back the sound that had risen in her throat.

"Well, my love?"

Another little shiver snaked along her spine—she was again unnerved, but not so frightened this time. Brett McGraff moved beside her then, settling an arm easily around her shoulders. She was ashamed to realize that his presence made her feel more secure in the shadowy dungeon, though still far from comfortable.

She was torn between clinging to him and shaking off his arm. As usual, she felt an amazing combination of emotions toward him. Sometimes he made her want to gag. Then again, she wasn't always immune to the purely sensual charm that had attracted her to him from the very beginning. Most of the time, however, she was only slightly impatient with him and fairly tolerant.

"It's very real," she murmured. "It actually scares me a little."

"Good."

"Why?"

"I think I want you scared."

"Oh?"

"Might make you a little clingy." He tightened his arm around her and lowered his mouth to whisper huskily against her ear. "We've each been assigned our own room in the castle—our host doesn't seem to remember that we were married—but I'd be happy to keep you company during the long, spooky nights."

"*Were*," she reminded him, "is the operative word here. We *were* married, once upon a time, more than three years ago—for all of two weeks."

"Oh, it took longer than two weeks to get a divorce," he said smoothly. "And don't forget how much we were together on our wonderful honeymoon."

"Brett, the marriage ended while we were still on that honeymoon," she reminded him.

He wasn't to be deterred. "And now we're getting to be such good friends again," he added with assurance.

Despite herself, Sabrina felt a rueful smile curving her lips. Brett was tall and good-looking, with unruly brown hair, dark bedroom eyes to match and a laconic charm that had made him a media idol. He wrote medical thrillers, with both commercial and critical success. He'd made a small fortune at his craft and still managed to be annoyingly arrogant only on occasion. Sabrina had met him soon after the sale of her second book before it had even been on the market—which had been soon after his divorce from his third wife. To say that she'd been naive was a terrible understatement. She'd also been healing from a far unhappier situation.

A whirlwind courtship had sent them on a honeymoon to Paris—at a time that happened to correspond with the French publication of Brett's latest thriller. She'd been amused, at first, by the number of women who gave him less-than-subtle hints regarding their carnal interest, then less amused when she realized how many of them he already knew. Carnally. Still, being an optimist who longed for a future, she'd decided she could live with Brett's past. It hadn't even been so bad that the women he'd known hadn't seemed to care that he had a new wife; she hadn't held other people's behavior against them. Ultimately, it had been Brett's indifference to the discomfort of her position that had disturbed her. He was a good lover; he could be amusing, charming. He'd made her laugh and love when she'd felt adrift and unsure.

But Brett could also be self-centered, selfish and downright mean. He'd disappeared with the voluptuous owner of a major bookstore for several hours and been totally impatient with his young bride when she'd demanded to know what was going on. Then he'd informed her that he was Brett McGraff, and opportunities were going to come his way. He'd told her she shouldn't mind; she should just be grateful he had actually married her, had made her his wife.

To Sabrina, his words had been devastating. She'd been stunned. Then furious—with herself. She'd been looking so desperately for someone to make her forget her past, to fill her life. And she'd been so wrong. She'd cared for Brett, believed things could work. But she'd been mistaken. So she was at fault, as well, for not seeing or believing that their visions of love and marriage were so wildly different.

Brett had seen the change, the new awareness, in her eyes, and he'd tried to placate her, to seduce her....

The rest had been hell.

She didn't want to remember. She'd learned some good lessons from that time, and maybe even taught him a few. To this day, he still couldn't believe that she'd left him and filed divorce papers, not asking for one red cent. In the months to come, when they'd met at various publishing events, he'd sought her out. He still referred to her as his wife, and she could actually smile sometimes now at the various lines he deployed to try to get her into bed. She should sleep with him because they had been married; because she'd already slept with him, and it wasn't good to sleep with strangers. Because she already knew him—and as a result there would be no ugly little surprises. Because he was good in bed; and she had to admit that he *was* good—naturally, because he was so practiced. Because surely *everybody* needed sex now and then, and since she was capable of being such a sweet, puritanical prude, coming from an apple-pie farm family and all, she was slow to form intimate relationships and therefore should simply indulge in a basic, necessary activity with him.

So far, she'd managed to resist.

She was certain that she wasn't alluring above all others; she was simply the one who had left him, and therefore she remained a challenge.

"Seriously, while we're here, wouldn't you like to share a room with me?" he asked now.

"No," she said simply.

"Admit it, I'm fun to sleep with."

"We have different ideas of fun."

"Look around you. This is a scary place," he urged.

"No, thanks, Brett."

"I can behave."

"That's doubtful. Besides, you remind me of a warning my mother used to give me. Don't play with toys when you don't know where they've been."

He grinned. "Ouch! But if you'd stayed with me, you would know exactly where I'd been."

"Brett, I never knew where you were when we were married, and I really didn't have all that much time in which to misplace you. I realize that it never occurred to you that marriage meant monogamy—"

"Do you think it means that to everyone?" he demanded.

"Brett, I can't tell other people how to be married. I only know what I wanted myself."

He sniffed. "If only you knew how many people slept around—people you would never imagine."

"Brett, I don't want to imagine."

"Your own friends!" he persisted.

"Brett—"

"All right, fine. Later you'll be begging me for gossip, and I won't tell you a thing. When you need to know, you'll be in the dark. Unless, of course, you want to forget the marriage thing for a while and just have fun? My intentions are honorable, though. I will remarry you."

She groaned. "As I said, we have different ideas on fun—and marriage."

"Fine. Play hard to get. But if things start getting spooky around here, you're going to want to crawl into bed with me, and it may be too crowded by then."

"That I don't doubt."

"Hey, I'm asking you first. And surely you wouldn't want to sleep with a stranger."

"Brett, I've slept with *you,* and I really can't think of anyone much stranger."

"Very funny. You'll be sorry, my pet. You'll see." He shook his head sorrowfully, returning his gaze to the display before them. "Amazing, isn't it?" he murmured, staring at the characters, his arm still around her.

"Yes, very real," she agreed.

He shook his head. "So real that in this lighting, she could fool even me. And I was married to you."

"What are you talking about?"

"What do you mean, what am I talking about? You've been staring at this tableau." He sighed with impatience. "Sabrina! Take a good look. That's *you.*"

"What?"

"Sweetheart, have you gone blind since you've been away from me? Take a look. That woman— she's you. To a T. The blue eyes, the blond hair, the gorgeous features. Nice body." He lowered his voice even further. "Great butt, too."

"You can't even see her butt, Brett."

"All right, all right, I'll concede that. But she's you. The spitting image."

"Don't be silly...." Sabrina protested, but her voice trailed away as she frowned.

Oh, Lord. Brett was right. The wax figure did bear an alarming resemblance to her. So much so that she felt chills begin to sweep up and down her spine again.

"Good!" Brett whispered huskily. "I can feel you trembling. You're getting uneasy, unnerved, good and scared. You're not going to want to be alone all night in this spooky old castle. You're going to want to come to me. Night will fall, you'll hear wolves howling, you'll run screaming from your bedroom and into mine, so you won't have to be afraid."

It was just a caricature in wax, nothing more, Sabrina told herself. Yet she still felt tremors racing through her limbs. It *was* her. The artist had executed the figure so well that the muscles and veins in the victim's arms fairly leaped into animation as she struggled to free herself from the ropes that tied her mercilessly to the rack.

The fear in the eyes was real.

The silent scream on the lips was far too eloquent. It could almost be heard in the air.

Brett whispered warningly in her ear, "You won't want to be alone."

From the darkness behind them, a deep, rich, masculine voice intervened. "Well, now, she'll hardly be alone, will she?"

Sabrina knew that husky voice.

She spun around to meet their host.

2

His eyes were on her, studying her. He smiled pleasantly as he continued, "Seriously, Brett, she'll hardly be alone, considering the fact that there are ten writers here—including ourselves, of course—along with an artist, my assistant and the castle staff, all in residence."

He sounded amused. Slipping from beneath Brett's arm, Sabrina stared at Jon Stuart. It had been a long time.

"Jon," Brett murmured, an unmistakable edge in his voice. The two were supposedly friends; still, it seemed that Brett was less than pleased with Stuart's timing.

"Brett, good to see you. Thank you for coming."

"It's always a pleasure. We were all damn glad you decided to do it again. Jon, you've met my wife, Sabrina Holloway, haven't you?"

Sabrina gazed at the mesmerizing owner of Lochlyre Castle, but Jon Stuart had already arched a dark brow Brett's way as he took Sabrina's hand. She resisted the odd temptation to wrench it away.

"Sabrina, good to see you again. I hadn't realized the two of you had remarried."

"We haven't," Sabrina said.

"Ah."

"Sorry. My ex-wife," Brett murmured innocently, smiling intimately at Sabrina as if there were still a great deal going on between them. "It's so easy to forget we ever divorced."

"Anyway, I'm glad you're both here. Thank you for coming," Stuart said politely.

"I wouldn't have missed it. You know that," Brett said.

"It was nice to be invited," Sabrina murmured.

"You've been invited before," Jon said pointedly.

"I...I was on a deadline last time." It was a lie, of course. An author's stock excuse for not being somewhere he or she didn't want to be.

"Well, it must have been worth it, then. Your last book was very good."

"You read it?" she inquired—too quickly. Instantly she wanted to kick herself. She was blushing, unaccountably pleased that he had been interested enough to read her work. Then she felt her flush darken, wondering what he must have thought of the book's graphic romantic encounters. And wondering how much her blush was giving away.

"I've loved all *your* recent work," she said quickly, trying to cover herself.

He smiled a slow, skeptical smile that clearly indicated he had heard the words before but somehow doubted them in this case.

"It's the truth," she murmured, wishing she could gracefully end her awkward monologue. Brett was staring at her now with real interest, having picked up on the tension between her and Jon Stuart.

"Really?" Jon murmured, either unaware of her discomfort or amused by it. It was disturbing to realize that he maintained such an edge over her both in maturity and in simple confidence. He had been a success since his first novel, a thriller based in World War II Italy, had been published soon after he'd graduated from college.

She forced a cool smile to her lips. She was not going to be intimidated. "Okay, so I hated it when you killed the priest in your last book—he didn't deserve it."

Her words didn't offend him; he laughed, apparently pleased with her honesty. "Good for you, telling me the truth."

"The truth is always different through different eyes," Brett interjected somewhat irritably.

Jon shook his head. "No, there's only the truth, maybe just shaded a bit differently," he said somewhat solemnly, gazing at Sabrina. Then he seemed to collect himself and said more lightly, "And the truth is, of course, that I'm delighted you were able to tear yourself away from your busy schedule to be here, Ms. Holloway."

"She knew I was coming and that she'd be comfortable here," Brett said proprietarily.

"Great," Jon responded.

"I have a number of friends here," Sabrina murmured, wondering why she cared if Jon Stuart did or didn't think she was still sleeping with her ex-husband. But she kept talking. "You know how it goes. We authors tend to stick together. You have an impressive guest list. I'm flattered to be invited."

"I very much wanted you to be here," he said politely. "As you may recall, I wanted you last time, as well."

Right. He had wanted her. She'd first met him just months before his last Mystery Week party. And in that time, she'd married Brett—and they'd divorced.

And he'd married Cassandra Kelly.

"I had only one book out on the market at the time. I could hardly be ranked among the pros you had here then."

He arched a brow, cocking his head. "Dianne Dorsey was even more of a babe in the woods at the time, and she was here," Jon commented.

"But it did turn out to be a tragic occasion, so it's a good thing Sabrina didn't come," Brett said. "Glad to see you seem to be bucking up, old boy," he added, punching Jon lightly on the shoulder with his fist. "We haven't seen enough of you lately. By the way, wasn't Cassie actually the one who told us all what a great book Sabrina had written?"

"Yes," Jon said evenly, still studying Sabrina. "Cassandra thought you had created superb characters in a compelling setting, then concocted the perfect murder for just the right dramatic twist."

"That was quite nice of her," Sabrina murmured uncomfortably. Cassandra was dead—and she felt incredibly guilty, because she hadn't cared much for the woman when she was alive.

All right, so she'd jealously despised her. The one time they'd met face-to-face had been a horror worse than anything in this gallery.

It was only natural that she had hated Cassandra Stuart.

A hot tremor snaked through her again, having nothing to do with the tableau in front of them. The way Jon was staring at her was unnerving. Despite the ridiculously possessive way Brett was behaving at the moment, Sabrina was suddenly glad of his presence.

For Jon Stuart was imposing. Even intimidating, in a way. Perhaps by simple virtue of his height and hard-muscled build. He was very tall, about six foot three, and strikingly handsome in a rugged way. His hair wasn't just dark, it was jet black, thick and luxurious, long past his collar though neatly combed back from his forehead. His eyes were a marbled hazel, truly unique, merging blue, green and brown into a compelling, moody mix that could appear golden at times, dark as night at others. His features were strong, arresting: firm, square chin; broad cheekbones; generous, sensual mouth; high, defined brow. At thirty-seven, he was a renowned master of adventure and suspense writing; in real life, too, he had been named by a prominent international magazine to be one of the world's ten most intriguing men. An American of Scottish heritage, he had never used fame or fortune to shirk duty; he'd served overseas in the National Guard during Desert Storm.

Though Stuart had recently lain very low, remaining in Scotland more often than not, he still appeared in news stories now and then, usually upon the once-a-year publication of his latest book or the reissue in paperback of the previous title. It didn't matter that he'd been something of a recluse for the past several years—that merely enhanced his reputation.

The mystery surrounding the death of his wife rendered him both fascinatingly dangerous and hauntingly sympathetic. Some journalists claimed he had gone into deep mourning for Cassandra, while others hinted he had retreated into guilt, that he had somehow killed her—even if he had been a hundred feet away from the balcony from which she'd fallen at the time. Some suggested she might have committed suicide, that her marriage had been failing and she had cast herself from the balcony in a moment of dramatic self-pity, putting the blame on her famous husband, creating a scandal that would torment him until the end of his days. Others thought that perhaps the cancer consuming her beautiful breasts had driven her to despair. Whatever had happened had certainly given rise to endless speculation. And Jon Stuart had endured legal hearings into the matter and been tried by the press, his peers and fans, as well. His annual Mystery Week, a famed writers' retreat orchestrated at his secluded castle in Scotland to raise publicity and funds for children's charities, had been halted.

Until now.

Three years after the death of his wife, he had opened the doors of Lochlyre Castle to the outside world once again.

"Come to think of it, Cassie's praise of Sabrina's work was noteworthy," Brett mused suddenly, "because she wasn't usually so generous. She supposedly liked my work, but she ripped *Scalpel* to shreds. Remember, Jon? She even blasted your work sometimes, and though I hate to admit it, that's hard to do."

"Thanks. That's quite a compliment," Jon said dryly.

Brett grinned. "I'm feeling chipper. Just got the word that *Surgery* is number two, the *New York Times* list, come a week from Sunday."

"Congratulations," Sabrina told him wholeheartedly. He always made the bestseller lists, but his position was rising steadily, much to his delight.

"Great," Jon said. "You can keep everybody's spirits up during the week. Remind them that, dire perennial rumors to the contrary, publishing is not yet dead. So...what do you two think of the chamber of horrors this year?"

"Ghoulishly wonderful," Brett said.

"Too real." Sabrina shuddered.

"Ah," Jon murmured, eyes pure gold with sudden devilish humor. "I wouldn't let your resemblance to the lady on the rack upset you," he said. "An artist named Joshua Valine created the figures for the exhibit. He's also done a lot of cover art—he met you at the booksellers' convention in Chicago and was duly impressed."

"Not very positively, if he has me on the rack," Sabrina commented.

Jon laughed, a deep, husky, compelling sound.

"Trust me, his reaction was quite positive. He always uses real people, whether he's painting or working in wax. And if you'll look around, you'll see that there really wasn't a pleasant situation in which he could have put anyone. Look to the far corner," he said, that glimmer still in his eyes.

As hardened as she told herself she had become, Sabrina could still feel the force of his charisma. He had just the slightest hint of a Scotsman's burr in his deep voice, acquired from all the time he had spent here. His features and build—his entire presence—were exceedingly masculine. Even his subtle aftershave seemed intoxicating.

Indeed, Jon Stuart was a dangerous man, she reminded herself. And a stranger, really, though she had once known him well—in a way.

"In the far corner over there," he said now, "Louis XVI and Marie Antoinette are off to face the guillotine, and Joan of Arc is about to be burned at the stake. In the next display, Anne Boleyn is ready to meet her swordsman, and over there, Jack the Ripper is in the midst of slicing Mary Kelly's throat." He shook his head in mock sadness. "Joshua is not fond of Susan Sharp, I'm afraid. Go take a look at Mary Kelly."

"So I suppose I should be grateful to be on the rack? Tortured for endless hours before death?" Sabrina observed.

Jon cocked his head slightly, amused. "Actually, Ms. Holloway, the beautiful blonde on the rack is the only victim in this room to survive. She is Lady Ariana Stuart, and before she could be stretched and broken—accused of an attempt to turn young Charles over to Cromwell's forces when his father was about to be beheaded—her brother brought a plea regarding her innocence before the young Charles himself, who was by then returned to the throne as Charles II, king of England. Charles, being the lusty fellow he was, instantly saw the waste in destroying so fine a damsel, so he ordered her out of the torture chamber and into his bed. Naturally, being the charming man he was, he made her one of his mistresses. She bore him numerous illegitimate children and lived to a ripe old age.''

"How comforting," Sabrina said.

"Very romantic," Brett sniffed. "I bet you made all that up to placate Sabrina."

"I swear it's God's own truth," Jon Stuart assured them.

"Well, Joshua certainly had a field day with Susan Sharp," Brett said, chuckling with malicious pleasure. "And what a perfect Ripper's victim. After all, she has been known to 'entertain' men for the rewards she might gain," he remarked.

"That's hearsay," Jon murmured, shrugging.

Sabrina gritted her teeth at Brett's boorish comment and silently applauded Jon's refusal to speak ill of others.

"Who did old Josh use for Joan of Arc?" Brett asked, unfazed.

"My assistant, Camy," Jon said. "She's actually

quite religious herself, I believe, and a good, hard worker.''

''How apropos,'' Brett said. ''I approve.''

Jon grinned. ''So far you do.''

Brett let out a groan. ''So there's something I'm not going to like?''

''Most probably not.''

''He used me?''

Jon nodded.

''As?''

Jon indicated the torturer about to twist the rack with the blond beauty upon it.

''Take away all the facial hair...'' Jon suggested with a touch of rueful apology.

Brett gasped. ''I should sue!''

Sabrina couldn't help but laugh, which irritated Brett still further.

''Come on, Brett, be a sport. You were just a model—and with the beard and mustache, no one will guess. And remember, the weekend is all for charity. Have a sense of humor,'' she suggested.

''Oh, very funny. I get to torture my ex-wife. So are you in this rogues' gallery?'' he demanded of Jon.

Jon arched a brow. ''Yes. Yes, I am.''

''Where?'' Brett demanded.

''Come on.''

Brett looked at Sabrina, shrugging. ''He's probably set himself up as a king—or as Gandhi.''

''Gandhi would hardly fit in here, and a number of kings weren't such great fellows,'' Jon reminded him. ''But I didn't have anything to do with Joshua's choice of models. He doesn't tell me how to write, and I don't tell him how to sculpt."

They followed him down a corridor to another display. A tall man in European dress of perhaps the 1500s stood above the sprawled body of a woman. Her head was turned to the side, hiding her features from them. The man was staring down at the woman with a mixture of anger and confusion on his face. He had long, light brown hair, but he was still quite evidently Jon Stuart.

"Who are they?" Sabrina asked, confused.

"He's not well-known to Americans," Jon said, studying the display dispassionately. "His name was Matthew McNamara. Laird McNamara. He was a Scotsman who did away with three mistresses and two wives."

"How?" Brett asked. "I don't see a weapon."

"He strangled them," Jon said simply.

"How did he get away with so many murders before he was found out?" Sabrina asked.

"He was never brought to justice. He was considered so powerful among the clansmen that executing his own wayward women was considered his right," Jon said.

He turned away from the figures to look at her again, and she saw that his marbled eyes had gone very dark and cold. A strange trembling touched her as he slowly smiled. Was he mocking her? Or himself? She was afraid, she realized.

And worse.

She felt like a moth attracted to a flame. Time

hadn't changed anything, nor had distance. That Jon Stuart was virtually a stranger to her meant nothing at all. She felt the same fierce and immediate fascination she had felt the first time she'd met him, a little more than three and a half years ago.

The first time...the last time.

"Who's the model for the wife?" Brett asked. Then, as if suddenly realizing that he might not want to hear the answer, he hurried on. "Joshua Valine is good. What an eye for detail."

"Relax, Brett. It isn't Cassie," Jon said, a dry smile curling his lip. "It's Dianne Dorsey. You can see her face if you look at the tableau from the other side."

"Dianne...well, yes, of course. I guess I thought of Cassie because of the black hair, but Dianne is dark, too...." Brett murmured, clearing his throat. He looked at Jon uneasily.

"Cassie's over there, Brett," Jon said, indicating a figure praying in front of mullioned windows. "Joshua used her for his Mary, Queen of Scots, contemplating the morning of the day of her execution."

"Yes, yes, that's definitely Cassandra," Brett said, staring for a long moment. His eyes jerked back to Jon's. "Doesn't that...bother you?"

"They all bother me—they're so real," Jon admitted. "But Josh is an artist, and that's how he works. Besides, I think Cassie makes a good Mary, Queen of Scots."

"They're all women, the victims," Sabrina commented.

Jon smiled. "Well, historically, it seems, lots of men were monsters. But I assure you, we have some lethal ladies here, as well." He pointed across the room. "There you have Countess Bathory, the Hungarian 'blood countess.' Allegedly she sacrificed hundreds of young women so she could bathe in their blood to retain her youth and beauty. V. J. Newfield is the model, as you might notice."

"Oh, you're in trouble there!" Brett warned.

Jon laughed. "V.J. will get a good laugh out of it. Besides, the countess was supposed to be quite beautiful as well as bloodthirsty." He pointed out another tableau. "There you have Lady Emily Watson, who poisoned no fewer than ten husbands to get their worldly goods. So you see, we do try to be an equal-opportunity chamber of horrors."

"Who's the model for Lady Emily?" Brett queried.

"Anna Lee Zane. And her victim is Thayer Newby."

Brett laughed. "Thayer, downed by a woman! He's going to love that."

Jon shrugged. "There's Reggie Hampton as Good Queen Bess, signing the death warrant for Mary, Queen of Scots."

"Who are the others?" Sabrina asked, indicating the rest of the tableaux receding into the shadowy depths of the castle's basement.

"Naturally Tom Heart and Joe Johnston are in here, but I'll let you find them. Joshua used a few of the household staff, as well, so don't be surprised if you find your breakfast being served by Catherine the Great.''

"Sabrina," Brett puffed, "we really should re-marry, and quickly! Jack the Ripper could arrive for your laundry!''

"Oh, I think I can manage my own hand laundry, and I'll make sure to have breakfast with a crowd," Sabrina told him. She wanted to kick him when she saw that Jon was studying her again.

Jon merely shrugged and seemed to ignore the exchange. "Joshua had lots of people working on this project for more than a year. We'll be donating the sculptures to a new museum in the north country when we're done here."

"You'll need releases from the models," Brett warned him.

Jon smiled. "I think I'll get them. The publicity will be phenomenal, you know."

"Great, I'll go down in history as a maniacal tor-turer!" Brett moaned, but the word *publicity* had won him over.

"Don't feel bad. One way or the other, I go down as a wife murderer. Well, if you'll excuse me, I have a few things to attend to. Enjoy yourselves. Brett, you know your way around. Ms. Holloway, please make yourself at home, as well. I'll see you at cocktails."

He turned and walked away with strong strides. In a moment the shadows swallowed him.

Yet somehow his presence seemed to linger, and Sabrina found herself turning to stare again at the wax tableau of Matthew, Laird McNamara.

Very tall, straight, broad-shouldered he was, with hands on his hips as he stood over the woman at his feet. Handsome, proud, merciless, powerful—laird indeed of his domain.

So powerful that he could kill and get away with it?

She forced herself to turn away, to look at the other figures as they engaged in their various dances with death.

The diffuse lighting made everything even more horrible. Shadows filled the room except where each scene stood, looming out of the darkness in eerie purple light, adding to the sensation of everything being *real.* Sabrina could imagine that the figures breathed. That they twitched, that they sweated. That they might move at any second...

Matthew McNamara stood over his wife, fists clenched.

Jack the Ripper wielded his knife.

And Lady Ariana Stuart continued to scream in terror and chilling silence.

A new wave of chills began a route through Sabrina's bloodstream, and she jumped again when Brett's hands fell on her shoulders.

"Let's get out of here, shall we?" he said.

And she realized that even he suddenly sounded afraid.

3

"**M**s. Holloway!"

Cocktails were being served in the library of the castle, just down the grand staircase from the guest rooms on the second floor and opposite the great hall, where everyone would gather for dinner. Sabrina found herself arriving rather late. She'd lingered in the modern bath for a very long time, drawing together the courage to dress and go downstairs. Her brief meeting with Jon Stuart had left her far more unnerved than she'd imagined it would. For once she had to be grateful for Brett's presence. He kept her from feeling too lost and alone, even if he was annoying.

She'd barely reached the doorway to the library when she heard her name being called. A small woman with short-cropped, shiny brown hair was moving toward her, offering her a glass of champagne. She had powder blue eyes, a pretty, heart-shaped face and a tentative smile that immediately set Sabrina at ease.

"Welcome, welcome, we're so delighted that you could come. Well, I'm delighted especially, since I'm a true fan.'' She pressed the champagne flute forward into Sabrina's hand.

"Thank you so much," Sabrina said. "And you are…?"

"Oh!" The young woman said, and flushed, making her appear even prettier and more delicate. "I'm Camy, Camy Clark. I'm Jon's secretary and assistant."

"Of course, Joan of Arc!"

Camy flushed more deeply. "Yes, that would be me. Joshua Valine is a good friend."

Sabrina laughed. "He must be. You look lovely, even being martyred."

"Well, Josh is a dear. He makes everyone look wonderful. You're definitely the finest looking victim I've ever seen on a rack."

Sabrina laughed again, lifting her champagne glass. "He's very talented, certainly."

"So are you. I love your work. The male writers can be so dry. You know, all action but no endearing characteristics to their people. I just love your Miss Miller. She's a delight. So real, so sympathetic, brave but not ridiculously so."

"Thank you again. Very much."

"Camy, Camy, Camy!"

A slim woman of about five-five, with short, artfully styled dark hair, was bearing down on them. Her off-the-shoulder cocktail dress was elegant designer wear; her shoes matched its soft mauve. Sabrina knew Susan Sharp, because Susan herself made a point of knowing everyone. Most writers both feared and appreciated the literary critic because she had so much clout, especially in the world of the wealthy, and thus, by word of mouth, could help make or break a book or an author. She had written two mysteries herself and done very well with them, since her characters were clearly based on her acquaintances among the rich and famous. But she could also be loud, opinionated and abrasive, drawing mixed reactions from friends and enemies alike. It was rumored that she had absolutely hated Cassandra Stuart, who had often been her competition in talk-show bookings.

"Camy, Camy, Camy!" Susan repeated, reaching out to curl her perfectly manicured fingers around Sabrina's arm. "You can't just pin Ms. Holloway down at the doorway—we're all waiting to see her. Authors get to be such good friends, you know."

"Yes, of course, Ms. Sharp," Camy murmured, flashing Sabrina an embarrassed look. Susan had put her in her place. She was just an assistant. The rest of them were *authors*.

"Camy, it was wonderful meeting you, and I look forward to getting to spend more time together," Sabrina told the young woman.

Camy lit up with a smile. "Thanks!"

Susan drew Sabrina on into the room. "How have you been? It's been ages since I've seen you."

"It was just last June, in Chicago," Sabrina reminded her.

"Yes, of course, you were doing so well. So many people adore that Miss Mailer of yours."

"Miller," Sabrina corrected smoothly.

"Yes, yes, Miss Miller. So tell me, what's up with you and Brett? Are you planning on remarrying?"

"What?" Sabrina demanded.

"Well, Brett does make it sound as if you two share so much passion, both of you being so talented and wild. I'll never forget how delicious it was when the tabloids ran those pictures of you running *naked* from your hotel room in Paris."

"Susan, maybe you'll never forget, but I'd like to. It was a very painful time in my life," Sabrina said firmly. "Oh, look, there's V. J. Newfield. I haven't seen her in quite some time. Excuse me, will you?"

Sabrina escaped Susan and hurried toward V. J.— Victoria Jane—Newfield. V.J. was somewhere in her fifties or sixties and had been writing forever, or so it seemed. Her work was dark and scary but far more psychological than graphic, always striking a resonant note on the human condition. She was very slim, tall, with silver hair and a graceful carriage. She was a stunning woman and doubtless would be so until the day she died. Sabrina had met her early on in her career at a group autographing, where V.J. had assured her that the nicest thing about doing signings with other authors was that there was always someone interesting to talk to if no one stopped to buy a book.

"Trip the customers as they go by, dear," she had advised. "When they think you're sitting at a table piled high with books just so you can direct them to the nearest ladies' room, trip them! Then apologize to pieces, and you've snagged them!" V.J. had been great. Already popular, she had convinced most of her fans that they simply *had* to buy Sabrina's book, as well, and Sabrina remained grateful to this day.

"V.J.!" she now said with pleasure, approaching the woman at the buffet table, where she was studying caviar-covered crackers and trying to decide whether or not to indulge.

"Sabrina, dear!" V.J. said, turning with a smile and offering her a warm hug. "I wanted to call and make sure you were going to come. I was so sorry when I learned that you turned down the last invitation, though that did become quite a tragedy. I just got back from a cruise down the Nile—do you remember my telling you how much I wanted to take one of those?"

"Yes, and I'm glad you got to go. How was it?"

"Wonderful. Exhilarating. Awesome. The sense of history is so intense, so chilling. And I do just love a good mummy."

"I've got nothing against loving mommies," Brett said, slipping an arm around Sabrina's shoulder and smiling at V.J. "Mommies these days can be just as exciting as the innocent girls. It's great to see you, V.J. You look splendid. Sexy as ever. A great mommy."

"My children are all long grown up!" V.J. reminded him.

"Mummies, my boy, mummies. We're talking about dead women, though from what I hear of your indiscriminate womanizing, that might not make any difference to you. How are you, Brett? A kiss will be acceptable, but just on the cheek. And quit mauling

Sabrina. The child has the good sense to be your *ex*-wife, and if the right man is out there, we don't want him being put off by your foolishness.''

Brett laughed, freed Sabrina and good-naturedly planted a kiss on V.J.'s cheek.

"I am the right man, V.J.," Brett protested in a mock-pitiful voice. "One moment's bad behavior, and she won't forgive me."

"My boy, I'm no marriage counselor, but I sense that it might have been a bit deeper than that. Still…" She smiled, lifting her champagne flute to him. "Congratulations, I hear you're just below Creighton on the list."

Brett bowed his head in humble acceptance. "Thank you, thank you. Creighton just had to put out another book the same month, huh? I might have made number one."

"Well, there's always next year."

"So there is. And since we're all together here, a fine assembly of mystery, suspense and horror writers, surely we can come up with some new ways to bump off the competition. What do you say?"

"I say it's in bad taste, considering where we are," a masculine voice stated softly, and Joe Johnston stepped into their circle. Joe was an Ernest Hemingway lookalike, a handsome man with a bushy beard and a pleasant way about him. He wrote a series about a down-and-out private investigator, charming and laid-back, who still solved the crime every time.

Joe clinked glasses with Sabrina by way of hello

and continued, "I mean, who really thinks that Cassandra Stuart threw herself from that balcony?"

"Joe, shush!" V.J. warned. "It was great of Jon to do this again after what happened last time."

"My point exactly," Joe said. "And that's why we can't talk about bumping off our competition."

Susan Sharp sidled into their group. "We can't talk about bumping people off?" she protested indignantly. "Joe, it's Mystery Week. One of us is *supposed* to be a murderer and bump off the others until the mystery is solved. That's the whole point."

"Right, but that's all pretend," Sabrina said.

Susan laughed dryly. "Well, let's hope that Cassandra's being dead isn't pretend. Can you imagine if she were suddenly to walk back into this room?"

"Susan, that's a horrible thing to say," V.J. admonished. "If Cassandra were to suddenly appear here, alive—"

"If Cassandra were suddenly to appear here, alive, more than half the people here would be thinking of ways to kill her again," Susan said flatly. "Cassandra was vicious and horrible."

"And smart, talented and very beautiful," V.J. reminded her smoothly.

"Oh, I suppose. And just think—everyone who was here when she died is back again. The guest list is exactly the same," Susan said.

"I wasn't here," Sabrina reminded her.

Susan shrugged, as if her presence were of little importance. "Well, you were invited, and the point is that those of us who were here then are here again.

All of us. Ready to defend ourselves if we're accused.''

"Accused of murder?" V.J. asked.

"Accused of anything," Susan said blithely. "We all have our little secrets, don't we?" she demanded, staring hard at V.J.

V.J. stared right back at her.

"Susan, if you're going to start implying things about the rest of us—" Joe began.

"Oh, come now, Joe, we're all grown-ups. Everyone knew that no matter how polite and controlled he seemed, Jon was furious with Cassandra. He thought she was having an affair—and she implied to me on several occasions that she was!"

"Susan, 'Pass me the butter' has made you think people were having an affair on at least one occasion," V.J. said impatiently.

"V.J., it's all in *how* someone says it. The point is, Jon thought she was having an affair, and *she* thought *Jon* was. If they were both right, then you have two other people involved. And God knows, Cassandra nearly destroyed some careers. Any number of us despised her at various points for what she said about our work."

"*You* might well have despised her," a soft voice said. It was shy, retiring Camy, who smiled apologetically at Susan. "After all, Ms. Sharp, you two were often in direct competition, weren't you?"

Susan arched a brow, staring at the girl imperiously. She didn't mind the accusation; she minded Camy's interrupting her. "My dear child, I have no real competition. But just for the record, I did despise Cassandra Stuart. She was an opportunist who used and manipulated people, and you should be grateful that she's dead, because she would have had you fired by now otherwise. Now please excuse me." She turned her back on the girl and spoke to the others. "You mark my words. Everyone here has a secret, not to mention a reason to hate Cassandra Stuart."

"Except Sabrina," Joe commented quietly.

Susan stared sharply at Sabrina. "Who knows? Maybe she had as much reason as the rest of us. But you couldn't have tossed her over the balcony, could you, Sabrina? You turned down the invitation to come here last time. Why? Most writers would kill—if you'll pardon the expression—for such an invitation."

"Fear of flying," Sabrina said sweetly.

Susan kept staring at her. "I'll just bet," she said. Then, whirling around, she left the group.

"I think *she* did it," Brett said with such simple conviction that they all laughed.

"According to the police, no one did it," Joe said.

"Cassandra didn't commit suicide," V.J. commented. "She loved herself far too much for that."

"But I thought she had cancer," Sabrina said.

"She did, but *maybe* it *was* treatable," Brett said.

"Maybe she simply tripped," Sabrina suggested.

"That's probably just what happened," another masculine voice interrupted. It was Tom Heart. Tall, lean, white-haired, handsome and dignified, he was the unlikely author of some of the most chilling horror novels on the market. He smiled, lifting a champagne flute to them all. "Cheers, friends, gentlemen and ladies, Brett, Joe, Sabrina...V.J. Good to see you all. And, Sabrina, you may be right on the money. From what I understand, Cassandra was shouting at Jon, who had simply had it with her mood of the moment and was walking away. Perhaps she leaned over to shout louder and leaned just a little too far. Ah, there's our host now, with the lovely Dianne Dorsey on one arm and the exquisite Anna Lee Zane on the other."

Sabrina looked toward the library door. Their host was indeed just arriving—in style.

He was in a tux, and achingly handsome. His height and dark good looks were enhanced by the elegance of his attire. His hair was slicked back, his crystalline eyes enigmatic as he talked and laughed with the two attractive women.

Anna Lee was a writer whose novels were based on true crimes. She was somewhere in her late thirties, very petite and feminine, and rumor had it that she happily chose her sexual partners from either gender.

Dianne Dorsey was considered the up-and-coming voice of horror. She was fond of creating alien beings with a bizarre hunger for human flesh. She was very young, having just turned twenty-two, and had published her first novel as a junior in high school, her second as a senior, and now, just out of Harvard, she was a veteran, with four books on the market. She was considered a genius and already had a huge following. Older writers had a tendency to be jealous of her amazing success at so tender an age, success acquired with what appeared to be so little effort. Sabrina was only envious because Dianne seemed to have acquired such self-assurance at so young an age. She would still give her eyeteeth for that kind of assurance. She had a feeling, though, that Dianne had had a tough childhood, that something had happened to make her a fighter even early on.

As she contemplated Dianne, Sabrina realized that Anna Lee was waving at her, smiling. She smiled and waved back.

Then Dianne spotted her, and she, too, grinned and waved. Sabrina lifted a hand in return. Dianne was into the Gothic look. She always wore black; her hair was jet-black; her lipstick was black; her skin was flawlessly white. She favored huge medallions, medieval-style jewelry and slinky clothing and yet managed her look with a sexy femininity that made her unique and appealing.

Still smiling, Sabrina suddenly became aware that Jon was watching her.

Once again, she was right next to Brett. Brett was, in fact, brushing up against her.

She quickly lowered her eyes. She told herself that she didn't want to get involved with anyone. She hadn't come here hoping to find something she had lost. She was a mature woman now, with a good career, lots of friends and a great family. She was here as a guest, participating in an important charity event, and it was icing on the cake that it might be a boon to her career, as well.

Liar! an inner voice taunted.

"Ladies, gentlemen, dinner is being served in the great hall," Jon announced. He excused himself from his two companions, and Sabrina bit her lip to keep from taking a step back as he walked purposefully toward her. "Ms. Holloway, you're the only one here who might not have had a chance to meet everyone. Excuse me, Brett, may I claim your ex-wife for a moment?" he asked lightly.

"Sure—for a moment," Brett replied in kind.

Sabrina was dismayed by the warmth that filled her when Jon took her by the arm, flashing his smile, and led her across the room to where a tall, slim man with curly blond hair and clean, handsome features was standing. He looked like an artist, impeccable in his dress clothing except for a tiny drop of paint on his tie. "Ms. Holloway, I'm sure you remember Joshua Valine, our sculptor extraordinaire."

"Oh, yes," Sabrina said, instantly remembering the man as his warm brown eyes touched hers. They'd met briefly in Chicago, at the booksellers' convention. She'd been signing books, and one of the sales reps had introduced him. "We've met," she told Jon, shaking Valine's hand. "How nice to see you again. Your wax work is incredible. But so real and scary! I'm going to have nightmares about being tortured by my ex-husband," she told him.

Joshua flushed and flashed a smile. "Thank you.

Forgive me for putting you on the rack. You do live, though, you know.''

She laughed softly. "So I've been told."

"You're rescued from the rack on the command of the king."

She nodded, adding, "I'm glad I didn't have to be one of Jack the Ripper's victims."

Joshua wrinkled his nose, lowering his voice. "Susan Sharp does it well, though, don't you think?"

"Shh. Susan has exceptional hearing," Jon teased. "Let's see, Joshua, is there anyone here that Sabrina might not know yet?"

"Have you met Camy Clark?" Joshua asked.

"Yes, she's charming. You're very lucky to have her, Jon."

"She's organized and incredibly competent, and I *am* very lucky," Jon agreed. "How about...?"

As he turned to look around the room, they were joined by a solid-looking man with his bright red hair in an old-fashioned crew cut. He flashed a smile at Jon and Joshua and extended his hand to Sabrina. "We've met, but only briefly, at a conference in Tahoe. I don't know if you remember me or not, but I'm—"

"Of course I remember you," Sabrina told him. "You're Thayer Newby. I went to every one of your lectures. You probably didn't see me, because the rooms were so full every time you were speaking."

Thayer Newby flushed to the roots of what there was of his hair. He'd been a cop for twenty years before becoming a writer, and his talks on police procedure were excellent.

"Thanks!" he said, staring at her and still holding her hand. He shook his head slightly. "How did McGraff ever let you get away?" he inquired. Then he suddenly blushed again. "Sorry, none of my business. I did see that picture, of course."

Sabrina gritted her teeth, trying not to blush herself. But she could feel Jon at her side, looking at her, and she knew that of course anyone who had ever seen that tabloid photo would wonder just what had caused her to go running naked from her honeymoon suite.

"Brett and I have different ideas about marriage," she said as smoothly as she could manage.

"But you've remained friends, huh?" Thayer said, trying to be casual.

Somehow the words didn't sound right. And Sabrina realized that he'd probably seen her with Brett most of the night and, like others, had jumped to the conclusion that they had remained more than just friends.

"Yes, we've managed that," she said flatly.

"Ah, there's Reggie," Jon said, lifting a hand. "Do you know Reggie Hampton?" he asked Sabrina.

Old yet somehow ageless, Regina Hampton might have been seventy or a hundred and ten. She had written scores of books about an amateur sleuth who was a grandmother and solved local mysteries with the help of her cat. Reggie was blunt, intelligent and a great deal of fun, and she had walked straight across to them as she came into the room. "Reggie," Jon began. "Do you know—"

"Of course I know the dear child!" Reggie exclaimed. She was tiny and thin and looked as if a breeze would blow her over, but she hugged Sabrina with an amazing strength that gave proof to the rumor that she was a tough old bird. "How lovely to see you here, Sabrina! Jon, however did you convince this lovely young thing to come visit a morbid, reclusive old man in his decaying castle?"

"The same way I convinced you, you old battle-ax," he teased her affectionately in turn. "I sent her an invitation."

"Well, it's just wonderful that you're here. We need new blood in on these affairs!" Reggie said.

"Ah," teased Susan, striding over to the group, "let's just hope we don't *shed* new blood, eh?" She smiled wickedly.

"Let's eat—I'm famished!" V.J. called from across the room. "Jon, you did announce dinner, didn't you? If we don't eat soon, we'll all expire, and not so mysteriously."

"Perish the thought!" Joe Johnston quipped.

"Perish! That *is* the thought," Reggie retorted.

"Right, Jon, let's eat," Brett said. "And by the way, think we could break out some brewskies? This champagne just doesn't cut it for me. How about you, Thayer?"

"There's a full bar in the great hall, with beer on tap and all kinds, domestic and imported, in the bottle. Go on in and help yourselves," Jon said.

He glanced down at Sabrina, his eyes strangely dark. She felt as if he were studying her, assessing her. And he looked as if he suddenly wanted to push her away from him.

"Excuse me, will you, please?" he said quietly. And then he was gone.

4

Reggie Hampton linked arms with Sabrina. "My dear, you are a breath of fresh air. Tell me, what's been happening with you since July?"

Sabrina tried not to watch Jon Stuart as he strode away from her. She forced herself to focus on Reggie, and replied with enthusiasm, "I've been home visiting my family."

"At the farm?"

"Yes. I have an apartment in New York now, but I've been staying at my folks' and my sister's for a while. She just had a baby, her first, a little boy. Naturally, we're all just delighted. I spent a few months out there to help when the baby was born."

"You should be having your own babies soon."

"Reggie, not every woman has babies these days."

"But you want children, don't you?"

"Yes, I do, when the time is right."

"Are you going to remarry Br—"

"No. Enough about me, Reggie. How is your family?"

Reggie told her briefly about her sons, grandsons and new great-granddaughter as they crossed the entry to the great hall, where dinner would be served. They all milled around the bar first, making drinks.

Brett popped up again to supply Sabrina with a gin and tonic, heavy on the lime, then whispered happily that he'd moved the place cards around at the dinner table and put her next to him. They sat down to a magnificent meal of pheasant and fish. As they ate, they all talked and laughed; it might have been a high school reunion. Then Jon, at the head of the table, rose, thanked them again for coming and reminded them that they were there not only for fun but also for the benefit of children's charities. Each writer had submitted a favorite cause, and the one who solved the mystery claimed the lion's share of the donations.

"When do we start?" Thayer called out.

"Tomorrow morning," Jon replied. "Those with the energy are welcome to catch up on each other's lives tonight. Those who are too exhausted from jet lag can get some sleep. Things will be pretty much the same as they were previous years. Camy and Joshua have worked out the particulars. I won't know who the murderer is any more than any of you will. In the morning, you'll all receive your character roles and a description of the situation. The murderer will discover who he—or she—is, and then he or she will have to get busy before being discovered. The murderer will have been assigned the order in which the victims are to be dispatched. The victims will be 'murdered' with a washable red paint, and naturally we'll take care of any cleaning expenses. Any questions?"

"Sure," Joe Johnston said, speaking up. "Even if I'm not the murderer, can I shoot Susan anyway?"

Laughter rose, then faded, as Susan stared them all down. "You're right at the top of my list, too, Joe," she told him sweetly. She pointed a finger at him and made a popping sound, as if she were pulling a trigger. "And you'll be covered in something a lot worse than red paint!"

"Come, come, children, behave," Anna Lee Zane drawled.

"Well, shit, I'm sorry!" Joe said.

Anna Lee shook her head, as if it were as impossible to deal with writers as with unruly children.

Jon rose. "If you all will excuse me, I have a few things to attend to," he said. "Please, make yourselves at home. We'll meet here at nine tomorrow morning. For the early birds, coffee will be on the buffet by six."

He exited the great hall, closing the double doors behind him. Sabrina stared after him, biting her lower lip, wishing suddenly that she hadn't come.

Brett's hand landed on hers where it rested on the table. "Want to see my room?" he inquired hopefully.

She withdrew her hand, smiling because he could be so much like a child, so eager, so unwilling to admit defeat.

'No. I'm going to bed."

That will work with me."

'To sleep. I'm one of those guests with jet lag. I

got to London late last night and came here this afternoon. I'm tired.''

"All right. I'm right next door to you, if you change your mind. If things go bump in the night."

"Thanks. I'll keep that in mind," she told him.

She waved a good-night to the others as she escaped the great hall.

The castle foyer and magnificent staircase were empty. With the doors to the library and great hall closed, she suddenly felt very alone in the ancient edifice.

She hurried up the stairs and down the second-floor hallway with its Norman arches toward her own room.

It was huge, retaining a historical feel yet updated to offer incredible warmth and comfort. The bed sat on a richly carpeted dais, and heavy draperies hung at the balcony doors to ward off cold drafts. The closet and bath were large, and an antique desk sat to the side of a massive hearth. A fire had been built and stoked, and it burned brightly as she entered her room, hesitated, then carefully shot the bolt.

She kicked off her shoes and stripped away her stockings, then found herself wandering to the glass-paned balcony doors that closed out the night beyond. She opened them and stepped outside. From this vantage point she could see rolling fields, the shimmering waters of a small loch and the purple crests of mountains in the distance. The scenery, even by moonlight, was breathtaking. This trip was the opportunity of a lifetime.

She never should have come.

Sabrina drew a long, shaky breath. "So," she asked herself aloud, "did you come to try to convince yourself that your brief, shining moment in his company is completely over and forgotten? Or were you hoping to sleep with him just once more, whatever the consequences?"

She felt her cheeks redden. How humiliating. Would he sleep with her again? She undoubtedly had a reputation for being rather...casual. Just think of the way she had left Brett, running away naked....

Funny. Brett was okay. She liked being friends. It was even flattering that he still pursued her. What he had done *was* terribly wrong, but what she had done was wrong, as well. She had married him without truly loving him.

Because, of course, she had been in love with Jon Stuart.

A cool breeze suddenly wrapped around her, and she remembered being in New York City for the very first time and winding up at a party for one of her publicist's other clients, who had just had a Broadway opening. Sabrina had had no idea who the handsome party guest was when she met him, other than that his name was Jon. He'd had her laughing, telling her about the terrors of the big city and how it might well be a death-defying feat simply to survive her first experience with a New York cab driver.

Admittedly, she'd drunk too much. She'd been exhilarated with the success of selling her book and excited at being in his company. He had a car, and he offered to drive her back to her hotel.

She'd fallen asleep on his shoulder in the car, and when they'd reached her hotel, she was still drowsy, intoxicated and giddy. She remembered opening her eyes and seeing his face above hers, his eyes dark, marbled, fascinating. "We're here," he'd told her.

And she'd nodded, though she hadn't moved, and then he'd said, "I can carry you up to your room. Which is what I should do. Because if I bring you home with me, I'll take advantage of you. I won't be able to help myself."

Even with the breeze caressing her now on the balcony, she could still remember her reply.

"Please do."

No amount of alcohol could forgive that, she told herself now. She hugged her arms around her chest. Yet it had been wonderful. The best time of her life. They'd driven to his apartment in the city, and he'd carried her upstairs. He had undressed her in his bedroom, and, still dressed himself, he had demanded to know if she was sure....

Then he had kissed her, and for the rest of her life she would remember his touch on her body, his lips, burning, intimate, demanding, everywhere. She would remember him, the feel of his flesh, the touch of his hands, the mole at the small of his back....

The night had been pure magic. The next day they'd cooked breakfast together, wandered through the Metropolitan Museum of Art and gone out for Chinese before returning to spend the evening making love again. Absurdly, after all that, it wasn't until the next morning that she'd asked his last name and learned that he was "the" Jon Stuart, the well-known author.

Jon had been in the shower when his "fiancée," Cassandra, showed up. Sabrina herself had been wearing a terry robe, her hair wet and plastered around her face. She'd been stunned when the door opened. Cassandra had stared at Sabrina, looking her up and down, not appearing angry—just amused. Then she'd made a comment about Sabrina being an annoying little whore, thrown some money at her and told her to get out.

One of the biggest regrets of Sabrina's life was that she had done so—after throwing the money back, of course. She'd come from the farmlands of the Midwest, and even with a college education, a little work experience behind her and a four-year relationship with the captain of her college debate team, she was incredibly naive. Every time she replayed the scene in her head, she was newly humiliated and newly furious with herself. Where had her backbone been? Why hadn't she challenged the woman? She should have—but she hadn't. Maybe she had just been too stunned, or too insecure. She'd grabbed her own clothing and left.

Jon hadn't made any promises to her. He'd been honest, asking about her life, admitting his involvement with Cassandra, saying that they were on and off more often than a water spigot. When Sabrina looked back at the situation, she realized that she had simply been too afraid she might lose if Jon had had to make a choice between the two of them. Life, she'd since learned, meant taking chances. She'd just learned it a little too late.

Jon had tracked her down, all the way to Huntsville. But she'd told her mother to tell him that she'd gone to Europe. He'd written to her, telling her that he wasn't engaged, and that he'd had no commitments whatsoever the night they met. He'd asked her to contact him, since he hadn't been able to convince her mother to quit lying for her.

Sabrina had just reached the point of deciding she was being a worse fool not to respond when she heard that he and Cassie had suddenly done the deed, marrying after a late night in Las Vegas.

Not much later, she'd married Brett.

End of story.

Until she'd run naked from her honeymoon suite. And Cassandra Stuart had plummeted from her balcony into the waiting arms of death.

The wind was growing sharp. Sabrina shivered and looked out into the darkness.

The moon was high, struggling to shine through the clouds. Outdoor lights slightly illuminated the courtyard below. The castle was built in a horseshoe shape, surrounding the courtyard. The maid who had brought her to her room earlier had told her that the far end of the left wing comprised the master suite, with balconies opening to the central courtyard and to the rear.

Glancing in that direction, Sabrina saw the shape

of a man standing on the far balcony in the moonlight. His shirt ruffled in the wind; his hair flowed back. He stood tall and still, staring at the moon.

Then he turned, and she knew he was watching her, and she was watching him.

It was Jon. And standing there, watching him, she wondered if he was in pain, if he was missing his wife, if he was reflecting on her death.

He lifted a hand, as if saluting her.

Sabrina backed away, right into the door, and for a moment a scream lodged in her throat as she thought that someone was behind her.

She felt a moment's strange fear. She was standing on a balcony. And whatever the situation, Cassandra had fallen to her death from a balcony not far away. She had plummeted into the arms of a statue of Poseidon below. His trident had torn into her, and she had died instantly, even before her husband had come running back to her. Poseidon still stood below that balcony, though the rosebushes surrounding his fountain were no longer in bloom.

It was so easy to feel that someone was standing behind her now, ready to push....

But when she spun around, no one was there. She went into her room and discovered that the bolt was still thrown.

The rooms were all supplied with brandy.

Sabrina hated brandy, but she poured herself a snifter, wrinkled her nose and swallowed a fairly large portion. "If you're going to survive this week, you're going to have to cool your imagination,'' she told herself.

She'd claimed downstairs that she was tired. And she was. Shaky, exhausted from the time change and lack of sleep.

But she couldn't seem to get drowsy.

She stayed awake for hours. She sipped brandy, making faces at the taste, and read some magazine she'd brought for the flight.

She had V.J.'s latest book, and after she finished the magazines she began to read, until she realized that she just couldn't concentrate. She finally lay down, determined that she had to get some rest.

But even when she finally slept, she tossed and turned and began to dream disturbing dreams.

In the darkness of the night, he moved down the steps, silent, a wraith. He tried to tell himself that it would all go well, that he didn't need to be afraid.

But he was afraid. Because he loved her.

They had prearranged their meeting, yet even so, he was suddenly, perhaps ridiculously, uneasy. In the ancient dungeon, he suddenly felt as if long-dead murderers had come to life, as if they were mocking him, telling him that he was no better, even if he hadn't actually performed the deed. The lighting was pale, purplish, seeming to cast a ghoulish fog over the faces of torturers, swordsmen and more. Executioners in their dark masks seemed to move, taunting him, warning him.

He came to the tableau of Lady Ariana Stuart upon

the rack, and for a moment he paused, forgetting both fear and reason. She was the finest of all the pieces. Something in her eyes was real, a touch of the innocence and sincerity that belonged to Sabrina Holloway. Startled anew by the resemblance to the living woman so nearby, he was tempted to reach out and touch her, to rescue the beauty from the beast who threatened her.

"My love!"

The whisper drew him back to the present, and he spun around. She had come. She rushed to him, and he wrapped her in his arms. "Why are you so afraid? Why did we have to meet in secret?" he queried gently.

She shook her head against his chest. "This is all so dangerous. I know that they know. I know that we're in danger. I just wish..."

"Don't be so afraid. Don't create trouble before trouble appears."

She shook her head and stepped back. "You don't know how vicious, how dangerous, they can be!"

"Our game is dangerous, my pet. We mustn't overreact. We must just wait, listen, watch...and see what comes."

She leaned against him. "I'm so afraid. Hold me."

He did, feeling the movement of her body against his, her touch. He felt her tugging at his clothing. Felt her hands...finding bare flesh. To his amazement, he hardened instantly, a streak of desire flashing through him. He looked around at the ghoulish setting,

*amazed, somewhat aghast, and all the more excited
because of it.*

"Someone could come. Look where we are...."

*They seemed to be staring at him. Headsmen in
their black hoods, murderers, executioners, rogues.
Joan of Arc, so saintly on her cross.*

*She laughed softly, and the sound washed over his
senses. He groaned and slipped down with her, and
within seconds they were sprawled out on the cold
floor. She was as naked as a jaybird as purple light
bathed them. She was insatiable, rising above him,
crying out. He tried to hush her, but she laughed, and
when they were both spent, she lay at his side and
looked up at the faces surrounding them. "It was fun,
like an orgy," she teased.*

"You worry me."

*"Come on. It was as if they were all watching. It
was an incredible turn-on."*

*He hesitated. "You liked to watch...her," he said,
suddenly realizing the truth of his own words.*

She shrugged. "So? That was a turn-on, too."

*"But this is dangerous, meeting here, like this," he
told her. "Everything we do now is dangerous. The
days to come are dangerous. We don't know what
people know, what they saw, what they might have
suspected...."*

*"We'll be careful," she whispered. "We'll be okay.
But I have to be with you...."*

He nodded slightly.

*She knew how to move him, how to make him need
her. Because he loved her, of course.*

He closed his eyes and opened them, then started.

She was looking at him. Lady Ariana Stuart was turned his way, and she was looking at him with her huge, wide, beautiful blue eyes.

She was watching.

He could feel her eyes. Looking at him, seeing him. Watching…

It was a turn-on.

And yet dangerous.

He was both aroused and afraid.

It was as if she knew….

She didn't want Jon Stuart; she'd told herself that time and time again. She wasn't absurdly, naively young anymore; she was older now, wiser. But in her dreams, she was lying in her bed, naked, waiting, wanting….

Because he was there. Tall, towering, dressed in black. Standing over her…

It was Jon.

It wasn't. The tall figure was surrounded by fog and changed with each slight flutter of a purple-gray breeze.

It was a torturer, intent upon her agony and destruction, and she was caught, tied, unable to move, to escape, because ropes bound her tightly, and all she could do was look up into the eyes of death with a silent, wax-cast scream….

She awoke with a start, shaking, drenched in sweat. She sat up wildly, looking around.

Her room was empty. The fire burned low; moonlight filtered in.

She could see plainly that she was alone, entirely alone.

And yet it seemed...

There was a presence, a scent, a feeling, something in the air. A feeling she couldn't shake that someone had been there. Jon? Or Brett? Or an artist's rendering of a medieval torturer in wax?

"Too much time in the dungeon," she told herself softly. But her unease persisted.

She leaped up. The bolt was still secure. She'd been dreaming, and she was alone.

Shaking, she curled back into bed and tried to sleep again. But the moon began to set, and soon daylight was filtering in.

She sat up again. "Oh, the hell with this!" she groaned aloud.

So she rose and showered and was the first one downstairs for the six o'clock coffee.

But not even coffee and sunlight could dispel the strange feeling that she *hadn't* been alone....

Someone had been with her in her locked and bolted room.

5

Sabrina had a pounding headache and felt so tired and wretched that she could barely sit up.

So naturally the first person into the great hall for breakfast was Susan Sharp.

"Good morning! Nice to see you up!" Susan said with a cheerfulness that was doubly irritating. "Don't you just love this place? I slept like a baby."

"The castle is beautiful," Sabrina replied.

Susan drew up the chair beside Sabrina's at the polished oak table. "Can you believe that Cassandra absolutely hated this place?"

Sabrina told herself that she didn't want to gossip, but with Susan there was little choice. And despite herself, she wanted to know everything she could about Cassandra Stuart.

"Did she really?"

Susan nodded grimly, stirring sugar substitute into her coffee. "Hated it. I never understood why Jon put up with her." She shrugged. "Frankly, I never understood why he married her."

"Well, she really was beautiful. And smart," Sabrina heard herself comment.

Susan wrinkled her nose. "Yes, but...well, Jon is

gorgeous himself. He could have dozens of women. *Has* had dozens of women. Why marry that one?''

''He must have loved her.''

''Well, maybe he did. But I can tell you this—he was ready to divorce her when she died.''

''How do you know?''

Susan added milk to her coffee. ''Because I was here, remember? They were fighting like crazy. Jon has always loved it here. He didn't grow up with money, you know. The family inherited this place, but it was a disaster, an albatross hanging around his neck when he first came into possession of the property. Cassandra's family was swimming with cash—she never wanted or needed for anything. Jon's dedicated to his children's charities, and these little Mystery Weeks of his make some really big money. Cassandra didn't like games, hated half of Jon's friends. She couldn't bear V.J., because V.J. would never suck up to her. She said whatever she damned well felt like saying—you know her. Cassie tortured Jon every time he held one of these. He'd be in the middle of something, and she'd supposedly be his hostess—and then she'd suddenly decide she simply couldn't bear it and throw a tantrum or be off. I know Jon had decided that he was done with her when she died.''

''Susan, maybe they had problems,'' Sabrina said, ''but how can you possibly know their marriage was over?''

''Because I know Jon,'' Susan purred. She leaned back, lifting her long-nailed fingers in a casual gesture. ''But then again, Jon wasn't the only one fighting with Cassandra. She and Anna Lee Zane had barely been civil to one another all week. For one thing, Cassandra had given a scathing review of Anna's last book on national television in the States. And, of course, Anna is stunning, and she and Jon have been good friends for a very long time. Cassandra never understood the concept of friendship, especially not between a man and a woman, even a woman who goes both ways. Then again, I admit, I don't quite get friendships, either. I mean, it's hard to like a man and *not* want to sleep with him.''

Susan shrugged. "But that's beside the point. Cassie also completely dished Tom Heart in a review that might have cost him a spot in a really important anthology that came out last year. And of course she was also afraid that Jon was sleeping with someone who was a guest here, and she herself was supposedly sleeping with someone else, as well. I don't know if she really was or wasn't, since she adored Jon. She really did. She just didn't know how to be a wife to him. She was always jealous but always taunting him. It was as if she thought she had to let him know at all times that other men found her desirable, that she was a special prize he needed to cherish. Jon never did take well to threats. But then, she threatened everyone all the time—she seemed to need to hold something over the head of every single human being she ever met.''

"And you fought with her, too, of course.''

"Of course,'' Susan said, smiling. "I've admitted I hated her. She was the worst bitch known to man.''

"Oh, come now!" Brett exclaimed, entering the great hall. He poured himself coffee and sat down at Sabrina's other side. "Was Cassie really such a bitch? Or was she misunderstood? Maybe it was hard being married to Jon Stuart and giving in to his every whim. She loved cities, glamour, excitement, and he liked to tuck himself away here in the country and watch the wind blow."

"That's not true," Susan said, staunchly defending Jon. "He has homes in London, New York and L.A., as well."

"Poor fellow," Brett murmured lightly.

"Poor fellow, indeed!" V.J. announced, sweeping into the room with an audible sniff. She ruffled Brett's hair. "As if *you're* going to be suffering financially after your next contract!"

Brett smiled sheepishly. "Okay, so I'm not a poor fellow, either. I'm a happy one right now. And I'm going to be really, really rich, as well. You truly should remarry me, Sabrina."

"Not a chance, I'm afraid."

"Sleep with me, then. Men always buy their mistresses better presents. And we were good together, right?"

Susan and V.J. were both staring at her.

"Brett!" she said, nearly strangling.

He ignored her protest, his eyes suddenly on Susan again. "Here you are, Sue, defending Jon now, but you seemed to be absolutely convinced he killed Cassandra when it happened."

"Don't be silly. He was outside when she fell."

"He could have paid someone to do the deed," Brett said, waggling his eyebrows.

"Isn't it rather rude, the way we're sitting around discussing our host as a potential murderer," V.J. queried.

"But it *is* a Mystery Week," Brett said.

As if on cue, Camy Clark came into the room bearing a stack of envelopes. "Good morning, everyone."

"Everyone isn't here," Susan said snidely.

Sabrina frowned, wondering why the woman was continually so rude to Jon's assistant. Camy didn't intrude; she was quiet and tended to stay out of the way.

"Well, it's still early," Camy said. "But if you'd like—"

"Ah, you have our character descriptions and our instructions!" Brett said, flashing her one of his devastating smiles.

Camy flushed, smiling. "Yes, I do. Now remember, everyone is to know one another's character but nothing else. You'll receive more instructions as we go along. The murderer will, of course, know who he or she is and where to get the murder weapons. And remember, the murderer may have an accomplice. If you're killed, you're dead, but you're a ghost, and you can still warn others of impending danger and help solve the crime."

"I'm dying for my envelope, darling," Susan told her, drawling the word *dying*.

The others laughed. As Camy began handing out the envelopes, more of their number began to arrive:

Anna Lee, looking fetching and slim in stirrup pants and a halter top; Reggie in her inevitable flowered dress; Tom Heart, tall and dignified in a smoking jacket and flannel trousers; Thayer Newby in a Jets T-shirt and slacks; Joe Johnston, casual in a golf shirt and chinos; Joshua Valine looking very artistic, with a paint-smudged denim shirt over a plain white T and baggy pants; Dianne Dorsey in a calf-length skirt and sleeveless knit top. And Jon.

Jon, too, was casual, in a navy denim shirt, the sleeves rolled up, and form-hugging jeans. His dark hair was damp, as if he'd just showered, and Sabrina couldn't help but wonder if he'd slept late...because he'd been up late, wandering restlessly around his castle at night. She reminded herself that her door had been bolted. And that just because she hadn't forgotten a reckless sexual encounter in her youth, there was no reason to assume Jon might have any remaining interest in her whatsoever. Her reputation wasn't exactly a sparkling one.

She rose for more coffee. V.J. came up beside her, offering her cup to Sabrina to fill, as well.

"Ah, you're watching our host," V.J. whispered to her as Jon greeted Camy and Joshua, listening to some of their last-minute instructions.

"He's an intriguing man," Sabrina said noncommitally.

"And, of course, the question remains—is he a murderer? Does Susan really think so? Except I'm sure Susan wouldn't think of Cassie's death as murder. To Susan, if Jon did kill his wife, it was justifiable homicide.''

V.J. shrugged, sipping her coffee. ''Honey, to half the people here, killing Cassandra Stuart would have constituted a public service.''

''Ladies!'' Reggie admonished from behind them. ''We're not supposed to speak ill of the dead.''

''Even if the dead caused tremendous ills?'' Joe Johnston whispered from behind her.

''Sabrina,'' Camy said, walking across the room to her. She stopped, flushed and corrected herself. ''Ms. Holloway.''

''Sabrina, please.''

Camy flushed again. ''Your envelope. You only get to know your character now. You'll get instructions later regarding what you're supposed to do and where you're supposed to go.''

''Great, thanks.''

''Do you have mine, dear?'' V.J. asked.

Camy gave V.J. hers, then handed Reggie her envelope, as well.

''Ouch!'' Reggie exclaimed, looking up. She smiled. ''I'm the Crimson Lady, a stripper, trying—or pretending—to reform.''

''Great,'' Thayer Newby groaned, flexing his muscles. ''I'm the effeminate male dancer, JoJo Scuchi.''

''JoJo Scuchi?'' Brett said with a laugh.

''Check yours out,'' Thayer warned him.

Brett read the letter in the envelope and made a face. ''I'm Mr. Buttle, the butler. Number two on the

New York Times list, and they make me the butler!'' he groaned.

Sabrina, reading her sheet, began to laugh.

''And who are you, my dear?'' Brett demanded.

''The Duchess. I run the church choir,'' she told him.

''Oh, now that is apropos. The lady who ran naked from her honeymoon suite,'' Susan said, staring at Brett. ''Neither of you has ever explained that situation,'' she reminded him smugly.

Sabrina had lived with what had happened for a long time now, but she still felt her temper rising and her cheeks reddening, especially since she realized that Jon had been watching the exchange. Waiting for a reply?

Or perhaps not, because he was the one who responded to Susan. ''And I imagine they don't feel they owe you an explanation, Sue,'' he said.

Susan opened her mouth, then quickly shut it, lifting her chin.

''Ah, but Susan,'' Joe Johnston said, reading over Sabrina's shoulder, ''the Duchess runs the choir by day—and a high-class call girl outfit by night!''

''Hey, it's a dirty job, but someone's got to do it,'' Brett declared. ''Does the butler get to be in on it?'' he asked.

''The butler always did it, you know,'' Reggie teased.

''I mean in on the sex,'' Brett said.

''You would,'' V.J. said with a sigh.

"You know I've always wanted to make it with an older woman," Brett stated.

"Older than what?" V.J. demanded tartly.

He smiled innocently. "Older than God, darling. That's you, isn't it?"

"Cute, boy, cute!" V.J. sniffed.

Dianne Dorsey suddenly started laughing. Sabrina leaned past V.J. to look at her. As usual, Dianne was in black. Black denim shorts, a ruffled black blouse, black socks and black hiking boots. "You'll never guess who I am."

"Who?" V.J. obligingly inquired.

"Mary, the Hare Krishna!"

They all started to laugh.

"Susan, who are you?" V.J. asked.

Susan shuddered and looked up at Camy accusingly. "I'm Carla, the call girl with the clap."

Another round of laughter followed, but Susan was not amused. She glared at Camy. "You did that on purpose!"

"Sue, chill!" Brett said.

"Camy didn't make these up, you know that. We hire writers from the game company," Jon said impatiently. He sighed. "Trust me, mine is worse."

"Why, who are you?" Susan demanded.

"Demented Dick," Jon said dryly. "Serial killer, supposedly cured by his cousin, Sally Sadist, the psychologist."

"That's me!" Anna Lee called out.

"And I'm Nancy, the naughty nurse, hired by Sally

Sadist to look after you. Nancy the naughty nurse!''
V.J. repeated with a shudder.

"You think that's bad?" Joe Johnston said, laughing. "I'm Tilly the transvestite, Demented Dick's mother!"

"Hey, Mom!" Jon said, and they all laughed.

"Oh, no!" Tom Heart groaned, looking at Joe.

"What?" Joe demanded.

"I'm Demented Dick's dad—which means you're my wife. Ugh!"

"Well, baby, you're sleeping on the couch," Joe told him.

As they teased, Jennie Albright, the housekeeper, with the help of two younger maids, brought in the food platters, setting them up on the buffet. Jon thanked them and announced, "Breakfast is served. While we eat, Joshua will show you the weapons with which you might be 'killed.' We'll wait until everyone is seated."

With a lot of talking and good-natured joking, they fixed plates of food and took their places at the table. Sabrina was glad to find herself next to V.J. rather than Susan, but Brett managed to remain on her other side. He was definitely trying to create the impression that they were a twosome.

Jon took a seat toward the end of the table between Anna Lee Zane and Thayer Newby. Anna spoke to him, and he lowered his head, smiling. Sabrina couldn't help but wonder if something *had* gone on between the two of them, since it was rumored that Jon and Cassandra had both been having extramarital affairs at his last Mystery Week. Still, so much about the past was speculation. What wasn't speculation, however, was the fact that Cassandra Stuart had died.

Joshua cleared his throat, smiling. "Ladies and gentlemen, here is the situation. Demented Dick is newly home to take over as heir apparent to the family fortunes, due to the untimely—and unnatural—demise of his older brother, Demented Darryl. Naturally, since he had the most to gain, Demented Dick is a likely suspect in his brother's murder, but since this is a whodunit, it's for you to discover who did in Demented Darryl and why. Everyone in the house has a past and is hiding a secret, and it will turn out in the end that everyone had a reason for wanting to do Darryl in. The killer—or killers—are naturally afraid of what everyone else may know, and therefore, one by one, they will begin picking off the others. Now, there are a number of murder weapons, since the killer is to continue his or her spree until he or she is caught or until the entire household has expired."

"So shoot," Joe said. "What are our weapons?"

"Fine, we'll start with the pistol," Joshua said, showing them the gun in question. "Shoots red paint." He proceeded to lift the other toy weapons as he described them. "Rifle, shoots red paint. Bowie knife, complete with 'blood' sack. Jackknife, bow and arrow, heavy vase, rope with noose, poison—actually, it's a grape drink guaranteed to turn your mouth purple for twenty-four hours—and last but not least, a candlestick. So that's it, ladies and gentlemen. There will be clues left around the castle, and instructions for your characters will be slipped to you at various times as the week moves on. I'll warn you all, the first murder is planned for sometime today, so everyone take care. Oh, and anyone who chooses—living or dead—can meet at seven each evening for cocktails, to be followed by dinner at eight, and at that time discuss the case. More coffee, anyone?" he asked blandly.

"Only if you drink it first," Anna Lee replied dryly.

"Sure," Joshua said. He procured the coffee carafe from the buffet, poured himself a cup, sipped it, then walked around to Anna Lee's place, pouring her more. Smoothing back his blond hair, he leaned close to her, a teasing light in his eyes. "One can't be too cautious around here."

"I'll take more coffee, too," Jon said, pushing his cup forward. "Late night," he explained.

"Death by poison!" V.J. said with a shudder. "Well, I'd been intending to go on a diet anyway. I can live without food, but never without coffee."

"Never without a good gin and tonic," Reggie argued.

"No, never without beer," Brett corrected.

"Well, as far as coffee and food—or even cocktails and beer—go, you can indulge now," Jon said dryly. "The game doesn't begin until we've all exited the dining room. Everyone is then to go to his or her room for the next hour, while Camy and our master sculptor make sure that the weapons you've just seen have been properly hidden. If someone finds the weapon with which he or she was to be murdered, it can be used against the killer. But for now, feel free. Indulge.''

"Well, then, let me have just a wee bit more toast," V.J. said, adding a touch of a Scot's accent to her voice.

"I'll go for the bacon," Joe said.

"Toast for me, too, V.J.," Sabrina called to her.

And suddenly everyone at the table was hungry again. They ate like a group of loggers about to head out for hours of hard labor. But, finally, one by one, they began to leave. Sabrina, seeing Brett ahead of her, purposely lagged behind, lowering her eyes as she sipped her coffee. When she lifted her gaze again, she was startled to realize that only she and Jon remained in the room. He was seated across the table, studying her.

"It really is good to see you again," he told her, voice husky, eyes firmly on her.

To her dismay, she felt a fluttering in her heart. "Thank you."

He sat back, still watching her. She felt as if his eyes were penetrating her skin, and she groped about quickly for something casual to say.

"So, are you the killer?" she inquired.

He arched a brow. "Are you talking about the game—or real life?"

She flushed. "The game."

"If I were," he answered slowly, "I couldn't tell you. Just as you couldn't tell me. It wouldn't be fair."

He leaned forward then, a dry smile curling his lips. "But don't you want to know about real life?"

She stared back at him, feeling as if her breakfast had suddenly sunk from her stomach to her feet. "Jon, I didn't come here to question you or to bring back unhappy memories."

"Why not? It's why most of the others did, both my friends and my enemies. Don't you want to know the truth? Or did you really run away from me simply because you didn't give a damn?"

She wasn't going to answer that, so she stared at him and demanded, "So did you kill Cassandra? What a question! If you had killed her, you couldn't tell me, could you? There's no real difference between the game and real life."

"Oh, there's a difference, all right. As far as the game goes, I can't tell you if I'm the killer or not. As for real life...no, definitely, decidedly, on pain of every torture God or the devil could inflict, no. I did not kill my wife. Do you believe me?"

"Yes."

He arched a brow, sitting back cautiously. "Why? Why should you believe me?"

"Well, I..."

"You what? You know me?" he queried, taunting slightly. He shrugged. "You know me," he repeated mockingly.

"I don't pretend to really know you," she snapped back angrily. "But you were nowhere near her when she fell—"

"She was pushed," he stated flatly.

She lifted her hands. "How do you know?"

"Because I knew Cassandra. Very well. She was far too fond of herself for suicide."

Seated at the huge table, his eyes dark and sharp, he looked like a medieval lord, powerful ruler of all his domain. But there was a touch of bitterness in his voice, and despite his harsh demeanor, she reflected that the years since Cassandra's death must have hurt him very badly. Had he really loved her, despite their fights? Or had there been another woman involved, an affair gone tragically wrong? Had there been another man, and did Jon Stuart still harbor anger deep in his soul?

He was still staring at her, his dark marbled gaze seeming to pierce through her, seeking something, giving nothing. The lines around his eyes had deepened since she'd seen him last; he had aged, and yet he was even more attractive then he had been, and she felt as if she could feel his power reaching out across the table to mesmerize her.

Was she a fool? Even if he hadn't pushed Cassandra himself, he could have been her killer. Plenty of people seemed to think it would have been a miracle if he wasn't the one to murder her....

He was still watching, waiting.

She shrugged. "From what I understand, nothing is certain. You can't be certain of anything, just because you think you knew her. She might have simply slipped and fallen. She might have been reckless. We none of us really ever know one another, do—"

"Cassandra didn't kill herself."

"Maybe that's what you want to believe."

"Maybe it's the truth."

"Jon, she had cancer. She might have felt that—"

"She was already undergoing treatments."

"But she was a woman, and women can be vain. Maybe she was afraid of losing her hair, her looks— or even losing you because of it."

He shook his head impatiently. "She knew about the cancer when we were married. She told me about it, so she knew I was aware of everything we might be going through. She didn't kill herself. And she was very coordinated. She didn't trip."

"Well, then, in your mind, you definitely believe that *someone* murdered her."

"Yes," he said.

"But who—"

He leaned forward. She could see leashed tension in the pounding of a vein in his throat.

"Someone killed her," he said harshly, "but I didn't. And the matter of who did is not your concern. I don't want you involved in any way."

"But—"

"Why did you run away from me?" he asked abruptly.

"What? I—I—"

"Don't stutter. And don't tell me that it was a long time ago, or that you don't know what I'm talking about."

She lifted her hands. "Cassandra came. I left."

"Why?"

Sabrina stared at him blankly. "It really was a long time ago—"

"Why?" he interrupted more heatedly.

"She said she was your fiancée. Apparently, she was."

He shook his head angrily. "We were broken up. I had no commitments. I told you that."

She shrugged. "But you married her."

"Later. Yes, I did marry her. She was beautiful and tempting and all the rest, and we did have a history between us. And she was afraid of facing her illness alone, and she wanted me to be with her, and yes, she was a bitch as well, and yes again, it wasn't working at all and I was planning on getting a divorce."

There was a strange anger in his voice, as if he were revealing intimacies under duress, as if the words were spilling from him against his will. Then his tone changed abruptly and he queried wryly, "And what about you? Running naked from your honeymoon suite in Paris?"

"That was a long time ago as well, and it's really—"

"None of my business? You're absolutely right. It isn't. But that doesn't mean I don't want to know." He smiled a little. "Whenever you're ready to tell me."

She stared at him, surprised to find that she was not offended. His words might have been blunt, even arrogant, but from the way he smiled, she suddenly realized that he understood a great deal.

"Hey!"

Camy Clark came back into the great hall and put her hands on her hips. "You guys are supposed to return to your rooms for the next hour—and that means you, too, boss!" she said firmly.

"Okay, okay, we're leaving," Jon assured her.

He got to his feet with a lithe, easy movement and managed to be at Sabrina's seat before she could rise. He stood behind her, graciously pulling out her chair. His scent was masculine and subtle—of soap and a hint of aftershave. He remained one of the most attractive and sensual men she had ever met, and even without touching, she could feel him at her back with every fiber of her being. She was tempted to turn around and throw herself at him.

Naturally, she didn't.

She rose, thanked him and smiled at Camy. And, leaving the great hall, she fairly flew up the stairs.

Yet as she reached her door on the second floor, she felt him behind her again. Knew he was there before he spoke.

"Good luck, Duchess."

She spun around.

As always, his dark gaze was unreadable.

"Good luck?"

"Catching the killer."

"Oh, the game."

"Of course, what else? Ah, but then, there is real life, right?" he queried. His voice was very deep, and he suddenly seemed very close.

"Are you angry with me?" she asked nervously.

"What do you think?" he said.

Then he pushed open her door, urging her into her room. His hand on her elbow, he led her outside. "Look around you," he said. "Feel the wind. Soon it will be cold and brutal. This is a harsh place, especially to those who despise it. Do you suppose the castle itself might have turned on Cassandra? The place was rumored to be haunted, you know. Well, naturally, now Cassandra haunts the castle, as well. Imagine how she must have felt, out here on a balcony, feeling a breeze...this same breeze. Seeing this land she so disdained. This same land. It must have been a terrible shock when she realized that someone had the audacity to be murdering her."

His grip on her arm was very tense, and Sabrina felt the heat and anger and frustration that emanated from him. He stared out on the day; he seemed to have forgotten how tightly he held her, how he had wedged her against the balcony rail.

She felt her heart pounding. And for a moment, she was afraid. She didn't know this man. Sleeping with a man didn't keep him from being a stranger.

Yet along with the fear rippling through her veins was a strange warmth, a static excitement. She liked the feel of his hand upon her, liked his being so close. She wanted him to stay; she was tempted again to throw her arms around him. She felt so strange with him. She had never known another man who could create such a sensual, aching hunger within her. She tried to tell herself that she was a fool, that women who fell for dangerous men were, quite simply, stupid.

But Jon hadn't killed his wife.

Still, he might have wanted her dead.

Yet lots of people had wanted her head.

"Imagine," he repeated now, drawing Sabrina closer to him, farther over the balcony rail. "Imagine looking, leaning, and then—"

"Jon!"

He jerked back at the sound of his name being called. Sabrina let out a long breath, then swung around with him to face her open doorway.

Camy stood there, smiling but shaking her head impatiently. "We've never going to be able to get this game started!"

"Oh, I am sorry," Jon said smoothly. Then he smiled at Sabrina. "Good luck finding the killer. It can be a matter of—"

"Life and death," she said softly.

To her surprise, he took her by the shoulders and kissed her forehead. Then he strode from the balcony and the room.

For a moment, Sabrina stood very still. Then she turned to look after him and saw that Camy was still there.

"We've got to get on with the game!" the young woman said somewhat impatiently.

And Sabrina's door was finally closed with a sharp little click.

6

Jon strode the length of the hallway to his room, aware that Camy was watching him, anxious for him to reach his room and shut himself in. He smiled to himself. She and Joshua took this all very seriously, which was why, of course, he had asked them to help host the affair rather than participate as players. For, along with the fun and publicity the writers would enjoy, the project was for charity, and he didn't want any more scandal. And who better to see that things ran smoothly than hardworking Camy Clark and meticulous, painstaking Joshua Valine?

Jon reached his room, waved at Camy and locked the door behind him. Alone, he stared at the bed. Why in hell had he ever married Cassandra?

He walked into the bathroom and doused his face with cold water. He stared at himself, noting the lines around his eyes. He'd been younger but still no kid when he'd married Cassie. She'd been a manipulator of the highest degree, capable of appearing pleasant, reasonable and loving when it suited her purpose. But what had truly snared him then, and haunted him now, was the feeling that she had really loved him. True, she had never given up the battle; she had wanted things her way. But as best as Cassandra could, she had loved him.

He walked out to the balcony and stared down at the fountain, remembering. Despite the time that had passed, he felt real pain. Poor Cassie. She had loved life so much.

She hadn't killed herself; he really did know that about her. Her death had been ruled accidental. Perhaps she *had* fallen?

No. He remembered the way she had called his name…remembered the change in her tone of voice. And he remembered that, at the end, he had failed her completely in a way he never should have.

Jon felt a sudden, terrible dread of this Mystery Week. He had thought about it, of course, weighed the grim idea over and over again—for nearly three years now. And it had seemed a sane, sensible, if chilling thing to do. Until…

The irrational unease had seized him when he was with Sabrina. In her room. On her balcony.

He stared down at the Poseidon statue that had cradled Cassie as she died. He'd thought to catch a killer this week. He'd never thought that, in one day's time, he might be wishing for a future rather than trying to resolve the past.

And it made him afraid.

Fear made a man weak.

He couldn't afford to be weak.

He heard a sound and turned. An envelope had been thrust beneath his door.

He reached for, opened it—and felt a chill sweep through him.

The note he'd received was a warning...and not part of the game....

The woman burst in on him while he was in his own room, at his desk, head in his hands.

He straightened, staring at her.

Her eyes were downright vicious.

And she pointed at him.

"I know what happened. I know exactly what was going on. Oh, maybe I haven't complete proof, but I've got the story pieced together nicely, and once I give out the truth, well, honey, you can kiss your wonderful little life-style goodbye!"

He stared back at her, filled with dismay, totally speechless at first. Then he got a grip on himself and sat straight and impassive. "Whatever you think you know doesn't matter."

"Doesn't it? Oh, come now, I can see that you've got a new passion in your life. Maybe an old passion. So hard to tell. But aren't you looking forward to the future?"

"I don't understand this. Why are you here? If you knew the truth—or suspected you knew the truth, why haven't you already shared it?"

Her smile deepened. "Because everything in life is negotiable."

"You mean you're blackmailing me?"

"Oh, dear, what an ugly word! No, no, no, not blackmail. I don't mean to torture you forever or any-

thing like that. But I will admit to having a slight cash-flow problem at the moment, so you see...''

''And what happens if you have another 'cash-flow problem' in the future?''

''Well, I do try to be reasonable. I seldom find my-self strapped as I am now.''

''And there are no morals involved here, I take it? You really don't give a damn that Cassandra Stuart was murdered?''

''Of course not. Many people would have been tempted to push her over. They didn't all get the op-portunity to do so. A mean, nasty woman died. Who cared?''

''There were those who cared,'' he told her angrily.

She shrugged with a total lack of interest. ''I wasn't one of them. This is a business negotiation, nothing more. I'll not be troubled by my conscience later or anything like that, so you needn't fear.''

''But there is the cash-flow thing.''

''So unlikely to occur again!''

''Name your figure.''

She did.

He nodded.

She smiled and left. After all, everyone was sup-posed to be in his or her own room.

He stared at the closed door long after she had gone, a wave of desperate depression washing over him. She would have a ''cash-flow problem'' at least once a year—that was simply the way she was. And what if he ran out of hush money?

But what choice did he have?
Of course, there was one *other choice....*

Alone, Sabrina tried to shake the unease that had settled over her. A feeling of intimacy had sprung up so quickly between her and Jon, yet it seemed he was trying to warn her away from him at the same time.

She phoned home, checking in with her parents, asking about her sister, brother-in-law and the baby, and telling them that Scotland was wonderful. She assured them that the rumors they had heard about Jon Stuart were just tabloid garbage and that she was in no danger at Lochlyre Castle. Finally she bid them a cheerful goodbye, apologizing for having called so early, and hung up. She tried to lie on her bed and close her eyes and rest. She was too restless.

She wandered back out to the balcony. For a moment, she couldn't go near the edge. How odd it had been to stand there with Jon! To feel a hint of fear. But he wouldn't have thrown her over the edge; he would have no reason to do so.

Had there been a reason to kill Cassandra? Silly question—everyone seemed to think there was a reason to kill Cassandra.

Sabrina gazed down the length of the castle toward Jon's suite. She wondered if things would have been different if she hadn't been so young when she'd met him, been with him. Not just young, but so naive. She felt her pulse quickening and bit her lower lip, admitting at last why she had come here. She was still in love with him.

But surely, that was absurd. She hadn't seen him in far too long.

And there were some who still hinted that he *had* been involved in the death of his wife, no matter what the findings at the inquest.

But logic was proving worthless at the moment. She didn't believe for a minute that Jon had killed Cassandra. Still, was she being hopelessly naive again?

She heard a noise and hurried back inside. A note, her first set of instructions, had been slipped under her door. She ripped open the envelope and studied the words.

Duchess, head to the chapel for choir practice at dusk. Meet with wayward girl. Show her the light. Directions to chapel included.

Studying the little map beneath the printed sheet, Sabrina shuddered and muttered to herself, "Great! The chapel is in the dungeon beyond the chamber of horrors!"

There was a tapping on her door. She answered it, to find Brett waiting with a smile. He didn't exactly push his way in; he brushed by her before she could stop him.

"So what were your instructions? What are you to do, Madame Pimp?" he asked. "Are you the murderer?"

"I can't tell you that. It will spoil the game, and you know it!"

"You should tell me," he said determinedly, hopping up on her bed, stretching out and lacing his fingers comfortably behind his head. "You should confide in me, and I should confide in you. We could catch the killer that way and become a real husband and wife sleuthing team. Then we could write stories together and get fabulously rich and famous."

"We're not married, Brett."

"Oh, that can be easily rectified. You're just being stubborn."

"Because I'd like a husband who'd like to be monogamous?"

"I can do that."

"Brett, I don't think you can, but that's beside the point. Now get off my bed."

"Come help me up."

She sighed with irritation as he stretched out a hand entreatingly. She took it, intending to pull him up.

He pulled her down instead. "Gotcha!"

He said the word with such childish delight as she landed on his chest that she didn't have the heart to either yell or slug him in the jaw. "Brett McGraff, you—" she began in laughing protest, trying to push away.

But she never finished. At that moment, they heard the explosive sound of shots being fired.

Brett clutched her, his eyes wide.

"Sabrina! What happened?" V.J. cried, swinging around the doorway. "Oh!" she gasped, seeing the two of them together on the bed. "Oh, I am so sorry, but the door was open, and—"

"How absolutely delicious!" Susan Sharp exclaimed.

There suddenly seemed to be a meeting occurring in Sabrina's doorway.

"Everyone in there alive?"

Sabrina felt her cheeks flood with color at the sound of the deep, slightly burred, masculine voice. Jon Stuart was now standing between V.J. and Susan in her doorway.

"Hey, who got shot?" demanded a second male voice. It was Tom Heart, peeking in over V.J.'s shoulder.

"No one in here. We're fine," Sabrina said irritably, trying to push free of Brett's grasp.

Brett held on. Tightly. He grinned at her wickedly. "I haven't been so fine in a very long time."

Sabrina gritted her teeth, tugged herself free at last and stood. As she straightened her clothing, she checked it and Brett's for red paint. "No, we've not been shot," she said with a false cheerfulness. Her cheeks, however, were as red as tomatoes.

"Well, I wonder who has been?" V.J. demanded.

"Let's go see," Tom suggested.

"What's happened?" Standing in the hallway, red-haired, muscular Thayer Newby had his hands on his hips, looking every inch the cop he had once been in Houston, Texas. His tone was sharp, and he was ready to question them all.

Dianne Dorsey stepped from her room into the hallway. Two doors down, Anna Lee Zane did the same.

Joe Johnston stepped out from behind Anna Lee.

"Oh, now, this is all just too rich!" Susan exclaimed.

"We were just talking," Joe said indignantly.

"Ah, then perhaps it's those two who are conspirators!" Susan said, pointing into Sabrina's room.

"Conspirators at what?" Sabrina asked. "A gun went off, but we're all alive, and none of us is wearing red paint."

"Now there's a fabulous investigative deduction!" Brett exclaimed, applauding. "We're all still alive."

"What happened?" Joshua asked, striding down the hallway. Apparently his room was at the end of the wing, near Jon's suite. He looked around with a frown. "Where's Camy?"

As he asked the question, Camy came up the stairs from below. She looked at her watch, then at the guests gathered in the ancient arched hallway. "I can see that we're going to have to keep a strict eye on all of you!" she declared. "The time is barely up, and every single one of you is out of your room!"

"Shots were fired. We were trying to figure out who had been killed first," Tom Heart explained.

Camy shook her head. "I think that you're all mistaken. It wasn't time for shots to have been fired."

"We heard shots," V.J. insisted.

"A car backfiring, perhaps?" Camy suggested.

"Whose car? What car? We're all here."

Camy smiled, shaking her head. "We do receive mail and deliveries here, you know. It's not the end of the earth."

They all looked at one another.

"Could it have been something other than gunshots?" Dianne asked.

"Well, it must have been," Tom Heart replied. "None of us was shot. Unless the murderer has horrible aim. Anybody's doors or walls covered in red paint?"

They all shook their heads.

"It had to have been something else," Camy insisted.

"Sounded like shots to me," Thayer Newby said.

He should know! Sabrina thought. He'd been a cop for over twenty years. Surely he recognized the sound of gunshots.

But the bottom line was none of them had been shot.

Sabrina saw Jon staring at Camy, neither agreeing nor disagreeing with her. His arms were crossed over his chest.

"I was actually working," Dianne said.

"So was I," Anna Lee said.

"Working on what, dear?" Susan queried, arching a brow toward Joe, who had exited Anna Lee's room with her.

"Joe recently did some extensive forensic research with a bone expert. He was giving me some really great ideas."

"Ah," Susan said archly, the one syllable dripping with doubt.

"Don't forget, we've actually got a bowling alley and a heated pool in the dungeon, just down from the chamber of horrors,'' Camy reminded them. ''For those not working,'' she added innocently.

''I haven't gone bowling in years,'' Sabrina said, looking at V.J., who was usually up for almost anything. That way she could return to the dungeon area and find out exactly where the chapel was—without being alone—before it was time for her to go down and play the mystery game at dusk.

''Great! It always takes one person to get things started!'' Camy said.

''If you and Brett aren't *working*,'' Susan purred.

''We're not,'' Sabrina assured her, trying to keep her voice level.

Jon arched a dark brow her way, murmured that he had some phone calls to make, and walked away without further comment.

''I wouldn't mind a dip in the pool, either,'' V.J. said. ''Why don't we put on suits so we can throw some heavy balls, complain about our aching arms, then relax in the water.''

''Sounds fine,'' Sabrina said. She turned away to get ready. And glared.

Brett hadn't left yet.

''I think I'll join you two,'' he said cheerfully.

''The amenities of the castle are open to all of us,'' she said, adding dryly, ''but you'll need your swimsuit, which I'm sure must be in *your* room.''

He reached over and pinched her cheek.

''Brett—''

''You really do love me,'' he assured her.

But at last he walked away. And she closed and locked her door.

Camy's room was near the grand stone stairway that led to the foyer and the library and great hall below. The hallway had emptied of writers when Jon exited his room to reach his assistant's, but Joshua stopped him on his way, calling to him from his own doorway.

"Jon, come in here, I think you should see this."

As Jon entered Joshua's room, the sculptor gestured at the large television set. A weatherwoman from a Stirling station stood before a large map of northern England and Scotland. Jon stood silently beside Joshua, watching as the meteorologist smiled her way through an explanation of the storm moving in from the North Atlantic. It was already hitting the islands, covering John o'Groat's with a blanket of snow and ice, and moving southward.

"What do you think?" Joshua said.

As if on cue, the weatherwoman smiled more broadly. "Due to atmospheric conditions, it's difficult to forecast the exact movement or speed of the storm, but it's possible that within the next twenty-four to thirty-six hours we could have snow and blizzard conditions across the midsection of Scotland, all the way down to Yorkshire, England."

"I think it's going to snow," Jon said. "The staff here are extraordinary—I don't think we've ever run out of anything. But I'll speak with my housekeeper and make sure we're doubly provisioned, just in case we wind up snowbound.''

"Good idea. I thought you might want to know," Joshua said.

"Yeah, thanks," Jon told him. He hesitated. "Josh, you and Camy are working together on all the clues and instructions for the game, right?''

"Yeah, why?"

"Did you slip the envelope under my door?"

Joshua shook his head, looking a little uneasy. "No, Camy was distributing the instructions today," he said with a shrug. "Why, is something wrong?''

Jon showed Joshua the message he had received.

The sculptor went pale, shaking his head. "Someone is playing a dirty game," he said angrily.

"So it seems."

"Do you think you're in any real danger?"

Jon shook his head. "No."

"But—"

"Never mind. I'm sorry I even bothered you with this."

"Sorry!" Joshua said indignantly. "Someone did this! We have to know who—"

"Josh, I can handle it. Hey, you're an artist, my friend, filling in as game master for the good of my charities. This isn't your concern. Excuse me, and thanks for the weather report. I'll check with Camy."

He left Josh and walked down the hallway to tap on Camy's door.

"Come in!"

He opened the door, strode to where she sat at her

desk and tossed down his note. "Not funny, Camy. What in God's name would induce you to do something like that?"

"Something like what?" she demanded indignantly. She stared at him, then frowned and lifted the note and began to read.

He watched her face go parchment white. "Joshua said you did the notes and slipped them under the doors."

"I did, but I didn't do this, Jon. Honestly. Honest to God, I swear! How could you think I would write something like that to you?"

"Is this what the other instructions look like?" he demanded harshly.

She nodded. "Yes, but—"

"Who had access to your office? This is castle stationery."

"Well, I guess anyone might have slipped in here. And there's more of this stationery in the desk in the library. I think it's even in the guest rooms. Jon, I can't prove anything, but, honestly, I've seen how you've suffered over all this, and surely you can't believe that I…" She trailed off helplessly.

Jon felt the tension in his shoulders ease as he watched Camy. She was so distressed. "No, I don't believe that you would be so cruel, Camy. I'm sorry. But it did arrive under my door."

She shook her head. "That's not what I sent you. Your note read, 'You're demented but cunning. Watch the proceedings, and listen well. Naturally, you're Demented Dick, which makes you a suspicious

character.' That's all that I said. And that's what I put
under your door.''

"Did you see anyone else in the hallway at the
time?" he asked her.

She shook her head strenuously, and he began to
feel guilty; huge tears were brimming in her eyes.

"I didn't see anyone at all," she said. "I went
downstairs to check on arrangements for dinner, and
I turned on all the lights in the cellar—dungeon,
sorry. I keep forgetting it's a dungeon, no matter how
long your family has owned this place! And then I
came back upstairs, and everyone was in the hallway.''

"Well," he murmured, "apparently, someone
doesn't think I've suffered enough for Cassie's death.
I would like to know who wrote this," he said, pock-
eting the note again.

"Some of your friends are a bit eccentric," she
suggested meekly.

"Some of them are simply bizarre," he agreed,
grinning. "Well, keep your eyes open," he said, and
he turned to leave.

"Jon," she said, calling him back hesitantly.

He paused, turning to look at her.

She cleared her throat. "I think...I think Cassie
really was having an affair. I mean, she loved you,
the best Cassie could love, but I think she was convinced that you had lost interest in her, that you were
seeing someone else. And I think that she was seeing
someone else. God knows, with Cassie, maybe she
was seeing more than one person.''

He arched a brow. "And...?"

"Well, if Cassie had a lover, maybe he blames you for what happened."

He nodded. "Was there something else?" he asked as she continued to look at him imploringly.

She flushed. "Well, if *you* were having an affair, maybe *she's* angry that you haven't pursued things, with Cassie now out of the way. Were you...having an affair with someone?" she ventured.

He crossed his arms over his chest, hiking up one eyebrow, a slight curl to his lips. "Camy, I'm not the type to kiss and tell. Never have been. So if I had been having an affair, I guarantee you, very few people would have known about it."

"Maybe that narrows down the question of who might have written that note," she suggested hopefully.

"Maybe. Except that I didn't say I'd had an affair."

"You didn't say you didn't, either."

He started to laugh. "Never mind Camy. Some of my friends are bizarre—let's leave it at that."

He left her combination bedroom-and-office suite and started down the hall. Then he paused, noticing an irregularity in the smooth stone wall. He reached out and touched it, amazed. He ran his fingers over the grouting.

"Sweet Jesus..."

7

The dungeon was a remarkable place.

Actually, the entire castle was remarkable, Sabrina reflected. A flawless combination of the new and the ancient. From the main foyer, a sweeping stone stairway curved down to a central hall; to the left were doors that led to the horror chamber, the chapel and the crypt, while to the right were doors that led to the recreation areas.

Sabrina stood next to V.J. staring at the sparkling water in the heated pool. Lounge chairs graced its deck, and at the far end was a complete bar taken from a turn-of-the-century Glascow pub. The bar had been modernized to offer a sink, a refrigerator, a coffee urn and a microwave. The ultramodern entertainment center at the rear of the bar, complete with big-screen TV, somehow blended artistically with the antique stained glass.

"This is living," V.J. commented with a soft sigh. "I do love Jon's invitations to come here. It was such a shame that something so terrible had to happen last time. I'm so glad he's decided to rejoin the world of the living. Imagine, a swimming pool in a dungeon!"

Sabrina had to admit that she was amazed as well.

The castle had so many sides, so many faces. It was so incredibly historical that it was possible at times to walk along its hallways and imagine that hundreds of years had faded away. Yet she had yet to smell any mustiness or even feel a draft.

"It must cost an arm and a leg to keep this place up," V.J. said, whispering suddenly as if someone might overhear.

"I'm sure. But Jon must make really good money with his books, don't you think?" Sabrina queried.

"Well, yes, he is really at the top of the commercial heap. And I understand he's also a smart businessman. He played the stock market extremely well, getting in very early on a number of computer and internet companies among other things. How on earth Cassie managed not to be happy with him is hard to imagine."

Sabrina looked around, certain that others—Brett, for one—would be coming down to enjoy the amenities soon. But at the moment they were all alone in the big rec room. Two billiard tables and a Ping-Pong table separated the pool area from the two-lane bowling alley and some comfortable chairs and love seats cozily set up around a woodburning stove. It all looked so innocent, so fun. Yet Sabrina wondered if, despite the contemporary atmosphere in this part of the dungeon, she'd feel so comfortable in the castle depths if V.J. weren't with her.

"I thought that Cassandra actually did love Jon," she finally replied. "I got the impression they had one of those passionate artistic marriages, that they were very much in love despite their quarrels."

V.J. shrugged. "There's only so many mysteries one can solve in a week," she said gaily. "Let's forget bowling; shall we? This pool looks just too delicious. I'm going in."

She slipped out of her terry cover-up and headed for the deep end. Still elegant with her long legs and trim, toned figure, she executed a beautiful dive and emerged at the far end. "It's wonderful in here!" she called to Sabrina.

"Look at that!" Sabrina called back. The television in the entertainment center was on, and though the volume was low, she could see that much of the country was being blanketed in snow.

V.J. swam to the edge of the pool and rested her chin on her arms on the tiled rim to watch. "Imagine! All that cold weather out there, and here I am, swimming in eighty-degree luxury. Indeed, our boy does know how to live!"

She pushed away from the ledge and continued swimming laps. Sabrina shed her own cover-up and dived in after her. She, too, swam laps for a while, then finally stopped to rest.

V.J. joined her, picking up the thread of their earlier conversation. "Cassie couldn't have been happy with Jon. All he had to do was say hello to someone, and she was instantly jealous and suspicious. She hated this place, hated it, and always came up with some excuse to try to make him leave it. Before she died…"

V.J.'s voice trailed off, and Sabrina wanted to scream in frustration. "Before she died?" she prodded.

V.J. shrugged her shoulders, smoothing back her wet hair. "They had an awful fight at breakfast. We were into the third or fourth day of the week, I believe. My character had already been killed off—a few of the others as well—and everyone was having a wonderful time. Susan was being a pain, naturally, but she was having fun, too. I think she actually enjoyed sparring with Cassie. And they did spar. Fur flew!" V.J. laughed in reminiscence.

"But what about Cassie and Jon?" Sabrina prompted.

"Well," V.J. continued, "Cassie seemed to be going out of her way to upset Jon. Dressing in outrageously revealing clothing, being provocative with every male in the place. But I think part of the problem was that she wasn't making Jon angry anymore." She reflected for a moment. "When they were first married, I think Cassie put on a good act. She could pretend to be gentle and sweet, an ideal wife. But she had a mean streak in her, and the more it came out, the more Jon lost interest. I remember her trying to sock his jaw once when they fought, and he just caught her hand, stared at her, then waltzed away. He wasn't fighting anymore. I suspect he'd long since fallen out of love with her."

"Maybe," Sabrina said. "But, V.J., how can anyone know what someone else is feeling?"

The older woman looked at her, arching a brow.

"Sabrina, love is something you can see in someone's eyes. And believe me, it was no longer in Jon's."

"V.J.! I never imagined you to be a closet romantic," Sabrina teased.

V.J. shrugged. "You just never can tell about people, can you?"

"Ah, correction, you can about me!" Brett called, striding into the pool area, wearing sandals, bathing trunks and a robe. He discarded the robe and struck a playful beefcake pose. "The entire world knows that *I'm* an incurable romantic," he announced. "Right, V.J.? Tell my wife that, would you? And remind her that I'm in supreme shape, too, please."

V.J. glanced at Sabrina, then back at Brett. "Sorry. But I imagine your ex-wife knows all about your glorious shape, Brett. Why don't you behave, dear? I'd love a mild vodka and soda, lots of lime. Why don't you go fix me a drink before you plunge in? I might find a few nice things to say about you."

"Make it two," called Thayer Newby, walking into the pool area.

He hadn't bothered with a cover-up; he had come down in cut-off jeans. Sabrina noticed that the ex-cop was wall-to-wall muscle. Thick-necked, broad-shouldered, and imposing, he looked a bit like the Incredible Hulk with red hair.

He plunked down into a deck chair, smiling. "Now all we need is a little sunshine."

"No sunshine in the dungeon," Brett said, "but there is a sauna back there beyond the bar, next to the rest rooms."

"A sauna sounds good. If I ever decide to move," Thayer said. He looked up at the entry to the rec area as Anna Lee Zane came in. She didn't need any sunshine, her tan was already perfect. She wore a white gossamer caftan over a white bikini, and she looked stunning.

She was followed by Dianne Dorsey, who was wearing a black open work cover-up over a stunning black suit.

"We could just lie on these lounges all day and imagine ourselves in a very strange paradise," Dianne said, taking the chair next to Thayer. "Brett, you brilliant novelist you, will you make me a drink as well, while you're at it?"

"Mine is vodka and tonic," Anna Lee advised him.

"Hey," Brett protested, "what do I look like here, the—"

"The butler, Mr. Buttle," Jon Stuart reminded him, joining them.

He was smiling, but in the strange light of the dungeon reflected by the pool, Sabrina thought that he looked tense and unhappy.

"But," he added, "since I'm Demented Dick, what do I know? Right, Sabrina?" he inquired.

She hadn't realized he had even noticed her there in the water. But he was staring at her, and the expression in his eyes made her uneasy. Then she started as a loud, crashing sound suddenly filled the rec room. Jon didn't flinch; he kept looking at her.

"Strike!" Reggie called out happily. And Sabrina

realized that Tom Heart and Joe Johnston had arrived, as well, opting to bowl rather than swim.

"So, Sabrina," Jon said, "will you trust me to fix you a drink?"

Now, here was a man in extremely good shape. His shoulders were handsomely broad, his waist tight and lean, his legs long and nicely shaped. And Sabrina couldn't stop staring at him, remembering....

She forced her eyes to his, about to refuse a drink. It was so early.

"Gin and tonic," she said weakly.

But he already knew her choice, and he'd already started for the bar.

She swam the length of the pool to step out at the shallow end. White-haired Tom Heart had left the bowlers and now offered her a towel as she walked up the steps. V.J. came out behind her, and Tom, in a courtly fashion, draped another towel over V.J.'s slim shoulders. Sabrina wrapped hers around herself and approached the bar. Dianne, Thayer and Anna Lee had already taken seats there and were laughing as Brett and Jon argued over the proper way to make a martini.

"Stirred, not shaken," Jon said.

"Oh, come now, that's a bunch of British rot," Brett protested. "This is the way!" he said, shaking a canister. "The ice just ever so slightly melts, giving the alcohol a perfect frost!"

"Speaking of frost," Jon said, addressing all of them, "I'm afraid we've acquired a rather grim weather forecast. It has occurred to me to suggest that we nix this Mystery Week and that I move you all into Stirling so that—"

"What?" Tom interrupted. "Nix the party now?"

"Some bad weather is moving in pretty fast," Jon said. "I'd like—"

"I'm not leaving," V.J. insisted. "Jon, dear, I've come all the way from California for this! A little bad weather isn't going to drive me away."

"I'm not going, either, old buddy," Thayer said firmly. "Hell, I don't make your kind of money yet, Jon. Maybe not ever. This is my vacation with the rich and famous."

"So what if we're snowbound?" Anna Lee demanded.

Jon hesitated. "I just have a bad feeling that—"

"Oh, Jon," Reggie said, joining them, her elderly voice full of grandmotherly empathy. "Jon, I thought when you planned this that you'd gotten over what happened the last time. We're all here for some fun and for a good cause, and we're not going anywhere."

"Cassie fell," Dianne Dorsey said firmly. "It was simply an accident, and that's what the coroner said."

"Exactly, Jon," Anna Lee added, an edge to her voice.

They both defended him so passionately, Sabrina noted, and she couldn't help thinking that either of them might have had an affair with him. Either of them might have really hated Cassandra, too.

Jon shook his head. "Thanks, but I'm afraid there's more to my concern than unhappy memories. Or even the snow. Remember the gunshots we heard this morning?''

Nods and a chorus of yeses met his words.

''I found a bullet in the grout in the stone in the hallway.

''What?'' Thayer demanded.

''Well, Jon, this place is ancient, much older than even I am!'' Reggie exclaimed. ''Perhaps—''

''It wasn't an old bullet, Reggie. It was a new bullet,'' Jon told her.

Tom Heart shook his head in puzzlement. ''Then it's part of the game.''

''It wasn't part of the game. It's a real bullet,'' Jon said somewhat impatiently.

''Adding a little spice to the mystery, Jon?'' Joe queried with a knowing smile, stroking his bushy beard.

''He's good at this,'' V.J. said in agreement. ''Jon, did you ever consider acting?''

''Ladies and gentlemen, we're talking a real bullet, really fired in the hall, and someone might have gotten hurt. Or even killed,'' Jon said grimly.

''Okay,'' Joe protested, ''so maybe one of us is an asshole who made it through the airport with a gun for protection in a strange country. God knows, we're all off-the-wall a bit. But I can't see ruining this whole Mystery Week because some moron mistakenly fired a gun in the hall.'' Joe sounded for all the world like the world-weary, no-nonsense P.I. in his books.

"All right, then, who fired the gun?" Jon demanded, looking from one of them to the next.

There was no confession.

"Well?" he said softly.

"Someone is trying to add to the mystery. No one was hurt," Joe mentioned.

"There's a bullet in the wall," Jon repeated flatly.

"Can you be absolutely certain it wasn't there from sometime before?" Thayer Newby asked, sounding, as he often did, as if he were grilling a suspect at headquarters.

"I'm familiar with firearms and bullets," Jon said.

"I'll take a look at it," Thayer said. "But I, too, say it's one of us adding a little spice to the Mystery Week."

"Please, Jon," Dianne said quietly. "We all just love doing this. Don't let what happened last time make you paranoid. Cassie didn't kill herself. She was very beautiful but maybe not particularly coordinated. She fell, Jon. She fell, you've gone through hell and that's that. It was a long time ago, we're all having a wonderful time now and we'll all be extremely angry with you if you make us leave!"

"And that's a fact," Anna Lee said determinedly.

"I'm just very concerned about you all, and—" Jon began.

"Jon Stuart, you are not going to throw an old lady out on the streets!" Reggie said indignantly.

And he was defeated. Sabrina could see his expression change as he looked at the elderly author. He took her hand and kissed it. "Never, Regina, in a thousand years would I think of putting you out on the streets.''

''Damn straight, dear boy!'' she declared, and she leaned across the bar to kiss his cheek.

Jon set down the drink he had been making. ''All right, ladies and gentlemen, let's leave it at this. If there are any more incidents, or if it looks as if the weather could present real danger, it's over.'' He poured himself a straight shot of bourbon and hoisted it.

Anne Lee smiled. ''Hear! Hear!'' she cried, and she too leaned over the bar, planting a kiss not on his cheek but on his lips.

''Whoa, hot one!'' Brett declared. ''Well, I'm awfully damned glad we're going to keep this party going, but I'm sorry, I'll be damned if I'll kiss you, Jon.''

''You'll be decked if you kiss me!'' Jon warned in turn, and the whole group laughed.

''You won't deck *me,* will you?'' Dianne Dorsey asked sweetly. ''My turn,'' she said, leaning over the bar and kissing him on the lips as well.

''Hey, ladies, I'm bartending here, too,'' Brett commented. ''Don't all fight to kiss me at once!''

''Silly boy, those are surely the most used lips in history,'' V.J. drawled.

''Oh, let's be nice,'' Anna Lee said, and she kissed him, lingering just a bit.

''Much better. Share the wealth,'' Brett told Jon.

Jon shrugged. ''Well, it is my house.''

"House!" Susan exclaimed. "He calls this a house."

Sabrina wasn't sure why—she didn't mean to be a killjoy in the least—but she suddenly wanted to be away from the crowd, away from the joking.

And away from all the well-used lips.

She felt strangely like an outsider. They had all known each other much longer—and much better. They had all been here when Cassandra died. They seemed to form an enclave, and she felt oddly excluded, yet at the same time a little relieved to be so. She needed to get away for a bit, to feel a touch of reality.

Jon had mixed her drink; she saw it on the bar. But she took her towel and silently slipped away, making her way upstairs to her room.

She showered, washed her hair, wrapped herself in a towel and curled up on the bed to call her sister. Tammy was two years her junior, an archeology major who had married one of her professors. Nothing in the world made either of them happier than digging in the dirt for ancient relics, unless it was their new-born son, Tyler Delaney. Though she was happy as a lark, Tammy was also feeling the confinement of new motherhood, and she was eager to hear all about Scotland.

"Aren't you having fun?" she inquired now.

"Sure. Why do you ask?" Sabrina replied.

"Well, you've already called Mom. Now me. Surely you have better things to do with your time.

So tell me, what's going on? Are you having problems with the master sleuth himself?''

"Who?"

"Oh, don't play innocent with me. You know I'm talking about Jon Stuart. Tall, dark and handsome. Man of mystery with the great accent. The faster-than-a-speeding-bullet affair of your life. So, did he or didn't he do in his beautiful, bitchy wife? Have you learned anything new over there?"

Sabrina stared at the phone. "He was cleared of all charges, you know."

"Lots of people have been acquitted on all kinds of charges. That doesn't make them innocent."

"No, I don't believe he did it," Sabrina said firmly.

"Oooh, listen to you. So the flame is still burning brightly. He remains tall, dark, handsome and totally enchanting! So where is he, and why are you on the phone with me?"

"Everyone's down by the pool—in the castle dungeon, if you can believe it. Jon was threatening to call the whole week off because he found a bullet in the wall."

"Well, it is Mystery Week," Tammy commented. "Isn't that the kind of thing that happens? Mysterious clues and all?"

"He says it's not part of the mystery."

"Is he telling the truth?"

"I imagine. He was trying to make us all go home. Reggie Hampton—she's a tough old bird who writes adorable mysteries featuring a cat—refused to go."

"Good for her," Tammy said. "Then again, maybe

you should come home. That way you could quit calling us long distance."

"Very funny. See if I call you for a friendly chat again."

"How's your ex, by the way? Brett is there, right? Honestly, I have to admit to being totally jealous. I'm sitting here with baby oatmeal, poo-poo diapers, and my boobs are swollen enough to burst. And you're off jet-setting in Scotland with the rich and famous. Not fair. Besides, Mom always liked you better."

Sabrina started to laugh at the old joke, glad that she had called. "Mom never liked me better, and you're being totally irrelevant." She and Tammy had fought like the dickens growing up, but now her sister was her best friend, and the only person other than herself and Jon who knew she'd had a faster-than-a-speeding-bullet affair with him.

"So how is old Brett?"

"Brett's fine. He's at the pool, too, whining because he isn't getting as many kisses as Jon."

"Ah," Tammy murmured, "so that's it. Those other writers—those hussies—are down in the dungeon kissing tall, dark and handsome. And you're jealous, so you ran to your room and phoned home."

"Don't be silly. I called to ask about Tyler," Sabrina protested.

"Our beautiful baby is fine. He's an angel, too—sleeps all the time. I'm waiting for him to wake up."

"Think you deserved such a good baby?" Sabrina teased.

"If you want me to suffer, I'm suffering. I'm going

to have to poke the kid awake soon. I'm not kidding—this nursing thing is killing me. I think I could do lethal damage with a jet spray of milk at the moment. But back to you and Mr. Mystery. Now seriously, pay attention to me here. Why not take the bull by the horns? Sleep with good old tall, dark and handsome again, and find out if you've been carrying a torch all these years for something imagined or something real. Just remember that it's Mystery Week, and make sure you know who you're sleeping with. Don't go sleeping with any strangers!''

Sabrina was startled to feel an uneasy sensation sweep over her as her sister jokingly, unknowingly, echoed what Brett had said in the chamber of horrors.

"I'm here as a professional fiction writer involved in a charity event, nothing more," Sabrina said. Yet to her own ears, even as she spoke the lie, she froze, certain she had heard a soft clicking sound on the line.

Had someone been listening in on her conversation?

"Sabrina?"

"Yes, I'm still here," she said softly. She didn't know why, but she felt the same deep sensation of unease again. It was unnervingly akin to fear.

It was a big house—castle—and she was certain it had several phone lines, but not necessarily one for each guest room. Someone had simply accidentally picked up in the middle of her conversation and then hung up again.

So why did she feel someone had been listening in?

"Give my nephew a kiss for me," Sabrina said quickly. "Love you. I'll call again in a few days."

"Great, bye, have a good time!" Tammy said.

Sabrina stared at the phone for a moment, then hung up. And suddenly she had the uneasy feeling that someone was behind her. She whirled around on the bed.

She was alone in her room, but the doors to the balcony were open.

She held tightly to her towel and rushed over to step outside.

There was no one there.

But she could see Jon Stuart, out on his balcony. For a moment, she was relieved to see him. He, too, had left the crowd and come upstairs. Okay, so maybe she had been jealous. And maybe she had felt out of his league down by the pool, realizing that he'd had many lovers in his life, and she had just been one of them. After all, it was rumored that he'd been having an affair at the time Cassandra died, and if so, that affair would have been with someone who was here now....

The thought hurt. Like a knife in the pit of her stomach. She gazed at him, wondering what was going on in *his* mind....

Then she realized that she was standing on the balcony with only a towel around her.

Maybe he hadn't seen her.

He raised a hand in a silent salute.

She waved back and retreated in a flash, anxious to get dressed.

At least, she told herself, if Jon had been on his balcony, he couldn't have been in her room. No one had been in her room. True, the balcony doors had been open, but no one had been out there, and, despite the celebrated guest list, she doubted there were any superheros among them who could have *flown* away.

Of course, Jon might have been on the phone in his room, listening in on her conversation, she thought.

No, he would have apologized, and he would have hung up right away.

Surely he would have done so. But how did she really know? Had she made of him what she wanted him to be? In fact, if she thought about it, maybe she didn't know him at all. And so much time had passed.

Maybe he truly was a stranger.

And some very strange things were happening here....

Stop! she told herself. Get dressed, and get ready to take part in Mystery Week.

It got dark so early, and now it was almost dusk. Time to head down to the chapel.

She loved the chamber of horrors.

It was just so good.

The people were so real. The fear and the terror were so real. And deep in the dungeon, with the recessed lighting, it was like a secret world where famous killers could come to life. Their victims could almost be heard in their silent yet eloquent screams.

Walking softly through the fantastic exhibits, she felt a pleasant sense of power.

No one knew.

"Here!"

She spun around at the whisper, trembling with a pleasant fear.

For a second, just a split second, she thought that one of the wax figures had come to life, that Jack the Ripper prowled the dungeon or that a headsman was stalking her.

The pale, purple-gray light was so eerie.

The figures were so real.

She could hear her heart slamming against the walls of her chest. Someone was moving, furtive in the darkness...stalking?

Then she heard her name whispered, and delicious chills cascaded down her spine. It was him. He had come.

Then she saw him, and she started to hurry to him, wondering at the stricken expression on his face.

"She knows!" he gasped. "She knows, and she intends to blackmail us. Oh, God, I don't know what to do. I don't—"

She threw her arms around him, hushing him, calming him. "Now tell me who you're talking about and what exactly happened."

He did, and as he spoke, he shook. He was afraid. Afraid for the future, afraid for her. She had never been loved so in her life.

"My God, I couldn't bear it if—" he began.

"Hush, hush, my love! Nothing bad will happen."

"But I don't know what to do!"

She smiled, shaking her head. "I do," she said softly. "Don't you worry." She held him close and looked around at the tableaux. Hooded headsmen, masked murderers. She smiled and soothed him. "Don't you worry. I know exactly what to do."

8

The castle was most definitely large, Sabrina thought, descending the main stairs to the foyer. It was full of people, guests and staff, and yet now, at dusk, as she hurried to her appointment, she didn't see a soul. Eerie.

She headed around the stone expanse of the main stairway to where the second set of winding steps led down to the dungeon beneath. She hadn't felt unnerved just glad that they were going swimming. Now, however...

Turning away from the cheerful recreation area, she came to a pair of heavy, brass-accented wooden doors and paused. They were open to the exhibits, of course, Joshua Valine's fabulous tableaux of lives—and deaths—gone by. The track lighting within allowed an eerie mauve glow to whisper out of the room like fog on a dark night. She shivered, then thought that she had heard someone inside.

"Hello in there!" she called. Her voice seemed very loud. She stepped in, following the path to where Jack the Ripper stood over his last victim, Mary Kelly. Sabrina found herself pausing again, biting her lower lip. Mary Kelly really did resemble Susan

Sharp. The sculptor obviously had an odd sense of humor—or esthetics. After all, he supposedly liked Sabrina and he had made her the victim on the rack. Then again, none of the women in the exhibit had fared any too well.

She heard a noise behind her, like a whisper of air, and she spun around. "Hello? Who—"

She broke off, looking around. She could see no one moving about at all. Camy Clark as Joan of Arc gazed heavenward from her stake. She herself was stretched out on the rack. Joe Johnston, shaved and wearing a white wig as Louis XVI, faced the guillotine with Anna Lee Zane as Marie Antoinette at his side. They all looked incredibly real, as if they had just been in action but suddenly stopped dead when Sabrina turned around.

Goose bumps broke out over her arms, and she took a step backward. She nearly screamed as she backed into someone. Then she saw that it was only the straw setup for the Joan of Arc display.

Face it, this place is scary as all hell, she told herself. No one had been in here, watching her, even if she had felt a presence, felt someone's eyes on her. It was just the eerily realistic wax figures "watching" her. All the figures, with their penetrating glass eyes.

Sabrina hadn't meant to run, but she did.

And as she did so, she thought she heard the sound of laughter. Soft, whispering laughter, like an airy breeze.

Okay, so you're losing your mind here, she told herself as she hurried toward the second set of wooden doors. She assumed they led to the chapel, and she pushed them open, entering the room.

It wasn't the castle's chapel, but the crypt.

Stone shelves and flooring housed ornate tombs, with angels hewn of marble, crosses, death's-heads and more funerary art decorating individual graves. Sabrina felt as if she had entered the catacombs of a great cathedral, there seemed to be so many dead from so long ago, stretching out at least the length of one wing of the castle. Only here, in the entry, was there dim lighting to show the unwary guest what he or she had stumbled upon. There was nothing awful about the crypt—no visible bodies decaying in shrouds, no skulls or bare bones upon the shelving. If she weren't alone, she'd be fascinated, eager to study the crypt's dates and art. And Terry would be in heaven here.

But, admittedly, Sabrina was spooked. Goose bumps were popping out on her arms again. She turned about, then paused, turning back. A stone sarcophagus lay dead ahead of her, a shiny new cross and fresh flowers atop it. Sabrina saw that a banner was tied to the flowers, and she approached the casket to read the words. *Rest in peace and God's love, dear Cassie.*

Sabrina backed away, startled and uneasy. She'd had no idea that Cassandra Stuart had been buried here, in this castle, where she had died.

Feeling suddenly as if the crypt were closing in on her, Sabrina turned and hurried out. She closed the massive doors behind her, and as she did so, she was suddenly certain that she heard the laughter again.

"Get a grip!" she whispered angrily to herself. If the creatures in the tableaux were coming alive to taunt her, they weren't magically making their way into the crypt, as well. This place was simply spooky as all hell.

"Great setting for a Halloween party," she murmured irritably, realizing that, of course, it was also a great place for a Mystery Week. They had taken place here before Cassie died, and they should continue to do so. She, Sabrina Holloway, was a mystery writer. She was supposed to come alive with excitement over this type of affair, the way the others did. This was supposed to be fun.

She leaned against the crypt doors. "Right. I'm having so damn much fun, I can barely stand it," she whispered softly to herself.

She straightened her shoulders and headed for the third pair of doors, which had to belong to the chapel.

They did.

She breathed a sigh of relief, looking in. The chapel was beautiful, with its stone arches, altar and ancient pews. The stations of the cross had been etched in stained glass along the walls, with special lighting set behind to show them off even in the gloom of the dungeon. Evidently a few Stuarts had their tombs in here instead of the crypt and these were between the stations, their occupants elaborately carved in stone atop their final resting places. Like the crypt, the chapel seemed to be immaculate, with nary a cobweb or spider. Tapers burned on the altar and from beautiful candlesticks at the end of each pew.

Sabrina started toward the altar. As she reached it, she heard footsteps behind her, and she spun around, thinking she'd scream and tear out her hair if no one was there this time.

But Dianne Dorsey, clad in a black cocktail gown, her neatly cut ebony hair swinging, was coming toward her, a smile on her face.

"Am I glad to see you!" the young writer exclaimed.

Sabrina smiled. "I'm glad to see you, too."

"Are you the murderer?" Dianne asked anxiously.

Sabrina laughed. "I'm not supposed to tell you if I am."

"Well, if you are, I'll be the first to go."

"And vice versa, of course."

"Your note sent you here?" Dianne asked.

Sabrina nodded. "I'm supposed to meet with one of my wayward girls. Choir practice."

Dianne laughed. "Well, despite the fact that I'm Mary, the Hare Krishna, by day, evidently I moonlight for your call-girl outfit at night."

"Oh, no, you mean you're not an angelic but misguided chorister?"

"Well, I'm sure I sing just as angelically as anyone, but my note said that I'm to be reprimanded for missing the last 'appointment' you arranged for me."

"With whom?"

"Demented Dick—who else?" Dianne laughed.

"Oh, well, consider yourself duly reprimanded."

"Not that I would have missed a date with Jon as Demented Dick had I had one!"

Her airy comment had Sabrina turning with curiosity about the nature of Dianne's relationship with their host, but Dianne had begun walking through the chapel, looking at the stained glass stations of the cross.

"These are really beautiful, aren't they?" the young woman observed.

"Gorgeous," Sabrina agreed.

"It's Tiffany glass," Dianne explained. "Jon's grandfather put them in, turn of the century. Jon told me the last time we were here."

Curious, Sabrina followed her. "That week must have been so awful. So tragic."

Dianne shrugged. "I hate to sound like Susan, but Cassie was so…hated." She flashed a small smile at Sabrina. "Mostly by women, of course."

"Apparently Jon was happy with her," Sabrina ventured, just a little embarrassed by her not so subtle fishing expedition.

"John was planning on getting a divorce."

"How do you know that?"

"He told me."

"He…"

Dianne smiled. "You're assuming I was sleeping with Jon?" she demanded.

"I wasn't assuming anything. I—"

"Actually, I adore Jon. He's a good friend, one of the best guys out there. Tough and rugged, willing to go to bat for a friend."

"So are you saying that you weren't having an affair with him?"

"I'm saying that I would, wouldn't you?" Dianne said pleasantly.

"I wasn't here," Sabrina reminded her without answering the question.

"Oh, I see. This is the mystery that everyone *really* wants to solve this week. So you're looking for the criminal, too. You're asking if I was having a mad, passionate affair with Jon, flew off the handle and threw his nasty wife over the balcony? No, Sabrina. Jon was a big boy, he could handle himself. He wouldn't have thanked anyone for interference on his behalf. Besides, he did care about Cassie. She could be dazzling when she chose to be. I think she was becoming rancid because she realized she was losing him, and she was trying desperately—and pathetically, perhaps—to win him back."

"You think so? Then you hated her but felt sorry for her as well?"

Dianne shook her head. "Nope. Don't go giving me any gentler emotions where Cassie was involved. I simply hated her. I had good reason. But don't think that *only* women despised the little darling, no matter how dazzling she could be. She did a few terrible things to men, as well. Then again, I must admit, there were those who absolutely adored her. Like your ex."

"Brett?" Sabrina said, surprised.

Dianne looked at her, arching a brow. "Oh, dear, I'm sorry—are you two getting back together? Brett does keep implying that you're a twosome, but V.J. told me it wasn't so.''

"V.J. is right—it isn't so. I had just never realized that Cassie was among Brett's…women.''

"Really?'' Dianne said, sounding startled. "Well, maybe he didn't want his feelings known…especially by you. You may not be back together, but Brett seems to wish it were so.''

"Dianne, are you saying that Brett was having an affair with Cassie? Here, in Jon's house?''

"His castle, darling. You mustn't call it a house,'' Dianne said, amused. "But yes, they were having an affair, in Jon's castle. They were discreet. Brett was in the midst of a wild infatuation—but you know Brett well, so you know how his infatuations come and go. Cassie probably wanted to irritate her hubby, but Brett really does value his friendship with Jon.''

"But not enough to avoid sleeping with his wife.''

"Now, that's a dangerous tone. Moralistic, even. How intriguing. But then, our host does have an impact on most women, doesn't he? We all instantly spring to his defense. Like Lucy defended Count Dracula even as he sucked her blood dry!''

"I'm not trying to be moralistic, and I hardly see Jon Stuart as Count Dracula.''

"Tall, dark, handsome…devastating,'' Dianne said. "I admit, I adore the man. He'd be welcome to my blood anytime.''

"But, Dianne, I can't see where, with any man, sleeping with his wife would encourage a friendship.''

"I told you, Brett was infatuated. Madly in love."

"Dianne, you bitch!"

Dianne and Sabrina both swung around at the sound of the voice coming from the doors to the chapel.

"Brett, this is a house of worship!" Dianne said. "He can't say that in a chapel, can he?" she asked, glancing at Sabrina.

Sabrina shrugged. "He said it, didn't he?"

"You could go to hell for that, Brett," Dianne taunted.

But Brett wasn't amused. He was striding down the aisle between the pews. "It's not true!" he stated furiously, glaring at Dianne, then looking more petulantly at Sabrina. "You know me, it's not true!"

Sabrina looked at him, slowly arching a brow. "What isn't true, Brett? Are you trying to tell me that you weren't having an affair with Cassandra Stuart?"

He didn't exactly deny it. He spun on Dianne again. "Where did you get your information? It's all a pack of lies!" He was clearly agitated, hands on his hips, handsome face contorted.

Dianne lifted her chin. "From someone who knew."

"Oh, come on."

"Someone Cassie confided in."

"She was delusional! Don't you dare go around spreading the story that I was sleeping with Cassandra."

"Is it a story, Brett?" Dianne challenged.

"Damn you, Di—" he began.

But Dianne interrupted him, black hair tossed back defiantly, hands—with long, black polished nails—on her hips. "Maybe *you* pushed her over the balcony, Brett."

"Me? Oh, this is rich, Dianne! Come on, I wasn't married to her. I didn't need to get rid of anyone. You were crazy about Jon. Always have been, always will be. And now you're pointing a finger at me, trying to make my wife think—"

"Ex-wife, Brett," Sabrina interjected.

He ignored her and kept talking. "You're trying to make Sabrina think that I was involved with a married woman—and then in the next breath you're accusing me of killing her!"

"Maybe you were afraid that she was about to tell your buddy, Jon, the truth of the situation. She was just using you, Brett. Oh, I know you're the great lover, but she was in love with Jon in her warped, sick way. And—"

"If anyone had a reason to kill her, it was Jon. So why are you trying to make me look guilty?"

"Jon wasn't in the room! He was outside."

"So someone else was in on it. One of the guests, his staff—a bloody stranger!"

"And maybe she teased you just a little bit too much, a little bit too long, and—"

"I should give you a black eye!" Brett exclaimed. "Not that anyone would notice, with your damn black makeup. What is it with you, Dianne? Are you trying to scare your readers into buying your books?"

"Oh, Brett, is that all you can come up with? Is

everything in your life about book sales, about securing a place on a list? We're talking about a woman's life here.''

"Yes! Life—not death. I mean it, Dianne. How dare you make such accusations? You want the truth, the real truth? I did care about her. I didn't want her dead or—''

The sound of a gunshot suddenly exploded in the quiet chapel.

Startled, Sabrina ducked, and Dianne, too, dropped to the floor.

Brett didn't move as quickly. And the back of his tailored blue silk shirt was suddenly soaked in red.

Bloodred.

The note had sent him to the crypt.

Not his Mystery Week instruction note, but the first note he had found thrust beneath his door—the note Camy had denied writing.

It had read:

"You are a demented dick, thinking that you're slick. You're only sick, you maggot tick. You must go below, lie with your wife, minus all life. If a night's sweet passion you still crave, you must go sleep down in her grave.''

And so he had come here, to the crypt, where his ancestors rested. Along with Cassie. Despite her alleged hatred of Scotland, her will had actually requested that she be laid to rest in Jon's castle. To avoid morbid scandal-and-celebrity seekers, he had allowed reporters to believe she was being buried back in the States. Her family, happy to comply with his wishes and to avoid prurient interest, had been vague about her burial.

So there lay his wife, in the center of Lochlyre Castle's crypt.

Apparently his guests knew where she rested. For on her tomb lay flowers in her honor.

He swore softly, staring at them. Were they truly in her memory, or a taunt to him? Did someone here really think he had killed her?

Or was someone suffering a brutally guilty conscience and trying to cast blame his way.

If he'd been with her, she wouldn't have fallen. She wouldn't have been alone. Alone for a killer to come upon in a precarious position...

The sound of a gunshot galvanized Jon into action. He raced from the crypt, certain the blast had come from nearby.

He ran straight into Thayer Newby. Tom Heart and Joe Johnston were close behind.

"Anyone else down here?" Joe demanded.

"The chapel!" Thayer shouted.

They ran the short distance to the chapel doors, bursting in together.

Dianne and Sabrina were there, hunched down by the altar.

Brett was on the ground. Between the two rows of pews.

Swearing, despite the fact that it was the chapel.

Brett looked up as the men entered. Jon realized that they were followed closely by Reggie and Anna Lee.

"Can you believe it?" Brett said, disgusted. "Me! I'm the first to go. Damnation! I didn't see a thing, didn't hear a thing. I was a damned sitting duck, an idiot, a fuc—"

"Brett! It is a chapel," Sabrina reminded him.

She was by Dianne's side, and obviously the two of them had been trying to make McGraff feel better about becoming a ghost. Sabrina's blue eyes were huge, her hair shimmering as it fell around her shoulders. Jon felt a strange pulse ticking against his throat and forced his attention back to the situation at hand.

His heart, he realized, was still pounding. The bullet he had found in the wall earlier had unnerved him. It had been real. And it hadn't been there before. He would have seen it. He walked that hallway every day of his life when he was in residence. He'd been afraid that someone was toting real fire power with real purpose.

Now he was so relieved to find that this gunshot was part of the game that he needed to sit.

Brett was flushing, staring at him. "Sorry, Jon. I suppose this place is sacred or something, huh? But the game instructions did tell us to come here."

"Well, it is a chapel, yes," Jon said. "But I think you can get away with 'damn,' especially if you've just been shot with red paint. So who did it?" He looked questioningly at Dianne and Sabrina.

Dianne smiled like a cat. Sabrina shrugged. "We didn't see. We were in the midst of an argument."

Jon frowned. "About what?"

"Oh, some silly thing. I don't even remember, do you, Dianne?"

The young woman arched a brow, then lifted her shoulders. "No...I can't quite remember. At the moment."

"Five minutes ago you were all arguing so passionately that you didn't pay any attention to what was going on, and now you can't remember what you were talking about?" Jon asked skeptically.

Sabrina shook her head. The color in her cheeks heightened, and her lashes fluttered before her eyes met his again.

She was lying, Jon knew.

"You are all acting like a bunch of lunatics!" Thayer accused.

"Well, what do you want?" Brett said irritably. "I'm shot all over with red paint. Damn! Damn! Shit! Ah, hell, sorry, Jon."

"I say it's cocktail hour," Reggie announced.

"Hear, hear," Tom agreed.

"Well, now, wait!" Joe protested, rubbing his bearded chin and looking at them all. "Let's check out the situation first. We're here to solve a mystery, Sabrina, what happened here?" he asked.

Sabrina looked at him, started to speak, then stopped. She glanced at Jon, looked away.

What the hell? he wondered.

Then she shook her head sheepishly at Joe. "Honest, you know how opinionated we all are, Joe. It was dumb, but we got so involved talking, none of us was paying any attention.''

"Well, this is a total loss!" Joe said, disgruntled.

"No, it's not," Tom argued. "We know that the butler didn't do it, since Mr. Buttle, the butler, is now dead."

"The butler is dead?" a new voice suddenly inquired. Susan Sharp, in a deep blue cocktail dress that emphasized her darkly attractive looks, swept into the chapel. She spotted Brett and burst into laughter.

"Well, you didn't last very long, did you, dear?"

"Susan, trust me, you won't last very long, either," Brett promised her direly.

"Oh, don't be a spoilsport. They killed you, and I'm alive and well."

"No, Susan," Brett informed her firmly. "Carla— the call girl with the clap—is alive and more or less well. For the moment."

"As Sherlock Holmes would say, 'The game is afoot!' Reggie informed them. "And the week has just begun. We are beginning to learn a few things. The butler is out of the picture. We now know that Sabrina isn't the killer, or Dianne."

"That's not true. We don't know anything, except that none of them will talk!" Tom protested. "Remember, the killer may have an accomplice. Someone to lure the victims to their dooms. That means that Dianne or Sabrina could easily be guilty of complicity in murder."

"But who pulled the trigger?" Joe demanded. "Let's see, everyone is here except... V.J."

"Excuse me—right here, at the chapel door," V.J. called, and they all turned to look at her.

Entirely elegant in a floor-length, sequined gown, V.J. was casually leaning against the doorjamb and watching them all with amusement as they argued.

"Ah, but where were you?" Tom demanded, smiling as he sauntered over to her.

For the first time it occurred to Jon that his two friends made a very nice looking couple. Tom Heart, too, looked elegant, in a dinner jacket, tie and vest, his silver-white hair gleaming. Interesting. Maybe something was brewing there. The two had always seemed so compatible. The last time they'd all been together here, V.J.'s husband had been living. No more. And rumor had it that though Tom was still married, he'd been separated from his wife of thirty years for several months.

V.J. lifted a champagne flute to them all. "Where was I? Where I was supposed to be. I was at cocktail hour—all by myself. I had no idea that the party was in the chapel." She looked around. "So the butler bit the dust. That kind of ruins the fun—we know we won't get to say that the butler did it! Well, the chapel is lovely. Much better than the crypt. If we're all going to spend time down here, at least it's with this beautiful stained glass and not with coffins and dead people." She winced. "Oh, sorry, Jon. I forget they're your relatives."

"I understand, V.J.," he told her. "I prefer cocktails with the living myself."

"I told you it was cocktail hour," Reggie said. "V.J. is the only one of us with any sense."

"Hell, I agree with that."

"Brett McGraff!" Reggie reprimanded him indignantly. "We're in a chapel!"

"Sorry," Brett muttered in resignation.

"Oh, Brett," Dianne warned, "that stuff is dripping onto your pants now."

"Hell, you're right, it is. Damn! Oh, shit. There I go again, swearing in the chapel. I wish I could stop that!" Brett said. He leaped to his feet, glanced at the crucifix on the altar and crossed himself quickly. The others were staring at him. "All right, all right, I was brought up in the Catholic Church. Do you mind?"

With that he spun around. "I'll be changing my shirt so that I can come to cocktails in ghostly white apparel." He stomped out of the chapel. "Shit!" he swore one last time.

The tension was broken as the others burst into laughter. Reggie started out after him. "Ladies, gentlemen, I'm going up for cocktails. Anyone joining me?"

"Definitely," Jon agreed.

"Joe Johnston, get up here and escort an old lady," Reggie commanded.

"Yes, ma'am!" Joe said, hurrying to her side.

The others began filing out. Jon paused by the door, waiting.

Tom escorted V.J. Dianne, Thayer and Anna Lee

exited together, Dianne still insisting to Thayer that she hadn't seen anything. Susan brushed by Jon.

Sabrina remained by the altar. She looked at him as if she was trying to figure out how to escape him when he stood blocking the only exit.

He walked toward her. "Were you intending to stay behind for some reason?" he inquired.

"No," she said quickly.

"Are you trying to avoid me?" he inquired.

"No," she repeated.

But she was lying again. And he thought he knew why. The argument between Brett and Dianne had been over him. Or Cassie. Or what had happened three years ago.

And Sabrina didn't want him questioning her.

Well, maybe it wasn't the time.

She stood very still, trying to keep her beautiful blue eyes level with his. Her hair was falling around her shoulders like silk, and he suddenly ached to reach out and touch it.

No, he admitted to himself, he wanted more than that.

There was so much in life that went by so swiftly. So much that a man barely remembered. But he remembered Sabrina. Her tentative smile. Her gentle touch. Her passion. The way she'd been so trusting way back when.

She was still tentative at times.

But not so trusting.

She was very wary, watching him.

He felt a renewed bitterness that she could suspect

he would cold-bloodedly kill his wife. He wished he could reach out, shake her and tell her he was innocent. No, he didn't want to shake her. He wanted to touch her. Hold her. Again. Hell, Brett McGraff was worrying about the things he'd been saying in the chapel. The things Jon wanted to *do* in the chapel were surely far less forgivable.

God, he could remember the way she looked naked, covered with a sheen of sweat, crystal blue eyes half shielded by the fall of her lashes, every curve of her body inviting.

"The others are way ahead. I guess we should hurry," she said, and she stepped past him, striding quickly toward the doors.

He followed her, and, unable to stop himself, caught her arm, swinging her back around to face him.

"We have to talk," he said.

The words came out sounding far more harsh than he had intended.

She gazed at his hand where it rested on her upper arm. Her long blond hair brushed over his fingers, soft as silk. To his dismay, that slight sensation was arousing.

"Not here, not now," she said nervously.

"We have to talk," he insisted.

"Later," she said, pulling free.

"I'm taking that as a promise," he told her.

He ushered her out. Aware that, though she had shaken off his touching, she was sticking very close to him.

And he realized that she didn't want to be left alone in the dungeon of Lochlyre Castle.

With him.

But then again...who did?

9

Amazingly, Sabrina didn't dream that night; she slept like a log. The evening had ultimately gone pleasantly, with everyone trying to figure out why the butler had died first. Dinner had been delicious, rack of lamb, and she'd been starving. She had opted for regular coffee rather than decaf with their late dessert, and despite even that, she had come upstairs, changed into a nightgown—and slept.

Only the persistent tapping on her door forced her to wake up. And by then it was morning.

"Sabrina, hey, wake up! Hurry!"

At her ex-husband's urgency, she catapulted out of bed and into her robe and hurried to her door.

Brett was in jeans and a heavy sweater. "Hey, sleepyhead, you've got less than a week now to find the killer. If you sleep the whole thing away, you'll never be the master sleuth."

"I'm awake. What's the rush?"

"Riding!"

"Riding?"

He nodded. "A riding party is going out. Come on, hurry, we're probably late already. The others might have headed out. Come on, you want to see the countryside before bad weather moves in, right? Get dressed. I'll wait for you.''

"I need coffee, Brett.''

"I'll get it for you.'' He waved his hands at her. "Go on, get moving. I'll bring you coffee.''

He closed her door and disappeared. She shrugged and decided that if the rest of the household was headed out riding, she didn't want to be left behind. She loved horses, and the countryside did look beautiful.

She hopped in and out of the shower, careful to bring her clothing into the bathroom with her. She emerged in jeans, shirt, jacket and boots to find that Brett had returned and was comfortably curled on her bed—offering her coffee.

She took the cup.

"Get up,'' she commanded him.

"Why?'' he demanded.

"You make it look as if you've been sleeping here.''

He frowned, studying her. "What are you so afraid of?''

"What do you mean?''

"What do you care what something looks like?''

"Brett, you're my friend, I care about you, but you are my ex-husband, and though I'll surely make lots of new mistakes in my life, I'm not going to repeat old ones. I'm not marrying you again, and I'm not sleeping with you again, and I don't want people thinking that we're a twosome.''

He was still studying her as he stood up. "So.''

"So what?"

"So there is something between you two."

"Who two?"

"You and our host. I was right."

"You were right about what?"

"You slept with him."

"Oh, Brett, please."

"I still love you, Sabrina."

"Brett, you never loved me."

"I did. I do. But don't worry, I'm going to prove to you that I can be good for you. Drink your coffee, and let's get going."

There was no one in the hallway, on the stairs or even in the great hall as they walked out of the castle into the front courtyard. The stables were ahead to the right. Two horses were saddled and bridled and ready for them.

"I guess the others have gone on ahead," Brett murmured.

"Are you sure?" Sabrina demanded, suddenly suspicious.

He laughed. "Well, since I'm already a ghost, you know that I'm not the murderer, so I'm not luring the Duchess to her doom."

"You've got a point there," she said. She walked up to one of the horses, a sleek bay that stood about sixteen hands high. She stroked the horse's velvety nose. "What a beauty. This is a great idea, Brett. Thanks for coming to get me."

"Yeah, sure, let's get started."

He gave her a hand before leaping up on the roan

that had been tethered next to the bay. He started from the castle at an easy lope, looking back a little uneasily. Sabrina thought he was worried about her.

"Go on, you know that I can ride!" she told him delightedly.

Riding had been one of the benefits of growing up in the Midwest. But this was some of the most spectacular scenery she had ever seen. The ground was rolling here in the valley, while majestic hills rose up around them. Leaving the castle behind, they came up on a little promontory. She could see the hills rising higher and higher toward the mountainous country to the northwest, the loch shimmering in the sun below them and a sea of grass and flowers seeming to flow all around them. The air was crisp and cold with the promise of strong weather to come, yet it felt delicious, and she was delighted to be out.

"Which way did they head? Do you know where we're going?" she asked Brett.

"Of course."

"How?"

"I was here before, remember?"

"Where are we heading?"

"That way." He pointed to the northeast.

"Oh. Race you to that copse!" Sabrina called out, and she nudged her mount. Her horse smoothly began to run. The animal was graceful, the air was invigorating, the world around her was beautiful. Sabrina felt a pure rush of exhilaration.

She heard Brett pounding up behind her, and at the copse she reined in, waiting for him.

"Remember when we went riding outside Paris?" he asked her. "There were flowers everywhere."

"There were women everywhere," she corrected him.

He shrugged that off, looking at her, his brown eyes sincere. "I've learned my lesson, Sabrina."

"Brett, you make sexual innuendos every time you're around anyone who's even remotely female."

"Even remotely female? I resent that!"

"Brett, you—"

"Sabrina!" He reached over, placing his hand on her thigh. "I only do that because I want you so badly and I can't allow other people to see just how much."

She stared at him. "Oh?" she said softly. "Brett, were you having an affair with Cassandra Stuart when she died?"

"Me?" he demanded, startled. Then he huffed, "This place is getting to you, Sabrina. You can't let it. Cassie is dead and gone. We need to let her rest in peace, forget the past and get on with our lives. Come on, I'll race you to that next little hill there!"

He took off; she followed. As they rode, the wind whipped around her, colder than it had been only minutes before.

She looked up. The sky had been a deep, striking shade of blue. Now it was darkening to mauve. She reined in next to Brett on the hill. "Looks like that bad weather is coming in. We should find the others."

"Maybe they're up ahead in that hunting lodge."

"I don't see any horses."

"Maybe the horses are in back. Let's get there and see."

He nudged his horse into a lope. With little other choice, Sabrina followed.

Jon's note that morning had read simply: "Attend the séance in the crypt at 11:00."

Joe Johnston and Tom Heart were in the great hall when he went down for coffee, and like the good game players they were, they were trying to figure out why the butler should be the first to die.

"He knew something. People who know things are dangerous," Joe said.

"He was blackmailing someone," Tom suggested.

"Obviously," Joe agreed.

"I say there's an accomplice in this. Not a single person acting alone," Tom continued to theorize.

"I say that there isn't enough information in as yet, but I agree with you—I think we have two people acting on this."

"Now the danger involved in having an accomplice to murder is that, even if you commit the perfect crime yourself, you have to worry about the other person. Leaving a clue. Panicking. Giving something away."

"Being an idiot and doing the wrong thing."

"Exactly!" Tom said, pleased that Joe seemed to agree with his thinking. "Especially when the murderer is a clever enough person but emotionally involved with the accomplice."

"And the accomplice is an idiot. Happens often enough."

"And naturally, a man can prove to be a real fool himself when he commits murder because of a woman—"

"Meaning," V.J. interrupted from the doorway, "that the woman, who is, naturally, the accomplice, is an idiot?"

"Now, Victoria—" Tom began.

"Oh, now, Tom, don't you 'Now, Victoria' me!" V.J. said sternly. "You were implying that the murderer must be a clever man with a female accomplice who must be an idiot."

"Both could be incredibly clever," Joe suggested diplomatically, but it was too late.

V.J. gave him a withering stare. "Perhaps a woman is the killer, and her bumbling assistant is a male," she said.

"Perhaps a woman is the killer," Tom said, looking at V.J., "and her male accomplice is a bumbling idiot madly in love with her, trying to keep them both from spending the rest of their lives behind bars."

"Either that," Jon interjected smoothly, "or both of our killers are women. V.J., my love, we know that women can be deadly. We grant you that!"

V.J. sniffed, shaking her head sadly at him. "I can see that I'm outnumbered. Excuse me, gentlemen. I have a date with destiny." She exited the room.

Joe glanced at his watch. "Well, excuse me, too."

"Crypt?" Jon asked.

"Séance?" Tom queried.

"The séance is in the crypt. We might as well head down together," Jon said.

"Sir, it's your castle," Tom said gallantly. "Lead the way."

Jon was surprised to feel an uneasy sensation prickling the back of his neck as his colleagues followed him down the back stairs to the dungeon. He was surprised to realize that having anyone behind him had become an unnerving experience.

They reached the crypt, however, without incident. V.J., Dianne, Reggie and Anna Lee Zane were already there. Candles had been lit, and a crystal ball sat on a low wooden table. Pillows strewn around it served as seats. The women were at their places around the table, which had been set as far from the tombs as possible, about ten feet away. Still, there was an eerie feel to the setup. Candlelight paled to shadows. Flames reflected in the crystal ball. Wisps of smoke vanished into the air. Cassie's tomb, one of the closest, gleamed dully.

"Join us, gentlemen," Dianne invited. Seated at the crystal ball, she was reading the game instructions propped in front of it. In black stretch pants and sweater, with her fashionable short black hair, pale skin and bloodred nails, she looked the part of a prophetess.

Her brooding eyes met Jon's, belying her light tone. "We're to contact Mr. Buttle, the butler," she said dryly. "Join hands and chant and ask the spirits of the castle to bring him to us." She made a face. "I assume that our boy Brett, the poor, deceased Mr.

Buttle, is hidden behind a tomb somewhere, about to make a 'spirit' appearance. Shall we start?'' she inquired.

"We're not all here," Jon said. Sabrina was among the missing.

"Well, here's Thayer coming now," V.J. said, curled comfortably on a cushion. "We'll wait a minute for Susan and Sabrina—"

"Well, we can't wait forever," Anna Lee said impatiently. "Maybe they weren't instructed to come to the séance."

"And maybe one of them is the murderer," Joe suggested.

"Conspiracy theory—they're both the murderers," Tom said.

"Well, maybe Sabrina can't be here," Anna Lee said with exasperation, "since she rode out of here with her ex-husband not too long ago."

"Rode out with *Brett?*" V.J. said incredulously.

"Rode out where?" Dianne asked.

"Rode out on what?" Thayer demanded.

Anna Lee looked at Thayer incredulously. "A horse, obviously. It doesn't take Sherlock Holmes to figure that one out!"

Jon strode to where Anna Lee was sitting, drawing her to her feet to question her. "When? When did they ride out?"

She seemed startled, almost unnerved, by the pressure he was putting on her. "I guess about an hour ago. I saw them leaving the stables at—"

"Alone?" Reggie asked.

Anna Lee nodded.

"How delicious! Rumors about those two must be true," Dianne said.

"Which way did they go?" Jon demanded.

"They were headed northwest."

"Oh, Jon, don't look so concerned. They'll be all right. They were married, and they're obviously getting back together—" Dianne began.

"And there's a major storm system moving in! The fools could be stranded in it. Even killed," Jon said angrily. "Excuse me." He turned abruptly on his heel to leave.

Jon didn't understand his sudden sense of fear. Sabrina could ride; she wasn't an idiot. And whether he liked it or not, she had been married to Brett and had evidently gone off with him willingly.

Still, he knew he had to find them. The weather coming in could be treacherous, and neither of them was familiar with what an early storm could be like in this wild countryside.

As he strode from the crypt, he heard the others commenting on his hasty exit.

"Well, he's in a bit of a mood, wouldn't you say?" Dianne murmured.

"He's concerned," V.J. said in his defense.

"Think he would have raced after the butler that way?" Dianne again, sounding resentful. He could just imagine her face tilted up, eyes staring at him, challenging, angry. "Out to rescue the lovely Ms. Holloway, right in front of her beloved ex. Cassie must be spinning in that grave."

"I think that Jon is a responsible man worried about his guests," Reggie announced impatiently. "Now, I'm an old woman contorted into a ridiculous position on this silly cushion. Can we get on with this thing?"

Bless you, Reggie, Jon thought.

Moments later, he was up the stairs and out of the castle, looking up at the sky. Gray clouds billowed in an angry pattern, rapidly darkening the day. The wind picked up even as he stood there. He hurried on to the stables.

The first drop of precipitation seemed mild enough—a little wet kiss on the face as Sabrina dismounted from her horse. "Snow!" she called to Brett.

"No, just a little rain!" he called back. "But that's okay, we'll hole up in the lodge!"

He came to her, slipped an arm around her, and they ran together to the door. Brett pushed it open, and Sabrina stepped inside, looking around for the others.

No one was there. The lodge was empty except for the furnishings and the cozy little fire that burned in the hearth.

It was an inviting if masculine place, a true hunting lodge, with rough wood paneling, a boar's head over the mantel, and a quilt-covered bed. The small kitchen area had a pump in the sink and an old-fashioned ice box. The entire look was rustic—except for the ice bucket and champagne that sat surrounded by finger sandwiches and chocolate-covered strawberries on a table by the bed.

Sabrina spun around to look at Brett. "Where is everyone?" she asked him.

He shrugged. "They didn't get here? Maybe they're lost."

She stared at him sternly. "Brett, where are they?"

He shrugged again, but then looked contrite. "Sabrin—"

"You deliberately lured me out here alone, didn't you?"

"I know that if we just had some time together—"

"Brett!"

He stayed across the room from her, staring at her. "I love you, Sabrina, you know that."

She shook her head impatiently. "Brett, you may think you love me, but trust me, you love anything female."

"Give me a chance. We'll take things slowly. Dear God, Sabrina, surely you must have needs, as well."

"Brett, you're my friend. Let's just stay friends."

"It's him, isn't it?" Brett said angrily.

"What?" she queried carefully, because it seemed as if something about him had changed. His devil-may-care bedroom eyes had a sharp, hostile glint to them.

He moved toward her. "It's him, our great, wondrous host. You've got some kind of an obsession going there. It's him, all right. You *would* sleep with me, except that you want to sleep with him."

"Brett, you've got to understand—"

"Well, there it is. It's true. You want to sleep with him—again. It is again, isn't it? Exactly when did you sleep with him, may I ask?"

"No, you may not ask! When you and I were married, I was faithful. You were not. So no, you can't ask questions. Brett, I want to stay friends with you. Don't make that impossible. Let's get out of here. Now."

She started past him, walking toward the door.

His arm snaked out; his fingers closed like a vise around her wrist. Startled, she saw the deep-seated anger glinting in his eyes.

"Oh, no," he told her. "We're not leaving. Not yet."

"Brett, let me go."

"Never, Sabrina," he said passionately. "It's you, it's all you. Everything—even Cassie—everything. I can't let you leave. Haven't you guessed?"

V.J. was anxious. Too anxious to sit silently at a table in the crypt. "Well?" she said.

"Well, I say Jon has been our basic killjoy. And it's his party," Dianne complained.

"He's worried, dear," V.J. said, studying Dianne. The girl was so restless. What had caused her strange mood? She suddenly looked very young and very upset. V.J. sighed, surprised to feel sympathy for a young woman who had stormed her profession at a ridiculously tender age. "Dianne, there's some fierce weather coming in, and neither Brett nor Sabrina knows this country at all."

"Snow is snow," Thayer Newby said. "Can't be much worse in one place than another. Why, I remember one year when I was in basic training up in New England, it was so cold and there was so much snow that people froze right in their cars. Can't be much worse here."

"How reassuring that a storm can't be much worse than one that killed people," V.J. murmured.

Tom placed a hand over hers, seeming to feel an empathy with her controlled impatience. "They may be in trouble," Joe agreed, rubbing his bearded chin.

"Think Jon needs help finding them?" Thayer asked.

"Think any of us knows this countryside well enough?" Reggie queried.

"Reggie, no offense," Tom interjected, "but you can't possibly mean to help Jon—"

"Hey," Reggie protested, "you're no spring chicken yourself, Tom. V.J., tell the boy he's an old man, will you?"

A moment's laughter rose among the group, then faded.

After an uneasy silence Dianne said, "I've been here to Scotland many times. I actually do know the countryside."

"You don't know it as well as Jon, dear," Reggie said. "He'll find Sabrina and Brett."

"Hey, where's Susan?" Thayer asked, as if suddenly noticing her absence and considering it highly suspicious.

Anna Lee, snickered. "Maybe she followed Brett

and Sabrina to spy on them. She's forever nosing into everyone else's business, and the more potential for dirt the better.''

"Okay, so should we leave Jon to the rescue and just get on with this séance?" Joe said. "Then we can get up from this stupid table."

"You're right, let's play the game," Anna Lee intoned.

V.J. looked around the circle. Dianne was definitely behaving strangely. Anna Lee was in a nasty mood. Reggie was in her Queen Victoria mode, and right now, scratching his bearded chin, Joe looked something like a cranky homicidal maniac. Thayer was staring at Anna Lee as if he knew something he shouldn't. Susan was missing, and it was true, she was probably nosing into somebody's dirty laundry. My friends, she thought. What a group! Then she felt Tom's eyes on her, and she calmed down a bit. "Yes, let's play the game," she said.

"You know," Joe said, "if Brett and Sabrina *are* out shacking up somewhere, at least they've found shelter and they're safe from the snow."

"If Brett is out shacking up with his ex-wife, he won't be playing the game as the dead butler. 'Mr. Buttle' will not be appearing here out of the tombs to make ghostly noises," Dianne said flatly. "So, you all still want a séance?" she inquired. She lowered her head and began swaying back and forth. "Spirits of the dead, give us a sign. Knock on wood, cry out!"

As if on cue, they suddenly heard a succession of eerie, muffled screams.

"What the hell is that?" Thayer demanded, leaping up.

They all rose, looking around. The sound seemed to fill the crypt, and yet wasn't coming from the crypt itself.

"Help! Help! Jesus, sweet Jesus, for the love of God!"

"Oh, Lord!" Dianne cried, pale as death herself.

"It's coming from—" V.J. breathed.

"The chamber of horrors!" Reggie finished.

They all stared at one another.

And raced from the crypt toward Joshua's excellent exhibition.

Brett let go of Sabrina's arm, and he was suddenly on his knees, clutching her. And she was unbalanced and startled.

"Sabrina, give me a chance! I can change. I've been wrong. I've been reckless ever since we parted. I've done things I'm not proud of. But I think I really love you, and—"

"Brett..."

"Sabrina, I had to see you alone. Please forgive me for—"

"Brett, what were you saying about Cassie?"

"Cassie?" he said blankly.

She was alone with this man. Alone and far from the castle. In a snowstorm. She told herself that she couldn't believe Brett would ever kill anyone, but he had said that everything was her. Everything. Even Cassie.

"Brett, did you kill Cassandra Stuart?" she demanded.

"No!"

"You said that—"

"My arguments with her," he mumbled. "Sabrina, okay, I lured you here dishonestly, but you have to listen to me."

"Brett," she protested again, trying to step backward. He was still down on the ground, his arms wrapped around her knees. The situation was ludicrous. A good percentage of the female reading populace would gladly have changed places with her; Brett McGraff was famous, charming, and rich—a number two bestseller, right behind Michael Creighton. But then, those women hadn't been married to him. And then again, how flattered could she be when he'd said, "I *think* I really love you."

Still, Sabrina couldn't really believe that Brett was a killer. He could be so childlike and endearing, and he seemed to be in earnest now. She didn't want to hurt him.

"Give it a chance, a real chance. I'm on my knees to you, Sabrina!"

"Don't Brett, please." Again she tried to back away. Again he clung.

"It is him, isn't it? I knew. I just knew that there was something between the two of you."

"Brett, you're tripping me."

"Sabrina, I can get past it. I can forgive you."

"You can forgive *me?* Brett—"

"Sabrina, I can't tell you how passionately I want—"

"Brett, you only want me because I'm saying no, and you're not familiar with the word where women are concerned. Please, Brett—"

She'd backed up until she struck something behind her. The bed. She lost her balance completely and fell backward.

And Brett was quick to take advantage. Up in an instant, he threw himself atop her. As she tried to crawl out from beneath him, she began to slide, the bed coverings coming with her. In seconds she was on the floor, entangled with Brett, a pillow, and the quilt. Another pillow fell on her head.

"Brett—" she began breathlessly.

But as more of the bedding tumbled down on her, she heard a crack like thunder as the door burst open.

"They're stuck! The doors are stuck!" Tom told Joe, leaning his weight against them.

More shrieking came from the other side.

"Do something!" V.J. commanded.

Dianne Dorsey stood back in the corridor, arms folded over her chest. "It's just Susan, being a melodramatic pain," she said.

"Oh, come on, she's frightened. Get her out," Anna Lee said.

"Help!" Susan pleaded. "Please, please, he's coming after me! He's going to kill me with his knife! Please—"

"Who's coming after you with a knife?" Reggie called to her.

"It's—it's Jack the Ripper!" Susan shrieked.

"Susan, Jack the Ripper is made of wax—he can't move. Just open the doors. I think you've got them locked," V.J. called.

Susan started screaming again.

"Step aside," Thayer Newby said firmly, all-cop. They cleared the doors.

Thayer stepped back and hunched his formidable shoulders. Tom and Joe joined him. Thayer nodded, and they all started forcefully for the doors.

Susan screeched hysterically, an ear-shattering sound.

Then she was silent.

Tangled in the bedclothes, Sabrina went still, listening as long strides brought someone close.

"What the hell—" Brett began.

The quilt was pulled off Sabrina's head. She found herself staring at Jon, who was hunched down before her. At her side, Brett struggled out of the tangle. "Excuse me for interrupting," Jon said smoothly, "but the storm is worsening. The snow—"

"Is just snow!" Brett interrupted. He sounded petulant, making Sabrina feel even more embarrassed.

"It's a big storm, Brett, and we're likely to be cut off from civilization, even at the castle. But at least there we've got real heat and supplies. You'd perish out here," he said politely.

Sabrina started to rise; Brett caught her hand. She

gritted her teeth. "Let me go." At her glare, he reluctantly released her, and she struggled to her feet. Both men also rose, exchanging suspicious stares.

"What the hell is going on here?" Jon demanded curtly of Brett.

"A reconciliation!" Brett snapped.

"Is that true?" Jon asked, looking at Sabrina.

"We're not recon—" she began.

"Damn you, Stuart, who the hell do you think you are?" Brett fumed. "The great lord of the castle? Just because you host this damn thing doesn't mean you—"

"I certainly don't host it for you to abduct women into the wilds and put their lives in jeopardy."

"You self-righteous bastard!" Brett countered, and he suddenly took a swing at Jon.

Jon's reflexes were excellent, and he ducked. But when he came up, Brett swung again, catching his chin. Jon swung back in a fury. He caught Brett on the jaw. Brett fell back on the bed, stunned, then shook his head and surged back into the fray like a maddened bull.

"Stop it, stop it!" Sabrina cried, trying to step between the two men.

Though testosterone was at work, and it didn't seem that either of them paid her the least attention, they took no more swings, settling, instead, for soothing words.

"So you think you're the great man to the rescue," Brett snarled, "telling me how to treat my women!

Why don't you tell the truth about how you've treated yours?'' he challenged.

"The truth? My past is none of your business, McGraff. But maybe you'd like to tell *me* the truth about the past," Jon growled in return. "After all, I was the one with a wife. You're the one who simply can't get over something that happened that had nothing to do with you!"

Both strong, fit, tense and all but flaring at the nostrils, the two stared at one another with clenched teeth, and Sabrina realized that something far deeper than the current circumstances was ripping through them both.

She heard a sound and was surprised to see that Joshua Valine was standing at the door.

He smiled crookedly, sympathetically, at her as the argument raged behind them.

"We must get back to the castle," he told her. "This storm is only going to get worse and worse."

Sabrina nodded. Leaving the warriors to Joshua, she walked outside to her horse and mounted.

Soon after she did so, the two combatants came out of the cottage, neither of them speaking. Jon's features remained tense, his eyes hard and crystalline. Brett, too, oozed tightly leashed anger. Joshua emerged a few moments later, having evidently seen to closing up the lodge.

In silence, the men went for their horses. As they mounted, Sabrina started moving. The day that had seemed so crisp and beautiful when she rode out earlier had undergone a startling transformation. The landscape didn't seem the same at all; she might have been riding into an endless world of nothingness. She couldn't see trees, foliage or even a distinction between sky and ground. In the short time they had been indoors, the snow had become blinding, and she was surrounded by a sea of white.

Jon apparently knew she was lost and had every intention of leading the way. He kneed his mount past hers without looking at or speaking to her. But she knew enough to stay behind him, followed by Joshua and then Brett.

The snow pelted harder and harder, icy crystals that hurt her face.

Jon turned back, shouting to them, "We've got to move as quickly as possible!"

They nodded, and Jon began to ride hard, taking advantage of an open field and level land. They followed closely.

Suddenly Sabrina heard a cracking sound and an abrupt cry. Turning back, she saw that Brett had fallen. His horse raced pell-mell past her.

"Brett!" she cried, reining in, turning back. She raced to his side, hastily dismounting. The snow was falling with a vengeance. "Brett!"

He lay facedown in the snow, seemingly stretched atop a red ribbon.

As she reached for him, she realized that it wasn't a red ribbon at all.

It was a splatter of blood, brilliantly crimson against the white purity of the snow.

10

Susan Sharp was lying just inside the doorway as the men burst through to the chamber of horrors.

She was sprawled on her side, her hair covering her face. Staring at her, V.J. felt as if her heart stopped, then slammed back into a frenzied beat.

"My God!" she breathed, hurrying to Susan, her mind racing with flights of horrible fancy. Had Jack the Ripper truly come to life to kill her?

She knelt by the woman's side, as did Thayer. The ex-cop, evidently accustomed to emergencies—and even to dead bodies—was calmly lifting Susan's wrist and checking for a pulse. He slowly smiled across Susan's body at V.J.

"She's not dead. She has a strong, steady pulse and easy respirations. She's just passed out. It seems she scared herself half to death."

"She's not hurt?"

"She doesn't appear to be," he said as he quickly and expertly guided his hands over her, checking for injuries.

"Well, how'd she get locked in here?" Tom Heart asked, studying the doors.

Thayer rose, looking over the doors with Tom and

Joe. "She didn't. We couldn't get in because the bolt wasn't completely free of the catch. As to why she couldn't get out, I don't know. Maybe she didn't realize that the bolt wasn't quite open. The doors themselves might be swollen, too. Damp weather causes stuff like that, you know. I don't think there's any great mystery here. Just swollen wood, a loose bolt and panic."

Dianne stared at Thayer. "She scared herself into thinking she was locked in?"

Thayer shrugged. "That's what it looks like. What else could it be? It's obvious, swollen wood can stick. It took the three of us slamming ourselves against these doors to get in. And we didn't break the bolt free. Look yourself. The wood is barely damaged."

"Strong wood, though," Tom Heart said dryly. "If someone was bolted in here…"

"But the bolt was only a hair over, right?" Dianne persisted.

"This really can be an incredibly creepy old castle!" Anna Lee said with a shudder.

"People are creepy, dear," Reggie said dryly. "And, at my age, at least, creepy and creaky and cranky. I'm old, I've had it, I'm going up for a drink and some lunch." She turned and walked out.

"Maybe one of us should go with her," Joe mused aloud.

"Reggie will be fine. Woe to the spirits who mess with her. But shouldn't we do something about Susan?" V.J. said. "She is lying on a cold stone floor."

They all looked at one another, slow, guilty smiles

on their faces. It occurred to V.J. that there probably wasn't a human being here Susan hadn't hurt in some way at one time or another. If they had found her dead, would any of them have felt deep sorrow?

"Well, she is quiet this way," Dianne commented. A chorus of grunts and chuckles from the others seemed to back the truth of her observations.

"Oh, come now!" V.J. said. "What are we, a bunch of monsters? If someone would just please—"

"I'll get her, I'll get her!" Thayer grumbled. "I can consider her my weight-lifting exercise for the day. Anyone know which one is Susan's room up there? She should be coming to soon."

Just as he began to lift Susan, her eyes flew open. "Put me down, you ox!" she fumed.

Obligingly, Thayer let go, and Susan's rear bounced back onto the cold stone floor. V.J. turned away, suppressing a laugh.

"You bastards!" Susan charged them all. "Who did this to me? What kind of sick joke is this? I swear, you should all be hanged. So, you think this is funny, Victoria Jane Newfield? You'll be sorry, I swear you'll be sorry."

"Quit threatening V.J., Susan," Tom Heart said angrily. "She was the one among us most concerned about you."

"She probably locked me in, or pretended to be Jack the Ripper coming after me!"

"Susan," Anna Lee said impatiently, "No one was pretending to be Jack the Ripper. Your imagination just got the best of you because you thought you were locked in.''

"I didn't *think* I was locked in. I *was* locked in," Susan said stubbornly. "And somebody must have taken the Jack the Ripper costume and come after me."

"Susan, Jack the Ripper is wearing his costume," Joe said, stroking his beard absently as he looked around the horror chamber. "If you take a good look," he said gently, "you'll notice that nothing has changed in here at all. You were a victim of your own imagination."

"Or your guilty conscience," Anna Lee suggested pleasantly.

Susan rewarded her with a look that could kill. "I'm telling you something sick happened here!" she snapped furiously, tossing her head. "I was locked in here and deliberately terrorized. I came because my note said to attend a séance here, and—"

"The séance was in the crypt," Dianne stated, slinging her hair back and kneeling down by Susan. "Didn't your note send you to the crypt?"

"No, to the chamber of horrors," Susan said. "So one of you bastards switched it and locked me in here. When I find out who did this—"

"Where's your note?" V.J. demanded. She looked around the room. All wore masks of complete innocence.

"I had it. It was right here," Susan insisted. She stood, looking around the area where she had fallen.

There was no note. "Whoever tricked me stole the note!"

"Maybe you were sent here as part of the game," Joe suggested, still trying to ease troubled waters.

V.J. glared at him with a bit of contempt. There would be no placating Susan Sharp, and she would be damned if she'd suck up to her or tolerate her nonsense, no matter what the woman might write in a column. She'd come too far to play the sycophant to the likes of Susan.

"Look," Thayer said with an air of practicality, "the other ladies were in the crypt when we came down, and we men all came down together, so no one of us could have done anything evil to you without someone else knowing it, Susan. I think you accidentally scared yourself silly and in your panic inadvertently locked yourself in."

"Oh, bullshit!" Susan snapped furiously. She dramatically paced around the room. "This old place is full of false doors and secret panels. Any one of you could have slipped in to torture me."

"Susan, frankly, if I were going to torture you, I'd do a more thorough job of it," Thayer barked.

"Maybe it was the master of the castle himself, Jon Stuart, who locked you in," Dianne suggested suddenly. "Jon was here earlier, you know. And he would certainly know the castle's secret passages, wouldn't he?"

"Jon would never do such a thing to me," Susan said affectedly, smoothing back her hair. "Where is he now? We're going to get to the bottom of this!"

Once again, everyone in the room looked away from her, evidently reluctant to give Susan any bit of information she might use against someone else.

Then V.J. shrugged, because it was no great secret that Jon had gone after Sabrina and Brett. "There's a storm coming in. Some of the others had gone riding, and he went out to make sure they made it back in," she said.

"Some of the others?" Susan repeated. Then she smiled like the Cheshire cat. "Could it be that Brett and Sabrina took off—to be alone? How positively darling. Perhaps they're the ones hiding guilty consciences!"

"Oh, right," Anna Lee murmured dryly. "After one of them locked you in here while the other pretended to be Jack the Ripper. An incredible feat, when you consider that both of them would have had to be in two places at the same time."

"Well, one of *you* bastards did this, and I will find out which one," Susan assured them bitterly. "Where's Reggie?" she demanded.

"Probably sipping a martini in comfort by now," Tom said.

Susan's eyes narrowed. "And that wretched Joshua, who made these horrid creatures—"

"He was never even down here this morning," Joe said.

"And that despicable little worm of a woman who works for Jon?" Susan asked.

"Upstairs somewhere," Joe said with a shrug.

"I wouldn't put it past that horrid little mouse to

have been in on something like this!'' Susan said. ''In fact, I'm sure she planned this, the sniveling wretch. I will demand the truth from her, and—''

''Susan, I'm telling you, it looks as if you accidentally locked yourself in,'' Thayer reminded her firmly.

''Oh, and dressed myself up like Jack the Ripper?''

''Jack the Ripper is wearing his own clothes,'' Joe Johnston said, walking impatiently to the tableau. ''Look, Susan. He's dressed, he's in place, okay? But fear is a terrible thing. It plays upon the imagination. We all know that—we make a living out of the concept. It's dark down here, scary, shadowy—easy to imagine things.''

Susan's eyes narrowed. ''Joe Johnston, you are an ass. I'm going upstairs, and I'm going to gouge Camy Clark's little eyes out!'' she announced, turning on her heel and stomping off rather dramatically for someone who had just been unconscious.

Joe groaned.

''We'd all better go with her and protect Camy,'' Tom advised.

''Actually, maybe questioning Camy isn't such a bad idea,'' Dianne said. ''We can ask her about the game note sent to Susan and find out if someone was maybe playing a trick with different notes.''

''Good idea,'' V.J. exclaimed.

Dianne smiled, pleased. To V.J., she suddenly looked very young again. Despite her outlandish determination to be different, she was really just a little girl cast into an intimidating adult world, V.J. mused. She determined to be a better friend to the young writer, even if she did happen to be stealing places on the all-important bestseller lists!

Well, that was life, V.J. reasoned. No one said life—or death—had to be fair.

"All right, then let's all go up—" Thayer began.

But at that moment, the room was plunged into darkness. And the only thing to cut through the wall of black was a hysterical scream.

Down by Brett's side in the snow, Sabrina suffered a wealth of fear and agony. Okay, so he could be a jerk. Their marriage had been over before it had begun. But she did love him in a way. And he was a friend. And she was suddenly so scared.

"Oh, God!" she breathed, looking at the splatter of blood, tenderly touching his cold face. So cold. "Brett!" she cried.

Jon rode back and reined in, snow whirling in the air around him. He came down by her side, Sabrina found the courage to feel for a pulse at Brett's throat.

A beat. Another beat. Another. He was alive!

Jon looked at her, and she nodded, tears brimming in her eyes. She saw the relief flood his handsome face, and she knew that whatever differences there were between the two, Jon cared deeply for his friend, as well.

With long, supple fingers, he carefully searched for the wound emitting the blood. "It looks as if he struck his head when he fell. We have to get him back to the castle and get him warm before we lose him to shock. I've had some emergency medical training, but not much. I hope to God he's not hurt too badly, since we're likely to be snowed in.''

"What about broken bones, or his neck?''

"No, I'm pretty sure his neck isn't broken,'' Jon murmured, carefully fingering muscle and bone. He began gently skimming his fingers over Brett's limbs.

"Wait, I've taken lots of anatomy,'' Joshua said, dismounting and joining them. He knelt down in the snow, studying Brett and touching him carefully with the gentle hands of an artist. After a moment he looked up at them both. "The only injury seems to be the crack to his head from that rock there. I can't find any breaks.''

Sabrina looked at him and Jon gratefully. Then Jon began lifting Brett. Staggering a bit, he rose to his feet. He must have seen the fear in Sabrina's eyes because he paused for a moment and gently teased her. "We'll get him back, and he'll be fine. But he sure is a heavy sucker. Must be the weight of a swelled head from his successes lately, huh?''

She was able to smile weakly in return. Then Jon turned to Joshua for help. They didn't sling Brett's unconscious body over his horse as they did in the old western movies. Instead, with Josh's aid, Jon arranged to hold Brett before him in his own saddle, almost as he might carry a child, sheltering him from the snow with a blanket from his saddlebag. Sabrina quickly mounted her horse and followed closely behind him at a walk.

When she realized Joshua wasn't with them, she glanced back.

He was kneeling by the rock where Brett had fallen, staring at it in a puzzled manner, then looking all around him, though what he sought in the snow-white landscape, she couldn't begin to fathom. There was no one, nothing. Then again, there might have been an entire army of Highland soldiers advancing over the next rise, and they wouldn't know it, the snow was swirling in such a heavy, windswept barrage.

"Joshua!" she called out. But he didn't seem to hear or see or heed her. Should she go back for him? But they couldn't turn back; they couldn't lose any time with Brett unconscious, facing shock and a long ride through the snow.

Biting her lip, she looked toward Jon, who was moving ahead quickly. Should she call out to him? She turned to glance back at Joshua Valine once again, and she was relieved to see that he had finally risen and was mounting his horse to follow them. She turned quickly away, for some instinctive reason not wanting him to know that she had been watching him.

They all rode on in silence until, finally, like a giant boulder cast down upon the snowy land, the castle rose out of the sea of white before them. They were almost home.

"Oh! It just fucking figures, doesn't it?" Susan swore from a few feet away, her voice sharp in the sudden total darkness. She hadn't gotten very far before the lights went out.

Then V.J. thought she heard something else. A

whirring or whooshing sound, as if a cape swept by her, nearly touching her.

A cape.

Jack the Ripper?

Jack the Ripper, real and running amok in the chamber of horrors? They'd all been so determined that Susan was dramatizing, that her imagination had been running away with her. But mightn't someone dressed up like the figure have been hiding nearby, gloating, laughing, thinking that he—or she—had only to wait for the power to fail, then they'd all be like lambs at a slaughter, helpless, perfect victims?

A second scream pierced the darkness, and V.J. thought she might perish of a heart attack.

But it was just Susan, and the sharp cry was followed by swearing. "You burned me, damn it!" she yelped.

"Well, damn it, you're standing right on top of me!" Thayer said as his lighter flicked to life, giving them a small spot of illumination.

V.J. strained her eyes in the darkness. The figure of Jack the Ripper was standing right where he'd been. Silly woman! she taunted herself.

"Here—a lantern," Tom said, lifting an old-fashioned candle lamp from a hook by the door. "They probably lose electricity in most of these storms. This thing looks as if it was in use not too long ago."

"There's another here," Joe stated.

With the lanterns flaring, the chamber of horrors

was alight again, actually brighter than it had ever been before.

"I'm telling you, someone is—" Susan began.

"Oh, Susan!" Joe protested, pulling on his beard in total aggravation. "Storms are acts of God, and power outages are failures of mechanics, and neither is a conspiracy against Susan Sharp."

"The hell with this storm. You haven't seen anything yet!" Susan assured them. She strode to Thayer, snatching a lantern from him. "There's going to be one big hurricane around little Miss Camy Clark."

She started once more out of the chamber of horrors, still determined that she'd been the victim of an evil trick. The others followed her.

V.J. found herself last in the chamber, with the blackness swiftly creeping in around her. She gazed at the wax figures as the light began to fade. It seemed that they were beginning to move, just waiting for the light to dim entirely before leaping fully to life.

"Wait!" she tried to cry. But her throat was dry, the sound barely a whisper. They were all going to leave her, and she'd be standing here, stupidly paralyzed, as the figures came alive and started menacingly after her, seeking her blood in the black void settling around her.

"V.J.?" boomed a masculine voice.

"Tom!"

Bless him. He'd come back for her, lifting a lamp high. Light flooded around her, and the wax figures stood obediently still.

"Victoria, you're not staying down here, are you?" Tom asked softly.

V.J. felt life and movement return. She flashed Tom a smile and hurried after the group with him. Susan was leading the way, striding ahead of them all. It was amazing to V.J. that a woman like her, who sometimes made an art out of the act of walking itself, could swing her shoulders and stride with the tough-guy gait of a trucker.

On the ground floor, candles gleamed all around them. The household staff had been at work.

And there, three of their number deserted the gang. As Susan started up the stairs to the second floor, barging along like the Wicked Witch of the West in search of Camy Clark, Thayer Newby followed her, but Tom Heart halted.

"You do your best with this one, Victoria. I'm not watching a lamb at her slaughter," he announced, shaking his head.

V.J. bit her lower lip lightly, knowing how he hated Susan.

"I'll be joining Reggie for a drink," Anna Lee interjected, walking toward the library. Over her shoulder she added, "Maybe Thayer can keep Susan from extreme violence. The rest of us should just huddle around the fire like the true chickens we are."

"I'm with Tom," Joe Johnston agreed.

V.J. looked at them both. They stood side by side: Tom tall, handsome, so dignified with his beautiful crop of silver-white hair, and Joe, bearded, heavier, coarser and a bit gruff. One dressed Versace, one Salvation Army. One was a second Sean Connery, the other a Grizzly Adams. They seemed strangely united now.

"Susan's going to do her best to humiliate young Camy," Tom explained. "And Camy might not want an audience," he added softly.

V.J. nodded, but stood her ground. "We don't all need to barge in on her, but I'll go and back up Thayer."

"I'm with you," Dianne said, her eyes curiously wide with excitement. They all looked at her. She tossed back her perfectly cut black hair. "Susan can be a real monster—we all know it. I'll be there to back up V.J. as Susan tries to draw blood, so V.J. won't have to take the heat alone."

"Just remember, after this weekend we may *all* be paying for the fact that Susan's a monster," Joe said dourly.

Tom was watching V.J., his thoughts held in check. She turned away and hurried up the stairs, Dianne right behind her.

Susan had already burst in when they reached Camy's room. As usual, Jon's diminutive assistant was sitting at her desk. Evidently power failures didn't daunt her. She was working by the light of a large battery-powered lamp.

"You stupid, miserable, little bitch, I will have you fired for this!" Susan raged at her.

Camy jumped up, shaking, staring at Susan. Her mouth worked, but no words came. Tears stung her eyes, and she looked helplessly past Susan to Thayer, V.J. and Dianne.

"I—I…" she began, stunned. She looked as vulnerable as a baby chick fallen out of its nest.

"Susan, do you at least want to tell her what you're accusing her of doing?" V.J. snapped firmly.

Susan swung around to glare at her.

Well, even if her next book were the Bible, V.J. thought wearily, Susan was still going to trash it in the media.

Susan swung back to Camy, her face contorted in fury. "She knows what she did. She wrote me a note, sending me into the chamber of horrors, then she snuck down one of the secret staircases and did her best to scare me to death. She shouldn't just be fired, she should be arrested, and I intend to see that it happens!"

"Susan," Camy cried in self-defense, "I didn't…I don't know…I swear to you—"

"Lying little maggot!" Susan said through gritted teeth, starting forward.

"Now, wait a minute there," Thayer interrupted angrily, taking a step to stop Susan.

"Oh, let her bitch," Dianne said casually.

"Oh, Susan, why don't you just quit being such a royal, self-righteous bitch!" V.J. blurted.

Oh, great. Mystery Week, and she'd turned suicidal. She was mincemeat in the press.

"I—I—I didn't give you instructions to go to the chamber of horrors," Camy said to Susan. "Everyone was ordered to the séance in the crypt. Joshua was supposed to make a tapping sound from behind the tombs, but he followed Jon in case there was any trouble—I mean—uh, in case someone was stranded or the snow got too bad.'' She stuttered and paused, realizing she was admitting that her boss was in a high temper when he rode out after Brett McGraff and Sabrina Holloway. "He—he thought Jon might need help in the snow, and that you would all amuse yourselves just fine in the crypt.''

"Oh, yeah, nothing like an amusing morning among the dead,'' Dianne said dryly.

Camy shot her a pathetic look. Dianne instantly looked contrite. "Well, it was definitely more important for Josh to make sure no one got lost in the snow,'' she added quickly.

The truth hung in the air. Or to make sure Brett and Jon didn't come to blows over Sabrina?

"Susan, I swear, if you had a note sending you somewhere else, I didn't write it,'' Camy said.

"Then just where did the note come from?'' Susan demanded.

Camy was still shaking and in distress. "I don't know, I don't know. I don't know where the other one came from either—''

She broke off, staring at them all, white as a sheet.

"Someone else got a note you didn't write?'' Thayer demanded.

"I—I—''

"God in heaven, quit stuttering like a complete ninny!'' Susan cried.

"Who else got a misleading note?" V.J. asked quietly.

"Yes, please, who?" Dianne asked softly.

"I'm not at liberty to—" Camy began defensively.

"Jon! It was Jon Stuart!" Dianne guessed. She appeared strangely excited again.

Camy remained white. She looked like a little lost doe, standing there shaking.

"You know what I think?" Susan demanded. "I think this is all a pile of B.S. I think you're a troublemaker. Who else could be giving people different notes and stealing the ones you had *really* written? You're doing it all, Miss Clark. The only question is why."

"No, oh, no, please, Ms. Sharp. I couldn't. I wouldn't. Honestly," Camy said, desperately trying to state her innocence. "I'm so sorry you were frightened, but—"

V.J. felt as if she were watching a puppy being slaughtered. She had to risk stepping in again. "Oh, Susan, get off your high horse! None of us is in chains. We're all free to sneak around the castle! It could be anybody playing tricks!" she said angrily.

Susan stared at her with pure venom in her eyes. "You weren't locked in with some awful monster breathing down your neck. He could have killed me. I know he would have killed me if you all hadn't gotten to me first!"

"He who? You're accusing Camy of sending the notes," Thayer said.

"He, she, little precious Camy here pretending to

be Jack the Ripper—what difference does it make? Someone meant to kill me, and I'm certain it was this little bitch right here!'' Susan accused.

"Oh, Susan, stop it. You really don't know anything at all," Dianne told her quietly.

The young woman seemed oddly disappointed, and V.J. belatedly wondered if Dianne had looked forward to this confrontation, hoping it would help her discover something that was eluding her. She was so young, V.J. mused again, watching her, and she suspected that life had given her a few hard kicks, not just early successes, along the way.

Susan looked from one of them to another. She remained furious, her face pinched and ugly. V.J. thought that, at that moment, any one of them would happily lock her away with Jack the Ripper.

"Well, fuck you all!" Susan said softly. And once again she looked around the room at them. "And trust me, you *are* fucked!"

She stomped out the door, slamming it behind her.

Once again, V.J. had an image of the Wicked Witch of the West.

Camy started to cry softly, Thayer looked grim, and V.J. realized that she was trembling herself from all the dramatic emotions swirling about.

"I think we all need a drink," Dianne announced. "Come on, Camy, come on down and have a drink with us."

"I—I—was working," Camy said, a ragged sniff following her words as she tried to control her sobs.

"That's all right, you can work later, dear," V.J. said gently.

"But I'm not one of you. This is Mystery Week, and you're supposed to be solving a whodunit."

"Oh, we've enough mystery going on without having to work at it too much," Dianne said. "Either that or we're capable of making a mystery out of anything. Come on. Jon wouldn't mind. He'd want you to take a breather after an encounter with old Medusa there."

Camy nodded. "Jon would never mind," she said softly. "I do know that."

"Then come on," V.J. said. "I need to sit down before I fall down, and right now, I want a martini when I sit."

She started from the room, and the others followed.

And just as they did so, a high-pitched, blood-curdling scream sounded from the first floor.

11

Never, in fact or fiction had Sabrina ever heard such a shriek. Following Jon into the house, she nearly jumped a mile at the sound.

It was Anna Lee, standing in the entry, her beautiful eyes huge as she stared at Brett, unconscious in Jon's arms. Clearly she thought Brett was dead.

"He's alive!" Jon announced quickly. "He's alive."

And at that, Brett stirred slightly. His eyes opened. He groaned. Then he looked up at Jon, the friend who was carrying him, and tried to smile. "Jon, we've got to stop meeting like this. Rumors will begin to fly."

"I think he's going to be all right," Jon said dryly, striding toward the library.

By then Reggie, Tom and Joe had rushed into the foyer from the library, and V.J., Dianne, Thayer, Susan and Camy had made an appearance, running down the stairs. Sabrina felt Joshua crash into her from behind.

"What happened?" Camy demanded.

"A riding accident," Sabrina explained quickly.

"Stupid horse threw me," Brett said, grimacing.

"Right onto a rock! I'm in pain, ladies. Be kind to me!"

Jon groaned wryly, seeing that his patient was coming to in good form. He called over his shoulder, "Someone get a cloth and cold water, please."

Camy rushed to do his bidding. Brett was soon ensconced on a sofa in the library, and among them all they determined that his only injury was the blow to his head that had knocked him out. Brett was lording it over them all nicely, wincing, playing on their sympathies, insisting that Sabrina be the one to bathe his wound and press cold cloths to his head. Dianne Dorsey produced some painkillers to relieve the pain and swelling, and Brett gave a dramatic rendition of how his wild steed had suddenly reared, sending him flying into the snow. Listening to him, Sabrina found herself newly curious about what Joshua had been looking for out there, and she turned to glance at him. He stood in the shadows by the fire, alone and watching.

"Electricity is gone?" Jon asked, looking up at Thayer.

"We lost power awhile ago. Actually, while—"

"Right after I was viciously assaulted!" Susan declared.

Jon, accepting a drink from Anna Lee, arched a brow at Susan. "Assaulted?"

"I was sent to the chamber of horrors, while everyone else was involved in that silly séance in the crypt. I was locked in, and Jack the Ripper attacked me!" Susan cried.

Joshua made a strange, choking sound.

"Jack the Ripper came to life?" Brett said politely, laughter just behind the words.

"Susan wasn't locked in," Thayer said firmly.

"The door had jammed," Joe explained.

"So they say," Susan stormed. "But I think *she* did it!" Very dramatically, she pointed at Camy.

Brett let loose with a snort of derision. Camy softly started to cry. Joshua pushed away from the fireplace, as if to come to Camy's defense.

"Camy?" Jon said very softly.

"I don't know what she's talking about, I swear to you!" Camy cried.

"Since it seems that no one really knows anything, I suggest we not point fingers at one another—unless it's in the fun of the game," Jon said firmly.

"Jon Stuart, you're not going to ignore me!" Susan declared. "I'm not crazy, and I assure you that—"

"That what?" Jon demanded grimly.

"Your guests are a pack of liars with plenty of secrets to hide," she said, staring at them, one by one. As she did so, she added furiously, "And I warn you all, I will not be ignored. Someone will pay."

"Susan, if you know something—" Jon began.

"Oh, I know everything!" she snapped. "But I'm not out to tell tales about anyone—yet."

"Susan, if you're afraid you're in danger," Dianne said, twirling a strand of black hair, "maybe you should stop threatening people."

"Yeah," Thayer added.

Sabrina thought that they all sounded and were act-

ing like a group of children, finally ganging up against
the neighborhood bully.

"Maybe you all—every one of you—should take
a look at your nice little lives and think about the
pathetic, hypocritical lies you're living!" Susan retorted.

Jon sighed deeply. "Susan, for the love of God, if
you'd quit playing games—"

"Oh, but we came here to play a game, didn't
we?" she demanded.

Jon shook his head, clearly leashing his anger and
aggravation. "If you're really scared, then the stakes
have gotten too high. Maybe we should call a halt to
the whole blasted week."

"Oh, no. The game is going to be played, all
right—or we're going to expose whoever it is who
wants to play outside the rules," she said. "And Jon,
I expect you to—"

"I'll take a look at the doors in the chamber of
horrors, Susan," Jon said. "But I imagine it is possible that you only thought you were locked in."

"The mind can play very mysterious tricks," Anna
Lee said in a soft, sultry voice.

"My mind doesn't play tricks," Susan said flatly.
"And again, I promise, someone will pay."

"Susan, I'll do my best to find out what happened," Jon repeated. "But I'm afraid we're in a
rather sorry situation. I warned you that a storm was
coming, and God knows how long we'll be snowbound. Now we've lost the electricity as well, and
though we've got generators and batteries, I'm afraid

we can't keep this place as well lit as I would like. There's only so much we're going to be able to see, and only so much we're going to be able to do.''

"But we do have a nice buffet set up in the great hall," Reggie said. "I think we should all get something to eat, and we'll feel better, and we won't be so prone to wild hysterics."

"I wasn't hysterical!" Susan snapped.

"Oh, Susan, you're always hysterical," Brett complained. "And you're stealing my thunder here. I need all the attention I can get, people flocking around me with wonderful concern. So get a grip. *I* am supposed to be the patient here," he reminded her petulantly.

"I hit my head falling, too," Susan said.

"Yes, but rock against rock..." Dianne murmured.

"I heard that!" Susan snapped at her.

"So you did," Dianne said smoothly, her eyes venomous as they met Susan's.

"Susan, we've generators for hot water," Jon said. "We need to use the water a little sparingly, but right now I think that a drink and a long hot bath might make you feel better."

Susan looked mollified at Jon's words. "Yes, a hot bath, a drink. A strong one. Make me something, darling, will you? And will you stay with me while I bathe? Stand guard? I'm so very nervous now."

"Susan, I'm going to take a look around below, search the chamber of horrors, the chapel, the crypt," Jon said. "You'll be all right. Someone else can—"

"I'll stand guard at Susan's door," Thayer volunteered.

"No," Jon told the ex-cop, "I'd like you to come downstairs with me."

"I'll watch over her," Sabrina heard herself say.

"No!" Brett protested, capturing her hand where it lay on the cold towel pressed to his head. "You can't desert me now. Please, Sabrina." He winced as if in great pain. Looking down at him, she had to admit that he did have a nasty gash, and she was glad that he was alive.

"I'll stand sentinel at Susan's door," Tom Heart offered.

Sabrina looked up and saw that Jon was staring at her. She felt as if his eyes were piercing through her. There she sat on the arm of the sofa, her hand on Brett's head, his hand now upon hers, as well. It must make a cozy, intimate picture.

"Help me up to my room, sweetheart, will you?" Brett asked then. "Please, I don't think I could manage alone. You could bring me a small lunch, make sure I don't have convulsions or anything."

By then, Jon had turned away. And, followed by Thayer, he was soon gone.

"Well, let's eat. I'm famished," Reggie said.

"Two people hurt, and you're famished?" Susan protested.

"Two silly, careless people, and yes, I'm famished. Susan, you're a mess. Go take your bath. Sabrina, go ahead and get that randy little rooster upstairs and come back and have some late lunch with us. It's going to be a long day!"

It would be a long day. Sabrina knew that right after she helped Brett upstairs.

His clothing was soaked, and naturally, he insisted that she help him out of it, thanking her as she dispatched his boots, his jacket and his shirt. She drew the line at his pants, however.

"Oh, come on, Sabrina, it's not as if it isn't familiar territory," he told her. He looked at her pathetically. "Sabrina, I swear, I haven't an ounce of strength. Help me."

"All right," she conceded. "Lie down, and I'll drag off your pants. And you'd better be wearing underwear."

He laughed.

"Just because you were hurt doesn't mean that you didn't behave like a slimy bastard, you know," she reminded him as she wrestled with the sodden trousers, which now seemed plastered to his legs.

Naturally, just as she fell against the bedpost, his pants in her hands, Jon came striding into the room, while Joshua and Thayer lingered in the hall.

"I decided I should come by to see if you needed any help, McGraff," Jon said dryly. "But you seem to be doing all right."

"Of course. Sabrina does know how to take my clothes off," Brett said.

Jon stared at her, arching a brow, then strode from the room.

Sabrina threw Brett's pants to the floor.

Brett caught her hand. "I wish I could figure out when you slept with him," he grumbled.

"Brett, stop, now."

Amazingly, he did. He looked up at her and smiled. "You're a great nurse, Sabrina. Now how would you like to help me out of my underwear?"

"Your only saving grace at the moment, Brett McGraff, is that you're *wearing* underwear!" Sabrina scolded him.

"Please, show some mercy, will you? Would you put that cold towel on my head again?"

She was angry, feeling that Jon condemned her, convinced she was sleeping with Brett because of her ex-husband's seemingly endless ploy to seduce her or, at the very least, to land her in compromising positions. But what could she do about it now? Nothing. She sighed. "Get under the covers and behave."

He did so. He closed his eyes and winced, and she realized that he really must have one pounding headache.

Angry with Jon, too, for leaping so easily to the wrong conclusions, she fussed over Brett a bit. But she refused to be drawn into another of his traps. "Don't you ever give up?" she asked him, plumping up a pillow and refusing his outrageous request for a drink. "Not with that knot on your head," she told him. "Don't drink, and don't go to sleep. Just rest, and if you get blurry vision—"

"We'll call the doctor, Nurse Sabrina?" he said, amused.

"I think you're going to be all right," she told him.

"Nothing a good whiskey wouldn't cure," he said wistfully.

"No alcohol today. You could have died, you know."

"Stupid horse! I wonder why it reared like that?" he complained. Then he sighed. "Stupid me, for not being a better rider."

"Hey, things happen," Sabrina said gently.

"Too many things happen around here," Brett said dully. He paused. "So what do you think happened with Susan?"

"How would I know? I wasn't here."

"Everyone hates her," Brett mused. "Any one of us might want her dead."

"But she's not dead, is she? And normally, just because people hate someone, they don't become homicidal."

"Ah, but think about murder. You have your psychopaths, and then you have your people who commit the crime in the heat of passion, your opportunists engaged in other felonies—the list goes on and on."

"Well," she mused, "I don't think Susan is the type to scare *herself* to death."

"Those wax figures are awfully scary, though, don't you think?"

Sabrina agreed wholeheartedly.

"God, I'm suddenly famished," Brett said. "Want to go down and see if there are some grapes you can feed me?"

"I'm not going to feed you grapes, but I'll bring

you up some lunch,'' Sabrina said. ''Rest now, and I'll be right back.'' Slipping from Brett's room, she started down the hallway toward the stairs.

Behind her, she heard a door close quietly. She looked around. She didn't know which door had closed, or indeed, if she had only imagined the sound.

The hallway was as quiet as a tomb, she thought. She shivered and hurried down the stairs.

Jon looked around the chamber of horrors. Absolutely nothing seemed amiss.

Thayer gave him his theory, showing him how the old bolt had been turned just a hair. ''And with the weather swelling the doors...'' Thayer shrugged. ''Let's face it, Susan is a powerful bitch, but something seems to be unnerving her. Do you think she just scared herself into a tizzy?''

Jon, too, shrugged, staring at the wax figures. Joshua had done such a good job. The figures were haunting and scary and all the things they should be. But they *were* wax and wire and fabric and mesh. They weren't inherently evil, and they weren't capable of coming to life.

And Susan was a bitch.

But he, too, had been the recipient of a nasty note unrelated to the real play of the game. And he was feeling especially tense because they were now likely to be snowbound and dependent on generators for power. For how long, he didn't know. And he was responsible for his guests' welfare.

''The thing is, most of us were at the séance,''

Thayer said. "You, Brett, Sabrina and Joshua were gone. Camy was working. Maybe someone on the staff had something to do with it?"

"My household staff? They're all hardworking and far too busy and responsible to play pranks on my guests. Besides, I'm sure none of them could care less about scaring Susan Sharp."

"So she had to be imagining things," Thayer said. Hands on his hips, he sighed. "Well, if we had the equipment, we could dust this place for prints, but, hell, we'd find everyone's. Everyone has been down here."

Jon went to stand before Jack the Ripper. He reached out to touch the figure. Still wax, he told himself dryly.

But Susan likely had received a different summons from the others; he didn't doubt it, since he had, too.

He did have to wonder if someone was just playing cruel tricks, however...or if they were all to be snowbound with a maniac. Hell, now *his* imagination was running away with him.

"I guess there's nothing more to be done down here," he told Thayer.

"I agree. There's nothing here to prove or disprove anything Susan said. It was something, though. I wish you'd been here. The power suddenly went while we were here, with Susan screaming that I was trying to burn her when I lit my lighter!"

"The storm must be surely an act of God," Jon said dryly. "I hardly think there's someone up there shooting down lightning bolts and saying, Oh, good, let's get Susan!''

Jon smiled wryly. "I guess there's only one way left to solve any of this."

"Oh?" Thayer inquired.

"Play the game," Jon said grimly. "Play out the game, just the way we intended."

The castle in darkness was utterly eerie.

It wasn't that Sabrina hadn't been places where the electricity had gone off before. She had. Storms downed electrical wires across the globe.

But the castle was different. Haunting shadows filled corners and crevices. Candles and kerosene lamps shot flickering patterns against the stone walls. Each nook and cranny seemed to hold a mystery, a dark, fluttering menace.

She all but ran down the stairs and hurried into the great hall.

It was empty. The others had eaten and gone.

The food was still out; chafing dishes were aligned on the buffet, though many of the Sterno heating fires were out. Someone had begun clearing the table, but a few plates remained.

She began to inspect the contents of the chafing dishes. Suddenly, a stark chill of unease raced down her spine. She spun around, certain that someone was watching her from the shadows.

Then she felt like a fool. No one was behind her. Like Susan, she had simply begun to imagine a cloaked figure ready to bludgeon her to death when she wasn't looking.

But she did hear footsteps from the foyer, heading toward the great stairway. She started out of the great hall and paused in the shadows of the doorway.

Jon was coming up from below. Anna Lee met him on the stairs to the second floor. She set a hand upon his arm. Her wavy hair fell forward, brushing her face. She smiled. A beautiful smile. But then she said something, looking worried. Sabrina couldn't make out her words. Jon took her hand in both of his. She looked frail next to his tall, muscular form, and as he took a step up and whispered down to her, he looked like her protector. Something tender seemed to pass between them. Anna Lee turned around, accompanying him as he continued up the steps.

Sabrina slipped back into the great hall, leaning against the wall, feeling weak.

"It wasn't Anna Lee," a voice said out of the shadows. Sabrina nearly jumped; she was amazed she didn't scream.

Reggie Hampton suddenly appeared, rising from a huge antique chair set into the recess of the kitchen doorway. She looked old and tired but very straight and dignified.

"What?" Sabrina whispered.

Reggie shrugged, smiling slightly. "I watched you watching Jon and Anna Lee just now. Watching people—that's what keeps me going. And keeps me good, too, by the way. You're wearing your heart on your sleeve, and—"

"I don't know what you're talking about, Reggie," Sabrina interrupted.

"Our host, dear," Reggie said kindly, her keen old eyes assessing still. "You just watched Anna Lee and Jon. And somewhere in your mind you were remembering the rumor that Jon was having an affair when his wife was killed."

Sabrina arched a brow. "Reggie, I really have no right—"

"They're friends, Anna Lee and Jon. But don't worry, dear. He doesn't care about her now. Sexually, that is."

"He's free to care about her in any way he wishes. Including sexually," Sabrina said.

Reggie smiled. "Certainly, dear. Whatever you say. I can see that you don't care in the least. Ah, well, then my lips shall remain sealed about what I know. So why don't I help you make something for your patient up there? The food is so wonderful here, isn't it? Let's fix Brett a plate of the lamb. He'll love it."

"Reggie..."

"Nope. My lips are sealed."

"Reggie, if you know something imp—"

"I know lots of things. Or I think I do. But some of them would hurt innocent people, so I don't talk. Truth will tell itself when the time is right."

"Reggie..."

"If you're going to be tiresome, dear, then you can fix your own plates." And, shoulders squared, back straight, Reggie walked out of the great hall, leaving Sabrina alone for real.

Or was she?

Again she turned around and peered into the shadows. No one.

She fixed two plates of food. And she tried to walk calmly, rather than run, back to Brett's room.

The storm was bad enough. Being snowbound was worse. But now they were snowbound without electricity, and though Jon could keep the castle functioning, not even he liked the shadows.

He felt that he could kick himself a thousand times over.

Why hadn't he insisted that they end the game? He should have forced them all out before the weather came—even old Reggie, whether she wanted to go or not.

But he hadn't.

And so now they were all trapped together for the duration. And like rats in a cage, they were starting to scurry around, ready to cannibalize one another.

Yet they were coming to him. One by one.

Anna Lee.

And as he approached the door to his room, she followed.

He sighed softly. "Now, what in God's name—" he began.

"Shh! Please, Jon!" she insisted, urging him into the room. She was clearly excited. "It's happening!

Don't you see? Everything is unraveling. The truth is out there and—''

He caught her by the shoulders, trying to steady her. "The truth is out there—but meaning what? Anna Lee, are you behind any of these threats against Susan?"

"No!" she cried, trying to wrench away angrily. He wouldn't let her go.

"Susan is a bitch, and she can certainly make up nasty tales. But this time I think she knows she is in trouble, is being pursued. I think she knows what happened three years ago, and I think you should force it out of her."

"Force it out of her? Beat her up, you mean? Straddle her and choke her and force a confession?" he demanded dryly.

"Don't you see? I think that she's threatened the killer—blackmail, maybe. And now she's scared and unnerved, and she's stirring up a commotion among the game players, keeping herself visible and safe, rather than admitting that she's blackmailing someone."

"What makes you so certain Susan knows the truth?"

Anna Lee shook her head. "I don't know. I don't know. Maybe I'm just grasping at straws."

"We still don't even *know* that there was a killer. And lots of people here were keeping secrets when Cassie died. Hell, probably everyone here was keeping a secret." He hesitated. "Cassie was sleeping with—"

"Speaking of sleeping with," she interrupted quickly, "you could easily seduce Susan and get the truth out of her that way."

"What?"

"You know she has the hots for you," Anna Lee stated.

"Out!" Jon said explosively.

"Jon..."

"Out! And you be careful, do you hear me?"

"Yes," she said sullenly.

"No tricks on your part to stir up the kettle," he warned.

She turned to leave, then turned back. "I do love you," she said very softly.

He nodded. "I love you, too."

V.J. opened the door to her room and looked carefully down the hallway. No one was about.

With no electricity, the hall seemed a frightening place. Shadows danced on the walls. Outside, the sound of the wind had become a low keening. It seemed as if the whole place had come alive, that the very walls breathed.

She gave herself a shake.

She left her room, a heavy flashlight clutched tightly in her hands. She didn't need to turn it on; kerosene lamps hung from ancient fixtures along the way, casting their eerie, flickering glow.

She moved quietly, step by step down the cavernous corridor.

She came to Susan's room and opened the door.

She heard the sound of the shower.

And before the closed bathroom door, Tom, tall and handsome, paced.

He didn't hear V.J. at first. When he did, he looked up at her.

She saw that he was carrying a pocket knife, flicking the blade open, then closed.

Open, then closed. Open....

It was a wicked blade. Surprisingly long. It looked as if it were sharply honed.

V.J. stared at Tom. He went still and stared at her.

He took a step toward her.

Reached for her.

"What are you trying to do?" she whispered desperately. "No!"

The water in the shower continued to run.

Sabrina returned to Brett's room, bringing his food, finding that she was ravenous herself. It was a very late lunch; it was almost three o'clock. Brett ate with a hearty appetite, and she was glad to realize that his bump on the head seemed not too serious. He was in good spirits, happy to have her waiting on him.

She was curious, though, about Susan, and about whatever Jon might have discovered in the chamber of horrors. She had thought he might come back to Brett's room with a report.

He didn't. Telling Brett that she'd be right back, Sabrina went to Susan's room and knocked on the door.

No answer.

As she stood there, she thought she saw a figure in the shadows near the bend of the hallway.

The bend toward the master chambers, Jon's private domain.

She hesitated, then began moving along the corridor, close to the wall, watching.

As she did so, a figure moved toward Jon's door, hesitated, then rapped. His door opened; the woman slipped in.

Sabrina held her breath, staying flattened against the wall. A few minutes later, the woman came out.

The figure was slim, graceful, wraithlike in the shadows. She moved in a supple flow of black, coming along the hallway, her head down. If she had looked up, she would have seen Sabrina, despite the shadows.

But she didn't look up. She passed within three feet of her.

It was Dianne Dorsey. Dressed in a long, black, flowing caftan, she seemed a haunt in the eerie light and shadows of the hallway.

A haunt very deep in thought.

"I do love you!" she whispered softly, and, suddenly stopping, she looked back at Jon's door. "I do love you."

A sheen of tears made diamonds of her eyes.

"So I have to do what I have to do!" she added in an anguished whisper.

Then she moved on along the hallway.

Never seeing Sabrina.

Staring after her, Sabrina waited. Dianne followed

the hallway to the stairs and descended to the floor below. For long moments, Sabrina just stood where she was.

Then she walked on to Jon's room and tapped on the door.

He threw it open irritably. "What?" he demanded sharply, then stepped back, eyes narrowed as he saw Sabrina.

"You were expecting me?" she said in response to his obvious displeasure.

"I wasn't expecting anyone," he told her.

"Not even Dianne Dorsey?" she inquired.

He crossed his arms over his chest. "Are you spying on me?"

She shook her head, yet felt absurdly guilty. "No. No, I just came to hear what you found in the dungeon. I happened to see Dianne leave your room."

"Nothing. I found nothing at all."

He didn't invite her into his inner sanctum. He stood at the door, jaw set, staring at her.

"She loves you," Sabrina blurted.

"What?" he demanded sharply.

"Dianne. She left your room muttering that she loved you but that she had to do what she had to do," Sabrina told him, studying him for his reaction.

He swore softly. "Excuse me," he told her, starting by her.

"Is she the one with whom you were having an affair?" she called after him.

He paused, turning around, scowling. "No."

"Anna Lee?" She wanted to kick herself.

"No, and you will have to excuse me."

"Sure. I have to get back to Brett, anyway."

His jaw tightened, but he said nothing more. Turning, he walked away from her down the hallway.

She started violently as she felt a tap on her shoulder. She spun around to see Anna Lee. Had she, too, just slipped from Jon's room?

"You've got it all wrong," she said, her beautiful green eyes assessing Sabrina with amusement. She looked exceptionally pretty and feminine in a pink sweater and jeans that hugged her slim, shapely figure. Her sandy blond hair curled around her classical features.

"I have it all wrong?" Sabrina said.

"Mmm."

"You weren't having an affair with Jon when Cassandra died, but you are now?" Sabrina inquired politely.

Anna Lee laughed. "No, actually, you still have it all wrong."

"Oh?"

"Yes. You see, I *was* having an affair when Cassie died."

"Were you?" Sabrina hated the fact that she sounded so stiff and jealous when she meant to be nothing more than competently curious and composed.

Anna Lee smiled, running her fingers through her hair. "But I wasn't sleeping with Jon."

"No?"

Anna Lee laughed, and Sabrina realized just how uptight she must sound.

Anna Lee reached out and briefly stroked Sabrina's cheek. "I was sleeping with *Cassie,* Sabrina." She shrugged, serious and sincere, yet still amused. "Ah, but don't go getting any wrong ideas. Cassandra hadn't given up men. I wasn't the only one sleeping with her. But I was one among many. Just like she was one among many with me. Variety can be the spice of life."

"Was Jon upset?" Sabrina asked softly.

Anna Lee shook her head. "He'd known," she said simply. "Cassie always played people against each other. She used to ask him if he wanted to do us both together. He wasn't interested. Not very flattering, eh? I always did have a crush on him. And Cassie...well, Cassie had her way of making people love her, too. With Jon, I think she just misjudged her man. Poor Cass. It was all awfully sad, really. She was a bitch, hell on wheels. But she *was* beautiful."

Smiling, her hips swaying, she started down the hall.

Sabrina's knees felt strangely weak. She was ready to slink back to Brett's room.

Maybe Anna Lee had explained herself—to a degree. But Sabrina didn't pretend to comprehend what was going on with Dianne Dorsey.

Or with Jon.

12

Sabrina stayed with Brett throughout the afternoon, suddenly glad of a friend she knew and understood and anxious lest he suddenly go into convulsions from his concussion.

She felt numb yet wired. She wanted to see Jon, yet she was furious with herself for wanting to.

For waiting.

And hoping.

That he would come to her.

Brett had brought a tape player with him, and they listened to the latest book by Dean Koontz—which might have been a mistake, since it was about a young woman being stalked by a maniacal killer. But the time passed quickly enough, and as cocktail hour neared, a note was slipped beneath Brett's door.

"What does it say?" Brett asked Sabrina. "Are we playing more games now? Another séance? It's a wretched enough night for one."

She shook her head. "No, no games tonight."

"What does it say?"

She read it aloud to him.

"Dear Guests:
Due to the storm, the lack of electricity and the

accidents that have already befallen us, dinner trays will be delivered to all rooms. Please lock yourselves in for the evening, and we'll meet for brunch tomorrow in the great hall. Characters dropped, we'll confess all our sins.

Your host, Jon Stuart.''

"Good. You're locking yourself in with me, right?"

She kissed him on the top of his head. "Wrong. In fact, I'm leaving you now. You're cozy and warm in bed, and I—"

"You can be cozy and warm in bed with me."

"Do you have another book you want to listen to? I'll set up the first tape for you."

Brett sighed, looking at her like a deserted bloodhound. "Michael Creighton," he said dourly.

"Great. That will keep you entertained."

"He's ahead of me on the list," Brett said sulkily.

"Better yet. You can study your competition," Sabrina said. Before leaving him, she slid the first tape of the audio book into the player. "Holler if you need anything. I'll check in on you before I go to bed."

He wrinkled his nose at her. "If you really love me, you'd crawl in here and keep me company until morning."

"Brett, I've been with you for hours. I want a nice long bath while the hot-water heaters are still going strong."

"You can take a bath here. We can save hot water—bathe together."

"Good night, Brett."

She let herself out of his room. As she did so, she ran into the housekeeper, Jennie Albright, with two fresh-faced young maids, delivering trays.

"Ah, there, Ms. Holloway, would ye mind, dearie, takin' this on in to Mr. McGraff?" Brett's name burred warmly on Jennie's tongue, and Sabrina took the tray from her.

"Certainly."

"Thanks so much, my dear."

"My pleasure. You'll be at this all night, Jennie. Can I help you downstairs?"

"Ah, lass, what a sweeting ye be! But no, my thanks, these were the last. Mr. McGraff, Ms. Sharp and yerself."

Sabrina pushed open Brett's door with her rear and brought Brett his tray.

He smiled happily. "You're back. I knew you couldn't bear being parted."

"Your dinner, Brett," she said, setting the tray by his bed. "See you tomorrow."

"Hey, room service stays longer than that!" he called after her.

She shut the door behind her just as Rose, the younger of the two maids, gave up knocking at Susan's door. "Jennie, there's no answer here," the girl said.

"Then just leave the tray outside the door, there's a good lass. There's your tray now, Ms. Holloway," Jennie said. "Cooked up fresh fish, come in just before the storm. Eat it while it's hot."

"Thank you. If you need help picking up—" Sabrina began.

"No, now, what a love, being so helpful!" Jennie said gratefully. "But Mr. Stuart said that the lasses and I are to take our suppers and lock in for the night. We'll pick up with the dawn, hoping we've got some natural light by then. This snow must stop sometime and the sun shine again. Take care, dear."

Sabrina accepted her tray from Tara, the second of the maids, with a soft thank-you. The housekeeping trio bid her good-night, and as she watched them go, she suddenly felt uneasy alone in the hallway.

She took her tray with her into her room and closed and bolted her door, wondering why she felt so edgy. The fish smelled delicious; it was flaky and perfectly cooked over an open fire. She ate it hastily, appreciating the excellent chablis served with it. When she was done, she found that she was strangely loathe to open her door; she had begun to feel safe within her room. She chastised herself, unsure why she should suddenly be so afraid.

The remains of a fish dinner, however, could smell. Determined, she set her tray outside her door, looked hastily up and down the hall and locked herself in.

With her door bolted, she gave herself a shake, went into the bathroom and liberally added soothing salts as she filled the bathtub, delighted to see that the hot water was holding out.

But neither the chablis nor the tub seemed to ease the restlessness in her spirit.

Anna Lee Zane had admitted to an affair with Cassandra Stuart. Diane Dorsey had come from Jon's room, whispering of her love for him. Susan Sharp had claimed she was attacked. And now they were all snowbound. They might all be in danger. And all she wanted to do was touch Jon Stuart, make love with him....

Impatient with herself, she rose from the tub, dried briskly and slipped into a soft silk negligee. She should have been chilly. She felt hot. She opened the doors and stepped out onto the balcony to cool her heated thoughts and flesh.

The snow had stopped. The air was crisp. The stars were unbelievably beautiful.

It was then, as she stood there, that she suddenly felt him behind her.

She should have been afraid. It had been a very disturbing day. And once, not so long ago, a woman had plunged from a balcony of this castle to her death.

His wife.

Sabrina wasn't afraid. Because she knew, intuitively, that it was he. Yet she held her breath. If he wanted to kill her, it would be easy. Come up behind her. Push. No real effort. She was fairly light. As Cassandra Stuart had been.

And there had been other women in his life. She wasn't a fool; she knew that.

But the facts no longer seemed to matter. She sensed that she knew this man, and that there was something right about her wanting him, no matter what the past. His or hers.

No matter, even, what she might fear about the present.

She didn't know how she knew that it was he, she just did, assuring her that people were indeed in possession of a sixth sense, hidden somewhere deep within the psyche. She wasn't afraid. He hadn't come to hurt her.

She didn't turn around. She waited. She tried to remind herself that what had been between them had been a long time ago, that he had had relationships with others, that she should show some restraint, some dignity.

She didn't hear him move, nor did she start when he touched her. He took her by the shoulders and turned her around. His marbled eyes held a strange frustration and a simmering, potent anger. She held her breath and waited for him to speak, to ask the questions so obviously on his lips. She needed to speak herself, to tell him that there were many things they needed to talk about. She needed to ask him about his other relationships.

But he didn't question her, and she couldn't find words at all. He swore softly and dragged her into his arms.

The hard, forceful passion in his kiss sent a wave of electricity shimmering throughout her body. She'd never thought a simple kiss could be so bluntly intimate, but the feel of his tongue lashing hungrily within her mouth seemed so sensually hot that her limbs began to quiver, her body to quicken. She felt the hardness of his erection through the velour of his robe and the silk of her nightgown. The intensity of his body heat seemed to fuse his length to hers, settling in her center as if she were stark naked and touched in the most personal, intimate way.

Then he abruptly drew his lips away a fraction, and his eyes found hers. "Are you still sleeping with McGraff?" he inquired huskily.

Anger, intense as her desire had been, flooded through her. She tried to draw back, but he held her too tightly. She didn't answer because he continued in what sounded like a mocking tone.

"Forgive me, but nearly every time I see you two, you're in somewhat suggestive situations."

"God knows who *you're* sleeping with," she responded angrily. "Today your room reminded me of Grand Central Station. Are you sleeping with all those women? And does that mean you killed Cassandra so you could continue to do so?" she countered.

She was instantly sorry. His body tightened like a bow string.

"All right, then, be a bitch. And I won't give a damn if you're still sleeping with Brett."

His eyes were sharp and damning as he stared at her. Then, abruptly, he spun her around again, and she felt his fingers and thumbs at the base of her neck. He began massaging her nape, her shoulders. She wanted to say something in response, to snap back at him, by God, to move away like a sensible person with at least a modicum of pride. She stood motionless instead, furious, but lulled by the sensual, powerful feel of his hands on her. He was so close behind her. Still aroused. Tense, hot. And seductive.

"If you're angry with me, suspicious, you could leave, you know," she finally managed to say.

"I could."

"You might have knocked."

"I might have."

"I could throw you out."

"No, you couldn't."

"I can tell you to leave."

"I wouldn't go."

"Then you're extremely rude."

"What a shame."

"And just how did you get in here?" she inquired belatedly.

"Secret passage. It's my castle, remember?"

"Right. That would make you king of the castle, master of all you survey," she murmured sardonically.

"One would think."

"Where's the entry?"

"Castle secret. My castle, my secret."

"My room."

"In my castle."

"You've come before," she murmured accusingly. "No fair. You don't play by the rules."

His fingers stopped moving. She couldn't see his face, but she could sense his frown. "No," he told her. "No, I've never come before. Why do you think that I have?"

She shook her head, aware that he had grown even

more taut, wired, tense. "It was just a feeling. Waking from dreams. A sensation."

"You felt it was me."

"I felt..." She hesitated. What had she felt? "I don't know. I just awakened thinking I wasn't alone."

"I didn't come to this room before."

"Really?"

"Did you think that I was uncontrollably lusting after you?" he inquired with a touch of amusement.

She started to pull away.

His hands clasped her shoulders more tightly, and he continued, "I was. But I didn't come here before— other than in lusting spirit, of course."

She smiled slightly, glad that he couldn't see her face. "Maybe someone else knows about your secret passage," she suggested.

"No one else should know. The passage I came by connects straight from my room to yours."

"Interesting. Did you plan it that way when you put me in this room?"

"Yes," he said bluntly.

"But you didn't come before?"

"No."

"Why now?"

"I gave up waiting for an invitation. And I quit giving a damn about your ex-husband." He sounded irritated again. And tense. She still couldn't see his face, only feel his robe against her. "And," he added softly, "the uncontrollable lust finally got the best of me."

"Oh, really?"

"I came for sex," he said very softly.

"Me too," she replied coolly.

"With which one of us?" he inquired.

"You are a royal bastard, and you should crawl back into your secret passageway and—"

"Not on your life, my love," he whispered with a quiet intensity that left her shivering, wanting, all over again, despite herself.

He was still, as if he waited for a response. She refused to give him one. Then she felt his hands moving again, along her nape, along her shoulders, beneath the silky straps of her nightgown.

The negligee began to fall. She instinctively caught the fabric over her breasts, yet inclined her neck and thrilled to the hot touch of his lips against her shoulder, the side of her throat. She felt the muscled form of him behind her, the movement of his fingers on the silk over her hip and thigh, his hard palm gliding low over her abdomen, between her legs. Her limbs seemed molten; her knees nearly gave. His heat seemed to radiate into her, enwrap and engulf her, and she thought that she would melt into the floor, with no will to halt the flow of sweet, wicked warmth that filled her.

Jon suddenly seemed to realize that they were still outside on the balcony, possibly within view of others, and he slipped his arms around her waist, drawing her back into the room. Once there, he turned her to face him and, gazing into her eyes, caught her hands, releasing her hold on her nightgown. Silk shimmied down the length of her, like a cool breath against her fevered skin. She seemed to ache, to long, to desire from every pore. He said nothing, surveying her, and it was as if she felt the very touch of his marbled gaze, and it felt like fire.

Cassandra's killer watched. From a distance, with binoculars.

They weren't paying enough attention to what was happening around them. Not that the killer was playing infantile tricks. No, the killer was serious.

The killer saw the balcony. Saw the woman beneath the stars, saw the man behind her. Watched the scene, riveted.

Saw both their faces.

Felt the eroticism.

The woman, tall, willowy, her nightgown flowing in the night air, her hair caught upon the breeze.

Jon Stuart. Enraptured. Touching. Tall, handsome, so masculine in his robe. His fingers, long, bronzed, moving seductively over the woman's flesh. Her breasts, nearly bared, him touching, touching, touching, and you knew there was a stroke of fingers between her legs, and you could almost feel the manly bulge against the cleft at her bottom.

Then…

He drew her inside. As if he were aware that there might be eyes on them. Watching. Torn. Wanting. Angry.

Still angry. Why the anger?

Why the longing?

The strange longing.

Wanting.
And wanting to…
Kill.
And kill again.
And actually…
It was nearly time to do so.

She felt herself trembling under his gaze. She was naked, cold, yet burning with infuriating, arousing anticipation. Oh, God.

Jon went down upon one knee, his muscled arms encircling Sabrina's buttocks, drawing her forward to him. His kisses glided over her abdomen, then slid to the very center of her sex.

His bold, aggressive intimacy was staggering. Electric currents seemed to rip through her, rendering her aware of nothing but sheer sensation. She cried out in protest and desire. Her fingers tore into his dark hair; her body shook, raced alarmingly toward a shattering climax and convulsed in a startling, swift pinnacle of saturating pleasure.

She was swiftly in his arms, tasting the sexy muskiness of his lips, feeling his nakedness beneath his loosened robe as he bore her down onto the bed. She was dazed, stunned, even embarrassed, yet ever more eager for his kiss, his touch.

Memory came to join the fever of passion he quickly awakened again. He had made love to her before, and she remembered every nuance of him—his touch, his lips, his scent. She had held them sacred in her heart, and the sheer joy of feeling him again was overwhelming. She should have been skeptical, aloof, angry, indignant. He'd had no right, master of the castle or no, to slip into her room unasked, to touch unasked. Yet logic and emotions didn't matter. Nothing mattered. He had come because he was done with waiting. He wanted her, and he had come for her, and he knew that she had no will to deny him. Perhaps he even knew that she had been dying for his touch, and dying to touch him in turn. Perhaps he had seen the hunger in her eyes.

She returned his kiss with equal passion, arms enveloping him, fingertips eager to reach his flesh. His mouth was hard, his cheeks slightly rough as his face moved against her flesh, tongue and mouth teasing her throat, the globes of her breasts, closing around her nipples, teasing, tasting, grazing, making them pebble under his assault. She dug her fingers into his hair, cradling his head to her, her body arching, small, desperate sounds escaping her lips. His weight was between her thighs; she felt the tip of his erection against her, slick, insistent, arousing, and then he was sheathed within her, and the shock of sensation was dizzying again.

He angled his hips, thrust and withdrew, slowly at first, filling her as deeply as she could be filled. Her fingers dug into him, holding him, clutching his back, his muscled buttocks. His hands were beneath her, lifting, guiding, bringing her ever closer with a heady, impossible intensity.

She buried her cries in his shoulder when climax seized her again. She shook, convulsed, held him, damp, seeking breath, feeling the thunderous pounding of her heart as if it were a kettle drum. His hands still cradling her hips, he arched his body hard against hers, into hers, and she felt his heat spill into her, permeate her depths. He didn't release her right away, nor did he withdraw from her, and their ragged breaths mingled, as did the drumming of their hearts.

People were out and about. Jon had instructed Camy to deliver the notes asking his guests to be careful and stay put. But the trickster had been at it again, writing new notes, and a number of guests had fallen for the second set of notes sent around, risking life and limb running around the darkened castle rather than remaining smart and safe.

Finding one of the notes that summoned guests to the 'dungeon below,' Camy was perplexed. Was everyone writing his or her own directions, playing new games?

The upstairs hallway was quiet. Jon wasn't in his room. She hadn't been able to find Jon; he wasn't in his room. She wanted to tell him that something was up, but she didn't know just exactly where he was right now. And so, despite the fact that she was shivering and frightened, she knew that she had to go below herself.

Descending the first set of stairs, she was certain that she saw shadows moving ahead of her. Wraiths in the night. She told herself that she wasn't afraid of the castle, of the crypt. She lived here. There were no ghosts, no goblins. Joshua Valine was a talented artist who had sculpted figures from wax and wire, nothing more. There was nothing to be afraid of.

She knew the castle.

Still...

She started silently down the next flight of stairs, to the dungeon. She was convinced that she heard furtive sounds. People guarding their secrets and their fears.

Secrets and fears that could make them want to kill?

There was a sound, like the scurrying of rats running about, afraid of the light, glad of the darkness and the shadows of the castle. Strange, she could almost see all Jon's guests as rats in her mind's eye. Big rats, little rats, frightened, dangerous rats. Reggie Hampton, for instance, would be a plump rodent with a flowered dress. Susan Sharp would be a scrawny creature with big rat teeth. Thayer Newby would wear a cop badge on rat patrol, while Joe Johnston would be a scruffy gutter rat. And good old Tom Heart would wear a top hat and cane, a Fred Astaire scurrying gracefully among the rest of them.

Camy felt a strange chill. What was going on? It was so weird. She could feel the secretive movements in the castle. She didn't like it. She was uneasy.

Furtive and careful herself, she entered the chapel. A single lamp was burning there to protect visitors from stumbling in the dark. She saw no one. Yet it seemed even there that the dim light set menacing shadows to flickering in every corner.

Where was Jon? Was he down here somewhere,

silently trying, as she was, to find out what his guests were up to?

She left the chapel, carefully looking out the doors before she did so, and slipped into the chamber of horrors. She wondered if Joshua himself could have known just how frightening this place could be even without his purplish lighting, with the eerie flicker of lanterns against the stones of the castle. She blinked, half expecting Jack the Ripper to lift his face to her and offer her an evil, taunting grin. She was convinced, for a moment, that Marie Antoinette turned to look at her. On the rack, Lady Ariana Stuart screamed in silent anguish, her eyes upon Camy, desperate, accusing....

She waited, barely breathing, thinking again that she heard the scurrying of rats. Was someone there, hiding among the wax figures? Or were the figures alive, moving each time she blinked, coming closer, closer, ready to strike?

Idiot! she accused herself. Chicken! How silly. She was a sensible adult. She knew better.

She eased back out of the chamber of horrors, leaning against the wall, breathing deeply. To her other side, barely illuminated, were the recreation areas. The pool, the bowling alley. Might she hear a splash? As her imagination soared, she pictured a murderer casting a victim into the pool, blood fanning out in rich waves. Or, rolling toward the ten pins, a phantom bowling ball that would prove to be a human head.

Ugh! She'd been hanging around those who dealt in death and the macabre for far too long, she told herself. There were no sounds coming from the pool or the bowling alley.

One more place...

She glided toward the crypt and tried to open the double doors there in silence.

Naturally, the doors creaked.

It probably wasn't that noisy, but it sounded loud enough to wake the dead.

She stepped into the crypt.

The light was so muted that she could see almost nothing in the shadows. She blinked, adjusting to the hazy glow cast by the single lantern hanging from an ancient wall fixture.

Then she froze, staring in absolute terror, chilled to the bone....

For there she was.

Cassandra Stuart.

Oh, Jesus Christ, Cassandra!

Beautiful in purple silk and gauze, the very gown in which she'd been buried, her pitch-black hair flowing around her shoulders. She lay atop her own tomb, hands folded over her breasts.

And then she began to move, sitting up, smoothing back her hair, staring at Camy with her haunting eyes....

They lay for a very long time, entwined, and at first Sabrina could do nothing but savor the delicious feel of him. His body still a part of her, his scent, heat, strength cloaking her nakedness.

Then, with a sudden, renewed burst of anger, she

shoved him from her, rolling to pin him down on the bed. He stared at her with surprise.

"You're a complete ass. Jon Stuart! Giving me a hard time about Brett. Yes, I was married to him. And you know what? I still care about him. Oh, he's capable of being an ass, too—it seems to be something men, especially egotistical writers, are quite good at. In a way, I suppose you could even say that I love him. But our marriage is honestly over, and if you want to keep believing otherwise, then you can just crawl back under whatever rock in this big pile of stone you came out from!"

His left brow arched, and a smile tugged at his lips. "Does that mean you came for sex specifically with me?"

She started to swear, swiftly pummeling his chest. He grunted with surprise and suddenly, easily, seized her wrists. Then he rolled and, straddling her, pinned her beneath him.

"Fine," he declared. "Let's be open as hell. You know what? Yeah, Cassandra was a royal pain in the ass, an incomparable bitch when she chose to be. But there was a time when she really loved me, when I loved her, and yes, in my way, I cared about her until the day she died, even if our marriage was over, and even if she was sleeping with half the castle, male and female. That's why I—" He broke off abruptly, his lips thinning.

Sabrina inhaled sharply, staring at him. "Oh, my God! That's it, isn't it? The entire reason you had this party. You did love her, and you're trying to catch her killer.''

He pushed away from her, sitting up on the side of the bed. He ran his fingers through his hair, shaking his head. ''I don't know that she was murdered. I saw her fall, that's all. I was there, and all I saw was Cassie pitching over the balcony rail. It was as if she were flying, and that damn Poseidon is so close to the damned balcony that she landed right on his trident,'' he finished wearily. ''I was grilled by the courts, but I also hired every expert I could myself, trying to find out if she possibly could have fallen onto the trident or if she would have needed the impetus of a push.''

''And?''

He grimaced. ''One scientist showed me mathematical angles that indicated she had to have been pushed. Another showed me a set of diagrams that showed why it was impossible to tell.'' He shook his head again. ''I wish I could have let it go, accepted it as an accident. I wish we all could have gotten on with our lives. But actually, it wasn't my choice alone, and in the end, the wondering, the not knowing, has been worse than anything in the world. Every day of my life since she died, the tragedy has haunted me. I just keep wondering…''

''But, Jon—''

She broke off, frozen, as a sound that seemed to shake the castle itself slashed through the night. It was a scream of terror so deep and unearthly, that it was almost like a banshee wail. It seemed not so much muffled by the thick castle walls as amplified by them.

Jon was instantly up and tying his robe.

"My God!" she breathed. "What—"

The sound came again, a howl of horror and fear.

"The dungeon!" Jon exclaimed.

Even as Sabrina scrambled for her nightgown and robe, he was hurrying swiftly out the door.

"Wait!" she cried, racing after him into the hallway. He'd taken a kerosene lamp from a fixture beneath an arch and was already moving down the stairs. She followed, trying to close the distance between them. The stone floors felt icy under her bare feet, but she knew she hadn't time to go back for shoes.

They were halfway down the stairs when a third bloodcurdling scream shrilled through the night.

And then...

There was the horrible sound of silence.

13

Thayer was just ahead of them, running into the crypt as they arrived below.

They followed.

Racing, Sabrina blinked in the dim light. Then she nearly screamed herself.

Cassandra Stuart was not inside her tomb. She was atop it, in all her beauty and glory. She was feminine and elegant and even as a ghost, in death, looked amazingly well, sitting up on the stone sarcophagus that bore her name.

Someone crashed into Sabrina's back and screamed with instinctive, primal fear. Anna Lee, Sabrina noted vaguely, still too stunned to move or begin to comprehend what was happening in the depths of the ancient crypt.

Camy Clark, she now realized, lay in a crumpled heap on the floor.

"Sweet Jesus!" Sabrina heard someone gasp, and she saw that Reggie had come in now as well, clasping her heart.

"Dear God!" Joe Johnston had come running in as well, only to stop short at Reggie's side. He was followed by Joshua Valine, still tying the belt of his terry robe.

Joshua's jaw dropped, and a strange sound escaped him.

Joe Johnston spoke again, repeating, "Dear God, dear God!"

Then Cassandra muttered a terse "Shit!" as she saw Jon, furious rather than frightened, striding across the crypt to reach for her, grabbing her forcefully by the arm.

"What the bloody hell do you think you're doing?" he demanded with an anger that caused his voice to shake.

"Let go, please!" she cried out. "I'm sorry. Don't be angry. I didn't intend—"

"You must have intended for someone to have a heart attack!" Jon declared, lashing out.

Sabrina just stared, certain that the world had gone insane. Jon had just been telling her remorsefully how he had nearly gone mad wondering about his wife's death. And now here she was, flesh and blood, and he was yelling at her.

It nonsensically occurred to Sabrina that she had just committed adultery, which bothered her greatly, even if she was in a castle where it seemed that a group of rabid, insane people played musical beds.

"Look what you've done to Camy!" Jon thundered.

By that time, Thayer was down beside Jon's fallen secretary, checking for a pulse. Joshua hunched down on his knees in concern, as well.

"She's all right," Thayer said. "Better than I am. I—I saw Cassandra dead, bleeding, three years ago," he said in agitated confusion.

"Cassandra *is* dead!" Jon said irritably, and as he did so, he reached out to the ghost who had risen from Cassandra's coffin, wrenching at the woman's hair.

The long, flowing tresses came away. It was a wig. And then, even in the darkness, it became evident that the woman on the tomb was neither Cassandra nor Cassandra's ghost. It was Dianne Dorsey. Despite the eerie light and chilling surroundings, something that should have been evident for years but hadn't been became startlingly obvious. Dianne Dorsey bore a stunning resemblance to Cassandra Stuart.

"My God!" Anna Lee breathed.

"This is the cruelest, most vicious trick I've ever seen played," Jon snarled angrily at the girl.

"I'm sorry, Jon, I'm sorry!" she cried. She looked at the group that had formed around her. Most of the household was there—Joe, Thayer, Joshua, Anna Lee, Reggie, Jon and Sabrina. The housekeeper and the two maids, with rooms in the attic, evidently hadn't heard Camy's screams, and V.J., Tom, Susan and Brett had apparently slept through them.

Camy, coming to, suddenly started screaming again. Sabrina knelt before her and the two men supporting her. "Camy, Camy!" she said, touching the woman's face. "It's all right. It's not a ghost. It's just Dianne, playing a trick."

"It's not a trick!" Dianne protested. "All right, I suppose it was a trick, but I didn't mean to be vicious or cruel, I was just trying to find out which of you hated my mother enough to kill her!''

"Mother!'' Joe grunted, sounding as if he was strangling.

Jon walked across the room to Camy and touched her hair. "You all right?'' he asked gently.

Camy nodded. Sabrina stared up at him accusingly before rising and helping Camy to her feet. Jon stared back at her, but offered no apology.

"Mother?'' Joe croaked again.

Anna Lee started to laugh. "Oh, this is really rich. Is it true?''

"Yes,'' Jon said, striding back toward Dianne. His anger hadn't abated, but it seemed to be in check. "Cassie had Dianne when she was very young. And to Cassie, no matter how young she'd been, having a grown daughter was something she didn't want to admit publicly.''

"You knew—all along?'' Joshua said, looking at Jon.

He nodded. "I thought you knew, too. I mean, I thought it would be obvious to you when you were doing their wax figures.'' He shrugged. "Cassie and Dianne had both asked me not to say anything, for their own reasons, and I respected their desires. But Dianne, evidently, has changed her mind.''

He stood in front of Dianne, glaring at her.

"But...I thought you hated her!'' Joe said to Dianne.

"I did,'' Dianne said. Then she started to laugh. But as she laughed, tears began streaming down her face. "I hated her because her looks and youth and image were everything to her, far more important than I was. I wanted you all to think that I hated her because that was the only way you'd talk openly in front of me, say what you were really feeling or thinking. But she was my mother, and when she was with Jon, he made her realize that I was her child, and she took an interest in me, and in my work, and we were like conspirators, both of us preserving her image of youth and beauty. And she could be so horrible and mean, but she had times when she could be loving... and...and...it didn't matter, she was my mother, and one of you killed her!"

Jon slipped an arm around her. His anger gone, he held her tenderly. "You don't know that anyone killed her, Dianne. And dressing up like Cassie wasn't going to help you, honey. It just scared Camy half to death and could have put you into serious danger."

She clung to him, suddenly looking extremely young, her makeup running, her eyes lustrous, the tough-girl image completely gone.

"If no one killed her, why would I be in danger?" Dianne whispered.

Jon was silent for a split second too long. "Because it's a dark and stormy night in a creaky old castle," he told her lightly.

"And we have a full moon now, too," Reggie said.

"Are you implying that we have werewolves about?" Joe murmured teasingly, also trying to lighten the mood.

It was a strange gathering. They'd gone through

shock, terror, disbelief and anger. Now they were banding together in sympathy because it was all too painfully obvious that Dianne had been deeply hurt by her mother, and just when she had finally begun to receive the love she had craved, her mother had been snatched away. She looked like a lost child; she *was* a lost child.

"I think vampires like full moons, as well," Sabrina offered.

"Especially when cats are leaping out of the bag," Anna Lee murmured.

"I think there are probably a few more cats ready to do some leaping out," Jon said sternly, staring from one to the other of them. "We'll meet tomorrow in the great hall and try to get to the bottom of all our little secrets, shall we?"

Anna Lee shrugged. "I've admitted mine."

"You have?" Joe said.

"Never mind, for the moment," Jon told him. "We'll get to all this in the morning, when everyone is present. We should get some sleep for what's left of the night."

"I'm sorry, Jon," Dianne said again, looking up at him. She still rested against his chest. His arm was supportively around her. "I suppose it wasn't a very smart trick. I just thought that someone might panic and shriek out the truth—that I couldn't be there, alive, because they'd killed me. It didn't happen. Maybe the right person isn't here. I'm sorry. I guess it really was dumb. Please don't be angry with me."

"It was stupid and dangerous, and I am angry. I'm

angry with myself, because I shouldn't have had you here this week," he said.

"Are we all here to confess our secrets and find out the truth about Cassie?" Anna Lee asked.

"We're all here for charity—and to find out the truth about Cassie, if there is a truth to be discovered," Jon said honestly. "I'm sure you all came for exactly the same reasons I arranged the Mystery Week."

"Amen to that," Joe muttered.

"I can't believe that V.J. is missing this!" Reggie said.

"V.J." Anna Lee snorted. "It's Susan who's missing her big chance—thank God!"

"Well, she'll know the truth about everything soon enough."

"Yes, the sins we know now and the sins we'll share tomorrow," Thayer said dryly.

"There's really no help for it, is there?" Jon asked. "There's apparently a lot we need to get out in the open—if we don't want any more startling performances."

"Susan will still be deadly," Reggie warned.

Anna Lee smiled. "We'll see, won't we? Maybe we can all tie her up and gag her—or wall her into the castle. What do you say?"

"I say it's better when the truth is out," Dianne said suddenly, passionately.

"Definitely," Jon said.

"So why didn't you tell us all the truth about Dianne?" Thayer demanded of Jon.

"I asked him not—" Dianne began.

But Jon, apparently, wasn't about to have anyone fight his battles for him. "I already told you, it wasn't my truth to tell," he said flatly. "Other than the obvious emotional reasons, Dianne wasn't certain that the truth wouldn't hurt her career now. She's worked very hard at her writing, and one of the reasons she hesitated about letting the truth be known after Cassie died was that she didn't want people thinking, belatedly and erroneously, that Cassie helped her write or helped her get a publisher or special considerations. Dianne has earned every accolade that has come her way. So I respect her decision."

Dianne smiled up at him. "I know why she loved you so much," she whispered softly.

He cleared his throat, obviously uncomfortable. "Let's let Cassie rest in peace now, shall we?" he murmured. With his arm still around Dianne, he helped her stand and led her from the crypt. The others stared at one another for several seconds, then followed him out.

They mounted the first step of stairs as a group, and they were still together as they reached the second floor. There they said their exhausted good-nights and departed for their own rooms.

Sabrina stood in the hallway briefly, looking after Jon. He was still talking to Dianne, walking her to her room. He glanced back at her.

She turned and entered her own room, closing the door firmly behind her.

She wondered if he would come back to her, and she paced.

After half an hour, restless, she stepped into the hall and tried Brett's door. It opened, and as she looked in on him, she worried that she hadn't a way to lock it from the outside. Nothing really bad had happened; still, she wished she could make sure that he was locked in. He was sleeping, and she checked his breathing and his pulse. With his bedroom eyes closed for the night, he had a strange innocence. He looked absolutely cherubic.

She kissed his cheek and left him.

She walked back into her own room, still unhappy about leaving her ex-husband so defenseless. She closed her door, locked it, hesitated.

As she did so, a hand descended on her shoulder.

She spun around, almost screaming, but it was Jon. Once again, his marbled eyes were dark and dangerous—and very suspicious.

"Going back to the ex?" he inquired softly.

"You! You have your nerve lecturing me when—"

"I'm not lecturing. I'm asking. You were just with him, right?"

She gritted her teeth, hating his cool nonchalance and the piercing feel of his eyes.

Which still left her wanting him. Against her will.

"He's sound asleep. I was just worried about him."

"Why?"

"I don't know exactly. You said we should all lock ourselves in. I can't lock his door."

"Oh." He looked at her for a moment, the released her, opened her door and stepped into the hall. She followed him and watched as he drew a key from his pocket and attended to Brett's door.

She stared at him, then tried the door. It was locked. With narrowed eyes, she stared at him again.

"It's a master key," he told her.

"Because you're the master?"

"Of course."

"Your castle, right? How could I forget."

"I don't know. How could you?"

She turned and stepped back to her room. She entered it and started to close the door. He followed, closing and locking the door behind him.

"So this is all to catch a killer," she said. "You know, there are those who believe *you* to be the killer."

"No one with good sense."

"You do have the ability to sneak up on any of us—whether we want company or not."

"Do you really want me to leave?" he inquired.

She stared at him, but then lowered her eyes. "Why didn't you tell me about Dianne? You knew that I was…" Her voice trailed off.

His hands fell on her shoulders. She felt their strength and warmth, and for the life of her, she couldn't help but remember how they felt when they were more intimately upon her.

"Why didn't I explain that she was my stepdaughter and that I wasn't sleeping with her?"

"You—you could have," she stuttered.

He shook his head. "No, I couldn't have. I had promised her that I wouldn't, though, of course, I would have forbidden her to come to Mystery Week or thrashed her hindquarters if I'd had any idea she meant to pull such a dangerous stunt."

"You care about her," Sabrina said softly.

"Of course. She was just a young kid, scared, unsure, who'd never known her father and wasn't allowed to have a mother. I liked her from the start. She's searched for an identity, done all sorts of ridiculous things, but she's worked hard, and, despite all appearances, she's become a decent young woman."

Sabrina nodded, her head down. "Dianne is your stepdaughter. And Anna Lee..."

"Anna Lee seduced Cassie. And Cassie was happy to be seduced. She wanted to be shocking, and titillating. She thought that I was interested in Anna Lee as more than a friend and colleague."

"But you weren't?" Sabrina said, looking up at him.

He shook his head, smiling slowly.

"The rumor is that you were having an affair, as well, with one of the guests at the party. Perhaps V.J.?" she inquired, thinking of her beautiful older friend—married at the time, but then, stranger things had surely happened.

"V.J.?" Jon exclaimed. "I do love her, but as a dear and cherished friend."

"Susan?" she whispered.

He made a face.

"Reggie?" she inquired incredulously.

"Oh, please!" he groaned.

"Well, that's the group, other than—"

"Has it never occurred to you that it might have been rumor and nothing more?" he asked softly.

"But—but you knew that your wife was having affairs—"

"Yes, and I had a life other than the week in which I had friends out here for a charity function," he said.

"Then you were seeing someone else?"

"I was seeing someone, yes. But neither one of us was deeply involved. She knew that I was married, and she knew that there were difficulties. We weren't in love—it was a brief relationship, that's all. I wasn't seeing anyone who was here at the Mystery Week. From what I knew and suspected, most of them were already pretty busy, and that's all there is for me to tell," he said.

And she knew that the matter was closed. "But, Jon," she ventured, trying very hard to sound determined, sure and matter-of-fact, "So much has happened, there's so much that we don't know, and—"

But he interrupted her. "Yes, so much has happened, and there's a million things between us to discuss. We could fight over a dozen things for a dozen weeks, but—"

"You came for the sex," she interrupted bitterly.

He went still, watching her. "I came to make love. Because I'm not sure that I've actually *made love* since you walked out on me years ago."

It might not have been true. It might have just been the right thing to say. But it didn't matter. He was tense, and passionate, as if he'd rediscovered a hunger that couldn't be simply sated. His energy was electric, and she wanted to feel him again.

Still, she hesitated.

"But, Jon, I don't know what I feel. Anger, fear…"

That last word did it. He backed away from her and started across the room toward the balcony. He touched a brick in the wall, and a slim doorway slid open with the silence of well-oiled if ancient mechanisms.

"You can slide the top lock on your hall door to keep me out," he said curtly. "And you can wedge this door shut by shoving the fire poker into the crack," he told her.

Then he was gone.

She was stunned. Then she suddenly, belatedly found realization. And regret. She had told him she was *afraid*. She ran after him, hurrying to the secret door. But she couldn't even see it anymore. The bricks hid it completely. "Jon!" she whispered, and she banged against the wall. "Jon!"

He didn't reply. She pressed brick after brick. No passageway opened to her.

She sank down on the foot of her bed. A minute later, she curled up on it.

She closed her eyes, feeling ill, wishing she hadn't thrown him away when she'd had him. If he came back, she would tell him…

Tell him what? That she'd never gotten him out of her mind? Her heart? That she was *willing* to be afraid, to risk anything, to forgive anything, to believe anything, to be with him?

She closed her eyes.

Uncertain how long she might have lain there, her mind numb, she suddenly became aware of him again. She jerked herself upright. And he was there, standing at the foot of the bed.

"You didn't put the poker in the door," he told her.

"No," she whispered, and she jumped up, throwing herself into his arms. "Jon, I—"

"I don't think that we should talk," he said roughly.

And for the moment, she agreed with him.

She didn't want to talk. Not now. She wanted to make love.

She opened her mouth, but said nothing, for he kissed her hard, forcefully, demandingly, leaving her no room for speech or argument. She returned his force, eager just to have him, touch him, feel him touch her.

His hands brushed over her clothing, and it was gone. And then he was naked with her, touching her, and in a few frenzied moments he was within her, and the taste, touch, scent and feel of their lovemaking was all she needed.

What remained of the night became a blur. She was sated, dazed, floating on clouds, and then he was within her again. And then, exhausted, she slept, secure in the arms that held her so tightly.

Yet later she awoke feeling cold, her teeth chattering.

She was alone in the darkness. He had left her.

Sabrina rose, seeking her nightgown and robe. She hurried to her door, and it was locked. He hadn't left that way. Why should he have? He had come by the secret passageway; he had surely left that way.

Yet she suddenly felt uneasy. She unlocked her door and looked out into the hall.

It was empty.

Strange what night, darkness and being alone could do. It seemed as if there were sounds, movements, coming from every dim corner, from the stairway, from below. The wind outside gave a low moan as it swept around the castle. She thought that she heard cries and whispers within that sound.

She stood in the hallway shivering, trying to tell herself that she was sensible, that the wind didn't mask the cries of ghosts, nor was death shooting across the night sky in a banshee carriage to take any of them away.

Yet he had left her. Jon had left her. And to her deep dismay, she was afraid.

Worried, she moved to Brett's door. She hesitated, then tapped on it.

She was startled when the door drifted slightly open at her knock.

"Brett?"

She pushed the door open.

In the very pale lantern light from the hall, she could see nothing but a mound upon his bed. She hesitated in the doorway, suddenly terrified to walk into the room, afraid of what she might find.

"Brett!" she whispered more urgently.

Still no answer.

She didn't want to walk into the room. It was dark; it was filled with shadows. She was tempted to run back to her own room, bolt her door, curl into a ball on her bed and start praying for morning.

Even if she bolted the door, however, she could have visitors, of course. Jon.

Jon had said that he hadn't come before. She hadn't pressed the point; she hadn't actually seen anyone. But she'd had that feeling, at times, that she hadn't been alone. So either she was highly imaginative, or Jon had been lying....

Or someone else was aware of a passage into her room?

It didn't matter, she told herself. She wasn't being threatened. But Brett *had* been hurt. And though he had seemed okay, she should make sure.

Still she clung to the doorframe.

Then she became angry. Silly fool, she charged herself. If Brett was hurt...

She gathered her courage.

"Brett!"

No answer still. She walked into the room.

And discovered why he hadn't spoken.

Susan Sharp was dimly aware of movement.

She was annoyed at first, and nothing more. She couldn't remember anything. She must have fallen asleep…somewhere. And now she was groggy. And angry. Though a little hazy, she knew she had a right to be furious. She'd been played for a fool, and now they were going to pay. Oh, definitely, they were going to pay.

Except that she didn't know where she was. Or why she was feeling…movement.

It seeped into her clouded mind that she'd been drugged. She should have known, should have been wary. She'd been so busy being furious, demanding that she be paid and that the tricks stop. Yes, definitely, drugged. The merlot?

It had made her eyelids heavy. She couldn't move them. She wanted to open her eyes, rip into someone.

But she couldn't quite force herself to move anything. Not her limbs, her mouth, her eyelids…

Yet she felt…movement.

Then, in the midst of her haze and anger, it began to occur to her that she really should have been more careful. Even dealing with sniveling cowards, she should have been careful.

Where on God's earth was she?

She became aware of being cold. Stone. She could feel stone against her flesh, and the icy cold that could settle into stone like nothing else. It seeped into her side, where she lay.

Then she heard laughter—nervous, desperate, edgy laughter. Voices so low she could barely hear them.

"There, right there, yes, perfect."

"This is madness. It will never work."

"It will for a while. What else is there now?"

"There's time to change—"

"No, there's no time."

"But…"

The voices trailed away. Susan had heard nothing but whispers, low, sexless whispers, yet she knew who her attackers were. And when she got the strength to get up, she'd kill them.

She finally managed to open her eyes, slowly, so slowly. And she was staring up into the face of a killer….

No! No, it was an image. Yet am image of evil.

Not a killer.

Not real.

Was she losing her mind? She couldn't move, could barely breathe. If she could just see a bit more…

Tremendous strain. She twisted. Half an inch. It was enough. Just enough…

For her to look into her own face. And, looking, she saw her own death.

Sheer terror seized her. Yet still she couldn't move, scream, make a single noise.

Glass eyes returned her stare. Painted blood covered a knife. Her own face, contorted in the agony of death, lay just inches away. She looked at it. It looked at her….

Inside, she felt the welling of a scream. But she couldn't scream, couldn't move, couldn't make a single sound.

She should have told the truth, told what she knew! She had thought that she could deal with this. She had thought that her fury, her power, would be force-ful enough to get her what she wanted. She had thought that...

"She's awake!" a voice whispered.

"She can't be awake."

"I tell you, she is! Look at her eyes!"

"Don't look at her eyes! Don't look at her eyes, you fool!"

Her eyes. She could see her own eyes. She could see her own scream. See her own death...

She had to scream. Plead, maybe, cry out, give promises. They'd never believe her; they'd know that she'd skewer them the moment she had the chance. Oh, God, no...

"Her eyes are open!" She heard the fervent cry once again. "We can't do this! There's got to be an-other way!"

"We have to do this. There is no other way. And, frankly, it's only what she deserves."

"You said she'd be unconscious."

"She is. She isn't moving."

"But her eyes..."

"Do it! Or do I have to do everything myself?"

A cry of impatience.

She tried to scream. Couldn't.

And so she stared into her own eyes, her own face. She saw the horror and the anguish.

She saw her own blood.

Watched her own death.

Powerless.

Couldn't move, couldn't scream, couldn't cry.

But then, at last, she made a noise. It was a terrible, gasping, choking sound....

14

Sabrina was furious.

Brett wasn't there. She was prowling around in the darkness, scaring herself half to death, and the little shit wasn't there. The mound on his bed was just a pile of sheets and blankets. Brett's door was open because he'd left his room.

In the middle of the night.

"Where the hell did you go?" she whispered, ripping back the sheets angrily, even though she knew he couldn't be hiding in some little ball at the bottom of the bed.

"Last time I worry about you," she muttered aloud. She ducked down, looking under the bed. Foolish. She rose and looked around the room, the bath, making absolutely certain that he wasn't there.

There were no closets in the room, but there was a huge wardrobe in the corner. She stared at it for a long moment. Almost floor to ceiling, it was enormous.

It could easily hold a few bodies, she found herself thinking.

She forced herself to walk to the wardrobe, telling herself how silly she was being all the while. When she reached it, she suddenly wanted to turn around. But she was standing right in front of it. Again she told herself that she was being an absolute idiot. Every time she watched a horror movie, she grew irritated because the foolish would-be victim was walking around some dark and shadowed and lonely place alone. When help could have been summoned so easily.

That was the way it was done, of course. It was a dark and stormy night....

She was being ridiculous. It hadn't been dark or stormy when Cassandra Stuart had died. It had been broad daylight. And probably she had simply fallen. In light of what they all did for a living, they had *made* a mystery out of it.

But Jon had been haunted all these years by what had happened. And he wasn't prone to exaggeration or hysteria. He still wanted to know what had happened.

Unless, of course, he'd been involved?

There was no one in the wardrobe, she told herself. No living person ready to leap out at her. No cold, mutilated bodies.

So open it, she commanded herself. She had no logical reason to assume that anything was amiss at all, she told herself.

She reached for the wardrobe door.

But before she could open it, a hand descended firmly upon her shoulder.

She started to scream in sheer terror, but a second hand fell over her mouth.

"Hey, Sabrina! Shh! What's the matter with you? Want to wake the dead? Or the whole household, at the very least? It's me! You're in my room, remember? I'm the one who should be screaming. Maybe with pure delight. Because you finally realized that you can't live without me. My God, what irony! You finally come to my bed—and I'm not in it! But I'm here now. Ready, willing and able. You did come to sleep with me, I hope?"

His hair was mussed; his eyes had never seemed more lazily sensual.

Her heart was still thundering faster than the speed of light.

She wrenched his hand from her mouth. "You scared me half to death!"

"How?" he inquired innocently. "You were in my room."

"I was worried about you!"

"That's so nice."

"I'm serious!"

"So am I. It's great that you care and I do appreciate it. But as you can see, I'm fine."

"What are you doing, skulking around the castle in the middle of the night?" she asked him.

"I went down to the great hall to see if there was any food around." His eyes narrowed. "What are *you* doing, skulking around the castle in the middle of the night?"

"I was looking for you."

He smiled again. "Honey, I'm here now." He reached for her, drawing her into his arms.

"Brett, let go."

"Sabrina!" he protested, hurt. "You just said you were worried about me. And you came to me in the middle of the night."

"Yes, and you seem to be just fine!" she told him. He grinned. "So do you. You feel great."

"Quit feeling me. Let me be, Brett, please."

He finally did so, though a bit sulkily. "What were you doing up?" he asked her.

"I—I'm not sure. I just woke up...cold."

Brett turned away from her. "You were sleeping with him, I bet," he said gruffly. "And he left you in the middle of the night."

"Brett, don't. I want to be friends, I think we can be friends, but don't meddle in my personal life. I came just now because I was honestly worried about you and—"

He spun around. "*I* wouldn't have left you in the middle of the night."

"You don't know that anyone did."

Brett shook his head. "He's moving around the castle, too, you know." He shook his head. "Strange night. You can tell that everyone is skulking around, and yet no one sees anyone else. Bizarre."

"How do you know?" she demanded.

"I have my ways," he said, jiggling an eyebrow.

She sighed with impatience. "Brett, what's going on? Who else is up? And how do you know they are if you didn't see anyone?"

He shrugged. "I was lonely, looking for company for a midnight snack. I tried Tom's door—no answer.

I tried Joe's door—no answer. Thayer—no answer. I even went so far as to tap on Susan's door. No answer there, either.''

"You tried Susan's door?" she inquired wryly.

He made an apologetic grimace. "I was desperate for companionship." He shrugged again, casual and handsome in a long velvet robe.

"So you ran around in the middle of the night, tapping on doors seeking company to raid the great hall for food?" she asked skeptically. "Why didn't you tap on my door?"

He looked at her, his face suddenly taut. "I did."

"I didn't hear you."

"Of course not. It was awhile ago. And you were making too much noise to hear me. I almost burst in on you, afraid you were being hurt. Then, of course, I felt like an idiot, because I, of all people, should surely know the difference between pain and your little cries of pleasure."

Sabrina was glad it was dark; she was blushing furiously. "Brett..."

"Sabrina, it's late. If you're not going to sleep with me, just go away."

"Brett..." she began again.

"Please. I'm fine. I appreciate your concern. I'm glad to be your friend. But I do love you and it's hard to—"

"Oh, Brett, we've been through all this. You love every woman!"

He shrugged. "Maybe I discovered how much I

wanted you too late. But you don't want me, so go back to bed now, huh?''

She turned around, feeling strangely sad, wishing she could make him feel better.

''Sabrina?'' he said suddenly.

She looked back. He was seated on the edge of his bed, examining a fingertip, then sucking on it.

''What?'' she asked.

''You did know him before, right? Before we were married. I was always convinced of it.''

''Brett—''

''Come on, Sabrina, just answer me. You met Jon somewhere and had an affair with him. I never really had a chance. I felt it all along. I resented him for it, you know.''

''Brett, I married you, remember?''

''But you didn't love me.''

''I did. I still do.''

He shook his head slowly. ''Not the way you loved him. Not the way you love him now. Even when you barely know him. When you've barely seen him for years. When you can't even be certain that he didn't kill his own wife.''

''He didn't kill his wife,'' she said automatically.

He shrugged. ''It's okay. I just wanted the truth from you. I always knew it, somehow.''

''Good night, Brett,'' she told him softly. He nodded and returned to sucking on his finger.

She walked to her own room, locked and bolted the door and started to take off her robe. She realized there was a small dark stain on one sleeve. Frowning, she stared at it, remembering how Brett had gripped her arms.

She threw the robe back on and rushed back to his room, entering without even knocking.

He was still sitting on the bed.

"Brett, you're hurt. You're bleeding," she told him.

He arched a brow at her and smiled. "Bad night," he told her. He lifted the finger he'd been sucking. "Cut myself on a knife while coring an apple."

"Let me see it," she said worriedly.

"Oh, don't go turning into Florence Nightingale on me," he said impatiently. "You're far too tempting when you play nurse. It's just a little cut. I'm sorry if I got blood on your robe."

"Brett, let me see it."

"Out!" he commanded. "Seriously, you either hop into this bed instantly, or you get out of my room!"

He rose, came to her and ushered her out his door and into the hallway. Accompanying her to her room, he said, "Look around, quick! No ghosts. No people. Empty. Kind of like one big tomb, eh? Too bad the great and mighty master of the castle isn't around right now. Maybe he'd think I got in a shot when he was done."

"Brett, I swear—" Sabrina began furiously.

"Sorry! Just teasing you. Now get into your room and lock your door."

"Why are you suddenly so worried about my locking my door?"

"Maybe I'm afraid of creatures who prowl in the night."

"You're prowling around in the night," she reminded him.

His eyes were suddenly hard on hers. "And maybe you should be afraid of me!" he said softly.

He pressed her back into her room and pulled her door shut.

"Good night, my love!" he said firmly. "Lock your bolt."

She did so, and she heard him walk away, enter his room, close and bolt his own door.

"Great. I was only gone an hour, and you go running off to him!"

Stunned by the sound of Jon's voice, Sabrina spun around. He was in his robe, arms crossed over his chest, standing in the rear of the room by the secret passage.

"Damn you!" she told him vehemently.

"Me?" he demanded, brow arching, clearly angry to have seen her with Brett.

She strode across the room to him, pointing a finger. "You walked out on me in the middle of the night."

"So you went running next door to be with your ex-husband?" he asked furiously.

"You must have heard what he said."

"No, I didn't. And I can't imagine what he could have said that would make this look any better."

"I wouldn't sleep with him, so he threw me out. He wasn't even in there when I went—"

"But you did go to him," Jon stated angrily.

"Stop it! Yes, I went over to make sure he was all right. Because I was suddenly scared—"

"Why?"

"I don't know. Why not?" she demanded.

"But he wasn't there?"

"No," she said quietly, suddenly disturbed by the tension in his voice. "Why?"

"Oh, I don't know. Maybe because I sent my guests warnings that, just to be on the safe side, they should all lock themselves in. And instead, the castle is suddenly busier than a beehive. So Brett—injured, poor baby—wasn't in his room when you went to check on him?"

She shook her head.

"Where had he been?"

"Just down to find something to eat."

"So he says."

"Where do you think he went?"

"I don't know."

"And why do you say the castle is so busy?" she asked.

He shrugged. "I saw shadows on the stairs."

"Did you look?"

"Of course."

"Well?"

"I walked around. I didn't see anyone."

"Maybe you imagined the shadows."

The gaze he cast down upon her was withering. "I don't imagine things," he told her.

"No, of course not," she murmured. "So where else did you go?"

"Just back to my room. For clothes. For tomorrow morning."

He was telling the truth about that, at least. A neat pile of his clothing lay on the chair by the bed. "I wasn't gone that long. It never occurred to me that you'd go out prowling around in my absence."

"I didn't prowl around."

"No, you didn't. You went straight to Brett's room."

"He was injured today."

"Yes, the poor fellow. And you're such an angel, despite the divorce, letting bygones be bygones. You're such a wonderful, gentle nurse."

"You're jealous!"

"Naturally, don't you think?"

"But I told you that I care about him."

"It's how much you care about him that concerns me."

"I've been with you," she said softly.

He cocked his head slightly. "Nice to think that tonight has solidified our relationship."

She crossed her arms over her chest. "I suppose I could be jealous of lots of people."

"If you weren't somewhat jealous, I would be entirely insulted."

"So I should be flattered that you think so little of me that you assume I could jump from bed to bed?" she inquired.

He smiled slightly, his eyes dark and marbled. She

felt a strange tremor streak through her. He was still a stranger, no matter how well she thought she knew him.

"I didn't say that," he told her.

"You suggested something very close."

He caught her arms and pulled her up against him. "Sorry. I am just...jealous."

She held herself stiffly, but she didn't want to resist him. She felt his warmth, his scent, the pounding of his heart. She didn't want to say more, but she heard herself ask, "You left my room and returned by way of the secret passage?"

"Yes." He held her close, his voice drifting over her hair.

She pulled back, looking up at him. "But you said you had been out in the hallway, chasing shadows."

He smiled, looking down at her. He rubbed his chin, saying, "I went back to my room to shave."

"You decided to shave in the middle of the night?" she asked him.

He smiled again and touched her cheek. "I noticed I'd given you razor burn. Sorry. But I've paid for my sin. Knicked myself incredibly."

He touched his own cheek, and when he drew his hand away there was a smudge of blood on his fingers.

"That's from a knick?" she inquired.

"Took out a fair hunk of skin," he admitted.

"I'll say."

"Sorry, looks as if I got it on your robe."

"No, no, you didn't—" she began, then broke off.

"Then who did?" he inquired, eyes narrowed.

"Uh...Brett."

"Brett bled on you? This is pretty wild. Don't tell me, he'd been shaving, too, before wandering into the night?" he said suspiciously.

"No, he didn't decide to shave in the middle of the night."

"He's just running around bleeding then."

"He cut himself coring an apple."

"How'd he get the blood on you?"

"Oh, please."

"Sabrina, how?" Jon demanded tensely, taking her arms again.

She sighed. "He caught my arms while he was talking to me, just as you're doing now."

"Oh?" he said, his voice grating.

"Jon, he knows that I'm—that I was—that we were together."

"How?"

She felt the color flooding her cheeks. "He heard us."

"Through the walls?"

"Through the door."

"What was he doing at your door?"

"Seeing if I wanted to raid the great hall for food with him."

Jon was silent for a moment. "This is a busy place," he said very softly. "You running around, Brett out and about. Susan won't answer her door—"

"So I heard."

"From whom?"

"From Brett," Sabrina said sharply. She offered him a hard smile. "And since we're busy casting stones here, why were you knocking on Susan's door?"

"To make sure she was all right. She was really angry today, and someone—Dianne included—has been playing some pretty mean jokes. Actually, Dianne and Thayer didn't answer their doors, either."

"Nor Tom," Sabrina murmured, "nor Joe."

"You were knocking on Tom Heart's door?" Jon demanded. "And Joe's?"

"No!"

"Then—"

"Brett. Brett was out knocking on doors. He was looking for company."

"In the middle of the night?"

"You were knocking on doors in the middle of the night," she reminded him.

"But it's my castle."

"Still, it's the middle of the night...." Sabrina sighed, relenting. "Brett was simply hungry and trying to find someone else who might be awake and about."

"We should have had a midnight buffet, like a cruise ship," Jon murmured.

"I think it's well past midnight."

"Hmm. And you sound as if you don't trust me."

"Why wouldn't I trust you?"

"Oh, a little thing like half the world thinks I killed my wife."

She shook her head. "I belong to the half of the world that doesn't think you did."

He smiled, smoothing back her hair. "Do you think that's smart?" he queried huskily. "You know how it goes in horror tales. The sweet, innocent, noble young heroine is sucked dry by the bloodthirsty vampire."

"I don't think you've been accused of being a vampire."

"Just Bluebeard."

"You've only had one wife."

"But, alas, they say, she is dead. Do you think I should leave?"

"Should you leave? Well, what good would that do? You left before—you simply return."

"That's true, isn't it?" he mused, and she realized that he was just slightly bitter, and just slightly mocking her, and himself.

"You could bunk in with Brett, your good buddy."

"He would protect me with his life," she agreed blithely, watching his marbled eyes.

"Ah, would he? But if I'm not a dangerous man, perhaps your ex-husband is."

"Maybe I would be best off bunking in with V.J.," she murmured.

"Well, you probably would be. But V.J. isn't answering her door, either," he said dryly.

She felt a strange shiver. He was taunting her, almost as if he had pulled her too close and now wanted her to step back and find fault with him.

To be afraid?

"It's your castle, isn't it? Couldn't you actually follow me almost anywhere I went?"

"If I chose."

"Would you choose?" she asked softly.

"Yes."

She lifted her chin, studying her eyes. "I take my chances then, with what's left of the night."

"Not much, I'm afraid," he murmured softly. "Want to try to get some sleep? No more wandering? We both stay put?"

"Sleep?" she murmured.

"Sure."

Sabrina slipped out of her robe and into her bed. The sheets felt very cold, but then Jon doffed his robe and slid in beside her, curling an arm around her, pulling her close. His hands slid beneath the hem of her gown, over her calf, her knee, her thigh.

"I thought we would be sleeping," she murmured.

"Just trying to get comfortable. I hate these things," he told her, tugging at her nightgown. "I mean, they have their place, just not in bed."

"Nightgowns don't belong in bed?"

He shook his head. "Most certainly not," he said. Then his marbled eyes grew very dark in the shadows. "I can't seem to leave you alone," he admitted.

She didn't want to be left alone. She didn't know if he got rid of her gown or if she did. But soon her arms were around him, and she wanted him. "Then don't," she told him.

"I let you go once," he told her, voice soft, lips muffled against hers. "I can't do it again."

She didn't reply.

It was a dark and stormy night....

He was a stranger.

But she felt such a keen sense of intimacy, and whether or not she should be afraid, she had no intention of allowing him to let her go.

Later, she slept. She roused slightly when Jon rolled out of bed and stood staring toward the balcony. She felt a stirring in the region of her heart. Warmth. Possessiveness. Her lashes slightly parted to allow her an unobserved surveillance, she studied him. Tall, handsome, ruggedly muscled, very nicely put together. She loved being with him, loved the way he made her feel, as if she were unique in every way, exciting in her slightest movement. So cherished, and so thoroughly explored, tempest and tenderness in one exciting touch. She had been falling in love with him the night she'd met him. She'd eaten her heart out when she'd lost him. And she'd tried to tell herself that she was an idiot, wanting him through time and distance. But she had fallen in love with him, and time and distance be damned; what she felt now was pure wonderment. He was beautiful to her, from his tousled black hair to his taut buttocks, relaxed penis, muscled legs.

He turned, and she closed her eyes, not wanting to be caught observing him.

He kissed her forehead, left her side, dressed.

Tangled in myriad emotions, unwilling to let them

all show, she allowed him to go. Then she opened her eyes to the weak shafts of sunlight filtering in.

She sat up, absently rubbing her arm. He must have really knicked himself shaving, there was dried blood on her arm. Seeing his robe thrown at the foot of the bed, she reached for it, stroking her hand fondly over the shoulder and collar of the maroon garment. It was slightly damp, slightly stiff.

She frowned. Peered at it more closely. And felt her stomach turn.

Blood.

Not just a spot or two.

The front of his robe seemed to be covered with it.

15

Had he hit a damned artery, for God's sake?

Despite herself, she shivered, and she forced herself to reconsider every dumb horror movie ever made.

The women always tended to be such fools. Believing in men. Falling for vampires. Monsters. Seeing what they wanted to see, trusting....

She cared about him, had been in love with him, was falling all over again, or had never fallen out of love with him. She believed in him. If you loved someone, it wasn't foolish to have faith in him. She did know him. He was an honest man who knew right from wrong.

But his wife had died mysteriously. Here.

And last night, he'd been covered in blood.

Stop, she told herself. Brett had been slightly bloodied as well. And to the best of her knowledge, they'd both left only their own blood, so what difference did it make? No one else was running around wounded or lying around dead. After Dianne's drama in the crypt, there'd been no screams in the night, no cries of foul play.

Sabrina didn't even know what she was worrying about.

She lay still, tired, closing her eyes again. Then a pounding on her door jolted her out of her daze, and she flew up into a sitting position.

"What?" she cried out.

"Hey!" It was Brett, calling to her. "It's me. Are you decent? I know you're alone—the king of the old castle is downstairs sipping coffee." He paused. "I'm glad you were so concerned about me earlier," he added plaintively. "Hey, Sabrina, come on out. Speak to me. Tell me you're alive and well. I'm alive and well, no complications from the bump on my head or even that little cut on my finger. It's nearly noon, Sabrina, and we're supposed to be in the great hall for a tell-all. Aren't you coming?"

She leaped out of bed. "Brett, I need to shower and dress. I'll be right out." She sped to the bathroom.

She wouldn't miss this tell-all for anything in the world.

In ten minutes she had showered and was ready. Brett had waited for her; he was leaning against the hallway wall, sipping a cup of coffee, when she came out of her room.

"Well, it's about time," he complained.

"I was very fast."

"I was about to desert you, since my coffee cup is nearly empty. I need more caffeine. Hell of a night. Frankly, you look bushed. I'm jealous as hell."

"Right, because you spend so many lonely nights yourself?" she queried skeptically.

He grimaced. "All right, not so many. But I'm seeking consolation for the fact that I lost you."

She shook her head. "Did you get any sleep? And how is the bump on your head, really?"

"Just a little sore. And yes, I got some sleep. Did you? Oh, never mind. Silly question."

"Brett..."

"Sorry."

"How's the finger?"

"Oh, a little tender, that's all. Want to kiss it and make it better?"

She sighed.

He grinned. "Sorry, I guess I can't help myself. Truce? I really do want to be friends. Of course, if you change your mind and want more"—he leaned closer to her—"or if you're ever afraid that your rich, lordly lover is planning on tossing you off a balcony—"

"Brett!"

"—feel free to call on me."

"Brett, I thought Jon was your friend."

"He is. But all's fair in love and war and mystery."

They had reached the bottom of the stairs and stood at the main entry. Through the long, narrow windows Sabrina could see that the snow was piled high and the day was gray, with a hint that the storm could start up again at any time. It was actually rather beautiful, in a bleak sort of way.

Kerosene lanterns continued to burn from their wall

fixtures, but with a little struggling sunlight seeping in as well, the castle seemed much brighter.

"Coffee, dear, is that way," Brett said, propelling her toward the great hall.

Jon was seated at the head of the table, coffee in hand, deep in conversation with Joe and Thayer. Jennie Albright, as calm and competent as ever, was busy setting the Sterno aflame under the chafing dishes. On one side of the table Dianne and Anna Lee were discussing the pros and cons of body piercing, while on the other Joshua, Camy and Reggie were lamenting the lack of artistic talent demonstrated in a new museum of the macabre in London.

"I still insist that there is no such thing as a female serial killer," Thayer was saying as Brett poured himself more coffee and joined Jon's grouping.

"Well, what does one call a woman like Countess Bathory?" Joe asked. "She killed dozens of young women, hundreds, perhaps."

"And there's that prostitute who began offing johns in Florida," Jon reminded Thayer.

"Okay, she may come close to the profile of a true serial killer," Thayer said. "The point is, the typical serial killer is a sexual killer. Predatory—and male. Seeking sexual fulfillment through violence."

"It's true that most of the sociopaths the criminologists and behavioral scientists and FBI profilers have studied have been men," Jon said, "But—"

"But I would certainly call that wicked old Countess Bathory a serial killer," Anna Lee said, sliding into the argument. "She killed all those poor girls for their blood so that she could be more beautiful so that she could have more sex.''

"Actually," Reggie interjected, "I read that Countess Bathory played with her victims before she killed them, as well. If that wasn't sexual..."

''In a different way,'' Thayer insisted, but he seemed a little quieter, as he'd been thrown a new twist to an old argument. He had been a hands-on cop, not a scholar, but he still knew plenty.

Joe jumped to his defense. "Male killers of the kind Thayer's discussing can only get off on feelings of control, domination and power. Countess Bathory lived hundreds of years ago, so it's unlikely we'll get any real insights into her murderous activities. In part, she probably simply believed she was above everyone else and had a right to kill peasant girls for her own sport.''

"One way or the other, she was definitely a monster," Dianne agreed with a shiver.

"Careful," Brett warned, "V.J. will be down Joshua's throat for fashioning her into the beautiful Blood Countess if she hears us bashing the lady with too great a fervor."

"Where is V.J.?" Sabrina asked.

"Not down yet," Jon said.

"The point is, the historical Countess Bathory isn't the same as the serial killers we track today," Joe continued.

"Not the same as a Bundy, a Dahmer, a Gacy and so on," Thayer assured them. "Trust me, please, on this one. I know."

"The cop speaks," Anna Lee murmured.

"From what I understand," Jon interjected, coming politely to Thayer's defense, "our ex-cop is basically right. Psychologists are always arguing heredity and environment in the creation of killers, but there does seem to be a relationship between testosterone and violently aggressive behavior. Damaged males who feel they've been degraded, violated, put down, et cetera, tend to become violent, while studies show that women turn the loathing against themselves and are more likely to commit suicide or become victims themselves when their self-esteem is low."

"But women do kill," Anna Lee said.

"True, some do," Joe said lightly, looking right at her.

"So, Thayer, why do females kill then?" Dianne demanded.

Thayer looked at her soberly. "Passion."

"Passion!" Dianne protested. "Always?"

"I'd say they kill out of fear more often than not," Sabrina suggested. She'd poured herself coffee but hadn't joined the others at the table. Leaning against the buffet, she looked at them all as they turned to stare at her.

She shrugged, looked at Brett, and then at Jon. He was watching her curiously. "Say that someone's driving a woman mad, and the opportunity comes by for her to do something about it. A crowded subway…a little shove. Or busy street and a car speeding along…only seconds to think! Do I push gently, just give a little shove…?"

The room was silent as they all stared at her.

Except for Thayer, who hadn't heard any deeper implications.

"Sure," Thayer agreed. "Some murders are so simple, it's pathetic. A husband freaks out because his wife has made leftovers three nights in a row. He yells, she snarls—boom. Blown away—assuming he has a weapon handy. Women—the husband is abusive night after night, day after day. Breaks her arms or blackens her eyes, digs, digs. She's no good, she does nothing right. He screams about the lamb at dinner, tells her the mint sauce sucks and isn't fit for swine. He drinks like a fish, comes in every night at two in the morning smelling of stale booze and rotten cigars and wants sex. She can't feel, can't think anymore. She's just scared all the time. Finally, one day, megabelly sticking out from under his ugly, stained T-shirt, he sits feet-up on the recliner, belching for another beer while he watches a football game at a million decibels—she freaks out. She doesn't bring him another beer—she comes in, shotgun blasting."

"He's gross and disgusting," Dianne said, smiling. "Is the woman charged with murder, acquitted for self-defense or given a medal for ridding humanity of a danger to the human race?"

Light laughter filled the room. It was a pleasant sound. Despite the serious subject matter, they finally sounded like a group of mystery writers having fun discussing their interests, as it should be at a retreat.

The retreat Jon had intended, with a finale that benefited children, Sabrina thought. She suddenly felt a deep sadness that something had so altered the proceedings.

And yet...sad or not, there still seemed to be an underlying touch of evil here.

Who was telling the truth? And who was masking something beneath the surface?

Thayer was too involved in the discussion to notice anything evil, said or unsaid, at the moment. He grinned, responding to Dianne. "Naturally, you know that there's always a motive to murder."

"Even if murder is casual?" Anna Lee asked. "Like someone pushing a stranger standing on a subway platform onto the tracks?"

Thayer nodded. "There's insanity—that's a motive in itself. The guys who hear voices. The paranoid who believes people are after him. There's always a motive." Thayer shrugged. "We've always had monsters. It just seems we have worse ones today—bastards who get a kick out of pain and can only feel pleasure and release through torture and killing. It's great that forensic science is coming so far. One tiny fiber, one microscopic drop of blood or skin cell, DNA matching—it's terrific."

"Of course, you still have to have a suspect," Joe reminded him.

"Sure—hey, it's terrifying to realize how many crimes go unsolved!"

"Well, thank God people do love a good crime solved, or we'd all be out of business," Anna Lee said. She smiled suddenly, glancing around at the group. "Speaking of which, aren't we all supposed to be admitting our own most horrible sins today—and discovering what trickster is sending people to the wrong places?''

"Susan will make mincemeat of us all, no matter what," Joe said unhappily.

Anna Lee shrugged. "We'll simply tell her that if she dares print a mean word, we'll do an Agatha Christie on her—we'll every one of us kill her with a rope, knife, gun, poison, garrote, et cetera, if she doesn't mind her manners.''

"Speaking of Susan, where is she?" Jon asked.

"Haven't seen her," Joe told him.

"Nor have I." Dianne shrugged.

"She's really, really mad at all of us," Thayer said with a grimace.

"Has anyone seen her?" Jon asked, looking around the table.

"Not since last night," Anna Lee said.

"Come to think of it," Thayer said, "I haven't seen V.J. or Tom, either. Tom was standing guard for Susan while she bathed last night, remember?''

"Maybe they're all still sleeping?" Dianne suggested.

"Well, Tom and V.J., maybe. But Susan?" Brett said skeptically. "I mean, Tom and V.J.—"

"We're supposed to confess our own sins, not go around casting accusations at others, young man," Reggie declared, chastising him sternly.

"Sorry, I just meant that—"

"Meant what?" a new voice demanded.

Tom Heart, freshly showered, dressed in perfectly

pressed gray wool trousers and a matching sweater, walked into the room. He helped himself to coffee, then realized that everyone was looking at him.

He lifted his coffee cup. "What's up?"

"We were getting worried," Jon said.

"Why?" Tom asked innocently.

"Because it's getting late, and we didn't see you," Anna Lee said. "Or V.J."

"Victoria—V.J. said she'd be right down. She was finishing dressing when I...tapped on her door. And here I am. So why the long faces?" Tom asked.

"Tom, no one has seen Susan," Jon said.

"And you're all depressed about that?" he inquired incredulously.

"We're worried about her," Jon said.

"Well, she was fine last night," he muttered. "She came out of the shower yelling that I was supposed to have been standing guard in the hallway instead of in her room."

"Sounds like Susan," Dianne murmured.

"Well, then what?" Jon asked.

Tom looked uneasy. He shrugged. "V.J. was in the room—she had happened by, and we were talking. Susan was totally obnoxious. She called us a couple of perverts and said that we were sick and after her."

"Oh, this is getting good already," Anne Lee purred. "What did you do?"

"I told her to go fuck herself, and V.J. and I walked out and—" He broke off.

"And what?" Dianne pressed.

"And—and we went our separate ways," Tom said firmly.

But he was lying. Sabrina was convinced that he was lying.

"Wow, Tom! What happened to your hand?" Anna Lee asked suddenly, rising and walking over to him.

"My hand?" Tom said, and then he glanced at his palm and saw the long cut, suddenly oozing new blood, to which Anna was referring. "Oh…that. Looks much worse than it is."

"Paper cut?" Reggie drawled skeptically.

Tom gazed at her, shaking his head with a rueful smile. "I broke one of those old kerosene lamps of yours, Jon. Sorry, I'm sure they're real antiques."

Jon waved a hand dismissively. "I have more lamps. But that does look like a nasty gash."

"Tom, where did you say V.J. was?" Sabrina demanded.

"She didn't answer her door last night," Brett said.

"What the hell were *you* doing knocking at her door?" Tom demanded angrily.

"Trying to find someone adventurous—and hungry—with whom to roam down to the great hall," Brett said indignantly.

"Is that all?" Anna Lee asked teasingly. Then she smiled at the group. "After all, we're on to a new game here, right? Kind of like kiss and tell. We confess our sins, and we figure out who killed Cassie— if she was killed, of course, since the official ruling was accidental death."

"I don't have anything to confess regarding V.J.," Brett said with an edge of anger.

"Not concerning V.J., maybe," Anna Lee said sweetly.

Joe leaned back. "Now wait, if we're looking for motive, V.J. hated Cassie. They never got along. Cassie was mean and crude to her, and V.J. never hesitated to say what was on her mind, either."

"V.J. didn't kill Cassie!" Tom scoffed.

"Ah, Tom, dear," Anna Lee said. "*You* might have wanted to kill dear Cassandra. She wrote ugly things about you, implying you were having affairs all over the place. Let's see, you are separated now, but not divorced yet. Cassie could have cost you a big—capital *B-I-G*—settlement, right?" she queried.

"Anna Lee, we're confessing things regarding ourselves, remember?" Jon said firmly.

Tom lifted a hand to Jon. "It's all right, it doesn't matter. I didn't kill Cassie. I know the law, and my obligations, and I don't hate my almost ex-wife, nor do I begrudge her half the income I made, because we both took a chance on my writing. I already give Lavinia all but blood, yet I give it with an open heart."

"Oh, is that the perfect man, or what?" Anna Lee said. "I still say you had motive."

"Since motive can be almost anything, I think we've all got something that could qualify as motive," Jon said dryly.

"Not me," Dianne said softly.

"No?" Anna Lee queried. "Oh, Dianne, darling,

no, I'm afraid you're not out of this at all. Let's see, Cassie was your mother, but she spurned you. She wouldn't acknowledge you to the world, you were a problem, a bother, someone who made her *old*. Perhaps you freaked out yourself, and she happened to be at the balcony and—''

"What a wretched pile of bull!" Dianne cried angrily. She circled the table, hands on her hips, glaring furiously at Anna Lee. "For you to say such an awful thing, when all you ever wanted was to cause trouble. You have the morals of an alley cat. You couldn't have Jon, so went for my mother. And God knows who else. You like to cause chaos wherever you go. You're desperate for attention, so you have to be outrageous. You have to intrigue the public with your exploits because you can't write your way out of a paper bag!"

"Ouch," Anna Lee murmured. "How did I ever miss the fact that you were Cassie's daughter?" She didn't, however, seem particularly concerned. "Well, now we all know where I was sleeping, but there's more to the story, boys and girls. Shouldn't we all fess up?" She swung around and stared at Joe. "Have you anything to say?" she asked him.

He lifted his hands, shrugged sheepishly. "I—I was caught between them," he said unhappily.

Jon rose slowly and leaned against the mantel. The sound of a pin dropping would have been like thunder, everyone had gone so silent. Yet Jon seemed calm, as if he weren't learning anything new at all.

Joe cleared his throat. "I was really mad at Cassie," he explained. "Yet no matter how mad I was at her—and I lost a chance at an important anthology because of her—I was still fascinated by her. She was married to Jon, so I kept my distance. But Anna Lee was having a good time knowing that I had my own little fantasy love-hate relationship going with Cassie. Anna Lee must have been in a rustic mood at the time, for she decided to forgo her caviar tastes and seduce me. And then…"

"And then what?" Jon asked, looking at Anna Lee.

Anna Lee shrugged, then a strange flash of pain went through her eyes. "Jon, you wouldn't see the truth. You wouldn't divorce her. I was only trying to show you what kind of a woman she was."

He crossed his arms over his chest. "You were trying to show me what kind of a woman my wife was?"

Anna Lee ran her fingers through her beautiful hair. "You wouldn't listen when I told you she was well enough to be sleeping around."

"Anna Lee, I knew Cassie, and I knew what she was doing, and I was at the end of the line with her, but in my saner moments, I knew she was running as fast as she could because she was trying to outrun cancer. I didn't always care what she was doing, except when she tried to hurt other people—something it seems she had a lot of help doing." He spun on Joe suddenly. "So finish your story."

Joe was so red he was almost purple.

"I—I—only once—we—I—"

"Oh, Joe, spit it out!" Anna Lee demanded, amused. "We had a ménage à trois!"

Joe put his head down. "I'm so sorry, Jon. I was so… It's just that…" He looked up at Jon. "You're a wealthy, respected, powerful, good-looking man. I've always looked like a bear with a hangover. They were suddenly both teasing me, and wanting me…and then," he added softly, staring accusingly at Anna Lee, "and then laughing at me."

Anna Lee shrugged, evidently not terribly penitent about her sexual exploits. "We were all adults, Joe. And we weren't laughing at you. You must have just felt that way."

"Inadequate?" Dianne queried softly. "Put upon? Maybe even used?"

"Oh, no," Joe protested, "I'm not taking that kind of a rap! No, I didn't feel abused, no, I never felt murderous because women had humiliated me, or anything of the kind!" He stared at Anna Lee. "Besides I couldn't have been that bad in bed. Anna Lee comes back now and then when she's in the mood."

Brett was suddenly standing, hands on his hips, staring at them both. "I don't believe either of you!" he cried out. "Cassie wasn't like that!"

Jon stood behind him, setting a hand on his shoulder. "Brett, she was."

"No. You're both making this up, and why, I sure as hell don't know! What, for a great story? Something to make you both look so sick and miserable that you couldn't possibly be guilty? You're making this up, I swear. I knew Cassie—"

"Brett!" Jon said more firmly. "You didn't know Cassie. You just thought you did. You knew what she wanted you to know, you thought what she wanted you to think. You fell into her trap, you cared too deeply."

"No!" Brett said. Suddenly he sank back into his chair, his fingers against his temples. "No, I..." Then he looked up again. At Jon, then over at Sabrina, in a way that made her heart seem to bleed. He looked at Jon again. "I was so jealous of you. I had been married to Sabrina. And she never admitted to even knowing you, let alone sleeping with you. And yet whenever your name came up, she would look a little sad...and I just *knew* that you two had had an affair and that—and that no matter what a good, loyal wife she was determined to be, I was being compared to you. And I came up short. And right after the divorce, I couldn't believe that my own behavior had caused her to leave, and so...so I wanted to get even with you. I blamed you for my divorce—it was as if you had seduced my wife. So...I set out to seduce Cassie. And she cared about me in her way. I know she did, because, because..."

"Brett," Jon said with a soft sigh, "you cared about her because it was easy to care about Cassie. Even after she stopped being alluring to me, I cared about her. She was in pain, she was desperately running. She wanted so badly to be beautiful and young forever. She needed to be loved, she was afraid to be alone and afraid to die. She was a smart woman, well-educated, her insights were often good, and she could be charming and at times even gentle and caring."

He hesitated, looking at Dianne. "She did know what she had done to her own daughter, and she donated huge sums to societies for orphans and sick children. She wasn't a horrible person. I did know her—I knew what she was doing. It just didn't matter. That I had married her to begin with was what was really wrong. We'd known each other for years. She'd gotten me my first agent, shown me a lot of the ropes. She was a beautiful woman, and we had lots of fun. We were on again, off again. Then she got sick. And she didn't want to be alone. And we decided to give it a try. Marriage between us was probably doomed from the start. But she was a friend. And I did care about her."

Jon paused, then lifted his hands suddenly, a wry smile curling his lips. "Okay, so who here *didn't* sleep with my wife?"

"Well, dear boy, I most certainly didn't!" Reggie exclaimed indignantly.

Jon smiled. "Should we have a show of hands? The yeas and the nays?"

"I'm a nay," Tom asserted.

"Me, too," Camy declared.

"Nope," Thayer said.

"Not me, either." Joshua, silent up until now, leaned forward in his chair.

"I wasn't here," Sabrina murmured.

"Well, we're missing Susan and V.J., so we'll have to ask them later," Jon murmured dryly.

"Do you think we've all bled enough today?" Anna Lee asked abruptly. Her voice was so changed that Sabrina stared at her, wondering if her casual bluntness regarding her sexual exploits wasn't partially show. Was she bothered by the things she had done?

Motives could be so strange. Brett had set out to hurt Jon, because Jon had inadvertently hurt him. Anna Lee had loved Jon, so she had seduced Jon's wife. Joe had fallen in love with Cassie and been swept into Anna Lee's intrigue. And as to the others...

Cassandra had held things over all their heads. Evidently she'd liked to threaten people. She'd believed she could ruin Tom Heart, destroying his career and his marriage. She'd fought openly with V.J. What about Thayer, Reggie, Joshua and Camy? And would Dianne have been so hurt by what her mother had done that she might have committed murder?

"Jon?" Anna Lee continued, pressing the issue.

He lifted his hands. "We're no closer to any answers, are we?" he said softly.

"Not true," Brett said. "We know who was—and wasn't—sleeping with Cassie."

Jon smiled ruefully. "That doesn't tell us who killed her."

"If she *was* killed," Anna Lee said. She leaned forward. "Jon, maybe we should just leave it be."

"But what about all these crazy, misleading game instructions going out to people? Who's the one playing tricks to scare us?"

"Dianne!" Anna Lee announced.

"Once!" Dianne cried. "Only once, when I wrote the notes for you to come to the crypt."

"So what about Susan's note?" Jon demanded.

"Dianne, if you did it, please, for the love of God—" Anna Lee began.

"I didn't write Susan's note!" Dianne said irritably. "I'm not going to confess here to what I didn't do."

"Susan is simply crazy," Brett said irritably. "Let's go by process of elimination. I wasn't here, so I'm innocent. Sabrina wasn't here. She wasn't even here when the tragedy happened. Joshua wasn't here, Jon wasn't here—"

"Any one of us could have written a note before leaving," Jon said firmly.

"But if we weren't here, how could we have tormented Susan in the chamber of horrors?" Brett asked.

"Accomplice!" Thayer said softly.

"If Susan was really tormented at all," Tom said. "She's such a dramatist, and she thrives on attention."

"Please, Jon," Anna Lee said, "I've a pounding headache. Could I go back to sleep for a while?"

Jon lifted his hands. "Of course," he murmured. He looked around the room. "We'll meet for supper-cocktails in the library. We can keep playing the game, but the case we solve may be about ourselves."

"But, Jon, what if there's nothing *to* solve?" Camy

asked. "What if Cassie's death was just a tragic accident?"

"Well, if that's what we discover—and hopefully it will be so—we'll still have solved the case," he said.

"Well! If we've gotten past the mudslinging and the fess up, I'm for cards in the library," Reggie said hopefully.

"Bridge?" Tom asked.

"Poker, dear boy! Poker!" Reggie said.

Joe laughed. "I'm in."

"Me, too," Thayer agreed.

They all rose. Anna Lee left the room quickly, ignoring the rest of them. Reggie, Joe and Thayer started toward the library. Sabrina began heading toward Jon, but she saw that Camy was talking with him, apparently upset. Brett hovered near, as if he, too, were anxious to get in a word with their host.

Sabrina started to leave the room. Tom Heart blocked her way, his injured hand wrapped in a napkin. "Cards?" he said.

She shook her head, suddenly uneasy. "No, Tom, thanks. I didn't get much sleep. I'm going up for a nap. Maybe I'll join in if you're still playing later."

"Sure."

She slipped by him. Anna Lee had already disappeared up the stairs. Sabrina headed quickly up behind her, started for her own room and then paused.

She walked across the hall to V.J.'s door.

"V.J.?" she queried softly. No response. She tapped lightly on the door. "V.J.?"

Still there was no answer, and she knocked harder. "Damn it, V.J., you're making me nervous here!"

There was still no response, so she hesitantly set her hand on the doorknob and twisted.

The knob turned. V.J.'s door wasn't locked.

Sabrina inched the door open. "V.J.?"

Nothing.

She pushed the door fully open and stepped into her friend's room.

And saw V.J.

She was stretched out on her bed, dressed in a simple, elegant dress. No frills or lace for V.J. Her head was upon her pillow; her hands were folded upon her chest. She was laid out as neatly as a corpse in a coffin for a viewing. A thin red line encircled her neck.

"V.J.!" Sabrina shrieked, and flew across the room to her friend.

16

Jon began to wonder just what kind of can of worms he had opened.

"I don't understand any of this, Jon, and if I had managed things better—" Camy began.

"Camy, anyone could have written notes—"

Joshua had come up behind her, his aesthetic eyes dark and disturbed. "Camy, I'm supposed to be helping you keep an eye on things—"

"Joshua, you're an artist and a friend. I'm the one who works for Jon."

"Camy, Josh, you've both done great work for me. There's nothing more you could have done. Please—"

"Jon, we need to talk, really talk," Brett said, barging past the two.

Jon lifted his hands, palms up. "Camy, you didn't do anything wrong. Quit worrying. The game was great, clever, you and Joshua were doing wonderfully, but with the storm, the darkness and everything going on, maybe we just can't play it anymore."

"Jon, I need to speak with you," Brett insisted.

Jon turned to McGraff. "Brett, I'm not angry. Honest. I understand what you did, and why. It's all right.''

''Damn it, Jon, it's not all right. Friends don't screw friends.''

''Well, Brett, literally, it wasn't me you screwed.''

''Oh, God, Jon.''

''Sorry, Brett. Couldn't resist that. But I'm dead serious—it just didn't matter anymore.''

''Jon, she was still your wife.''

''Brett, it's over. I don't feel anything—no anger, no pain, nothing. Try to understand that there was just too much pain going on at the time with everyone. And try to see that it's all right because I've said it's all right. And I need to get by you and get outside.''

''Outside?'' Camy protested. ''But the cold and the snow—''

''Won't hurt me now,'' Jon interrupted. ''It will feel great. Excuse me,'' he said. Then he hesitated, turning back to Brett. ''How's the head?''

''The head?''

''Your injury.''

''Oh!'' He felt his temple and shrugged. ''Just a little sore, I guess. It's all right.''

''Good.''

Jon started toward the door, eager to feel the cold, clear air outside. The sun wasn't exactly pouring through the clouds yet, but at least the light outside was natural and the air would be fresh.

He didn't make it to the door. Joe stopped him. ''Jesus, Jon, you've been a good friend, and I'm sorry, honest to God. It was only once, you know, and there wasn't really even any...you know, not with me and Cassie. But what I did was wrong, I admit it, and I'm sorry. You've been a stand-up kind of friend, and I was a fool.''

"Joe, I need you to try and understand this. I knew what Cass was doing. I didn't always know with whom, but I didn't care anymore. She used people because she hated these Mystery Weeks of mine— she was even trying to get me to leave when she died. So quit worrying. But if it makes you feel any better, if I ever marry again and you so much as look at my wife, I promise to beat you to a pulp.''

Joe half smiled.

"Joe, honest. It was over between the two of us, okay?''

With his grizzled face and sad eyes, Joe looked at him steadily. "No, I don't guess it can ever really be okay, because I don't know if I can forgive myself.''

"Joe, for the love of God, *I* forgive you. You have to forgive yourself. It didn't matter then, it doesn't matter now. Unless, of course, you pushed Cassie off the balcony?''

Joe's eyes widened. "No, Jon, I swear, I never went near Cassie that day. I wouldn't have hurt her. I never would have hurt her....''

"Yeah, well then, let me by, will you?''

Joe stepped aside. Jon could hear some of the others gathering in the library across the way and he hurried toward the castle doors. He paused at the coat tree for his jacket, patting the pocket and finding a pair of gloves.

Snow had piled up, so he had to slam his shoulder against the door to open it.

He stepped out quickly. It was damned cold. But the cold embraced him, the air was fresh and the castle grounds were encased in a crystal glaze that was as beautiful as it was deadly.

He walked along the snow-covered gravel path, sinking at least a foot with each step. Walking out toward the stables, he saw old Angus MacDougall with a shovel.

"Morning' sir!" the groom called out.

"Mornin', Angus. Are you and the horses doing all right in this?"

"Aye, sir, that we are! I've got the stables warm as toast, burning wood in the stove. In fact, if you get too cold in that lofty castle, sir, you come on over and join me. Ah, me boys will surely be along within the next few days, and we'll have the place shoveled up fer ye, Mr. Stuart."

"Sure, Angus. Got another shovel? I'll set to the pathways with you now myself."

Within minutes he was shoveling snow, and it felt good. Good to move his shoulders, to use his arms, to feel the movement of his muscles.

Sabrina had nearly reached the bed when she heard the voice, deep, husky, menacing.

"What the hell do you think you're doing?"

She came to a stop and spun around.

At first she couldn't see who had come into the room. Mere slivers of light penetrated the narrow windows, and for a second she couldn't place the voice. Then she realized who it was, and she remained frozen in place, her heart thundering.

"What am I doing?" she retorted with a show of fury, her heart pounding a million miles an hour. V.J. lay on the bed. He stood in the doorway, blocking it.

There was no way out.

"What are *you* doing?" she demanded. "V.J. is... V.J. is..."

He started moving toward her.

Strange morning, Jon thought as he worked. The simple manual labor of shoveling—so often nothing more than a royal pain in the butt—felt really good. He could think and shovel mechanically. And expending his tension was good—it just might keep him from sending a fist, or his head, into a wall. He had suspected many things. Now he knew them for facts. And actually, he hadn't been lying; none of it really mattered. It was strange to think back. He'd been so young when he'd first met Cassie. Oh, he'd had his share of relationships, had his heart broken a few times and broken a few hearts in turn. Then he'd met Cassie. She'd known the ropes about life, about publishing. She'd been fun, wild, and when she'd been busy, he'd seen other people.

He'd met Sabrina.

He'd known that love at first sight was unlikely, that emotions needed to be explored, but he'd loved every little thing about her. Her naiveté, her charm, her strange wisdom. He'd loved touching her. And he'd thought that he'd been equally good for her. But she'd left, and no matter what he'd tried, she'd refused to see him.

That's when Cassie had come to him, with cancer, and she'd been so afraid, hadn't wanted to be alone. He'd been wrong to marry her, because he hadn't really loved her that way, and maybe her knowing that had caused her outrageous behavior. They had just kept hurting one another, and it was damned sad, because he had meant to be strong for her, meant to be, if not the husband and lover she had hoped for, the friend she really needed. But the games had become too much.

"Hey! Got more shovels?"

Jon looked up. Thayer was outside, flexing his arms.

"Sure. Angus, we've got more shovels, right?"

Angus nodded happily.

Thayer started shoveling; a few minutes later, Joe joined them, as well.

Then Brett appeared. He watched for a while, then he started shoveling, too.

Pathways quickly came into being. Then Reggie appeared. "So there's where you boys go when you can't ante up!" she called from the castle steps.

Brett saluted her. "Come on out and shovel, Reggie."

"Don't you dare!" Jon warned her firmly.

Dianne stepped out behind her, followed by Camy.

"Maybe Reggie's a bit—" Joe began.

"Don't you say it!" Reggie warned.

"I wasn't going to say old—I was simply going to say mature!" Joe protested.

"The hell you were!" Reggie chastised.

"Diane's young and strapping. Come on out here and work, woman!" Joe challenged her.

She was dressed for it—in black pants, black boots, heavy black sweater. She walked out into the snow, heading toward Joe, who was ready to hand her his shovel. But as she reached him, she smiled, bent down to pick up a handful of the white fluffy stuff, and pelted him right in the face.

"Hey, man, she got you!" Brett called out.

Joe wasn't about to take it lying down. He squatted, whipping up huge snowballs to cream first Dianne and then Brett.

Jon started to laugh. He was hit in the shoulder. Dianne had turned her attack on him. He started to throw a snowball back at her and felt a thud on the back. Spinning around, he saw that Camy was slinging snow as well. The white stuff began soaring everywhere. In minutes the group had grown. Anna Lee—so desperate to run up and take a nap—was back. Joshua had joined in. And it was, in fact, hard to tell who was who anymore, they were all so covered in snow.

Even old Angus got in on it. He had a mean curve and was dishing out more than he was getting.

In the midst of the fight, Jon began to look around. Where was Sabrina?

Almost everyone seemed to be there.

Except Susan, V.J., Tom and Sabrina.

Susan, V.J., Tom.

And now Sabrina.

Jon began to dust himself off, running toward the house.

"V.J. is sleeping," Tom stated with annoyance.

"Sleeping!" Sabrina exclaimed.

"Yes. She's tired. Why are you trying to wake her up?"

Sabrina looked from Tom to V.J.—the way her friend slept, like a corpse laid out in a coffin, hands folded over her chest. She started toward the bed again, not trusting Tom's words.

If V.J. was dead, Tom had killed her. And now she was alone with Tom. And there was no way out....

"Why do you want to wake her up?" Tom demanded again, irritated.

"The red...on her neck..." Sabrina heard herself say. Stupid! She should have turned, walked away, gotten help. Let Tom think that she believed V.J. was sleeping.

"The red on her neck?" Tom said.

He frowned, striding into the room. Sabrina shrank back from him, going to the opposite side of the bed to keep something bulky between them. Yet when she looked down, she realized that V.J. was merely wearing a cameo at her throat, on a red satin ribbon that nicely accented the color of her navy and red dress.

Her chest was rising and falling.

Her eyes suddenly opened. She saw Sabrina on one side of her, and Tom on the other. She jerked upright.

"Good God, what is going on here? Does a woman have to suffer an audience when she wants to take a nap?"

"I don't know what Sabrina was doing!" Tom exclaimed, throwing up his hands. "She came in here to wake you up!"

V.J. frowned, looking at Sabrina. Sabrina shrugged with a rueful smile. "I was worried about you."

V.J. stared at her blankly, then smiled. "Oh, I guess I missed the confessions. I'm sorry. I was dressed, I was ready.... I just stretched out to catch a few winks, and I guess I went out like a light."

"Sabrina!"

Sabrina jumped, startled to hear her name bellowed with such ferocity from down below.

"Sabrina!" Again, closer.

She turned from V.J. and hurried to the door just in time to see Jon throwing open the door to her room. She stepped into the hallway.

"Jon!"

He spun around. She saw the naked concern in his marbled eyes as he stared at her down the length of the hallway. She was suddenly ecstatic. V.J. was alive, Jon was in love with her and all of their fears were unfounded.

"Jesus, I was worried!" he said, walking down the hallway to her, a smile on his lips.

She smiled, too, because he was ready to embrace her. But he was covered in snow.

"You're all wet!" she exclaimed.

He nodded—and took her determinedly into his

arms. "We were having a snowball fight, and I realized you were missing. And V.J. was missing. And Tom."

"I seem to be missing everything," V.J. said dryly, stepping into the hallway.

"She was sleeping. Sabrina barged right in, acting as if she were certain I had throttled V.J.," Tom said, shaking his head. He slipped his arms around V.J.'s middle, and his voice became husky as he spoke. "Don't you know? I could never hurt V.J. I'm in love with her."

Sabrina was silent. V.J.'s husband had passed away, but wasn't Tom still a married man?

As if reading her mind, Tom said, "My wife and I are separated, amicably. And when the divorce is final, V.J. and I are going to be married, and we're going to spend the rest of our lives, however long that may be, together."

Sabrina found herself smiling, stepping away from Jon to place a kiss on Tom's cheek. "Good for you." She gave V.J. a big hug.

V.J. was blushing slightly. "I guess I dozed off again this morning because I'm not as young as I used to be. And last night Tom and I were up for hours and hours, talking and...well, you know, talking and—"

"Oh, my God, the old folks were shagging away!" someone announced from the other end of the hall. Brett, hands behind his back, was walking toward them.

"Brett..." Tom began angrily.

"No, no, dear, I'll take this one," V.J. said gaily. "Brett McGraff, don't you dare call us old folks. *Reggie* is old. We're merely on the downside of middle age," she huffed. "And just what are you doing here, anyway?" she asked.

"We had this perfectly good snowball fight going, and all of a sudden I see Jon here realize that he's been away from Sabrina for more than ten minutes. I figured she was snug and warm in the castle, so..."

"So?" Jon demanded, hands on his hips, a brow raised, a slight curl to his lips as he took a step toward Brett.

Brett grinned like a cat. He drew one hand from behind his back and threw a snowball at Sabrina.

Perfect aim.

It caught her on the chin, and snowflakes danced around her.

"Jon!" V.J. said. "Are you going to let him do that to her?"

"Certainly not," Jon said.

"Oh, I can take care of myself on this one," Sabrina announced, already heading toward Brett.

Brett turned to run. As he did so, he said, "We missed you, too, V.J.!" And he caught V.J. with the snowball he had carried in his other hand.

They all tore after him.

Brett was fleet, and he made it out of the house. But once there, he was in trouble. The others, who had still been pummeling one another, saw the attack on Brett and joined in. Within seconds he was unable to return fire. He was laughing, down on his back.

V.J., her dress sodden, knelt on one side with Sabrina on the other, all but burying him in snow.

Laughing, Sabrina realized that Jon was standing back a little, amused by the whole thing.

"Jon!" Brett whispered to the two women. "I'm mush already. Get Jon!"

And so they did. It was fun to see his expression change as they turned their focus on him.

He sprinted a good distance away and kept up a steady barrage of return fire for an admirable amount of time. Old Angus was the one who finally helped them get him. "Back him against the stables yonder, bur-ry the boy!" he suggested.

So Jon, too, wound up flat in the snow, Sabrina straddling him. He was laughing so hard he couldn't ward off her snow assault—but then he suddenly shifted, rolling, and Sabrina was the one on her back in the snow, pelted by handfuls of the soft, light, fluffy stuff.

"Cry uncle!" he warned her.

"Never!"

More snow. "Cry uncle!"

"Not on your life!"

She was nearly buried alive. "Come on now, give in, cry uncle!"

"Never, never, never—uncle, uncle, uncle! You will get yours!" she told him.

He smiled and answered softly, "I'm counting on it."

He stood, drawing her to her feet. The entire crowd was completely soaked, except for Reggie, who had apparently been issuing battle instructions from the castle steps. Laughing, they stamped their feet and shook themselves off.

"That was great fun. Maybe we should all be snowbound more often!" Dianne said.

Smiling, friendly, natural, she looked her age—just barely an adult, young and fresh and enthusiastic. Sabrina found herself thinking that Dianne might be capable of a few macabre pranks, but never murder.

But then, everyone in the group was laughing, having fun, with a strange innocence.

Yet even as she considered how innocent they all seemed, she noticed that there was blood in the snow by her feet.

"Someone is bleeding," she said.

"Tom, your hand—maybe you've split it again," V.J. said.

"Don't think so," Tom said, stretching out his palms. "Nope. My hands are freezing, but no blood. It's probably congealed!"

"We should all get warmed up—only half of us were wearing gloves," Jon said. "Someone has cut himself—or herself—good. Is everyone all right?"

"Your cheek is bleeding," Dianne mentioned to him.

"Old shaving wound," he said.

"Brett, how's that finger you cut?" Sabrina asked.

"I don't think I'm leaking blood," he said. "But then, I've actually got several wounds, you know."

"Yeah, right!" V.J. exclaimed. "Poor, poor boy!"

"Maybe it was me," Thayer said, rubbing his chin.

"You cut yourself shaving, too?" Ann Lee asked.

"Yep. It was like a gusher—caught myself right under the chin," he announced.

"Maybe we should all attend a barber's convention next time," Joe said sorrowfully. "I did a number on myself yesterday as well. It was the shaving by candlelight, I think."

"That looks like more blood than a shaving knick," Sabrina murmured.

"Whoever is injured will surely find his or her wound," Thayer said.

"We need to get in and warmed up before someone suffers real frostbite," Jon said.

"Have we got enough wood to keep the fire in the library burning?" Thayer asked him.

"Yep," Jon said. "There's a storage room in the dungeon. Want to lend me a hand?"

"Sure."

"I'm for a hot shower," V.J. told them. "You men just go ahead and be men and make the place nice and warm and cozy, and we ladies will be down shortly."

They all moved into the castle, Jon and Thayer and Joe heading straight for the stairs to the dungeon.

Sabrina started to follow Reggie on in, then noticed that Joshua had lingered behind and stooped down to see the blood in the snow.

"What's the matter?" she asked him.

Startled, he looked up at her. "Nothing," he said, and gave her a slightly baffled look. "I just hope that whoever is hurt realizes it soon. This is a lot of blood.''

''Maybe it just looks like more than it is. Why would anyone want to hide an injury?''

Joshua grinned at her. ''I don't know—tough, crime-writing guys. Maybe they don't want to look like sissies. Me, on the other hand...well, my hands are my life, my work. If I have a paper cut, I nurse the damn thing.''

Sabrina laughed, then sobered. ''Joshua, when Brett was thrown, you went back and kept looking around where he fell, as if something was wrong.''

''Well, something was wrong. Brett had been thrown, and he'd hurt himself.''

''No, no, I mean...''

He hesitated, his eyes blank for a minute, then he shrugged. ''It was nothing, really. I just needed to look. The artist's eyes, you know.'' He shrugged again.

But Sabrina thought he was lying. There was something. Something he didn't want to tell her.

''Well,'' he said, rising. ''You should be doing the lady thing in the shower while I go do the manly man thing with the wood in the basement.'' He grinned.

She smiled in return. ''I can help with the wood.''

''Nice of you to offer, but you don't think that six strong guys can bring up enough?''

''Well, I was trying not to be sexist.''

Joshua shook his head. ''Do it V.J.'s way. Be sexist when it's convenient. Go warm up. Your lips are blue, and your teeth are chattering.''

Sabrina took him up on his advice. She saw V.J.'s door closing as she reached her room, and down the hallway, Dianne's door closed as well. On a hunch, she walked across the room to Susan's door and knocked. "Susan?"

No answer.

"Susan, it's Sabrina. You can't stay angry with all of us forever. Please, come out?"

There was no reply. She twisted the handle. The door was locked.

She exhaled thoughtfully. Evidently Susan was still royally pissed off. And it seemed that there was nothing she could do. She turned and slowly walked to her own room.

Brett came up behind her.

"Save water, shower with a friend?"

"Brett!"

He grinned and disappeared into his own room.

Sabrina went in and headed for the shower. Once again she was grateful the hot water was holding out. It felt wonderful on her hands. She had idiotically, rushed out without gloves. She was probably lucky she didn't have frostbite. She might have been the one bleeding all over the snow. The snow fight, however, had been fun.

Except for all the blood she had seen afterward.

She frowned as the water cascaded over her, wondering why the blood bothered her so much when no one appeared to be seriously injured.

There had just been so much of it.

Still, everyone seemed to have a cut. And every man here seemed to have forgotten how to shave.

Including Jon.

He hadn't just bled a little bit. His robe had been drenched with wet, sticky blood.

From a shaving cut?

And despite herself, she couldn't help but be haunted by the thought that...

He had lied to her last night. And if he had lied to her last night...

Might it all be a lie?

17

With plenty of wood piled by the hearths in the library, and the great hall, Jon went upstairs to shower. He stopped by Sabrina's room, but she wasn't there. His heart started pounding, and he berated himself, wondering why he should feel fear every time he didn't see her. Of all of them here, Sabrina was the least likely to be in danger. She hadn't been here when Cassie was killed. She hadn't been part of any sex or revenge games. She wasn't a danger to anyone.

Hearing Sabrina's laughter from V.J.'s room, he sighed in relief. Apparently the two women were deep in pleasant conversation. He went on to his own room, wondering why nagging suspicion still plagued him. Dianne had been certain that someone had killed her mother. Jon had never felt more uncertain about anything in his life. Had Cassie been killed? Or had it been a tragic accident?

Strange things had happened here since this week began, yet what, exactly, did they mean? Anyone—not necessarily guilty of murder—might have wanted to torment Susan Sharp. She had tortured all of them at one time or another, and she could be, even as a female, such a pompous prick. There was also the note he had received. But again, maybe someone not guilty of murder had sent him the note just to make sure he paid—either for Cassie's death or for just not loving her enough. The gunshot in the hallway, however, was not so easily explained.

But what did these odd events add up to?

Nothing! he prayed.

In his own room, because he seemed to be growing paranoid, he made sure that the door to the secret passage was secure. It was. Then he showered and attended to other details of running the castle.

It was early evening when he walked back down to the library, and once again it seemed that he was hosting a group of pleasant, normal, *innocent* men and women.

A poker game was in full-tilt. Reggie was winning, taking pennies, nickels, dimes, quarters and the occasional dollar bill from Joe, Tom, V.J. and Thayer. Joshua, Sabrina, Brett, Anna Lee, Camy and Dianne were involved in a game of *Uno*.

Only Susan Sharp seemed to be missing. Again.

"Hey, Jon!" V.J. said, smiling as he came into the room. There was a new glow about her now that she and Tom were out in the open about their feelings.

"Jon, join us!" Reggie said.

"She'll fleece you!" Brett warned. "Come play *Uno*. It's more cutthroat but cheaper."

"Brett, pay attention. Draw four cards," Anna Lee said.

"Oh! You monster! You did that to me?" Brett cried.

"You don't know the half of it, honey," Anna Lee returned in a mock Mae West voice.

"Reverse!" Sabrina announced.

Jon caught her eye as she glanced up at him. There was something different about the way she looked at him. He frowned.

Had all this sordidness finally become too much for her? No, it wasn't like Sabrina to judge. And yet…

She was looking at him differently.

Guardedly.

"Aargh!" Brett cried. "Help! These women are out to get me."

"Uno!" Camy announced.

"Someone get that woman," Dianne commanded. "She's about to win!"

"Well, that is the point of the game, isn't it?" Camy asked. She smiled and looked at Jon happily.

"That's the point of the game," he said lightly. In a way, it was nice that Susan wasn't around, saying things that hurt people and stirring up trouble. Still, at this point, he was beginning to get worried.

"No one has seen Susan yet?" he asked.

"Nope," Thayer said, studying his cards. "But she left us a note."

"Left a note? Where?" Jon asked with a frown.

"Out!" Camy cried. She rose from the round oak game table and walked to the mantel. "Jennie found this when she came to set us up with drinks." She grimaced. "Want me to read it?"

"Go on—do. Jon will enjoy it as much as the rest of us, I'm sure," Joe said dryly.

Camy read aloud.

"To all you murderous, pathetic little pricks— leave me the hell alone. I don't wish to see or talk to any of you, and don't begin to imagine that any of you could ever suck up to me again after what has happened here. You're sick, all of you. I warn you again—while we're stuck here, stay away from me! Otherwise, I will prosecute, and if I can't land your sorry asses in jail, I'll see to it that none of you ever writes for a legitimate publisher again.

                                        Susan."

Camy looked at Jon apologetically.

"She sure does sound pissed off," Dianne murmured.

"Bully for her," V.J. said.

Tom shrugged. "I say what I said before. Fuck her."

"Really," Brett said, "who the hell does she think she is? I've never heard anything like it! Threatening us that way. As if she has the power to keep all of us from ever writing again."

Joe played a card. "Funny, you'd think Susan would know better. She might stick a few knives into us, the way Cassie could, but she'd never in a thousand years convince a publisher not to go to contract with an author who was bringing in the bucks."

"All right, all right," Jon said. "We've established the fact that Susan is a bitch. But I'm still worried about her."

"Jon," Sabrina said, looking up at him. Blue eyes liquid, hair streaming gold in the firelight, she was wearing a royal blue knit that clung to every curve of her body. He could pick out the subtle scent of her perfume, and he suddenly wanted to forget the hell about Susan Sharp and everyone else as well.

Except that there was that something different about Sabrina now....

"I knocked on Susan's door," she said. "I tried to talk to her. In fact, I carried on something of a conversation with her locked door. I don't think I've done anything to make her angry with me, but she wouldn't respond at all."

"Well, she can't stay holed up in her room for days," Jon said impatiently.

Brett looked up. "Why not?" he asked hopefully.

"Please, let's just leave her?" Dianne asked.

"Maybe she'll eventually starve to death," V.J. commented happily.

"No, she won't," Dianne told her. "She wrote another note, 'To the servants,' ordering that a tray be set in front of her door twice a day until this wretched, snowbound event comes to an end."

"Jon, it sounds as if she's really fuming and doesn't want to be disturbed," Joshua told him.

Jon lowered his head, smiling slightly. They were all more than willing to leave well enough alone where Susan was concerned. He looked up again.

"Sorry, guys. I'm still worried. We've got to go check up on her."

"Oh. Let's not," Reggie said.

"Well, I'll check on her then."

"Oh, we'll all go," Thayer said. "I'm out of nickels anyway, thanks to this old card shark."

"Card shark, yes, but I'm the only one who gets to call me old!" Reggie warned him. "But wait, Jon, let's enjoy our dinner first, and then we'll go and eat some crow with Susan. It will be easier on a full stomach."

Jon arched a brow. With a mischievous glint in her eyes, Dianne abruptly dropped to her knees, clasping her hands as if in prayer and looking up at him entreatingly. "Please, please, sir, just dinner. Let us have dinner in peace."

"Come on now, Dianne," he said, laughing. But then Joe Johnston was down on his knees as well, "Oh, yes, yes, please, sir, just give us some supper…in peace."

"Really, if you think—"

"Puh-lease!" Anna Lee added dramatically, kneeling, too. Laughing, Camy, Joshua and Brett joined the other supplicants on the floor.

"Dinner," Jon said firmly, shaking a finger at them, "but no more delays."

"Oh, thank you, thank you, sir!" Brett cried.

"Get up, the lot of you," Jon said, chuckling. "Dinner—and then we go upstairs and talk to Susan and at the very least make sure that she's all right."

He turned around and strode into the great hall.

Jennie was seeing to the Sterno fires beneath the chafing dishes. "We are getting quite inventive, sir!" she told Jon cheerfully. "Everything tonight was cooked upon the open flame. Well, except, of course, the salad, and that wasn't cooked a'tall! But we've lovely steaks and chops. No electric, but the snow itself is pr'sarving our food."

"Thank you, Jennie," he told her.

His guests remained in high spirits as they filled their plates and sat down by candlelight. A fire burned merrily in the hearth. Sabrina was quietly elegant, smiling, laughing, responding to the comments around her—but not to him. She wasn't exactly ignoring him, but she was somehow avoiding him, even though she was sitting beside him. What the hell had happened? he wondered.

Then he found himself wondering, as well, what would have happened if she hadn't disappeared years ago? Might they have stayed together then, eventually married? Hosted these parties, both enjoying them? Sabrina complemented the castle, and, he thought, she complemented him. She brought out the best in him. And if they had somehow stayed together, wed, would Cassie still be alive, a guest here tonight?

And would Sabrina be looking at him differently, as she had earlier, before…

Before what? He was baffled.

Sabrina suddenly looked at him and smiled, though her gaze still seemed guarded. Her blue eyes were dazzling, caught by the firelight. "What are you thinking?'' she asked him, under cover of the chatter and laughter.

"That I wish you'd never run away. Maybe we could have changed fate.''

She flushed slightly, looking down at the table. "Maybe you see more in me than is really there.''

"What do you mean?'' Jon protested.

"Well,'' she said quietly, "I'd like to think I have some strength, the courage of my convictions. But when Cassie came to you that day—''

"What?''

"I folded like an envelope,'' she said ruefully.

"But that was a long time ago. And it's my turn. What are *you* thinking?''

"Nothing, really.'' She looked away.

"You're lying.''

She shrugged.

"Tell me.''

"Nothing…really.''

"Something, really.''

She shook her head slightly. "There's just suddenly…so much blood around!''

"Really?''

She looked at him steadily. "Yes.''

He arched a brow.

"There was blood all over your robe.''

"I told you, I cut myself shaving.''

"Then it looked as if you cut your throat shaving.''

Startled, he sat back. "What is it you think I've done?'' He lowered his head, closer to hers, lest the others hear their conversation. "My wife wasn't stabbed to death—she went over a balcony. And to the best of my knowledge, we've no other corpses around, other than the long-buried ones in the crypt.''

Sabrina didn't answer. She was looking at Anna Lee, who was studying them with a frown.

Anna Lee smiled when she caught Jon's eye. ''You know what's a dreadful shame?'' she queried generally.

Before Jon could answer, Brett did. ''Yes. We didn't get our host to confess to any deep, dark sins.''

Anna Lee laughed. ''That's not what I was referring to, but, yes, well, there's that, too, of course.''

''I had no sins!'' Jon said lightly, lifting his wineglass to Anna Lee.

''Bull,'' Brett objected. ''Cassie told me you were seeing someone.'' He flushed when the words were out. ''Sorry, I, uh…'' He stiffened in his chair and shrugged, then couldn't seem to resist asking, ''Who was it?''

Jon sat back. ''It wasn't—''

''It wasn't me!'' Reggie announced, fluffing her hair.

''Nor me!'' V.J. assured them, laughing.

''Not his stepdaughter,'' Dianne said dryly.

''Well, I was trying, but it wasn't me,'' Anna Lee murmured.

''*Susan?*'' a number of them said in unison.

''No!'' Jon protested. He shook his head, sipping his wine again, glad to see that Sabrina seemed amused rather than horrified. ''I wasn't seeing anyone here at all.''

"But someone, somewhere," V.J. guessed. "Who was she?"

Jon gave in. "None of you know her, and it was only an occasional thing, as we both traveled frequently. Her home base was Edinburgh, but we met in the States. She's an interior decorator, and she'd done some work for me in New York. Are you all happy now, or do you need more specifics?"

"Well, I'd love to hear every last detail!" Anna Lee teased.

"I think he's making it all up, protecting someone here!" Joe announced.

"Well, we've all denied it," V.J. said. "I had a husband at the time, and that was it for me. I haven't young Anna Lee's stamina. Sorry, no offense meant, Anna Lee."

"None taken," Anna Lee said dryly.

"He wouldn't dream of touching his stepdaughter," Dianne said, gazing at Jon. "Even if his stepdaughter might have been willing," she added softly.

"Don't you all go looking at me!" Reggie declared.

"I wasn't here," Sabrina reminded them quietly.

"So that leaves..." Joe began.

"Susan!" Tom said again, making a face.

"Right. Why would he be protecting Susan? Who in his or her right mind could think that Susan needed protection?" Thayer demanded.

"Ah, but maybe Jon wasn't behaving quite so innocently. Perhaps there was some forbidden affair, the castle laird's seduction of some sweet young thing

from the village who came in to cook or clean,"
Joshua suggested, teasing, his eyes dancing. They all
laughed.

"Indeed! We should check out the chamber of horrors for some young, innocent, unknown face!" V.J.
suggested, waggling her eyebrows.

"You may look wherever you wish," Jon said.
"But since it wasn't my 'sins' you were really after
to begin with, Anna Lee, just what were you referring
to when you said it was a dreadful shame?"

"Oh, just that we never solved the whodunit. It was
really great fun, and so well-done. Who did kill your
brother, Demented Dick?"

"Let's solve it now," V.J. said.

"We don't have half the clues. We didn't play the
game," Thayer protested.

"Then we'll just talk it through, lay out the suspects and the clues, and we'll each make a determination!" Dianne said. "Jon?"

"Sure, why not?" he said.

Sabrina leaned forward. "Two of us are guilty,
right?"

"Well, I'm innocent, seeing as how I was killed in
chapel," Brett murmured.

"Right," Sabrina said. "Mr. Buttle, the Butler,
was killed—probably because he saw something."

"My guess," Brett said, "is that it was Thayer's
character, JoJo Scuchi, who killed Demented Darryl—because of an affair gone awry. Or…JoJo Scuchi
was having an affair with Susan's character, Carla,

the call girl with the clap, and he killed Demented Darryl for having given her the disease!''

"As demented Dick's and Demented Darryl's dad, I'm innocent,'' Tom Heart said. "I'm certain of that.''

"And as Tilly Transvestite, I know that I'm innocent, as well. Number one—I'm not sure how, but I'm their mother. And I'm just too weird and caught up in my own psychological problems to kill others,'' Joe said with certainty.

"I think the Duchess—Sabrina—did it,'' Dianne surmised. "Demented Darryl tried to ditch out on back payments he owed her. She's been pretending to be a dignified duchess, when we all know that she was the queen of sleaze. The butler knew about her transactions. He'd had seen too much, and he had to go.''

"Sabrina was in the chapel when Brett bought it, remember?'' V.J. said.

"So we're back to her needing an accomplice,'' Joe stated.

"Okay, Camy,'' Jon said, looking at his assistant. "We need a few more clues from the game. Are there two murderers?''

Camy glanced at Joshua, evidently sorry to part with information and give up the game. He shrugged at her. "Well, tell them.''

"Yes, there are two murderers. I'll give you that much. You all figure out the rest.''

"Give us this, too, please,'' Sabrina persisted. "Brett—Mr Buttle—is dead, and therefore innocent.

And I don't think that Carla, the call girl, is guilty, either. I think that her character was supposed to be the next to go.''

"Maybe," Camy said.

"But Susan's character isn't the murderer," Jon stated. Camy shook her head. "No, she's not."

"And my character is innocent, too. Mary, the Hare Krishna—she's innocent, right?" Dianne demanded.

"A Hare Krishna? You're daffy, not guilty," Joshua teased.

Dianne smiled at him. Josh smiled back. Jon wondered if his stepdaughter didn't seem to be growing more and more fond of the artist.

"Well, we're eliminating suspects, at least," Tom said.

"As Tilly Transvestite, the dear boys' mum. I am innocent, aren't I?" Joe asked. "You don't need to answer, Camy. I can see by your face that it's the truth. After their miraculous births, I surely wouldn't do in one of my children."

"You are in the clear," Joshua said with a shrug.

"And that's it, the last clue we're giving you tonight," Camy said. "Joshua, no more hints!"

"But the game is over isn't it?" Sabrina said quietly.

"Yes and no," Reggie argued. "We don't know who is guilty, but we do know who is innocent. I would personally like to work on it a little longer. What do you say?"

"Well, you know, the game isn't really over," Camy said, "since no one knows the truth at all."

"I'll say!" V.J. murmured.

Reggie looked sternly around the table. She fluffed her gray hair. "I want to solve this. I can't help it. It's in my blood!"

Despite his unease over Sabrina's comments about the blood on his robe—there hadn't been that much—Jon found himself laughing. Reggie was one great old broad.

"Okay, let's leave it at this," he said. "The innocent? Mary, the Hare Krishna. Mr. Buttle, the butler—he's a goner. Carla the call girl and Tilly Transvestite. That leaves us with Sabrina, the Duchess, Reggie, the Crimson Lady, V.J. as Nancy, the naughty nurse—"

"*Very* naughty nurse," Dianne teased.

"Hush, young woman!" V.J. admonished.

"V.J., dear you've already given us one confession, and we don't want any protestations of innocence now, thank you," Reggie said playfully.

"Besides, just like the rest of us," Dianne drawled, "V.J. could be lying."

"She could be," Jon said. "And Anna Lee, as Sally Sadist, could still be guilty, along with Thayer as JoJo Scuchi, Sabrina, the Duchess, running her covert operations, and, of course..."

"Who are we missing?" Joe asked with a frown.

"Me," Jon said simply. "Demented Dick. I think I'll be guilty till the end, don't you?" he asked lightly, gazing at Sabrina.

She looked away.

"Everybody happy with the way we've ended things for tonight?" he inquired.

"No," Reggie said. "I want to solve a mystery."

Jon pounced. "Good. So do I. So let's go talk to Susan."

"Susan isn't a mystery," Dianne complained. "Just a bitch."

"We had our peaceful dinner," Jon said firmly. "And now…" He rose determinedly. The others looked unhappy, but he knew they would follow suit.

He left the great hall and started up the stairs. He was aware of Sabrina's scent as she fell in slightly behind him, of Tom murmuring something to V.J., of Brett bemoaning the fact that the evening had been going so nicely and now they were going to go and spoil it all.

He reached the second floor and Susan's room. They were all silent. He rapped sharply on the door.

"Susan!"

No answer.

He looked at the others, rapped hard again. "Susan, it's Jon. I'd like to talk to you, just to make sure you're all right!"

Again, no answer.

"I told you!" Sabrina whispered. "She doesn't want anything to do with any of us."

"She thinks we're all monsters," Anna Lee said.

"Well, on that score," Brett considered, "she just might be right. I mean, we can be pretty horrible."

"Speak for yourself!" Reggie told him.

"I think he is speaking for himself," Anna Lee teased.

"Hush, woman," Brett commanded.

"Hush, all of you," Jon said sternly. "I can't hear if she's giving me an answer or not. Susan!" he called out again.

"Let's just leave her," Dianne pleaded.

He shook his head. "No, Dianne, we can't." He rapped his fist against the door with determination. "Damn it, Susan, if you don't answer me, I'm coming in!"

Still Susan didn't reply.

"Do we break the door down?" Thayer asked.

Jon smiled. "No, we use the master key. Susan!" he called, giving her one more chance, in case she was in the bathroom, or naked, or doing a mud facial, or something equally personal.

She'd kill him.

What if she had on head phones or something of the kind and simply couldn't hear him? He'd be invading her privacy. And maybe she did just hate the hell out of all of them and want to be left alone.

But he was worried.

Totally, completely uneasy.

This just wasn't right.

What if she had hurt herself? What if she had fallen, cried out for help, and none of them had heard her? What if she had slipped in the shower? What if she lay, injured and bleeding, on the shower floor, her blood trickling with water down the drain?

There were too many what-ifs to be concerned about her right to privacy.

He felt a sudden shiver rake his spine, an unpleasant sensation that made him more and more concerned that something was really wrong.

Sabrina was upset about blood.

Too much blood, she'd implied.

There hadn't been that much blood. But it had been on his robe. What the hell did that mean?

Was there a killer among them? In his mind's eye, he could suddenly see the worst. The killer had gotten to Susan, and she was lying on her bed, blood dripping down the sheets from the stab wounds that perforated her body.

He frowned, looking at the others.

"We've got to do it."

He turned the key in the lock and opened Susan's door. And, stepping into her room, he looked around.

A collective gasp sounded behind him.

And he saw what was there.

18

Nothing.

No body upon the sheets.

No endlessly running water.

No blood.

No grisly scene.

Nothing at all. No sign of Susan whatsoever.

"Well, where the hell is she?" V.J. demanded.

"Susan?" Sabrina called. She glanced at Jon, then walked farther into the room, pushing open the bathroom door, which already stood ajar. "Susan?"

"She simply isn't here," Dianne said flatly.

"Well, where the hell could she be?" Joe asked impatiently.

"She's probably been tiptoeing around, spying on us, trying to see how we reacted to her disappearance so that she could really do a number on us all," Anna Lee said.

"It's a big castle," Sabrina said. "She could be anywhere."

"That's just it. She could be anywhere," Jon said.

"Why are we so worried about her?" Tom demanded irritably. "Let's let her wander around and fume and be a bitch. I tried to be decent to her. I stood guard while she showered, and she went ballistic at me anyway, calling me and V.J. perverts for bursting in on her privacy. I'm sorry, Jon, but I've just about had it with her. She's beginning to make Cassie look like a goddamned saint."

They all stood very still, looking at Tom, who was seldom so passionately angry or bitter.

V.J. slipped her hand into his. "But, Tom, maybe she's hurt."

"We can only hope," he muttered.

"You don't mean that," V.J. said.

He sighed and threw up his hands. "All right, let's go search for her, Jon, if that's what you want."

"We should divide up, I think," Thayer suggested.

"Yes, I think so," Jon agreed. "We'd be ridiculous, all of us trooping behind one another around the castle, crashing into each other."

"I'm not going anywhere alone," Dianne said determinedly.

"No, of course not," Jon said impatiently. "We'll go in groups of two or three." He paused. "Reggie, maybe you should lock yourself in and—"

"Jon Stuart, quit acting as if I'm an invalid or so old that I should be stuffed!" Reggie protested.

"All right, then—" Jon began.

"Reggie, we just don't want you getting hurt," Dianne said gently.

"V.J. is almost as old as I am," Reggie insisted.

"Not nearly!" V.J. protested, appalled.

"Ladies, ladies!" Brett said.

"How do we split up?" Camy asked.

"Well, let's see," Jon said. "Thayer, Joe and I will take the different dungeon areas; Tom, you and Brett can check the first floor and then help V.J., Sabrina and Anna Lee search the rooms up here. Dianne, maybe you and Reggie can provide a liaison point for us in the great hall."

"I'll help you in the crypt and the chamber of horrors," Joshua said. "I know the area well."

"I'll help, too," Camy offered.

"No, Camy, why don't you hang out with Dianne and Reggie in the great hall. Or, better yet, you could go up to the attic and tell Jennie that Susan has disappeared and have her search up there."

"You know," Joe said, "being Susan and stubborn and ornery as a bull, she might have just taken off out of here, leaving us to worry about her."

"How?" Jon asked. "We're snowbound."

"Maybe she took a horse?"

"If there had been a horse missing from the stables, Angus would have said so."

"Maybe she sneaked out since we came back in," Joshua suggested. "The weather has improved a lot."

"It's a possibility, but I doubt it," Jon said. "Susan was never suicidal. The snow is deep, and it's a very long way even to the village. And if I remember right, Susan is not overly fond of horses. Tom," he said, reaching into his pocket, "here's the master key. Let's start searching, shall we?"

He stared at Sabrina, then turned and led the way down the stairs.

* * *

Sabrina didn't want to be a doubting Thomas. The way Jon had looked at her made her feel terrible. His gaze had gone cold, hard, his eyes like marble defenses that kept her from his heart or soul. She didn't want to throw him away again....

But she didn't want to toss aside her own life either. Logic argued that she had to be mistrustful. She didn't want to be a fool. And the more she thought about it, the more bothered she was. There had been blood on Jon's robe, much more blood than there should have been.

She was afraid, as well, that his robe still lay on the foot of her bed, that the others would see it—and the blood. She was afraid, yet she wanted to protect him at the same time.

"Well, how should we do this?" Brett asked.

"Stick together and go room to room," V.J. said. "You're welcome to rip mine apart first."

"Are we supposed to think that one of us has Susan hidden under a bed?" Brett demanded. "Not me, thank you. I have been known for some rather shameful sexual exploits, but I have never sunk so low."

"Well, that's questionable," V.J. murmured.

"Children, children, no squabbling," Reggie said.

"You and Dianne get to the great hall, where you're supposed to be. Camy, head on upstairs and see Jennie and the girls, and we'll get started here," Sabrina said.

"Right," Camy said. She, Dianne and Reggie started out. V.J. walked to her door and opened it. She strode into the room with the others behind, going so far as to lift the bed skirt. "No Susan, you will note."

Anna Lee walked into the bathroom, pulling back the shower curtain. "Susan?"

"She's not here," Brett said. "Not unless V.J. managed to dismember her and so totally roast her in the fireplace that there's nothing left of her but ash."

V.J. stared at him.

"How dare you—" Tom began.

"I was just teasing!" Brett protested. "I mean, it's obvious that Susan isn't here."

"Let's move on," Sabrina suggested.

"Jon's suite is at the end of the hall. Let's start there and work back this way," Tom said.

"Sure."

The five of them headed down the hall, Tom in the lead.

Sabrina hadn't been in Jon's room before.

She liked it very much.

A four-poster, king-size bed on an elegant dais dominated the main room, which was done in shades of deep blue and crimson. Antique tapestries and family arms adorned the walls.

There was nothing left of Cassie here.

There were two dressing rooms. One contained Jon's clothing. The other, exceptionally large, he apparently used as his office. The room overlooked the courtyard and had a doorway to the balcony; it was complete with word processor, printer, fax, phone, copier, shelves and files. Books he was currently using for research were piled atop his desk, along with notes and memos. Sabrina found herself wanting to touch his swivel chair, riffle his papers, delve into his very thoughts.

"Check this out!" Anna Lee said. She was standing at the door to the bathroom.

"Why? Is Susan hanging in the shower?" Brett demanded.

"No, just look at this place!" Anna Lee said.

They walked over to see.

"God, it's divine!" Anna Lee gushed.

It was. It boasted a huge whirlpool, sauna, shower, beautiful fixtures, black, gold, red, and white tiles, handsome mirrors, and fluffy towels on warmers.

He had lived here with Cassandra, Sabrina thought. It was wonderful, rich, and she could just imagine having all this with someone she loved. Except...

Cassie had gone off the balcony just steps from this place....

"You mean, you haven't seen this bathroom before?" Brett quizzed Anna Lee.

"No. What would I be doing in Jon's bathroom?" she inquired, puzzled.

Brett stared at Anna Lee. "You were sleeping with Cassie, right?"

Anna Lee stared back at him, her hands on her hips. "Yeah, right. But she came to me." She hesitated a minute, biting her lower lip. Then she sighed, her shoulders drooping. "She wouldn't see anybody here. It was...kind of sacred to her, I guess."

As Sabrina stared at Anna Lee, V.J. began to hustle them along. "Well, come on, let's make sure Susan isn't stashed here anywhere and move on. Tom, let's be thorough. Check under the bed. Girls, look everywhere.''

They went through the master suite again, then they all stared at the balcony doors.

Evidently no one wanted to walk out them.

Sabrina sighed. "I'll do it."

She stepped outside.

The night air seemed frigid, and she wrapped her arms around herself. The wind had risen again. It was keening. If Susan had decided to take off and leave the castle, she was surely an icicle by now.

There was nothing on the balcony. No one. And yet, of course, it was from here, the exact place where Sabrina now stood, that Cassie had plummeted to her death. Sabrina was disturbed by the sensation sweeping through her, a sudden, uncanny fear that someone was ready to push her. She spun around.

The others were where they had been. Waiting for her.

She remembered that somewhere in this room was a door to a secret passageway.

Maybe there were other secrets.

Maybe someone *was* watching her.

And maybe she was losing her wits.

"No one here. Let's move on, huh?" she said.

"Yeah, right, let's," Tom said.

"Dianne's room is next," V.J. announced.

"I'll just run down the hall to the top of the stairway and shout down to Reggie and Dianne and see if they have any messages from the boys down below," Anna Lee said.

"Okay," Tom agreed.

Four of them stepped into Dianne's room.

Dianne was not a neat freak. Her dressing table was strewn with brushes, combs, makeup and assorted toiletries. Her notepad computer was set up on a table by the window.

Clothing was scattered on the bed and chairs; shoes littered the floor.

"Susan couldn't possibly be in here," Brett said. "No room for her."

"I'll look in the bathroom. You boys check under the bed," V.J. told them.

Brett lifted the bed skirt. He suddenly yelped, and the others came crashing around him.

"What, what?" Tom demanded. "Brett, are you all right? What did you find?"

Brett drew himself up from his position by the bed. "Her dildo bit me."

"Oh!" V.J. cried in aggravation, belting him on the shoulder. "Will you be serious!"

"Actually, I was trying not to be so serious," Brett told her. "V.J., I am positive that Dianne isn't hiding Susan in this room!"

"But maybe Susan is hiding herself for some reason, slipping from room to room, place to place," Sabrina suggested.

"Let's keep going. At this rate, it will be the end of the week before we get anywhere at all!" Tom said, disgruntled. "And I want to get some sleep."

"Sleep? Oh, bull. The cat's out of the bag. You want to get back into the sack with V.J.!" Brett said.

"McGraff, you bloody—" Tom began, but V.J. stepped in, a hand on his shoulder.

"Tom, be understanding. Brett is merely jealous. He's not accustomed to being the only one without companionship. Poor dear, night after night he lies there, twiddling his thumbs—and whatever else— while right next door the love of his life is—how did he put it?—in the sack with someone else."

"Low blow," Brett protested.

"Then learn to be nice," V.J. warned.

"We need to keep going," Sabrina reminded them.

"All right, love of my life, let's move on," Brett said.

They moved on.

Joshua's room revealed art tools, a covered easel, a work in clay. But no Susan. Camy's room, with her big desk and tons of paperwork, was kept neat and tidy. But no Susan appeared.

Anna Lee rejoined them. Nothing had been reported from below.

They looked into Joe's room—a total disaster. Thayer's room, regimental, his toiletries sparse, his clothes neatly hung. Tom's room, neither as haphazard as Joe's nor in such precise order as Thayer's. Still no Susan.

Anna Lee's proved a very personalized room, the scent of her perfume on the air, scarves here and there, jewelry in a tangle on the dresser, clothing draped gracefully about. No Susan.

Sabrina led the way into her own room, anxiously looking at the foot of her bed for the robe Jon had been wearing. The one covered in blood.

It was gone.

She didn't know whether to breathe easy or feel a greater sense of panic.

The others weren't commenting at all, just walking around, looking.

Anna Lee checked under the bed; V.J. searched the bath. Tom went out on the balcony.

"This is ridiculous," Anna Lee said. "Obviously, no one is hiding Susan in his or her room."

"I agree," Sabrina managed to murmur, sitting at the foot of her bed. "But maybe Susan is playing a trick on us, trying to hide."

"And if she is, she can hear us coming from room to room," V.J. said.

"But could she keep disappearing, just one step ahead of us all the time?" Sabrina asked.

"Who the hell knows what Susan is doing?" Tom demanded irritably.

"And," Anna Lee said, "the place is riddled with secret passages. The Scots have always been ornery— and Jon's family, being Stuarts, were into protecting the Stuarts, hiding the young prince Charles II, and, I understand, losing a few heads themselves when they supported the Jacobites. They hid priests and ministers, outlaws and so on. Maybe Susan knows more about the castle than we do."

"Well, Jon certainly knows the place," Brett said. "It is his castle."

"Hmm," Anna Lee mused. "But I did some research on so-called haunted castles in York once, and there were lots of instances where the 'hauntings' were caused when someone other than the owner knew about secret passageways and the like. Maybe Susan has discovered some deep, dark secret about the place. Better yet, maybe she's walled herself up within it somewhere."

"Now that would be fitting. Susan has never appreciated the genius of Edgar Allan Poe," Tom said.

"We've only got one room left—mine," Brett said. "Then I, for one, am going down for a drink. Then I'm coming back up to bed. Sadly, V.J., yes, alone. But I'm tired, so I'll accept my fate."

"Onward," V.J. said.

They entered Brett's room, together. Standing in the middle of it while the others walked around, Sabrina stared at the wardrobe, remembering how afraid she had been the night before.

Brett had been gone. Jon had been gone. Everyone, it had seemed, was walking the halls.

Shaving—in the middle of the night.

Or cutting themselves on lamps or the like.

But she had stared at the wardrobe, afraid, thinking that there might be someone inside it.

Someone ready to jump out at her.

Or someone unable to do so. Someone who lay cut, slashed, still bleeding...

"Under the bed?" V.J. asked Tom.

"Nothing."

"Bathroom's empty," Anna Lee said.

Sabrina suddenly felt her heart pounding. The wardrobe still haunted her.

She walked toward it.

"Sabrina!" Brett said sharply.

She ignored him and threw open the wardrobe.

It was his castle. The crypt contained his dead relatives.

Jon had never been afraid of the dead. Years and years ago, when he'd been a young child, his father had reassured him after he'd seen a horror flick. *Don't ever be afraid of the dead, son. They're the safest people around, they can't do you harm anymore. Ever. Sometimes, son, you do, however, need to be afraid of the living.*

Jon believed in God, in a supreme being, but he didn't believe that God had people come back as spirits to haunt the living. He wasn't superstitious. He'd never felt the least fear while walking any part of this, his family's ancient castle. He'd loved it since he'd come into his special inheritance. There was no part of the brick, stone, mortar or wood that had ever made him uneasy.

Until tonight.

The chapel was evidently empty. Nevertheless, they combed the pews, looked behind the altar, peered through all the shadows.

They walked the bowling alleys, even checked the mechanisms for the pins, and approached the pool area together.

"Well, she didn't drown," Thayer said as they gazed into the water.

"Nope, apparently not," Joe agreed.

"Did you look in the men's room?" Jon asked Joshua.

"And the ladies' too. Rest rooms are empty," Josh reported.

"Well, the crypt is next, I guess," Joe said. He actually sounded uneasy.

"Yeah, I guess." Big, tough ex-cop Thayer sounded uneasy, too.

Jon led the way. They came in with kerosene lamps, lifting them high to dispel the gloom around the tombs. They methodically began to walk along the rows of the dead.

"Susan isn't here," Jon said at last.

"I never thought she would be," Thayer said gruffly. "She's got a big mouth, but she can be your basic chicken. Dianne might have the balls to come down here alone and pretend to be her mother's ghost, but Susan wouldn't be caught dead in a place like this."

Silence followed his words.

"Dead, you have no choice," Joshua finally said. He turned to Jon. "There is no sign of her whatsoever, Jon. As furious as she was, maybe she did take off into the snow. Maybe she did make it down to the village, and maybe she's sipping a hot toddy and watching the latest flick on the telly."

"Yeah, maybe," Jon said. But he didn't believe it.

Not for a minute. "Let's move on to the chamber of horrors."

"Oh, yeah, let's, can't wait," Joe said.

The words broke the ice. The four laughed, recognizing their false machismo and owning up to a certain unease.

Joshua led the way into the chamber.

The others began to walk around.

Jon stood by the entry, staring down the rows of frozen tableaux. Nothing looked out of order. Nothing at all.

It was very cold. The temperature was supposed to be kept cool here to preserve the wax figures, and with the power gone, the rooms were shut down completely. But the cold wasn't what bothered him, though he couldn't quite say what was.

He walked into the room, moving among the tableaux. The others moved about as well, lamps held high.

"Susan, here Susie, Susie!" Joe called.

"Come out, come out, wherever you are!" Thayer added.

Their words seemed to ricochet off the stone walls. The men took different aisles, crossed each other's paths. It was eerie, the way the wax figures stared down at them.

So very real.

Joshua was standing in front of the tableau of Lady Ariana Stuart being tortured on the rack.

"I am good," Joshua said, realizing that Jon stood by him. "Damn good." He shrugged. "Either that or it's a dark and stormy night, the lighting sucks, I'm a scaredy cat and I'm beginning to see my own work come alive.''

Thayer came up to them, clapping Joshua on the shoulder. "You're good. You're that damn bloody good. V.J. over there looks as if she's about to have us all for supper. I hate to admit it, but this place is giving me the chills. Cold as a witch's tit in here. Jon, think we can go back up? Nothing's stirring down here."

"We've walked every aisle," Joe said, reaching them. Despite the cold, little beads of sweat had broken out over his brow. "No one is here."

"So where the hell do you think she is?" Thayer asked.

"I don't know," Jon said, moving at last to exit the chamber. The others managed to squeeze out ahead of him. He almost smiled, but as he closed the double doors as they left, he felt a curious chill along his spine, and he paused, reopening the doors and lifting his lamp one more time.

Nothing. And yet something subtle was plaguing him. He didn't know what. But something was just slightly wrong. He had a sense of...

He didn't know what.

He closed the doors, shaking his head impatiently. And he followed the others up the stairs to the ground floor and the great hall.

Dianne was playing solitaire, a huge glass of wine in front of her.

Reggie was sitting at the table, drumming her fingers, looking entirely peeved. Camy, too, sat at the table, her head resting upon her folded arms. She looked up when the men came in.

"Jennie and the girls say they haven't seen hide nor hair of Susan," Camy said.

"Nothing down below," Thayer said cheerfully.

"And nothing here except for three tired, bitchy broads," Reggie informed them.

Jon smiled. "Anyone for a drink?" He started to pour himself a whiskey.

That's when they heard the shriek from above.

Sabrina screamed, jumping back as a head bounced out of the wardrobe at her.

Long hair splayed everywhere.

"Sabrina! It's a mannequin head—and a wig!" Brett said, coming up behind her, slipping an arm around her.

It was.

A white plastic head, a black wig.

"Hey, honey, it's okay!" V.J. told her.

Sabrina felt like an idiot. It was, indeed, just as Brett had said. She stared at the wardrobe. Why the hell had she gotten in into her mind that something awful was going to be found in that wardrobe? It was simply so stuffed with clothing that opening it had caused the head to bounce from a top shelf.

As she stared at it, still trembling, the others burst into the room, Jon in the lead, Thayer behind him, Joshua, Joe, and even Dianne and poor Reggie, puffing away to keep up.

"What? What is it? What happened?" Jon demanded.

"Nothing, nothing," Sabrina said quickly. "I just scared myself silly."

Jon walked over to the fallen foam head and picked it up and the wig. He looked at Brett. "Not yours, I take it?"

Brett shook his head. "Not my color."

Jon walked to the wardrobe, surveying the contents. "I hadn't realized these things were here," he said.

"They were Cassie's?" V.J. asked.

"Yeah. Sorry, Brett, we didn't leave you with much space for your things."

"My needs are few and simple," Brett said.

"Yeah, right!" V.J. exclaimed with a laugh.

"Well…no sign of Susan, right?" Tom said to the others.

"Not a single hair off her head," Joe answered.

Jon stopped in front of Sabrina. "Are you all right?"

She nodded. "I just feel like a fool."

"We're all on edge."

"And you were fixing drinks, remember?" Thayer reminded him.

"Yeah," Jon said, his eyes still curiously dark on Sabrina's. He turned then and left the room. Everyone traipsed after him.

Joshua helped him mix drinks. "Believe it or not," he commented, "we're finally running low on ice."

"I don't need ice," Joe told him, and he helped himself to two shots of bourbon.

Sabrina opted for a Tia Maria. As she accepted a glass and moved away, Jon said, "We've still got to find Susan."

"But not tonight!" V.J. told him.

"No, I suppose not," Jon said with a sigh. He glanced at his watch. Sabrina looked up at the clock over the mantel. Nearly 1:00 a.m.

"Joshua, Thayer, tomorrow we'll take the horses out and see if she did wander off somehow. Within another twenty-four to forty-eight hours, the roads should be cleared, and the electricity and phones should be back. But if she's out there..." he began unhappily.

"If she's out there without heat and shelter, she's already dead. And we'd probably freeze to death looking for her if we tried it now. And we'd never see a damned thing in the dark anyway," Joe said.

It was true, Sabrina thought. They were done for the night. Jon knew it; he just didn't seem to like it.

"Well, then, everyone, let's call it a night, shall we?" He looked at Sabrina.

She drew her eyes from his, not wanting to face him. *The robe was gone!* she wanted to shout. *Your robe, with the blood all over it.*

She started for the stairs instead.

An hour later the old castle was silent except for the creaks and groans that haunted its ancient stones and timbers every night.

Sabrina paced her room.

They were all locked in, weary, in need of a night's rest.

She waited. Afraid that he would come. Afraid that he would not.

They had searched the whole castle.

Except for the secret places. The places only Jon knew. She wanted to shout at him, and she wanted to run away. Except that…he didn't come.

Then, when she had walked toward the balcony, she suddenly felt his presence, and when she turned, he was there.

She kept her distance, staring at him. Tall, imposing, handsome, sexy, he was in a different robe, dark hair damp, with a fluff of hair showing at the V of his lapels.

He watched her gravely. "Do you want me to leave?" he asked.

"Your robe was gone," she stated. "The one with the blood all over it."

"My housekeeping staff is very good," he told her.

"Ah…you didn't make sure it was removed?" she asked him.

"No," he said, walking toward her. "Did you find a bloody corpse anywhere, and you're simply not sharing that information with us?"

Her eyes fell. He was in front of her. She could smell his soap, his aftershave, something more uniquely him. She felt an instant melting sensation within, and she knew that she wanted him. And if he touched her…

"Where have you been?" she demanded suspiciously.

He tilted his head. "Trying to make a thorough search of the place. I've just been through all the hidden passageways."

Logical. She had been thinking herself that the passageways should be searched.

However...

He had done so alone.

"Are you afraid of me?" he asked her.

"Should I be?"

He shook his head, looking at her. "No," he said firmly.

She bit her lip, not moving.

He turned around and started to leave.

She might be a fool, but she couldn't bear it. "Jon!" she cried, and she raced after him. She threw herself against his back, her arms encircling him, her chin resting against his robe. He went still for a moment, then turned. And as he did so, she fumbled for the belt of his robe, tugging it free. She buried her face against his chest, slid her hands along his ribs, over his hips. He was naked beneath the robe. The brush of her fingers brought him to an immediate erection, and she cradled it with her hands. She looked up at last, ready to meet his lips as he lifted her chin and kissed her.

She sank against him, kissing him everywhere, barely aware of his guttural moans as she slid down his torso and closed her mouth around him. He cradled her nape, fingers tangling into her hair; then he was drawing her up, lifting her, pressing her down on the bed. And he was everywhere then, bathing her with the hunger of his lips and tongue. He allowed her no inhibitions, granted no mercy. He delved into her most intimate places, slowly, with fire, until she thrashed beneath him with a violent frenzy that brought him atop her, staring down as he slowly penetrated her, watching her eyes, feeling himself sink within her, feeling her sheath him. Then she closed her eyes and felt the searing exhilaration of his passion as he began to move with an ever increasing pace within her.

When it was over she lay spent and exhausted in his arms, thinking that she loved him desperately.

And wishing that she did not.

He didn't speak. He kept his arms around her.

Thus entangled, they slept.

Almost two hours later Jon awoke with a jolt.

He sat up and looked around. For a moment, he was confused. What had awakened him?

Then he realized that he'd had the uncanny feeling of being watched.

He gave himself a shake.

Sabrina slept on, sweetly, beautifully at his side, her naked body curved to his.

And still…

There was nothing. No strange sound in the night. No strange scent. Just a feeling that they hadn't been alone, that someone had stood there, watching them sleep.…

He rose, donned his robe and slipped into the secret passageway.

Reggie was old but not dead. Yet.

And they were all missing something, the fools.

When she was certain that everyone was asleep, she rose. She buttoned her velour robe warmly about her and donned her comfy yellow slippers. She had a really good flashlight, and she reached for that.

Thus armed, she left her bedroom.

The hallway was silent.

Dead silent.

There weren't going to be any clues on this floor, she was convinced. She went down to the main level, glancing into the dimly lit great hall, then the library.

Not a creature was stirring, she thought. Except for maybe a few mice, she decided with some humor. And maybe a few great big rats! It was a very old castle.

In the great hall, she plucked up one of the heavy candleholders from the table. Brass bludgeon in one hand, flashlight in the other, she was ready to take on the world. Not that she thought she needed to take on anyone. Even monsters had to sleep. She just wanted to be prepared.

She journeyed down to the level below.

The pool rippled in the dim light. The bowling alleys were silent.

In the chapel, she crossed herself.

In the crypt, she prayed for the dead.

In the chamber of horrors...she met the murderer.

She was deep into the room, looking...for what, she didn't know. She liked mystery, loved mystery, and she intended to solve this one.

She did.

And then...

She heard something. A slight sound. And she turned. And faced the killer.

She never screamed. Nor did the killer even touch her. She didn't give the murderer the satisfaction of killing again.

The explosive pain in her chest ripped into her with the power of an atom bomb. Thankfully, the agony was fast. She couldn't breathe. She stared; she felt her eyes popping.

Then she fell.

She heard the killer's laughter, and she knew she was dying.

The killer thought she was *already* dead.

But not yet...

Not yet.

19

Sun streamed through the window.

Sabrina awoke slowly, aware of dazzling rays of light penetrating the room. She was aware, as well, of the warm body beside her, and she twisted, glad that Jon was with her. Yet, as she turned, she saw that he was awake already, staring up at the ceiling with a frown.

The frown left his face when he realized she was studying him, and he turned to her. "Hi."

"Hi yourself."

"You made it through the night," he told her softly.

"Yes. Meaning...?"

"Well, you don't really trust me, do you?"

"Yes...it's just that..."

"There was blood on my robe." He shrugged. "Well, we should be out of here soon. We can have a forensics expert check it out."

He sounded bitter. She didn't want him to be bitter.

"You'll admit, there's a lot of unusual stuff going on around here."

"A lot of mysteries to be solved. People are confessing to all kinds of things, but we still seem to be missing one simple truth.''

"What really happened to Cassie? And now, of course, where the hell has Susan gone?''

She sat up, hugging sheets and knees to her as she looked at him. "I was actually really tired and slept through the night. Were you here all night, or did you disappear?''

He arched a brow, hesitated, then admitted, "I disappeared for a while.''

"Oh?''

He nodded. "Remember how you told me that you thought someone had been in this room watching you, and I told you that it hadn't been me?''

"Yes, of course. I never saw anyone, though. It was just a feeling.''

"Well, I woke up with that same feeling.''

She arched a brow at him. "It is your castle, and you're the king of it, remember? Who else could have been in here?''

"I don't know. But I didn't like the feeling. It was very uncomfortable.''

"So you went running around in the dark to see if anyone else was up again, right?''

"Yeah, more or less.''

"Well, were other people up, running around the castle?''

He nodded grimly.

"Who?''

"Well, actually, you were one of only two people to sleep through the night.''

"Oh?"

"As I left here, Anna Lee was just coming from Joe's room."

"Why?"

"I don't know, and I didn't ask."

"Go on."

"Camy was up working, and V.J., Tom, Brett, Dianne and Joshua were in the great hall, chowing down on midnight snacks. Apparently, you and Reggie were the only people sleeping. I seem to be hosting a party of night owls."

"So you all had a party without Reggie and me, huh?"

He nodded, then grinned. "They decided that I was the killer."

She felt her heart pound against her chest. But they were talking about the game, of course. "Are you the killer?"

"I can't tell you. We decided not to admit or deny anything until we were all together again."

"But when—" she began.

"Later, this evening. I've got to get up and get going. I'm going to take Joshua and Thayer with me and see if we can figure out if Susan did try to leave here. Though why she would leave notes to people if she meant to walk out into mountains of snow…"

"Why would she?" Sabrina asked.

"I don't think she would."

"Then where could she be?"

"I don't know. And I admit I'm growing more and more afraid of finding out. Still, after searching the castle last night, it only makes sense to ride around the general area and look for her. So I guess I should get up, huh?''

She nodded. He kept staring at her. She laughed suddenly and moved into his arms. It seemed a unique opportunity, waking up beside him. One not to be wasted. To just slide into his arms and make love was a temptation not to be resisted.

Yet afterward, he didn't linger. He rose, showered quickly, kissed her, walked away, came back, kissed her once again, then hurried out by way of the secret passage. When he was gone, she bounded to her feet, showered and dressed in jeans, a cashmere pullover, boots and a heavy jacket.

She hurried downstairs and found that she was the last to arrive in the great hall. Despite their lack of power, Jennie Albright was still whisking up wonderful meals. As Camy handed her coffee, she saw that the others were already dining on eggs, ham, salmon, crispy potatoes, and toast cooked in little metal baskets that went over the open fire.

''You look as if you're ready for the outdoors,'' Brett told her.

''Yeah, I am. Cooped up too long. I want to take a walk down to the stables.''

''You're not coming with us,'' Jon told her.

She arched a brow. ''Why not?''

''Because Joshua and I know where we're going, where to ride, where it's dangerous and where it's not.''

''I know how to ride.''

"But you don't know this terrain."

"What about Thayer?"

"I spent a lot of time riding last time I was here," Thayer told her apologetically. "Before..." He looked away uncomfortably.

"Before Cassie was killed," Jon said bluntly. "Let's go," he told the others, and they left the great hall.

Sabrina watched them go. Brett came up behind her. "He's afraid for you."

"Why?"

"That's easy, isn't it?"

She turned around and looked at him. Brett smiled. "He's in love with you," he said. He shrugged. "Anyway, want to build a snowman?"

She hesitated for a moment. "Yeah, sure, why not."

The went outside. The air remained icy, despite the sun, but still, it felt good. Once again the others began wandering out. V.J. and Tom remained by the doors, but Camy, Anna Lee, Dianne and Joe came out and joined them in creating a huge snowman. Then when Dianne missed while in the process of adding a wad of snow to their creature's midsection, sending the snow all over Brett, their artistic endeavors deteriorated into another major snowball fight.

Finally, though, Sabrina realized that she was way too cold. And looking up, she saw that the sun had fallen, and they were heading into late afternoon. "Hey, we're going to be frostbitten Popsicles if we don't get inside!" she called.

"I think my nose is already gone. I can't feel it!" Dianne claimed.

"Mine was too big anyway," Joe said. "But I need my feet, and I can't feel them anymore, either!"

Laughing and drenched, they returned to the house. By then, V.J. had gone in. She was pacing in the entryway. Sabrina smiled at her. "I'm soaked!"

"That's what happens when children play," she said, but she looked distracted.

"What's the matter?"

"Reggie hasn't come down yet."

"Well, I'm going to take a shower and change. Walk up with me and see if she's in her room."

"All right."

In the hallway, they parted, Sabrina heading for her room, V.J. walking down the hall to Reggie's. Sabrina heard V.J. knocking, but then closed her door.

Well aware that the hot water wouldn't last forever—and that several of them were thawing in it right now—Sabrina showered quickly. As she wrapped a towel around herself, she heard a banging at her door. "Yes?" she called out.

"It's me. V.J."

Sabrina opened her door, and V.J. walked in, tense and worried. She was carrying a kerosene lamp, and she lit it as she spoke. The shadows were taking them from afternoon to evening.

"Reggie isn't in her room," V.J. said.

"What's going on?" came another voice. Brett, freshly showered as well, had just come into the hall and stood at Sabrina's open doorway.

"I'm worried about Reggie," V.J. said.

"Hang on, I'll get dressed, and we'll start another search party," Sabrina said.

She grabbed her clothing and hurried into the bathroom. Brett had followed V.J. into the room, and the two were talking.

"I mean, Susan might choose to disappear, but not Reggie," V.J. announced firmly.

"V.J., calm down," Brett said.

As Sabrina zipped herself into dry jeans and stepped from the bathroom, V.J. was shaking her head. "You don't understand. Reggie pretends to be so tough, but she's on all kinds of heart medication."

"Does Jon know that?" Sabrina asked.

"Jon always seems to suspect when something is wrong, but Reggie's so stubborn. I think she lied like crazy to Jon, telling him she was in wonderful shape so he wouldn't leave her out of things—which he would have if he thought she was failing in the least. But I know something has happened to Reggie. I just know it."

"All right, where might she be?" Brett asked.

"Well, she's not in the great room or the library or her room," V.J. said.

"I guess we go downstairs. To the dungeon," Sabrina said. She wondered why she was more and more loath to do so.

"Let's go," Brett said.

V.J. and Sabrina followed him out into the hallway. Joe, also freshly showered, was coming from his room. "What's up?"

"We can't find Reggie," V.J. said. "Want to help us on another hunt?"

"Sure. Where's Tom?"

"In the library. He probably thinks I'm with Reggie now," V.J. said.

"Well, let's get Tom and start searching again," Joe said.

"Sounds good," Brett agreed.

They went down to the library. Tom and Dianne were playing gin rummy at a table by the fire. Sabrina noticed the way Tom's face lit up when V.J. entered the room, and she wondered how either of them had ever managed to fool anyone for as long as they had.

But then, seeing the expressions on their faces, Tom frowned. "What's wrong?"

"I can't find Reggie," V.J. told him.

"We're going down below on a hunt," Joe said.

As he spoke, they heard the front doors open. Sabrina walked to the library door, looking toward the main entrance. A great blast of cold air came sweeping in along with Jon, Joshua and Thayer. They looked worn and freezing. All had red noses and runny eyes.

"No luck?" Brett asked, though the answer was obvious.

"No luck," Jon said, unwinding a scarf from around his neck. "You can see down the cliff, though, that the road crews in the village have dug through some of the major blockages. We could be out by tomorrow." He sounded relieved.

"Damn, I gotta get to the fire!" Thayer exclaimed,

making his way through to the library. "This is terrible. I may have to sue. I think my balls are frozen."

Sabrina smiled as he hurried by her. Then she met Jon's eyes, and she saw the hard, dark concern in them.

"What's going on?" he asked carefully as he looked at her.

"V.J. is worried. We can't find Reggie."

"Jesus! Reggie?" he repeated.

"Yes, we were about to go down below and see if she's there for some reason."

"Damn!" Jon swore. He drew off his coat and gloves, dropping them on the hall tree. Heedless of the snow he tracked in he headed around the main staircase to the second set winding down below. Sabrina followed him, Brett at her heels and the others close behind him.

He picked up one of the lamps from a wall fixture as he hurried down the steps. "Reggie! Shit!"

"Jon?" V.J. called anxiously. "Is there something wrong, something you know?"

He paused briefly, turning back. V.J. nearly plowed into him. "Yes, there's something wrong. I should have known Reggie better. We asked her to sit in the great hall while we were looking for Susan, and I think she was insulted. She might have decided to do her own search after we went to bed. She just won't realize her age!"

V.J. went white. She was right on Jon's heels as they hurried on down the rest of the steps.

"I'll take the chapel," Joe called.

"I'm with you like glue," Dianne told him.

"Crypts," Thayer offered.

"Crypts, fine. I'll do the tombs with you," Tom said unhappily.

"Brett, try the pool, the bowling alley," Jon said, already heading into the chamber of horrors. Sabrina and V.J. were on his heels.

"Oh, Jesus, dear God!" Jon breathed as they walked into the chamber.

Because there was Reggie. Crumpled on the floor, right in front of the tableau of Lady Ariana Stuart and her torturer.

"Reggie, Reggie!" He was instantly down on his knees, carefully testing her pulse, her breathing.

"Reggie!" V.J. shrieked, dropping down beside her.

By then, the others had come hurrying in.

"Oh, God, she's dead," Joe said.

"Was she cut? Shot? What?" Thayer queried.

"No...I think it was her heart," Jon said. He still knelt by her. "Reggie, Reggie..." The emotion he had borne the writer was evident in his voice as he leaned over her again.

"She's dead, oh, God," Dianne breathed.

V.J. looked at Jon. "CPR," she said.

He shrugged. Reggie was dead. But...

V.J. bent over Reggie's face, counting, giving her oxygen, while Jon worked her heart. Suddenly, there was a strange look in his eyes. "Wait... I think...oh, God, there's a pulse. Faint as hell, but she may be breathing. V.J.! Damn! She may just be breathing!"

"We've got to be talking serious brain damage here," Dianne said. "Maybe we should just—" She broke off, because V.J. was glaring at her. "Just let her go," Dianne finished very softly.

"She may pull out of this," V.J. insisted.

"What?" Tom exclaimed.

"She may only be in a coma. She may be in shock." V.J. said impatiently. "If we can just keep her warm…"

"Let's get her upstairs," Jon said.

He lifted Reggie as if she were a small child. He carried her up both flights of stairs to her room and laid her gently on the bed. V.J. adjusted pillows, took off her slippers, began chafing her hands. Jon covered her in blankets. He hovered over her.

By then, Camy and Anna Lee had both come from their rooms to see what had happened.

"What's going on?" Camy asked.

"Reggie…" Joe began.

"Reggie's dead!" Anna Lee announced.

"No…just mostly dead," Brett said with a sigh.

"I'm going to have to go down to the village, get help up here now," Jon murmured. "It's her only chance. V.J.—you'll stay with Reggie?"

"Of course."

"But not alone. Three people with her at all times," Jon said.

"I'll take first shift," Dianne offered.

"Just keep three people with her at all times. And the rest of you, lock yourselves in or hang together."

"Jon, I can come with you," Joshua told him.

"No, I'll go faster alone," he insisted.

He turned, leaving the room. His eyes fell on Sabrina as she stood just outside the doorway, watching. He mouthed the words "Lock yourself in!" and swept on by her.

She heard his footsteps as his long strides took him swiftly down the hall.

She hesitated, then followed him.

When she reached the main floor, he was nowhere to be seen, but he hadn't yet taken his coat from the hall tree. She frowned, puzzled, then realized that he had gone back down below.

Jon hurried back down to where he had found Reggie. In his concern to grasp at any hope of keeping her alive, he had ignored something right before his eyes.

Something that hadn't registered until she had been laid out on her bed.

A kerosene lamp remained where he had left it when he had knelt down next to Reggie. It spilled its light across the floor.

Reggie's hand had lain in a little pile of dust and straw that had spilled from the tableau.

And he searched for what had nagged at him, he found it. Yes. She had tried writing in the dust. It was difficult to read—it might have just been hand spasms. But no. There were definitely letters there, formed in the dust. *R...I...P...P...C*—no, *E. RIPPE...R.* Ripper.

He sat back on his haunches, frowning, then looked toward the tableau of Jack the Ripper.

He stood, realizing what his previous sensation down here had been. It smelled like...

When an animal got caught inside and died. It was cold down here, very cold, but still...

Shit.

He started walking to the tableau. There was Jack the Ripper in his stereotypical cape and black hat. And down below him was his victim. Mary Kelly.

Not Mary Kelly.

Susan!

Dead and decaying, dressed in the clothing that had adorned the wax figure. It was real blood, not paint, that now caked the slashed throat of the victim.

Her eyes were open and staring.

There was no mistaking her condition. No hope, no chance.

Susan was dead.

"God!" he breathed aloud, and the stench and the horror of it all suddenly gripped him. He doubled over so as not to be sick. And as he did so, he realized that he was hosting a killer far more dangerous and psychotic than he had ever imagined.

There was no question now that Cassie had been killed. And that Susan had known something...

That had cost her her life.

"Fool!" Jon charged her corpse, gritting his teeth. "Susan, why didn't you just tell us the truth? Why did you play games?" He was angry with her. He was horrified. She had played with cravings to be powerful, and she had paid with her life.

"Jon?"

He heard his name called. Sabrina. Oh, God.

"Sabrina, no!" he called.

But she was there, hurrying to him.

And staring.

At Susan's open eyes. The dried blood around her throat. The horror...

And then she looked at him. And there was terror in her eyes.

20

"Oh, Jesus, oh, God!" Sabrina exclaimed. She backed away, suddenly aware of the stench of blood, of death.

She opened her mouth to scream. "No, no!" Jon commanded, his hand clamping hard over her lips. Hard, smothering.

No, no.

She'd been a fool. He *was* a murderer.

"Damn it!" he whispered to her furiously. "Don't be ridiculous. I didn't do this. I only found her now because Reggie must have had a heart attack stumbling upon the truth down here herself. She left us a clue. *R-I-P-P-E-R,* written in the dust. I've got to get her to a hospital, get help up here and get the rest of us out. She knows who the killer is. Reggie knows, do you understand?"

As he spoke, Sabrina could still see Susan. See her throat. However had they missed this? That the vicious slash, and the blood, were real? How had they not seen it before?

Because the wax figures were so good, so real. You had to be right on top of this, you had to be *smelling* this to realize. Nothing had been different here, nothing at all…except that wax had become flesh, and paint had become blood.

Jon hadn't done it. So he said. But if he had done it, he could strangle her here and now….

His hand was easing from her mouth. "I've got to get moving."

"What are we going to do? Tell the others?"

"We have to. If we don't let everyone know that we're aware Susan is dead, Reggie alive becomes even more dangerous to the killer."

He took her by the hand, and they rushed up the steps. Jon burst into the library. V.J., Tom and Dianne were absent, upstairs in Reggie's room. The others were all present.

Jon looked around at them. "We've found Susan," he said simply.

"Is she—?"

"Dead," Jon announced.

Anna Lee stood uncertainly. "Not another heart attack?"

"No. She was murdered. Her throat was slashed."

"Where?" Thayer demanded. "Why didn't we find her body before?"

"Because she's in the Jack the Ripper tableau," Jon said.

"Lord!" Joshua exclaimed. He had been drinking tea by the fire. He set down his cup, stood and raced for the stairs.

"Wait!" Jon called, following him. "Wait, Josh, don't touch her! I'm going to get the police in here!"

But Joshua was on his way down the stairs, Jon

and Thayer right after him. Joshua reached the tableau and touched Susan before they could stop him. They pulled him back, and he let out a horrible, keening sound. "Oh, my God, oh, my God..."

Sabrina had followed but remained in the doorway. Anna Lee, at her side, started to cry. "Oh, God, oh, hell, oh, God, oh...I'm going to be sick."

She turned around, hand clamped over her mouth, heading for the ladies' room.

"Don't! Don't touch her! No one touch her!" Jon said forcefully. "Joe, Thayer, help me get Josh out of here. Camy, get Dianne. Everyone, out of here!"

He ushered them all out and closed the doors. Sabrina was still feeling sick herself. She met his eyes, and he reached out a hand to her. She hesitated just briefly, then took it.

Camy had an arm around Anne Lee. Together, they headed up the steps. They moved into the library like automatons.

Jon poured Anna Lee a drink, handed it to her. He looked at Camy. "You all right?"

She nodded. "I need a brandy, but I'll get it. We'll all get drinks."

"Get your drinks, and lock yourselves into your rooms. Now. Before I go," Jon told them.

"What about V.J., Tom and Dianne?" Joe queried.

"They're together. V.J. can't be guilty. I would never have noticed Reggie's faint pulse if it weren't for her," Jon said.

"But what about Dianne?" Joe asked.

"Whoever killed Susan killed Cassie. You can

make up whatever scenarios you want, but Dianne drove me crazy to do this Mystery Week again. She isn't a killer. She certainly didn't kill her own mother. So the rest of you get to your own rooms and lock yourselves in.''

"Can I lock in with Joe?" Anna Lee asked softly. "If you'll have me," she said to Joe.

Joe smiled. "Sure, you know I will."

"Everyone up," Jon said.

They started up the stairs, paired off. Jon asked Joshua to explain the situation to Tom, V.J. and Dianne, and directed Camy to go up and tell Jennie and the girls to keep themselves locked in as well.

Joe and Anna Lee walked, hand in hand, to Joe's room.

"Guess you don't want me guarding Sabrina?" Brett said hopefully.

"Guess you'd better both just lock your doors," Jon said.

Brett stopped Sabrina. "You know I'm not a killer. A womanizer, yes. But not a killer. If you do need help while hero-man is away…" He left it at that and went into his own room.

Jon came into Sabrina's room with her. He wedged a heavy chair in front of the panel leading to the secret passageway, then hit a brick in the fireplace that caused another brick—with a drawer behind it—to pop out. A small pistol lay inside.

"Know how to use a gun?" he asked her. She shook her head. He picked up the revolver and demonstrated. "The safety is off. Grab, aim, pull the trigger. Aim, pull the trigger. It's a six-shooter."

She nodded, moistening her lips. He set the gun back in the drawer and shoved the stone back into place.

"Open it for me," he told her.

She did.

He nodded, then drew her into his arms and kissed her hard. "I'm sorry, so damn sorry!" he said after a moment. "I should have ended this whole week long ago."

"And let a killer get away? To kill and kill again? This killer is psychotic. Maybe he can be caught now."

"And Susan is dead, and Reggie may die."

"God forgive me, no one deserves a brutal death, but Susan obviously knew something, and she should have told us all what it was. And Reggie—"

"Reggie is one of the finest people I know," he said.

"And she may live."

"As may we." His eyes studied hers. "This isn't a great time, but you do have a way of disappearing on me, and so let me at least get the question in. Will you marry me?"

She opened her mouth to reply, but he set a finger on her lips. "Don't answer yet. Wait until I get back."

"Oh, God, it's so late. It's freezing out there. You'll—"

"It's all right. I could see all the road clearing

that's been done below. Damn I just knew Susan hadn't gotten that far. She hadn't gotten far at all," he said bitterly. He kissed her once again. "I love you, you know. I have since I met you."

She smiled. "I love you. And maybe Brett did have a right to seduce Cassie. You did ruin all other men for me."

"You know I'm not a killer, right?" he said, brushing her cheek.

She nodded.

"But you know that someone here is."

She nodded again. "I'll keep the door locked against everyone. And I know where the gun is." She shuddered a little.

He gazed at her, kissed her, drew away. "I've got to go."

He didn't look back. He left the room, ordering her gruffly to lock the door.

She did so.

His footsteps faded, and the castle became silent.

For a while, she paced. Then she sat. Tried to read. Time seemed endless. She looked at her watch, certain that hours had gone by.

Thirty minutes.

It would take forever for Jon to get back.

She started pacing again, then hesitated, certain she had heard a sound. She had. A scraping sound. Very soft. Almost indiscernible. She walked to her door, laid her ear against it, closed her eyes, listened.

A squeak. A scrape. Like a door sliding open.

She realized that the sound wasn't coming from outside the room, but inside.

She spun around. And she knew why she had felt she was being watched before. She knew why Jon had felt the sensation.

There was a second false panel, on the other side of the room, flanking the right side of the balcony. It was open, and Brett stood there now.

His face was chalk white. Drawn. She watched in horror as he started walking toward her.

"Brett…Brett…what…?"

So it was Brett! He was the killer! Oh, God! She had to scream, get to her door, get help….

Jon had his horse saddled in the stables when he felt a touch on his shoulder. He spun around, mentally bracing himself, aware that the murderer could have followed him to stop him.

But it was old Angus. "Sir?"

"I've got a dying woman in there, Angus, and something worse. A murderer."

"Yer wife's killer, sir?"

He looked at Angus and nodded slowly.

"We'll get him, sir. We will."

"I have to ride out, Angus."

"Sir, there's something you should know first," Angus told him gravely, a very slight smile playing at his lips.

Sabrina never got the chance to scream.

Brett pitched forward into her arms, crying her

name. "Sabrina!"

His eyes closed. And she realized that he was covered in blood from a wound in his back.

"Brett!" Stumbling beneath his weight, she got him to her bed. Frantically, she tried to staunch the wound. He was unconscious. She was so involved with her frenzied efforts that she didn't see or hear anything at first as she wadded a pillowcase, her nightgown and then bedcovers to bind his wound.

Then she heard the sound.

And she realized that someone had come in after Brett.

Someone in a cloak and a top hat, wielding a huge knife that dripped blood.

Standing at the foot of her bed.

She couldn't see a face, just a scarf tied over the nose and mouth, the hat brim pulled low. The figure blocked her exit. And it was moving toward her.

She could scream, but she'd never get help in time.

There was only one way out. The secret passage.

And she had no idea where it led.

No choice.

She screamed as loudly as she could for good measure, then sprinted toward the open panel and the passageway.

Jon reentered the castle by way of the basement storm doors that led through a short passage to the furnace, the water system and then into the chapel.

Among the old vestments there he found a large

black hooded cape. Wrapped in it, he made his way back into the chamber of horrors. He surveyed each tableau, deciding where he should wait.

He turned.

And from the corner of his eye, he saw movement.

A wax figure was moving. The torturer from the Lady Ariana Stuart display. The figure suddenly jumped out at him.

Wielding a knife.

He caught the figure's arm. They grappled to the floor, exchanging blows. The knife rose and fell. Jon moved quickly, yet felt a slash against his thigh. He gritted his teeth at the pain, praying he wasn't losing too much blood. The killer was aiming at him again. He shielded himself with a blow to the creature's arm and got in a good shot to the jaw. The knife flew across the floor. The killer rose, ran after the knife, turned.

Footsteps. Someone was coming. From somewhere within the walls of the castle.

The accomplice?

If he was attacked by two of them...

He heard gasping, crying, screaming. Someone running from someone in pursuit.

Jesus!

He swung his fist again.

Despite the dark and her staggering, desperate terror, Sabrina knew where they were headed.

The dungeon.

It was still dark where the winding stairs ended,

with nothing but hard wall in front of her. In a panic, she began beating at it.

Miraculously, a panel gave. She burst out from the passageway...

And into the chamber of horrors.

Jack the Ripper was gone. Susan still lay dead.

She heard movement behind her. The killer. Jack the Ripper, come to life!

"No!" she screamed, and she turned to run. He caught her by the hair, spinning her back around. She struggled desperately, fighting, scratching. She heard a grunt, a groan.

He forced her against a tableau. She saw her own face as she was pressed downward. Saw more rope as the killer struggled to reach it, bind her so that he could kill her at his leisure....

She screamed and screamed...

And realized that the torturer above her was alive as well.

Jon.

He suddenly leaped down upon her assailant, and the two went flying across the floor, battling intensely.

A knife went flying. Sabrina scurried to retrieve it, but it slid into the straw beneath the wax tableau. Jon and the figure pummeled one another with their fists. Sabrina scrambled through the straw, gave up the search and looked for something else with which she might attack the killer.

Then she heard a sickening crunch.

One of the cloaked figures went down. The other turned to her, drawing back his cowl.

"Jon!"

She cried his name and went racing toward him. He caught her in his arms. "Oh, God, oh, God!" At first, she just kissed him. Then she drew back. "But who...?"

"Joshua," he said softly.

"Joshua killed Cassie?" she said incredulously.

"No!"

The downed figure struggled up to his elbows. Joshua's handsome face was sporting mean bruises. His eyes were both blackening; his nose was crooked and swollen. Talking was obviously an effort. He was winded, broken.

"No, I didn't kill Cassie," he said. "But..."

"Camy killed her," Jon finished. "And you killed Susan to protect her."

Joshua laughed, then choked. "No, Camy killed Susan, too. And Reggie...but..." He looked up, tears in his eyes. "You've killed Camy, haven't you? That's her, in that pile at your feet, Jon."

Sabrina thought Joshua had lost his mind. Then she realized that he was talking about a crumpled form at the feet of the wax figure of Jon on display.

"There—that's Camy. Where I immortalized you in wax, right, Jon?" Joshua asked.

"She isn't dead. She's unconscious."

"But it doesn't matter, does it? She might as well be dead. We'll be locked away forever."

Staring at him incredulously, Sabrina asked, "Why, Joshua? I don't understand."

"It's kind of hard for me to swallow, too," Jon

said dully. "I trusted both of you. With everything. With my life."

"At first…it just happened," Joshua said. "Because Cassie meant to have Camy fired, and ruin everything between Jon and me. You see, I am good." He smiled awkwardly. "But you know, art is like writing. Good doesn't necessarily mean fame or fortune. All my renown came from Jon's interest, no matter how good I was." He grimaced with pain and looked at Jon steadily. "Camy told me she killed Cassie by accident. But since then…there have been other accidents. A girl I was friendly with in the village went over the cliff last year and—" He broke off, shrugging. "Then…you were right about the bullet in the hall, Jon. Camy did it. I told her she was being crazy. She said it was part of the game. Then she shot at the horses when we were riding. I don't know if she meant to kill either of you or Brett, but the rearing horses would have been blamed for any deaths. She wrote the note to you that she lied about, accusing you of being the murderer, to create trouble among all of you. To deflect attention."

Joshua frowned, his pain evident once again. "How did you know, Jon? How did you know to come back? How did you suspect that Camy and I…" His voice drifted off; he lifted his shoulders. "I thought that we might just get away. Obviously, with all the forensic techniques available now, someone might have discovered who killed Susan. But it wouldn't have mattered. We would have disappeared by then. Gone to Mexico, Guatemala, Africa—somewhere. But then Brett there just had to play boy wonder and get nosy. He came back down. He found Camy and me here. I had to try to silence him. But how did you know what might be happening here, Jon?''

"Angus had seen you two together, Josh. You and Camy."

"Why didn't you leave?" Joshua asked pathetically as he used the wall to slowly pull himself up off the floor. "Why didn't you leave to get help for Reggie?"

"Angus's son had finally made it up to the castle to help his father, and he rode down to the village for me," Jon said. "And when Angus told me that he'd seen you two together—often and secretively—I began to fear that something worse would happen if I left."

"Something worse is still going to happen!" a voice suddenly said heatedly. Sabrina and Jon spun around. Camy, whose ostensibly unconscious form had lain at the feet of Jon's wax image, was up. She fumbled in her cloak pocket and produced a gun. "I know how to use this—I made a point to learn. A woman frequently alone in an old castle in the wilds... I needed to be armed, to protect myself, you know," she said. "Damn you, Jon, you just couldn't let the bitch die! I really never wanted to hurt you. You knew that Cassie was a monster, and Susan was even worse, and—"

"What about the village girl?" Jon asked her softly.

Camy looked as if she was about to lie. Then she shrugged. "She was in the way. I don't like competition. Joshua thought she was beautiful. Get up, Joshua. I'm sorry, Jon, but you've got to die now, too."

Jon stared at her, then folded his arms over his chest. "No, I don't think so. Joshua knows now that you're psychotic. He's not going to help you. And I'm not going to let you kill me."

"You can't kill us all, Camy!" Sabrina protested.

She looked at Sabrina and laughed. "Honestly, I'm sorry you just had to get so involved. You seem fairly decent. And old Reggie, if she just hadn't been such a nosy old puss! Still, it was fun to haunt you. You all think you're so clever. Jon thought he knew all the hidden passages in the castle, but I was the one who knew them all. And used them. Yes, it amuses me to watch people. I even watched you sleep. I thought you were the smart mystery authors, but I was the one with the power, the power of life and death, over you. It was tremendously amusing to use Jon's robe to clean the blood off me after I'd offed Susan. You were so intriguing. So desperately in love—and feeling such a fool that you might be in love with a wife-murderer! Weren't you still suspicious of him, right up to this very minute?"

"No," Sabrina said. "No." She crossed her arms over her chest as well and announced, "No. We're getting married."

"You're getting dead!" Camy said, and started laughing.

"Camy, you are a monster," Jon said. "Sabrina, we are getting married?"

"As soon as possible. Life is too short to waste any time," she told him.

Camy, disgruntled that they seemed to be ignoring her, exclaimed, "You don't know how short!"

"You are the one and only real monster, Camy, and you've played havoc with my life long enough!" Jon announced. He limped toward her.

"Keep your distance, Jon. I'll shoot you."

"Then do it! And you'd better aim well!" he said furiously. "Shoot to kill, because if I get my hands on you—"

"Wait, Jon! Camy, we've got to stop. We're done—" Joshua began, but Camy was grimly taking aim.

"No!" Sabrina shrieked.

The gun went off.

"Jesus!" Sabrina swore.

Camy had shot Joshua. With a bullet in his shoulder, he slammed against the wall, sinking down to the floor.

Sabrina started toward Joshua, and Camy turned the gun on her, firing. She missed. Sabrina dove to the ground while Jon rushed for Camy.

Camy fired two haphazard shots, diving behind one of the tableaux as she did so.

"Jon!" Sabrina shrieked, rising.

"Stay down!" Jon commanded.

She couldn't stay down. Jon knew as well as she

did that they should make Camy keep firing wildly until she was out of bullets.

And Sabrina had to pray that the gun was a six-shooter.

Sabrina started to streak across the room again. Camy fired again. Missed.

One bullet left.

"Damn you, Sabrina, stay down!" Jon commanded.

At the moment, she did. They were all hiding among the wax tableaux, no one knowing exactly where anyone else was.

Then Camy suddenly rose from right behind Sabrina. She smiled, taking aim. "I kill you, and Jon is just as good as dead," she said softly.

Her finger started to move on the trigger.

But Jon suddenly rose from behind Lady Ariana Stuart like a wave, a force of nature, a vengeful phoenix rising from ashes. He came hurtling across the room, tackling Camy at the ankles.

Camy shrieked, trying to aim and shoot.

But she teetered. Falling, she tried to take aim at Jon.

Her gun exploded.

So did a second weapon from somewhere else in the room.

Camy went limp, her eyes open, staring. Dead.

Brett, white as a ghost and still festooned in Sabrina's makeshift bandages, stood wobbling at the entry from the hidden passage.

"Jon?" he said quietly. "Jesus, am I too late?"

"Just a flesh wound or two," Jon said, rising, his hand on his upper arm.

"I know you're a fighter, buddy," Brett told Jon. "And you might have disarmed her, but I couldn't risk losing my best friend." Brett smiled, then crumpled to the floor.

Jon walked to Sabrina, reaching to help.

Camy lay dead. Joshua was wounded or dead. Brett was on the floor, passed out cold. She and Jon were alone among the carnage.

"It's over," he said softly. "Jesus, it's over," he repeated. "See if Joshua is alive, if he has a chance. I'm going to get Brett upstairs, stop the bleeding again, get him stabilized. Amazing, isn't it? He did just turn out to be my best friend." He knelt by Brett, carefully lifting the other man.

Then he looked up at Sabrina. "Did you really believe in me?" he asked.

"Always, in my heart."

"But you were suspicious."

"Logically, in my mind. But…"

"But what?"

"My heart would never listen," she told him.

He smiled and, limping, led the way out of the chamber of horrors.

_____ Epilogue _____

"Jon!"

He heard his name called, and he looked back.

There she stood, on the balcony. Calling to him.

He paused, smiled and waved back.

It had been two years since the night the medics and evacuation team had rushed up to the castle and the police had followed.

Both Reggie and Brett had made it. Jon's own wound had healed easily, leaving only a tiny scar. Joshua had died on the operating table.

The media had hopped on Joshua Valine's death, having a field day with the pathology of the unusual artist. His work garnered great publicity and attention—posthumously. But the gossip made Jon sad. Joshua had been guilty, but more of falling in love and refusing to think with his mind instead of his heart. He had become an accessory to brutal acts, though, and Jon often wondered if the artist could have survived year after year in jail. Camy's bullet and Brett's determination to protect his host and friend had written _finis_ to the case before it ever went to a court of law.

Sabrina had left with the medical team that night

to be with Brett—as a friend. And as soon as the police had finished with him, two weeks after the event, Jon had taken off from Lochlyre Castle, as well. He had needed to get away. To come to terms with everything that had happened. And he'd needed to do it alone.

Then, at last, he'd managed to go after Sabrina. And it was only with her that he'd broken down. He thought he had forgotten how to cry, and he hadn't realized that he'd blamed himself for Cassie and for Susan and for all the pain suffered in his castle. But that first night back with Sabrina, he'd begun to forgive himself. And to fall in love all over again.

They were married quietly, with her folks, her sister and brother-in-law and baby nephew in attendance. He'd never been happier.

On their first anniversary, they were gifted with the birth of a son. And soon after that, Sabrina had insisted that they leave the States and come back here. To Lochlyre Castle. The castle wasn't evil, she reminded him. Only some people were. She loved the estate, and vowed that it should be a place of happiness. That they could make it so.

And she had.

"Jon!"

"What?"

"You're just staring at me."

"Well, you called me."

"I got a card from V.J. and Tom. They're in Spain, and they want to come here for a week to visit."

"Great! Tell them to come!"

He was surprised at the happiness he felt. He did love his castle. And, thank God, others wanted to come back, as well.

"V.J. says we need to host another Mystery Week sometime soon."

"We'll think about that one, okay?"

"Okay!"

Sabrina's eyes were dancing in the sunlight. The breeze stirred her hair, making it flow around her face. She looked gorgeous, seductive, on the castle balcony. He'd gotten rid of the Poseidon statue, and the courtyard was planted with a vast variety of flowers.

She smoothed her hair back. "Jon…"

"Was there something else?" he asked.

"Yes!"

"What?"

"The baby is sleeping…."

"Yeah?"

"I thought you might want to come back for a while…."

He grinned, waved and started back to his castle. It was exactly where he wanted to be.

Take 2 of "The Best of the Best™" Novels FREE

Plus get a FREE surprise gift!

Special Limited-Time Offer

Mail to The Best of the Best™

3010 Walden Avenue
P.O. Box 1867
Buffalo, N.Y. 14240-1867

YES! Please send me 2 free novels and my free surprise gift. Then send me 3 of "The Best of the Best™" novels each month. I'll receive the best books by the world's hottest romance authors. Bill me at the low price of $4.24 each plus 25¢ delivery per book and applicable sales tax, if any.* That's the complete price, and a saving of over 20% off the cover prices—quite a bargain! I understand that accepting the books and gift places me under no obligation ever to buy any books. I can always return a shipment and cancel at any time. Even if I never buy another book, the 2 free books and the surprise gift are mine to keep forever.

183 MEN CH74

Name	(PLEASE PRINT)	
Address	Apt. No.	
City	State	Zip

This offer is limited to one order per household and not valid to current subscribers.
*Terms and prices are subject to change without notice. Sales tax applicable in N.Y.
All orders subject to approval.

UBOB-98   ©1996 MIRA BOOKS

Watch for this title by bestselling author

JOANN ROSS

*He didn't want to come to Ireland—
and she didn't want a boarder...*

Jaded and bitter scriptwriter Quinn Gallagher isn't happy
about being marooned on location in a sleepy Irish town—or
renting a room from young widow Nora Fitzgerald. He doesn't
know that the only way she can keep her home is to offer him
one—for a price—or that the happy endings he writes about
so cynically can actually happen offscreen, as well.

A Woman's Heart

On sale mid-June 1998
where paperbacks are sold!

MIRA

Available from bestselling phenomenon

DIANA PALMER

It all started as a joke! Sabina was only pretending to be engaged to her best friend, millionaire Al Thorndon. He'd talked her into this scheme as a way to trick his older brother, Thorn. But what Sabina thought would be one night of trickery turned into much more once Thorn began digging up her long-buried secrets and accusing her of being a gold digger. And revealing those secrets now would destroy everything she'd worked so hard to put behind her....

After the Music

On sale mid-June 1998 where paperbacks are sold!

MDP452

MIRA

Also available by
New York Times bestselling author

HEATHER GRAHAM POZZESSERE

Order these books now by one of MIRA's most popular authors:

#66000	SLOW BURN	$5.99 U.S.☐	$6.50 CAN.☐
#66005	A MATTER OF CIRCUMSTANCE	$4.99 U.S.☐	$5.50 CAN.☐
#66019	KING OF THE CASTLE	$4.99 U.S.☐	$5.50 CAN.☐
#66038	STRANGERS IN PARADISE	$4.99 U.S.☐	$5.50 CAN.☐
#66089	EYES OF FIRE	$5.99 U.S.☐	$6.50 CAN.☐
#66069	ANGEL OF MERCY	$4.99 U.S.☐	$5.50 CAN.☐
#66079	DARK STRANGER	$4.99 U.S.☐	$5.50 CAN.☐
#66146	BRIDE OF THE TIGER	$5.50 U.S.☐	$5.99 CAN.☐
#66160	NIGHT MOVES	$5.50 U.S.☐	$6.50 CAN.☐
#66171	FOREVER MY LOVE	$5.50 U.S.☐	$6.50 CAN.☐
#66285	IF LOOKS COULD KILL	$5.99 U.S.☐	$6.99 CAN.☐
#66296	A PERILOUS EDEN	$5.50 U.S.☐	$6.50 CAN.☐

(quantities may be limited)

TOTAL AMOUNT	$
POSTAGE & HANDLING	$
($1.00 for one book, 50¢ for each additional)	
APPLICABLE TAXES*	$ _____
TOTAL PAYABLE	$ _____

(check or money order—please do not send cash)

To order, complete this form and send it, along with a check or money order for the total above, payable to MIRA Books, to: **In the U.S.:** 3010 Walden Avenue, P.O. Box 9077, Buffalo, NY 14269-9077; **In Canada:** P.O. Box 636, Fort Erie, Ontario L2A 5X3.

Name: _____

Address: _____ City: _____

State/Prov.: _____ Zip/Postal Code: _____

Account Number: _____ (if applicable)   075 CSAS

*New York residents remit applicable sales taxes.
Canadian residents remit applicable GST and provincial taxes.

MIRA

Look us up on-line at: http://www.romance.net   MHGPBL13